GENTLEMAN OF STRATFORD

Also by John Brophy

Novels

THE WOMAN FROM NOWHERE
PORTRAIT OF AN UNKNOWN LADY
IMMORTAL SERGEANT
SPEAR HEAD
TARGET ISLAND
MAN, WOMAN AND CHILD
THE RIDICULOUS HAT
GREEN GLORY
GREEN LADIES
WATERFRONT
FELICITY GREEN

Short Stories

THE QUEER FELLOW
SELECTED STORIES

Belles Lettres

THE HUMAN FACE
ENGLISH PROSE
BRITAIN'S HOME GUARD
(with ERIC KENNINGTON)

August 1946

Many Happy Returns

All My Love

Isobel

Margaret L. R. Banks.

Gentleman of Stratford

A Novel

by

JOHN BROPHY

COLLINS
14 ST. JAMES'S PLACE LONDON

FIRST IMPRESSION	AUGUST, 1939
SECOND IMPRESSION	SEPTEMBER, 1940
THIRD IMPRESSION	APRIL, 1946

CONTENTS

ACKNOWLEDGMENTS

I am indebted to Dr. W. P. Barrett, of King's College, London, for reading the proofs and giving me the benefit of his specialist knowledge. My thanks are also due to Mr. F. T. Smith and Mr. Milton Waldman, who read the book in typescript and made some illuminating suggestions which I believe have improved it as a story. These gentlemen should not, however, be held responsible for any surviving defects of history or art.

J. B.

Book One

ANNE

I

THE LIGHT was fading in the schoolroom which stretched, long and low, over the Gild Hall. At one end, where the older pupils sat to their tasks at a table ink-stained and scored with initials and crude designs, two of the boys were whispering, heads together. Another, broad of face, already sturdy for his years, sober and industrious like all the Sadlers, bent over his book of syntax wherein Master Francis Lily had of his generosity provided much explanation in the vulgar tongue. The fourth boy, giving him a sidewards glance in which affection was somewhat mingled with pity, marvelled that his friend could so patiently apply himself to the rudiments of Latin, from which he should have been emancipated long since. But that he would look a whale among minnows, and but that his father, and still more his uncle who leased the Town mills, were men of substance in Stratford-upon-Avon, Hamnet Sadler, now nearing the close of his sixteenth year, would still be sitting at the far end of the schoolroom, among the restless young breeching scholars now being regimented by Master Jenkyns.

Hamnet desired nothing more than to be free from the Grammar School, to venture forth upon the estate and burdens of manhood. His interest was all in millings and markets and prices, in nicely calculated though honest profits. What availed Latin to one destined a prosperous baker ? Hamnet learned by painful diligence of memory, scarce understanding the moiety of number and declension his mind retained after many grapplings with his book, and plainly puzzled that his torments should be augmented by lines from the ancients set out to exemplify the rules of grammar. Will Shakespeare, his friend, declared that these quotations were hard come by, for

most of the ancients wrote as if they had never heard of Francis
Lily and defied his rules. Will, purely for love or for wanton
fancy, would read his way through the Metamorphoses of
Ovidius Naso, and Hamnet considered him a nonpareil of
scholarship.

This opinion was not upheld by Master Jenkyns, the Welsh
schoolmaster, not long graduated from St. John's College in
Oxford. Nor was it Will Shakespeare's view of himself. He
could learn by rote and speedily, and his wits ever leaped ahead
of the teaching offered him : yet his mind was of such a
quality, as the schoolmaster deplored, that information which
did not excite him was quickly cast forth and forgotten. "A
poy of your age," Master Jenkyns would admonish him, "and
inteet you are like soon to be a man, should be aple to think in
Latin. To hafe thoughts in Latin is everywhere the mark of a
scholar." Inwardly rebellious, though his tongue kept courtesy,
Will was already resolved to become neither a burgess like
Hamnet Sadler nor a purveyor of grammar like Master
Jenkyns. Ovid's tales enchanted him, and he would bend his
mind to wrest the meaning out of the long verses—but the
meaning always emerged for him in English. There were, he
had heard, books being newly printed in London which would
make futile all this toil, for they rendered the poems and
histories of the ancients into forthright English. He intended,
and soon, to procure such books for his own entertainment.
And why not ? A man does not fetch about five miles through
a muddy marsh, and weary himself into a sweat, when there is
a firm and short turnpike road at his service.

At the moment he took no pleasure even in Ovid : he had
the tale which he had begun to read through again clear in
his memory, and in English. Spring was not yet to be, except
in books. He stared up at the cross-beams and arched rafters
of the schoolroom, shifted himself for comfort on the wooden
bench, stretched his legs under the table till his toes in his shoes
kicked against the under side, and then looked out of the
window at the thatched roofs of the houses on the other side of

Church Street, scarce to be discerned through the blue gathering dusk. February had come in bleak and blusterous: the primroses, under the hedgerows in the riverside walk favoured by Stratford sweethearts for their evening dalliances, must needs hold back their appearance this year. It was a cold durance sitting here at school the day long. Will Shakespeare, luckier than many, wore two linen shirts, and his russet doublet, which he had outgrown so that it scarce reached below his waist and the skirt oft escaped the belt's confinement, was quilted and padded, like his round hose. He was warm to the knees, tolerably warm: below that his flesh shivered and his bones ached. His feet had almost lost sensibility. Yet if he shuffled them on the floor the schoolmaster would round upon him. Had all Welshmen such quick hearing, as well as such a talent for maltreating the sounds of English and Latin?

It could not be much longer now they would be kept in school and, as the light dimmed across the pages of his Ovid, he decided he would work no more. Hamnet Sadler, though he believed himself to be conning his subjectivos earnestly, was all but asleep in mind and body. The other two boys of the senior class went whispering on, plotting some mischief for their evening leisure. Will Shakespeare had taken the measure of their clumsy country minds long since. Indolently he turned his head and listened to Master Jenkyns examining the junior class in their rudiments.

"You, poy," he demanded, "you shall inform me how many numbers is in nouns?"

The boy knew the answer. "Sir, there are two."

Baulked of the opportunity for reproof, the schoolmaster asked again: "What is lapis?"

"Lapis is a stone, sir."

"And what is a stone?"

"Why, sir, a pebble."

This was heresy to Jenkyns. "No, poy. You are stupid. We consider not meanings in English. A stone is, in Latin, lapis. What for is your memory?"

Such dreary reiterations stupified the mind. Will Shakespeare felt compassion for the poor boy caught in these academic toils. It was not in this fashion he had himself been inducted to the mysteries of learning by Master Simon Hunt who had conducted the school before this Jenkyns and, suspect of Papistry, had had his windows broken, had fled the country, and was now, some said, a Jesuit. It would be unpolitic, so Will had been warned by his father, the alderman, to belaud the name of Hunt in general company these days: yet Will had heard his father maintaining that, traitorous priest or not, Master Hunt was the best schoolmaster to grace Stratford these thirty years. And Will himself revered the memory of the pale young man, new come from Oxford, who had accepted him as a seven-year-old pupil, already disdaining the horn-book alphabet and able to prove himself worthy his entrance to the school by reading aloud from the printed page. Eight years now Will had made his attendances in this upper schoolroom next the Gild Chapel. Eight years was a long time: he had learned much from good Master Hunt and, latterly, by his own endeavours in despite of the new dominus. He felt weary now of Master Jenkyns and would not protest were his father, who was not so prosperous as formerly, to make good his threats, further him not to the university, and withdraw him speedily from school.

At last Master Jenkyns dismissed them all, and at once Will Shakespeare's spirits surged up again. It was ever thus with him: either he enclosed himself in his secret thoughts, dreaming while he waked, or else he was all for action, ploys, jests, games and the bantering give-and-take of schoolboy rivalries. He snapped his book shut now and threw it into his satchel, stamped his feet to make them tingle to warmth, and hurried to lift his cloak from the pegs at the end of the room. He found that young Gilbert, who sat in the junior class, had got there first and was endeavouring to remove the cock's feather from his brother's velvet cap.

"Thief!" cried Will.

"Nay, brother, I did but set it firmer in the clasp."

"That is a lie!"

The second insult, smilingly given, had no more effect than the first. "Dost fancy," Gilbert demanded, "I would demean myself to wear such a bedraggled worn-out trophy to my head?"

"Ay, an I gave thee opportunity. Hence, thou egg! Out of my sight! Back to the cradle!"

And Will, pushing his brother out of the way, swung his cloak round his shoulders and settled his cap neatly over his short brown hair.

"These bantlings are insolent," he remarked to Hamnet Sadler as they walked down the stairs together. "When we were of that unripe age we dare not so use ourselves towards our elders."

"Gilbert means no harm."

"I trust not. Else should there be chastisement forthcoming."

At that moment Gilbert, clattering downstairs behind them, stretched out a foot, knocked his brother's heels together so that he stumbled, and ran off, shouting for joy.

Will cursed aloud as he bent to rub his ankles, and Master Jenkyns, gowned and grave-faced (he was a young man but Will would have it he had been born with a white beard and a grammar book in his hand), stopped to reprove him for setting such a profane ensample before the younger boys.

When, with Hamnet at his side, he was out in the street, dark now and the wind whistling under the eaves, Will complained against the injustice of the world.

"But it cannot be gainsaid," his friend protested, "they were terrible words fell from thy tongue."

"Wouldst have me unloose my wrath in pretty nothings? The pain was great and came sharp and unexpected. 'Tis a natural thing to curse upon such an occasion. And if one must curse, let him do it to the top of his ability."

"But there is moderation in all things," said Hamnet.

Will mocked him. "This is news! Moderation in all things! How so, pray thee? Expound to me this doctrine."

"Nay, thou knowest my meaning."

"If I do 'tis with no help from thee. 'Tis a miracle. But divert me not from my purpose. This irreverent brother of mine must be punished. His bare feet this same night shall find a thistle in bed where he sleeps. And Jenkyns, what shall I do to teach him the ways of equity? Would I could force him to eat a raw leek. But the fellow is Welsh. I fear me he would relish it. Out upon him! 'Tis punishment dire enough to possess such a dull mind as his. I shall bestow on him—my pity."

They walked on down the narrow muddy ways of Chapel Street and the High Street, the afternoon's rainwater still dripping from the thatch of the roofs, the wind stinging their ears, till they came to the High Cross where five roads met and the triple line of houses in Middle Row sloped down to the Clopton bridge and the full-flooding Avon.

"I am hungry," said Hamnet.

He made this announcement each evening when they reached the High Cross, and always with an air of astonishment.

"And I am cold," said Will, folding his cloak about him to begin the ritual game he had imposed upon his reluctant friend for the conclusion of this, their daily parting.

"Vale, Brutus," he pronounced now, drawing himself up in what he took to be the dignified senatorial fashion of the old Romans.

"Vale, Cæsar," Hamnet responded. "And shall we meet again?"

"We shall meet again. Upon the plains, at Philippi."

It was part of the understanding that after these farewells, remembered by Will from some of Master Hunt's early instructions, neither he nor Hamnet should look back. All was to be done solemnly, after the high Roman fashion. So now Will stalked off down Henley Street until he came in sight of his father's house, built with three gables upon a groundsill of clay set in a framework of pitch wood, and close-timbered on the upper storeys. Alderman Shakespeare, coming into the town from Snitterfield village, had first lived only in the eastern portion, but, as his family grew and his gloving trade prospered, he had bought in the other two houses, transforming them into one. It meant little to Will that of late his father wrinkled his brows over his account books, declaring that too much was spent, and, sometimes, his customary joviality all gone, that he feared for what would become of them.

The adult world, in which men and women were ever concerned with moneys and marriages and contracts, quarrels and trading friendships, and stories their children must not hear, was set apart from the ambit of Will's chief interests. He was fifteen years old, and whiles some of his age were already sweethearting and in other ways apeing their elders, Will was content with his boyhood lot, save in so far as he was irked six days a week by Master Jenkyns at the Grammar School. Life to him was above all acceptable; while he was free to move where he pleased or to set his mind on its fanciful wanderings, he was never dull or unhappy. Or if he was sometimes unhappy, he had of late discovered a new allurement in sadness.

In Stratford he was known as the son of John Shakespeare; he lived in this enlarged house, solid and comfortable, not new, not old. He knew whence every part of it came: the timbers hewn in the Forest of Arden and shaped by men employed by Hamnet Sadler's uncle: the stone from the quarries at Drayton; the sand from the Gild pits behind the house; the plaster mixed at Welcombe; the roofs thatched by an old man from Shottery village; the ironwork, little of it, latches, hinges, hooks and firebars, wrought next door in Hornby's smithy, beside the mere.

In spring, summer and early autumn Will could spend his holidays wandering with other boys in the meadows beside the river, swimming when the fancy took them or roving further into the greenwood or the Forest itself, which, to tell truth, was not so dense a forest as it had been, or so the old men said. He learned the country names for many flowers and birds and beasts. He watched the hunt assembling and in full cry. Once he had seen a stag brought to bay, trembling and asweat with weariness and fear: he had felt more pitiful than enthralled. He talked to the men who worked in the fields, to the hedgers and ditchers and shepherds with wrinkles deep-drawn in their sun-darkened faces, to the milkmaids and the foresters, gleaning from them the lore of their crafts, strings of new names for things, and tales of the fairy folk and Hobgoblin that some called the Puck. Sometimes he would choose to go forth alone, to lie in the sun and dream the hours away, betwixt sleep and waking. And sometimes it was his pleasure to steal up on some fluting song-bird, and observe it as it perched; to watch the hares in the corn or the water-voles in the shallows, light-footed and bright-eyed as they poised upon the streaming green bannerets of the weeds just below the river surface. In winter, as now, he was perforce town-bound, for the forest trees were bare, the fields all fallow, the lanes impassable, deep in mud, which often so beset the main roads that for weeks together no strangers came and went in Stratford. In winter his mind would divert itself, upon its occasions of freedom, with such books as he could borrow, for his father kept none in the house, with remembering old stories, and with devising new ones.

It came to him now that, when he was warm again and replenished with food, he might take a rush-light, or even a candle, if he were fortunate enough not to be observed, and, finding some unoccupied room, set himself to profit from an apt mood and the necessary solitude ; in brief, to cover some of his small stock of paper with a tally of verses. Of what he would write he had at present no notion, but he did not doubt that the purpose, and the words to accomplish it, would come. Were he a scholar by natural endowment he would write Latin hexameters, more compliant to the grammatical rules than Virgil or Ovid, and so earn the commendations of Master

Jenkyns. But he had no desire to turn verses except in English, nor yet to disclose this his new and precious recreation to any other. His scripts were all hid away behind a loose brick in the chimney of his room. In truth, such poetry as he brought to a final shape rarely pleased him. He would keep his fair copies a day or two, enjoying an afterglow of creative zest which did not long endure, and then burn them. It was the exercise of his mind he took delight in, the chase of stubborn, evasive thoughts, the reluctant bending of rhymes and measures to his intention. He lived, when he wrote, not so much in the present as in the ever hopeful future. There had been poets in ancient times: there were even poets in this year of grace fifteen hundred and eighty. Mostly these were great gentlemen. Yet one might, with the aid of time and due diligence, grow to emulate them. Meanwhile, Stratford, inside and out of his home here in Henley Street, was not like to appreciate his prentice endeavours. Secrecy must be his tutelary angel.

He went in by the front door, pushing it to behind him against the buffets of the wind, and then latching it. The hall, which served his father as his place of business, was furnished with a long table and a bench along the wall on which were stored hides, dressed and cut, gloves, leather jerkins and doublets in varied stages of making. Here the Alderman was at work, by candlelight, running his shears through a fine doeskin marked to a pattern for falconer's gauntlets. He was a portly man with apple-red cheeks, his hair and beard already flecked with grey.

"Thou'rt late, Will."

"Ay, sir. Jenkyns will wring his last minute of labour out of us."

"'Twould become thee better to speak of him as Master Jenkyns. And Gilbert hath been home these ten minutes or more."

"Gilbert runs."

"And canst not run as well as he?"

"Marry, that I can. But wherefore?"

The Alderman cracked out a laugh. "Why, son, for thy supper. It hath been said, a lad who will not run for his supper deserves to go hungry."

"Yet," said Will, "supper is not ready, as I perceive, or thou wouldst be sitting to thy silver dish. A lad who will run for his supper ere it be prepared is but a fool."

"Well answered."

Mistress Shakespeare called from the parlour, the room beyond the hall and the angled staircase leading to the upper floor. "An that be Will returned from school, we are all met and the meat is on the table."

"Behold, father, how timely is my arrival. Nay, leave that to me." And, throwing off his cloak and his satchel, Will snuffed out the candles one by one, making no haste and putting the last aside, in the darkness, for his own purposes. Then he followed his father through the open doorway, drawing the curtain across after him to exclude the draughts from door and windows, and took his place at the old-fashioned trestle table in the parlour.

There were four children in the family. Two daughters had died, infants, before Will was born, and nearly a year ago Anne had sickened and was quickly dead, ere she came to her eighth birthday. It was a fortunate family in which half the children survived to become men and women. Yet new births came to balance the conflict with death, and now Will's mother was with child again, heavy-bodied and slow-footed.

Only the Alderman and his wife had joined stools. The children sat to table on worn wooden tripods, and, except Will, the eldest, they ate from wooden trenchers. The floor was of beaten clay, strewn with rushes. The Alderman carved their portions from a loin of veal, dressed and spiced with saffron: to vary this fare they ate bread and afterwards spread what was left with butter. Richard, who would be six next month, had a cup of milk set before him; the others drank ale from pewter tankards, which had lately come into favour, displacing bowls, beakers and the German stoneware jugs.

They spoke little till the first fury of appetite was stilled. Then John Shakespeare, in easy mood, began to recount stories of his own boyhood to entertain his children. When he felt called to admonish them, he was wont to conjure up a picture of himself as a boy paragon of virtue, obedient to authority in all things, industrious at school, helpful about the house in his leisure hours. But now, it seemed, he had been famed for mischief, a truant in summer, a boy apt to push a poor drunkard into the horse-pond or to snatch the stool from under some old beldame as she thought to sit, crying Tailor in her behalf when she collapsed cross-legged, and, called to account, laying the blame upon the fairy Puck. The Alderman told his memories at length, pausing often to laugh deep in his fat chins, and plainly admiring his past self. Gilbert and Joan rounded their eyes to see their father exhibit himself so near to their own gamesome philosophy, but Will had heard it all before: he sat quiet, with folded hands, forgetful of his meditated vengeance on Gilbert, wondering how soon the maid-servants would come to clear the table. When the assembly broke up he hoped to repair, with pen, paper and ink-horn, and his illicit candle-end, to solitude.

His mother, who had gone to sit next little Richard and persuade him to finish the last remnants of his bread, glanced at her eldest son and trusted that the thoughts which smoothed his face to this privy contemplation were not of girls. Only last week she had seen a bold-faced hoyden in Rother Market roll her eyes at Will: but the boy noticed nothing. He was still safe, still too young, but fifteen years as yet, neither over-tall nor short, comely and clear-eyed. Trust a market wench to take heed of his graceful mien, his fair complexion, his soft hair, reddened among the brown, and very fine, his fresh lips, his merry hazel-coloured eyes. But there were no concealments, she was assured, in her Will. He had the look of a boy and the mind of a boy, turned all to pranks and exercises, and anon to his books at school. For him a female was but another sort of human kind, and not the most interesting. There were signs of warning to bid a mother be on guard, and they were not yet to be discerned in Will: would forget to wash, often enough, were he not put in mind of it, and was apt to brush his hair with his fingers. Not that he failed in cleanliness. He had Arden blood from his mother, and the Ardens were gentle-born and gentle-bred: the Ardens had the right to bear arms. It would be time enough to fret over Will, and seek him a suitable wife, when he was full-grown a man. At this present, an unbearded schoolboy sitting locked in his own privy thoughts, he roused all her pride and tenderness, and brought her no perturbation at all.

When the servants came to lift the dishes, to push the table against the wall and the stools under it, Mistress Shakespeare busied herself, giving directions, sending Gilbert upon an errand, and bidding Joan take Richard up to bed and stay with him till he slept. Then she went to sit beside her husband on the settle next the fire, while he re-filled his tankard and put it down on the hearth for the ale to mull. Neither of them noticed Will as he went tip-toe out of the parlour to the darkened hall and groped his fingers round a shelf till he had found his candle-end in its wooden stock and the tinder-box beside it.

But as the boy, still holding breath and moving softly, reached the staircase and prepared to mount without setting foot upon either of the two treads which creaked, he heard his father's voice, no longer jovial, but relaxed into the tone which those of mature age use in converse among themselves.

"I heard today a sad tale from Tiddington."

Will Shakespeare, one foot already on the first step, paused on the far side of the curtain drawn across the doorless portal. It did not occur to him that he was overhearing what was not intended for his ears, else he had hurried on at once. His father spoke of a tale, and a sad tale: such things were mightily to his liking. He stayed a moment to listen.

"Dost remember," his father's voice continued, "a Tiddington maid was missed some while since, and feared drowned?

'Tis proven truth now. They have taken her corse from the river. Some say she killed herself for love. Others have it she lost balance as she leaned over the bank to draw water. Which be in the right is not yet known, till the coroner holds his inquisition."

"What was her name?"

"Hamlet. Kate Hamlet."

"I never heard of her," said Mistress Shakespeare. "But 'tis no uncommon name. John Sadler's boy was christened after that family, or one akin to it."

"Hamnet! He spells it differently, however."

"Spelling is neither here nor there. 'Tis the same name. If the girl went to draw water from the river, she must needs take a pail with her. Have they found a pail?"

"Nay, wife, that's more than I know or thought to ask. But 'tis said in Tiddington this Kate Hamlet was strange in her ways. Would sing melancholic songs and make garlands of meadow flowers and hang them on the trees. Her corse was found hard by a willow that overhangs the river."

"I trust the crowner's jury will be charitable. 'Tis hard to die young, but harder to be buried in unconsecrated ground, a suicide."

Will listened no more. He had stolen away, rapt with the desire to compose verses, but his mind void of a theme to versify upon. And now by the bounty of chance a rare tale was delivered to him. A poor maid drowned for love! 'Twas certain she drowned for love and not by a clumsy slip of the foot. Melancholic songs! Garlands of flowers hung upon the drooping branches of a willow tree! This was all fine and pitiful. It demanded instantly a worthy chronicling.

He hurried, but still cautiously, to the bedroom he shared with Gilbert, put down his lighted candle on the table by the window, unstopped his ink-horn, brought out his paper and his quill, and sat to commemorate the tragical tale of Kate Hamlet. But the verses came slow and halting; the pen split and, being sharpened, would not convey sufficient ink. Almost as much as he wrote he struck out again. When Gilbert came whistling up the stairs to bed he had scarce time to hide his papers away. He felt frustrate and angry. Yet, when at last he drowsed to the borders of sleep, his mind was still intent upon a maiden he had never seen, victim of the river, all for love under a garlanded willow tree. Some day, he was resolved, he would write her elegy, in verses, and it should be a memorable elegy, to boot, piteous and memorable.

"WILL! A plague on the boy! Where art thou, Will?"

The stout, quick-eyed, red-cheeked alderman listened impatiently for an answer while his voice still resounded under the low ceiling. The hall was rush-lighted, for the morning was dark, with a river mist curling heavy and slow along Henley street and leaving trickles and beads of damp on the window panes.

His legs, still slender and well-formed under the heavy bulk of his body, moved jerkily as he went to the back of the room. There he raised his voice again and sent it echoing up the angles of the stairs.

"Will, I say! Will, come hither! The boy's a knave and a wither-wit. His mind is as far absent from this earth as I, poor distracted creature, am from Tartary. Will, I say! Rouse up! Taste thy legs! Make speed!"

"Nay, I come now. Look how I come. Swifter than the arrows despatched by thine aldermanic bow to the targes on Butt Close."

And, light and dainty, Will came skipping down the stairs, book in hand, smiling, graceful, comely, at ease with himself, with his own ready courtesy.

The merchant, as often lately, was bewildered by this his eldest surviving child, bewildered but delighted. He could rarely bring his mind to grips with Will's mind. The boy was doubtless spoiled by education, and hardly a week passed but one of his father's friends predicted that no good would come of such a day-dreamer. The boy lagged behind his years: but trees of slow growth often rooted deepest and lasted long. Eighteen years old last month, the rogue had an air. Doubtless he hid himself behind a smile and a jest. Doubtless he was hiding now, book in hand, waiting with that gentleman's grace of his, one hand resting on the post at the foot of the stairs, and one foot advanced, like a knight in a tapestry picture. Or like one of those harlotry players, all bombast, breeches and ale-laden breath? Well, he had good blood in his veins. Arden pride and the wit of a Shakespeare—no poor inheritance, that!

"Hast stopped thy ears?" his father enquired now. "Here am I with a throat dusty as a midsummer road from calling thy name about the house. Aldermanic arrows, no less."

"Art not an archer, and an alderman to book? Where is thy pride this morning."

"Cease pribbling, lad. I have employment for thee. Here is a parcel to be taken forthwith. Three pairs of gloves, fine buckskin, and marvellous daintily embroidered. They are to be delivered to the Swan Inn, to a gentleman who lies there on his way to London. His name is—'tis written here and thou canst decipher it thyself."

The young man's face lost its smile, the large, clean-shaped hazel eyes darkened, and the mouth, pushed forward, became pendulous and sullen.

"Is there no serving-man," he demanded, "more apt than I for this mean office?"

His father's good humour vanished as quick as his son's.

"Nay," he said. "There's none I can dispense with now, and none that I would if I could. Thou hast thought mounting above thine estate, Will. If this world is too poor for thee, shouldst have turned priest. But go to! Take the gloves and despatch."

The boy stared out through the streaming window panes of thick circled glass, and when he turned again to his father his body was alert as before, held slim and easy, his eyes lighted, and the long lines of dissatisfaction had gone from the high pale temples.

"It is equitable," he admitted. "I do little enough to earn my bread."

"That's my son that I recognise. Make speed, and keep thy

wits tethered to the gloves lest the vapours bewray thee to the wrong road. 'Tis a sorry morning for May, but the sun will have his way anon. The day will be fair and warm. Trust me. I have lived with mine eyes open. I know."

"The mists shall be my enveloping guardians. None shall see me come and go."

Even so, the father reflected, suddenly as twinkle-eyed as his son: that's the way of it. On a foggy morning this fine gentleman will perform a menial task without protest, all because he trusts none shall spy him as he goes by.

Lending his voice a dramatic intonation, Will declared: "Good father, this high majestic office shall be discharged in full conscience. Presto, without delay. In brief, three pairs of gloves to the Swan."

"Ay, Will, but I'll never make a merchant of thee. The price, lad! The fee! The money in return! This gentleman lies at the Swan. Tomorrow, even today perchance, when the sun puts the vapours to flight, he is up and away. See to it thou hast full value in thy hand before he receives the gloves. 'Tis all written there, fair and clear, in the scrip. Six shillings and fourpence."

"It seems I am become a bailiff as well as a hired messenger," Will muttered. "But no matter. Shalt have thy six shillings and fourpence, or else I fetch back the gloves."

He lifted a feathered hat from a peg and opened the door. "No cloak, lad?"

"Not I. The mists will clear. Who said it but thee?"

John Shakespeare laughed. "Wag thy head ever and anon, to rid thy beard of the dew. There are half of a dozen hairs on thy face will almost bear an atomy of water, if only thou proceedest with care."

He looked affectionately after his son swinging out of doors. Will would pass scrutiny in his damson red doublet, good buckskin it was, corded blue and ornamented with crystal buttons. His tall hat with the tilted crown had a green feather, and his long round hose, French fashion, reached from the hips to below the knees. Even if the stockings, gartered—again in green—were worsted instead of silk, many a gentleman was content with wool for informal occasions, and the wool on the boy's shapely legs was soft and thin, and close-woven. Two washings had not paled the yellow dye. Will had the figure for fine clothes. With so many debts on the house, it had been a folly to yield to his importunities for a new habit head to foot, but the boy had a sweet, smooth tongue, and a man who remembered the privations which ambition had set on his own youth had his secret excuses for not resisting the demands of a son now setting foot on the threshold of manhood. Will became his fine feathers.

The time would soon be when he would put poesy and dreams out of his head, anchor his abilities to earth, and make another generation of Shakespeares respected in Stratford. The eldest son of one who had moved into the borough from Snitterfield (a pleasant nook, but with little beyond a prospect over the river valley to the far hills to recommend it) and had served his office as chief magistrate and justice of the peace, and might do so again!—the son of such a personage could not be expected to face the world in drab habiliments or the blue fustian of a serving man. Marry, with such clothes to his back, with such a gentle-born air, and such a nightingale's tongue in his head, Will might make a match would set the gossips throwing up their hands and nodding their astonished heads together. His father had taken a wife (and a good wife, too, though always proud and lately with a nettle at the end of her tongue) who brought property with her to the marriage feast, property and money. Will might do better even than that, and, the truth of it was, a substantial dowry, always useful, would be doubly welcome in Henley Street at this present.

William Shakespeare, lapsing into the meditation from which his father's call had aroused him, became another person as he walked along the footpath, beside the damp stones of the cobbled centre way of Henley Street, towards the Swan Inn. The morning mists, pearly grey and white, enclosed

him in a dell of privacy, lit with a diffused radiance, neither
light nor darkness, as he walked. The vapour was cool on his
brow, and, as his father had prophesied, it condensed on the
fine, unshaven down which reddened his chin, his cheeks and
his upper lip. He had hopes of growing a beard: many a man
of his age, who had been schoolfellow with him under the
Welshman Jenkyns, was now black-avised as a pard. A razor
would promote the growth, but turn it to coarse stubble. He
preferred to wait upon the silken sloth of nature.

The mists this morning were running deep through the
streets, hiding the thatched roofs and the forward thrust of
the upper storeys of the houses, revealing doors and windows
and walls first as darker shadows in the grey and white, then as
random delineations behind a veil, without depth or solidity,
till he came abreast and could see the shapes of things for what
they were. This magic of the mists, this imposition of silence,
this subtle transformation of the familiar into a narrow and
changing scope, enchanted him. Almost he was persuaded
to take a citizen's pride in the town of his birth, to be content
with the future apparently cast for him there.

But within a few moments his thoughts were far away
from Stratford—Stratford-super-Avon it was written in the
maps—and, haphazard, waywardly and restlessly as the wind
without which the river vapours would not be dispersed, his
fancy went wandering behind the introspective glaze now
spread over his eyes: he was in Rome, the Rome of Cæsar and
Brutus; in Egypt with Cleopatra and Ptolemy; in Athens and
Troy; in sun-drenched Italian towns where everyone spoke
poetry, where manners and costumes outshone the jewels that
fine ladies wore, listening at their windows to the melancholy
plaints, chanted to the dulcet tunes of hired musicians, by their
lovers.

His mind was in London, too, as unknown to his eyes as
legendary Greece and Rome. But London was not so far
distant; over Sir Hugh Clopton's bridge the road divided,
and either way, by Banbury or by Oxford, you could reach

London, had you the means and the will and the purpose.
Never a week, except perhaps when the rainstorms and snows
of winter made the roads impassable awhile, but there would
be travellers lying at the Swan or the Bear; gentlemen with
their servants; post-messengers; merchants with pack-horses
to be stabled; some years, in the late summer, companies of
players who would send a man to cry round the town the news
of their performances. And all would talk of London as easy
and free as his father might speak of Rother Market. Will had
read and heard much of London town; of East Cheap and
London Bridge with its cornmills and shops; of Leicester House,
the Savoy, and the great towered and pinnacled cathedral of
St. Paul's; of the Tower and the Abbey at Westminster across
the fields. In London the Queen's Majesty might be seen this
day or that; in London monarchs had been crowned and
deposed, slain and conspired against; in London poets were
welcomed without ridicule. Almost he could believe, in such
a solitary communion as this, he was himself a citizen of
Cockaigne. Twice within the last year a traveller, holding
converse with him, had assumed him a man of London, and it
had not been difficult, with a little evasion, a deft turning of
awkward questions, to let the flattery stand.

To be in Stratford all his life, or to hoist sail, he who had
never seen, save in pictures, any vessel larger than the boats
which trammelled, for carp and trout and eels, in the fishing
grounds beyond John Sadler's mill? To rusticate, salved by
dreams which earned him the contempt of ponderous Stratford
wits, or to leap the occasion and plunge himself into distant
London? That was the question, oft put in speculation, never
answered in action. Dick Field, whose father, the tanner,
dwelt but a few yards further on in Bridge Street, was now in
London, apprenticed to a printer in the Blackfriars. Dick sent
books to his father, and Will would beg the loan of them, new-
printed, precious, to be handled with care, kept under lock
between reading times. Was Dick Field, at one remove, to be
his only communication with London, and through London

with poesy, with the gentle world, with fine ladies and fine imaginings, with Greece and Rome and the Italy of a thousand lovers' tales? The thought was ignominy, and Stratford, mist-enchanted though it was at the moment, a prison-house; a town not of the first order even in the county of Warwickshire, yielding place to Coventry; a town with not even a castle like Warwick; a town without a history; a town of clodpole fools and small beer.

The curve of the road had brought him to the crossways, where Wood Street came in at an angle and met Bridge Street, divided down its length by Middle Row. But all that was hidden now in mists, and looking along the High Street Will could scarcely make out the square wall, the inward-sloping tall roofs and the weather vanes of the High Cross. Shifting the cloth-bound package of gloves from under one arm to the other, he was silently thankful that the weather kept people within doors. Not a creak or a rattle of a farm-cart; no crack of whip or slide and clatter of horses' hooves; neither man, woman nor child abroad to give him good day and ask his business. But the pleasing thought came too soon. As he stood a moment pushing a finger into the purse at his belt to make sure he had still the paper there, written with the accompt for the gloves, his ear responded to the sound of feet, firm and clear, coming from beyond the High Cross. He had no wish to stand and parley, so he made off at once over the crossways, intending to keep close under the eaves of Middle Row, and to cut through the Chure, past the stinking Shambles, into Back Bridge Street and on to the Swan Inn. While he was still in the midway of the road, a voice hailed him, by name, but enquiringly. He recognised with relief the deep intonation of Hamnet Sadler, and stopped.

Hamnet had his short cloak pulled forward over his shoulders, which were wide and square, and thick from front to back. Will would say he had a chest like a barrel, and when he grew old in trencherman's years the barrel would slip down to his stomach. Hamnet, tall, burly, with patient bright blue eyes in a face built all, it seemed, on one plane, square-browed and square-jawed, never took his friend's jests amiss. "A portly man is a godly man," was his invariable retort. When he had acquired a dictum, and the more staid and sententious the better, he never wearied of it. And if Will taunted him about these familiar pronouncements, he would answer with another: "A good cloth will bear much wearing." They were vastly unlike, these two, lead and quicksilver, but fixed in friendship.

"Where away now, Will?" Hamnet enquired, as he came bulking up out of the mist.

"I have affairs at the Swan. And thou?"

"I go to mine uncle's forestry. Nay, 'tis my cousin's now, or will be when the notaries have done."

"I'll step with thee so far, Hamnet."

So between the mist-shrouded houses of the High Street they went, stopping a moment to look at the herbs and drugs and the new clay-pipes displayed in the window at Philip Rogers', the apothecary's house. Will held that tobacco smoking was an uncleanly practice, not befitting a gentleman, although gossip declared it fashionable with the younger sort in London, and some argued it a matchless specific against the ague and the infection of disease. Hamnet thought the price of tobacco excessive, and, like other commodities fetched from the Indies, a proper gee-gaw for landed gentlemen who had not to count the pence: for himself, he was a plain man, and could sustain his energy on Stratford ale and bread and cheese. A cup of sack on festive occasions was a sufficient adventure for him in foreign manners.

As they crossed the further end of Chapel Street, the Gild Chapel was no more than a suggestion of buttresses and windows through the mist, the great square tower entirely lost. They could not see the Gild Hall at all, or the upper schoolroom where they had both listened so long to Jenkyns and his Welsh exhortations. Almost at once they came to the several houses, the stables, the orchard and the garden belonging, till two months since, to John Sadler, Hamnet's uncle.

But the younger John, the heir, was not to be found at the timber yard, called the forestry. He was abroad, beyond Lime Close, they learned.

"Being interpreted," said Hamnet, "that means he is at the Mill argumenting the tenancy. He'll not return till the fog lifts. I'll come with thee to the Swan, Will. What's thy business there?"

"A paltry matter, but one I would further disclose to thee," said his friend, drawing him out into the street again. "Thou canst do me a service."

"Readily, Will."

"Am I thy Will? Then thou shalt be mine. Hamnet's will and Will's will—twin cherries on a single bough."

Hamnet thought that a marvellous fine conceit: Will Shakespeare could toss and catch words like a jongleur with polished oranges. Not that this was the first time he had made play with his own name, nor would it be the last, but Hamnet was never the man to tire of repetitions or cry for novelty every hour.

"Tell what is required of me," he demanded.

Will Shakespeare looked importantly, suspiciously, over each shoulder, and then, his hand on the crook of his friend's elbow, led the way across the street, past the almshouses and the Gild Chapel again, its tawny stonework, clean-carved, and iron-studded door plainly visible as they came close to Walkers' Street. They had to leap the narrow, muddy-banked mere to gain the other side, and before he opened his exposition, Will glanced at the wall and the ironwork of the gate to the New Place garden. The house had been built, like the Bridge and the Gild Chapel, to the order of Sir Hugh Clopton, experimentally with brick, instead of wattle and plaster, between the timbers, and for thirty years it had stood in abandonment and decay.

"The river is kindly," Will observed, "sending the mists, like a white shroud, to hide such an unseemly corpse."

"Mine uncle was of opinion the time will come it shall be

inhabited again. It belongs to Underhill of Idlicote now, but he lacks means or ambition to undertake repairs. He thought to make profit, and now the house is like the stone the old Greek (or was he a Roman?) would push uphill and ever it rolled back on him."

"'Twas old before it ceased to be new," Will declared. "But the garden might please the eye with a little care. Let it pass. I have a theme more important to discourse upon. Attend my words."

Hamnet turned to him his earnest and friendly blue eyes.

"Under my arm I carry three pairs of gloves, and I am charged by my father to deliver them to a gentleman at the Swan. See, here's the scrip."

"That's no occasion for whispering."

"No? But what if I dare not enter the inn?"

"And why not?"

"That I may not tell. It is an affair of honour, an affair of peril. I charge thee, Hamnet, keep my confidence."

They stood facing each other, two young provincials closeted in the mist exhaled from the river flowing broad, but now invisible, beside their native town. Not an extraneous sound disturbed their colloquy on the rutted road fenced off from the riverside pastures.

"Will, if that's the way of it, walk with care. I like not drawn swords. Fighting, though doubtless necessary for the state, is but barbarity among the Queen's subjects. 'Tis not of this age. At least, it is not for such as I to meddle with. Keep thy skin out of danger. Leave swordplay to gentlemen."

"And am I not a gentleman?" Will Shakespeare cried. "Is not my mother an Arden? Hast never heard my father hath applied for a coat of arms?"

"Ay, and got no fair response."

"That's a matter shall be mended."

"As maybe. But I tell thee, Will, for all the friendship I bear thee, I'll not spit myself on any angry gentleman's sword."

"Would I ask such a service? When the fight is on, I'll draw in my own behalf. In brief, good Hamnet, all I require of thee is that thou takest these gloves and this scrip yonder to the Swan Inn, present them, and receive the moneys due. Is that a burden on thy strength or they conscience?"

"Nay, that's an asking easily quit. But what a pother of mystification about so little! Give me the gloves and the scrip."

"That's my good friend. I'll with thee so far, and wait till I see thee again."

They walked on, side by side, down the road. Thus close to the river, the mist was rolling thick and white, curling over their heads like great waves of the ocean, which they had read and heard of, but never seen. Yet already the mist was spinning upwards, turning slowly back on its course as it rose, its curving crests losing shape, thinning and fading as they ascended. It would not be long now before the sun was through: the vapours were the reluctant promise of a warm, unclouded day.

When they came to the lower end of Sheep Street, Will stopped, for now could be heard the noise of horses' hooves clanking on cobble stones, and men shouting and whistling.

"They bestire themselves at the Bear," said Hamnet.

"And at the Swan beyond, I doubt not. Speed thee now, good friend, lest my fine gentleman lose patience. The morning fog will not be with us long, and perchance he too desires to depart with his new gloves. I'll thank thee for this service anon. Meanwhile, expect me yonder in the common pastures. I'll keep company with the kine till thy return."

Hamnet nodded, and trudged off, the gloves held in one hand, towards Butt Lane and the Swan Inn. Shakespeare turned aside from the road, climbed a stile, and walked over the wet grass of Bank Croft towards the river. Ten paces took him out of sight of the road, and the chance of an encounter with some passer-by who would not refrain from idle questioning. To live in Stratford-on-Avon, he decided, was to be cursed with public inquisitions : everyone knew Will, John Shake-speare's eldest son. Many liked him: all respected him because of his parentage, few for what he was. And what, to fetch up facing the question, was he? A youth with a quick tongue and a head perpetually jostled with fancies he could give no body to. A youth who lived in the past, other people's past, and in his own uncharted, boundless, incredible future. And, for the present, a youth notably lacking in industry, of whom many predicted that, once out of his father's fostering care, he would become no better than a charge on the parish. A rogue by predestination. A comely vagabond, with no resource but his reading, a trick of matching word with similar word to strike out a spark of new meaning, and another trick of devising stories. And now he had imposed a menial office, from which he himself drew back, upon his trusting friend. Had Hamnet required fuller reasons, a rounded tale, varnished with romantical lies, would have been proffered him, out of a wastrel's stock of idle fancies.

Truth is, Will Shakespeare arraigned himself as he walked slow and aimless through the meadow mists, I am but a poor fish tramelled up in the net of poesy. I am the fish: a poet authentic would be part of the net. I read, I dream, I have noon-day and moonlight fancies; but when I write them down, they glow for a while, for a day, for a week, and then, conning them over, they are cold and colourless. I am a stranger to myself. I seek and cherish these solitudes of inturned com-munion. I have my secret ecstasies. But they are barren. I am as a wife doomed to still-births. I produce not even mon-sters, merely cold little corses with never a breath of life, and stamped with the paternal lineaments of other men's inven-tion. I should have been born to a gentleman's estate. Thus had I pleased myself and the world. The stars were cursed that plotted my parentage. My mother was an Arden: she should have married within her degree. She did me a wrong ere she conceived me. Nay, that wrongs my father, and ignores the love I bear him. He is a worthy man, and hath wit. Perchance, had he not sired me, I should have lacked this my faculty for words. And then I had gone without a great and grievous burden. I had faced the world with a laugh in my heart to match the smile on my lips. I should have been born a gentleman, with a retinue and estates, and no coil to make concerning money. I could have been well esteemed as a gentleman. Merchants, John Shakespeare himself among them, would have doted on my commands. I should have been a figure at Court, a favourite of taffetaed ladies, a patron of poets. And here am I a poet without a patron, and what is worse, without poetry I dare show to the world.

Walking inattentively, paying no heed to the plaintive noise of the cows and sheep close at hand but mist-hidden, aware only of the despondent course of his own introspection, he had come almost to the brink of the river. The pollarded willows ranged along the bank stirred softly, for a little breeze was ruffling here. The branches, new-leaved, were pencilled dark against the silver-grey and white of the mist drifting past. As he looked at them, Will remembered a maid who had drowned herself, for love, at Tiddington, not so far away on the other bank. More than two years ago, that was, and in a cold February. Some said she drowned herself for love; some that she lost balance as she bent to take up water in a pail. She had sung sad songs and hung garlands of flowers on the willow branches. Once he had it in mind to write a poem about her. It came to naught, like all the rest of his projects.

It was high time to turn back and seek Hamnet Sadler who by now must have delivered the gloves (dear fellow, scorning no low service!) and was perchance wandering the mists calling for his Will, with six shillings and fourpence fastened in his purse. The river and the willows were melancholy playfellows, and suicide no subject for a young man's consideration.

But as he turned away from the river he saw a shadow there, a shape tall and of a piece, impossible to determine through the wispy interventions of the mist, but certainly the shape of no willow tree. And as, stockstill, poised with back-bent head and shoulders upon the arrested width of his stride, he stared, the shadow in the mist moved.

"Hamnet!" he called. "Here am I. But what a plague dost thou so far from the road?"

At the sound of his voice, the shadow moved again, quickly now, and then receded, dissolved away into the mist.

With a curse and a laugh, Shakespeare hurried after it, and fetched up in a few yards on the very brim of the river, leaning his hand against a tree trunk, bewildered. Here, almost underneath his feet, he could see the dark water with the vapour steaming off it, flowing past soft and slow, death-dealing, amorous of golden maids lacking love, and of poets lacking poesy.

He shouted again: "Where art? Stay till I come to thee!"

No answer was returned to him. A moment later, however, as he listened in the fog-bound silence, he heard a sound as of moving feet, and he plunged off again inland, the dewy grass soaking through his yellow hose above the shoes. He called as he went. But when he came up with the source of the noise that had guided him, he found a pair of sheep, wandering and cropping. They looked up at him with mild, incurious eyes, and then bent their heads to the grass again.

The Bank Croft is bewitched, this morning, he thought. An I were simple and believed on fairies, I'd home and report the Puck was tricking me. Yet it was no sheep he had seen poised beside the river. It was Hamnet surely. Who else? And yet again, it was not in Hamnet's custom to play such foolery. He was not gamesome save on gamesome occasions, and then his wits were slow tinder.

There seemed nothing to do but find a way back to the road and wait for Hamnet there, so Will began to trudge through the mist, and had hardly made ten paces when again, dim and indefinite, he saw a human shape wavering among the grey and white obscurity ahead. This time he did not speak, but plunged forward at a run, his feet slithering on the grass. The

figure wavered again as he drew closer, turned as if to evade
him, but too late, for he leaped with outstretched arm and
found his fingers closing on the cloaked shoulder of a woman,
who looked at him with wide eyes and opened her mouth as if
to scream.

"Cry your pardon, mistress," he exclaimed. "I am grievously at fault. I took you for my friend."

He dropped his hand, uncapped, bowed, and carefully
replaced the hat with the green feather aslant. The woman, he
saw, was young and comely, tall and fair-complexioned. She
wore a long blue cloak of linsey-wolsey, and held it gathered
tight about her. Under the shadow of the hood he could not
detect the colour of her eyes, but they were large and lambent,
very grave as she watched him now.

"You affrighted me, Master Shakespeare," she said at last.
She knew his name! But that was nothing untoward. He
was, after all, a figure of some prominence in the borough. And
certainly he had seen her before this moment, though never as
now, with this perplexed but gracious loveliness in her mien.
The clandestine secrecy of this vaporous encounter (though
the mists were rolling swifter past them now, as they stood,
a yard apart, facing each other) stirred excitement in his blood.
Could it be that Venice, Verona and Rome were coming to
Stratford, dreams being transmuted, by some alchemy, into
waking reality?

"I cry your pardon, again, mistress."

She took pity on his dilemma, and with a modesty which
delighted him said: "My name is Hathaway. Anne Hathaway."

"It was on the forward end of my tongue, sped there from
the retiring chamber of my brain."

Anne Hathaway! Nan Hathaway of Shottery. Three, four,
perchance a round dozen times he must have seen her about
the Stratford streets. The gossips were full of professed compassion for her. Now why? Her father was dead, had died
within the past year. But that was not the reason. There was
a scandal of sorts. The girl was still unmarried. She lacked

dower and would not wed beneath the estate of a gentleman. Nay, that was no just cause for scandal. The girl held to her pride. And she was beautiful. It could not be she had gone without suitors. His heart warmed to champion her against the gossips.

"I had fixed a meeting here," he explained, "with Hamnet Sadler." She nodded her head at the name. "Then I wandered in these mists. When I saw someone move at a distance it seemed it could be none but Hamnet."

"But you did not call. You came running, all silent, all eager. I am but a maid, Master Shakespeare, and I should not be here alone. You almost made my heart to stop."

"But it beats fair and true, now, I trust? See, I am all penitence. And I am confounded, also, to think that even in the mists I could mistake you for Hamnet. He is large-built, a solid man, though a worthy, and none but a dolt could mistake his bulk for your slender shapeliness, Mistress Hathaway."

She did not smile at the compliment, nor did he tell her he had chased a sound of feet through the murk and found only a pair of silly sheep. Some follies are best left to perish in oblivion.

"It was you, then," she asked, "who called to me yonder by the river bank?"

"Ay. And it was you, Mistress Anne, it seems, I mistook for a person of twice your bulk and a mere moiety, too small to be discerned, of your graciousness. And the wrong sex, to boot."

"The error was not all on your part. When I heard that cry by the river brink, though I understood no single word of it, for I was privy with my own meditation then, I bethought me it was the voice of Meg Candler, who attends me."

"Yet you answered not? You slipped leash, you dissolved in the mist?"

"Master Shakespeare, I had a desire then to be alone."

Now why should a maid, and a comely maid, nay, more than comely, desire to be alone with her meditations, obscured in mists, among the willow trees on the banks of Avon? It was an offence against nature. It lifted discomfortable thoughts into the mind, of cold deaths, and wet deaths, of burials in unconsecrated ground, of the poor Hamlet wench with her garlands at Tiddington. A lady so fair as this Nan Hathaway, with eyes of a probable blue and hair so fine and, for all the damp darkening it, almost certainly gold in hue (though the close hood made discernment difficult without unmannerly peeping); a lady by entitlement (for was it not said she turned away suitors base-botched in their blood heritage?); a lady, moreover, of pride, with no rustic gigglements, head-bendings, finger-claspings as she confronted a man alone in the mists; such a lady should not be wandering by the grisly brink of a river, companioned only by melancholy!

"Mistress Anne"—this was the second time he had ventured on her first name, and again he escaped reproof, even the reproof of a frown—"we have been the hapless victims in a comedy of errors. The mists have had their sport with us, but look! Already the sun gilds them. The day is up at last. The vapours are in rout, like ghosts at cockcrow. The pride of summer will soon be here, all hot with victory, to salute you."

"I had heard you were a poet, good sir."

"And now——?"

"And now I'll say you make fair speeches."

"I owe you recompense for an unwitting discourtesy."

Here he waited, expecting her to respond provocatively, to ask if penitence were the only reason for his gay compliments. But she said, urgent with anxiety: "I have tarried overlong. Meg will scold me. She has had me in her care since I was a child, girdle-high. She grumbled when I declared I had a whimsy to wander the Croft in the mist, and only followed when I slipped her and away over the stile. And then we parted. The truth is, I had a desire for solitude. I evaded. Nay, I trust Meg has come to no harm. I am idle and thoughtless. A poor old woman, with aches in her bones, lost in the river fogs. Nay now, I trust she has come to no harm."

"Never fear. She turned back before a wet sheep could wag

his tail, I'll take warrant o' that. Come with me, and we shall find her in converse with my Hamnet, high and dry on the roadway yonder."

A maiden passing strange, thus to walk the Croft alone. Most would have too strict a care for their reputations. But wilfulness was the mark of a true lady. Wilfulness and disdain of fear. Mistress Anne had them both, and bore them proudly.

He offered his arm, and she took it with a smile. They set off to walk through the mists, but the mists dispersed before them, thinning into tatters and tendrils that floated waist-high over the grass. The sunshine came, gold, sudden, joyful to their eyes, and there behind the palings they saw Hamnet with a beldame at his side.

"There is your Meg, Mistress Anne."

"I see her, and I can hear her tongue clattering already."

Hamnet stared and pulled off his cap as they came up, but the old woman bustled forward to the stile, holding out her hand to her mistress, scowling at Will Shakespeare, and scolding incessantly.

"So, my pretty Nan, this is the way of it. I am like to be abed with the ague in my bones, while thou keepest assignations under cover of the devil's darkness. Hadst a fancy to see the river's vapours at close quarters! How white they are, the mists, sayst thou! How exquisite! How rich in loveliness! Nay, 'twas not vapour grappled thee yonder, I'll warrant. Art still a maid?"

Anne Hathaway paused upon the topmost step of the stile, and answered coldly: "Cease thy prattling, Meg. An I knew not thy ways, I'd be put to the blush. Explain why I was deserted."

"Deserted, quotha! Didst not abandon me? Didst not give me the go-by? And I, poor deceived old woman that I am, took thee for as honest a maid as ever broke bread."

"Peace!"

Anne came lightly down into the roadway and, turning her head towards Will Shakespeare, who nimbly followed, declared:

"Render thanks to this gentleman who courteously discharged the office of custodian neglected by thee."

"Good day to you, Mistress Meg."

"And you, sir. Heed not my tongue. It ever runs apace, and speaks an old woman's thoughts to shame her. Are you not Master Will Shakespeare, son of the Alderman?"

"I am. And this is——"

"Ay, Master Sadler. We have had converse the while we waited and wondered were you both in the river."

"But I," Anne put in, "have not made Master Sadler's acquaintance. Sir, I am sorry if I have detained your friend. But you may know he has spoken kindly of you."

"Marry," Meg Candler chuckled, "if that was the only employment for your time while you were lost in the mist, there's no harm done. How long away! Ten minutes? Twelve minutes? Time enough for some I could put name to, but my Nan, pretty chuck, she's innocent as a babe unborn. I'd swear it on the book."

"You must forgive her, Master Shakespeare," said Anne, throwing her cloak open so that he could see the grey gown, with its braiding of silver lace, beneath.

"What's to forgive? We are all met, and all's well."

"A gentleman! A gentleman declared by his tongue. Nay, chuck, had the mists held another hour and hadst thou still kept me awaiting here, I'd not blame thee. A proper gentleman, sweet-spoken and comely."

The old face, apple-red in the cheeks, wrinkled, quick-eyed, bristled grey on chin and upper lip, leered at Will. But he turned away quickly, for Anne was putting back the hood from her head, and now he could see that her hair was indeed golden, or golden by glints, where the fine curling hairs sprung loose from the waving mass of brown, centre-parted and coiled over the ears. He had guessed well: her eyes were blue, the blue of periwinkle flowers and, when she turned away from the sun, the deeper, incarnadine blue of violets. She was tall, as tall as himself, very tall for a woman, strong, and she held herself erect. There was more than a country comeliness in her face: it was composed in curves, but curves drawn long and subtle; the brows arched dark over the full splendour of those blue eyes, candid and calm; the nose, not small or pert, faintly aquiline but spreading to the firm span of the nostrils; the cheeks a little plump: the ear tips pink, shewing under the coiled hair; the mouth wide, neatly shaped, soft-lipped, tender; the chin rounded; the throat a proud column descending to the lace collar. This was how he pictured her, inch by inch of careful observation, in his memory afterwards. At the moment he knew only that she was beautiful in his eyes, and that to be with her was joyful; to look at her wakened a tumult in his blood.

"Mistress Hathaway," he said to Hamnet, "heard me crying in the mist and thought to find her Meg. And I, seeking thee, found a lady in distress. 'Twas a comedy of errors."

"And all for the best," exclaimed Meg. "Never doubt it. All for the best. 'Tis a merry first encounter, between two creatures I could not find it in my heart to denounce. And perchance it will not be the last."

"You go too far, Meg," Anne broke in. "The gentleman has done me a service, and I thank him for it, and there's an end."

"I trust not so," said Will. "I do desire your better acquaintance, Mistress Anne. In all courtesy and honesty."

"That's easy accomplished," Meg exclaimed, renewing her reedy chuckles. "At Shottery we reside."

"And that's not at the other end of the world," Shakespeare retorted. "I take your meaning. I will present myself, with your leave, good Mistress Anne, as soon as may be."

He and Hamnet stood back, with doffed hats, as the two women moved off towards Sheep Street.

"Nan Hathaway!" murmured Hamnet. "I wot of her, but never before today have I spoken to her."

"Hadst little enough to say e'en now," his friend retorted.

"I left that to thee. Nan Hathaway! Now 'tis passing

strange a maid like that stays still unwedded. 'Tis not for lack of encouragement from her nurse."

"Oh, Meg? Meg's a bawd."

Hamnet looked astonished, and presently said: "I have discharged thine affairs at the Swan. Here's the money."

"Thanks, good friend."

But Shakespeare did not count the coins or even glance at them as he tilted them into his purse. He was staring over the pasturage of the Bank Croft, exposed beneath the sunshine now, to the willow trees and the broad Avon, smooth and gilded, to the long stone causey and the length of the Clopton Bridge, stretching span after span to where the far bank was wooded with elms and ash trees. Then he turned on his heel, glanced left along the Bank Croft side, over the leafy tree tops, to the little wooden spire of Holy Trinity Church showing thinly pencilled against the blue sky. Again he looked up at the roofs of the Stratford houses, thatched and eaved, built on the slope, and again to the corner of Sheep Street where Anne Hathaway, with flowing cloak and gold-glinting hair, had disappeared without a backward glance, though old Meg had not failed to turn and wave a skinny, promissory hand.

"Thy gentleman," said Hamnet, "expressed himself well satisfied with the gloves."

Will Shakespeare, it seemed, heard nothing.

"It was an unworthy device," Hamnet continued, grumbling, "to send me off on such an errand, that thou shouldst keep an assignation with Mistress Hathaway. Had but to say the word, and I would have left thee alone."

Will Shakespeare stared at him.

"So that's how it seems? I am putting deceptions on thee and on Meg Chandler?" He began to laugh.

But Hamnet's displeasure was not to be turned with a jest.

"I tell thee, Will, 'tis not worthy. 'Tis not honesty. 'Tis not plain-dealing."

Shakespeare laughed. "Thou sayest well. And for thy better assurance, here's my word on it. When I went down on the Bank Croft I had no hope to find another human creature there in the mists. I never spoke to the lady before this morning. But I trust I shall do so again."

The frown, like the shadow from a wind-driven cloud, swept from Hamnet's broad face.

"Give pardon if I wronged thee, Will, but the fault is in part thine own. Should'st not riddle in thy speech. And yet I could wish it were not Nan Hathaway had taken thy fancy. She goes too long unwed. She will be twenty-seven years, or I'm a pagan."

"How dost know that?"

"The time will come soon when I must marry. I keep count of all personable and proper maidens."

"In a book?" Shakespeare demanded, amused. "Tell me, Hamnet, dost keep a chronology of female births and properties in a book? Like a tally of accounts?"

"Laugh, an it please thee. But when a maid attains so ripe an age, and is personable, and yet unwed, there's something amiss somewhere. The gossips are in the right of it."

"But what's amiss?"

"Nothing I know of. But something there must be."

"I'd fain," Shakespeare declared, "trust the witness of mine own eyes and ears rather than the clatter of old wives' tongues."

Hamnet regarded him soberly. "There's wisdom in old wives," he muttered. "And none in thee. Thou'st a brave wit, Will Shakespeare, and thy mind sails round mine like one of our English frigates round a Spanish galleon. And yet thou could'st benefit by attending to my advice."

"Wouldst play guardian to my good behaviour, lad? Thinkest I need a nurse? Wouldst be my Meg? My ancient nurse? My nurse and gossip and bawd?"

"These saucy jests are out of season. Collect thy thoughts. Thou'rt no gentleman of the court to take love so lightly. Unless thou'rt careful, this will end in marriage."

But Will, with a touch of his hand on his friend's elbow, went off crying: "And why not, Hamnet, why not?"

III

THE SEPTEMBER sun was warm on his face as he sat on
the stile at the Shottery end of the footpath, and waited, the
incarnation of patience hard achieved, patience worked against
the grain. The mowers had ceased work, put up their bright
scythes, and were stretched in the shadow under the far side
of the hedge, thirty yards away. He could hear them cracking
broad jests as he sat on, shifting his hands from time to time
on the round wooden bar of the stile. They talked of country
matters over their bread and cheese, in slow country voices.
Their laughter rumbled. The kitchen wenches who had
brought the jars of ale lingered, cackling under their sun-
bonnets at what the men said to them, sometimes throwing an
answer back.

Will could hear their voices plain enough, though he was
not able to distinguish word from word. No matter. An it
pleased him, he could invent the substance and the manner of
such conversations: rough fooling, a gabble of clumsy mockery and bawdry. In another mood he would have joined them,
and excelled them, disdaining their broad jests but making
them gape at the fine conceits he would weave around their
sluggard wits. The common sort were all for bawdry. They
even gave names to hedgeside flowers with their thoughts hot
on the bed or the loose-spread bottles of hay whereon they
achieved their couplings. And their betters no better. The
world was a coarse and fleshly rendezvous, and delicate spirits
must walk with care through it, lest they soil their garments.
A poet in love was cloistered like a friar, and must not look
for understanding save from his mistress. Surely Anne understood him? Surely she knew he kept his tongue from unseemly
jests and his thoughts averted from lust? In her presence, and
indeed with no more than the image of her shrined in his

memory, he lived like a prince, exalted, impassioned, cleansed of the dross of this world.

Nan was tender with him; not proud, neither. She had given him her lips to kiss, and blushed awhile afterward. She knew his love for her was reverent, and esteemed him no less for that he did not urge his desire upon her, like other gallants, all eager to despoil. Nan's blood was cool, as an honest maid's ought to be. It constrained his own furious rages: they needed constraint. Perchance she charmed him most when she sat a little remote, straightbacked, with her head inclined, her eyes grave, and listened to his new-composed poems. She liked them, too. She liked them all. Truth was, they pleased her better than they pleased him. But then she read little: she could not discern semblances, she could not detect whence he filched this phrase and that. It was as well. Not a line he wrote but seemed to him a se'enight later stale and stiff, vassalled to another man's art, and out of all relation to his present self. Fancy danced lithe in his mind, but would not stir beyond the tip of his pen. The time would come when that should be mended, and then Nan's blue eyes would open wide in astonishment, and she would know she had no ordinary sweetheart.

Meanwhile, he must wait as calm as might be on this stile in the hot September noonday. He was not welcome at the house beyond the curve of the road in Shottery village, for the which Nan was bitterly ashamed. His father's affairs were in some confusion, and all Stratford and beyond knew it. There were debts and lawsuits, and money to seek for food and clothing. His mother wept, full and oft, these days. His father kept up a brave show, and his jesting grew louder and broader. But between times, John Shakespeare's good humour would split. He would curse, and lament the number of the family, saying that he was pressed about with children—Gilbert, Joan, and three years' old Edmund, besides Will, the eldest, bringing no grist to the mill. The house in Henley Street was full of unease, and all Stratford knew of it. They knew of it, too, in Shottery, and Nan Hathaway's uncle, himself ridden with debts, made it plain that Will Shakespeare was no welcome suitor there.

So Nan had begged him, her eyes brimmed with tears, to keep away; not to abandon her; to be forgiving and kind, but not to intrude. All his communications with Nan were through old Meg Candler, and half-an-hour since he had walked slowly past the wall of the Hathaway house, which was stepped up the slope, end-on to the lane, and slowly back again. All he had got for his pains was a glimpse of Meg under the orchard trees, on the high ground beyond the Michaelmas daisies and the tall hollyhocks in the garden. Meg had nodded her wicked, wise old head, and presently, he knew, she would find an occasion to totter through the village and out to the stile with a message. He needed that message sorely: a week had passed since he set eyes on Nan and had converse with her.

The minutes went by full slow till at last he saw Meg coming towards him in her bonnet and shoulder cape, one hand on the cord girdle at her waist, muttering to herself as she often did. She affected surprise to see him there, and for a time would disclose nothing.

"Why now, Master Will, what do you here in Shottery?"

"I wait on your coming, Meg, as you well know."

"Marry, and I had thought me past the age for young men's gallantry! I fear you'll find me stiff in the sinew and, to speak truth, not so soft to the kiss as a newborn babe. But a willing heart, young sir, a willing heart."

"All cats are grey in the dark, Meg, or so I have been told. The pity of it is, the day is not dark and I have ever misliked grey cats. But come, tell me of Mistress Anne. How fares she?"

"Passing well. Which is to say, she suffers not of the ague like me. Could I rid me of pains in my bones, and see a little more clear, and sleep sound o' nights, I'd not complain. Argal, say I to pretty Nan, what hast thou to plain for? Wherefore melancholic?"

"Is she so?" Shakespeare broke in eagerly. "Is my Nan sad?"

"Ay. Ever and anon she'll sit with never a clack from her knitting needles, and eyes round as an empty platter and as blank, and ever and anon a will breathe a sigh on the air, no more than would stir the wing of a butterfly."

"And then?"

"And then she'll fall to her knitting again. What else? What would you? Winter comes nearer and will not stay for man or maid. Women must knit, for we shall need scarves against the cold."

"I am glad that she is sad betimes."

"That's unkind."

"Nay. Would you have me wish her to sing like an ousel-cock when she and I have not met this se'enight?"

"But I forgot," said Meg mischievously. "She doth sing, loud and oft and joyful."

"That's when she thinks on me, when she recalls our last meeting and looks to the next."

"Perchance. But I should do wrong an I concealed from you, young man, this sober fact: the maid was given to singing ere ever she met you that morning in the mists on the Bank Croft Close."

"Meg, stand to it."

"That's more than I can do, being but female."

The youth smiled to conceal his abashment, but Meg, wrinkling her sharp nose and narrowing her eyes, laughed in his face: "Out upon it, there's blood in thy cheeks. Not so innocent as to mistake my meaning, but a maid yet, I'll swear. I could embrace thee when I see thy ready blushings."

"No more, I pray. Deliver thy message, good Meg."

"What message?"

"Why, the message Mistress Anne hath charged thee with."

"Did she now? I wonder. Perchance I have forgot?"

"Meg, an thou delayest longer, I'll not answer for my impatience. Wouldst have me take thy shoulders and rattle thee like a dice box till the message fall out along with thy last few teeth?"

"What's this? Violence? But I am not afeared. In my time I have been shaken by stronger men than thou, Master Will, and I do not recollect that any teeth fell out. But I am an old woman, and my recollection not what it was. Perchance I did lose something? Perchance it was only my maidenhood? Yet that could have been but the once."

"Thou'rt a bawd, Meg."

"Nay, if that is thy mode of address, I'll no more. I'll back to the house. There's tasks a-plenty there for Meg."

"Cry pardon. Not thou but thy tongue's the bawd."

"A proper distinction, Master Will. And who shall be answerable for his tongue? 'Tis a naughty member, and froward. A woman can but reprove it and hope for better behaviour in future. In brief, I'll shame thy young apprehension no more."

"And thou'lt give me the message?"

"Forthwith. Cruelty's not in my nature. I have sins a-many without that. My mistress, and, for the matter of that, thy mistress—in all innocence, forsooth!—sends you her duty, and bids me say this afternoon she walks abroad by Lime Close. 'Tis an excursion commanded by her aunt, and for pleasure, for the exercise of the limbs, for the dispersal of certain melancholic humours which have troubled her of late."

"That's brave news, Meg."

"Is it so? But wait. My mistress hath an aunt."

"That's no news at all. Plague on the woman."

"Season thine impatience awhile. This aunt intends to accompany her niece while she walks abroad. Thou'rt discomfited? But wait yet awhile. Meg is kind. Meg was not born the day before yesterday. Meg hath a different plan."

"But what? Would'st dare poison the odious woman?"

"I could. I know the simples necessary. But I would not, having a fancy to die in my bed. Besides, poor creature, though she hath a tongue with a tang and griddles me like an over-baked pastry, I wish her no ill. 'Twill suffice thy purpose, good Master Will, if the meddlesome aunt be unable to make the excursion this afternoon?"

"Ay, indeed. But how? What's in thy mind, Meg? A draught to procure sleep? I have heard of such drowsy syrops!"

"Those, too, I could procure and mix."

"Thou'rt a witch, Meg."

"First a bawd and now a witch! Have a care of thy tongue, young gentleman. 'Tis passing strange I take such trouble to do thee service when all the reward I get is fine epitaphs."

"Pardon. And I promise I'll see thine epitaph, when the time comes, not yet, I trust, is fair and courteous. But tell me, dost plan to administer a sleeping draught to Nan's aunt?"

"If I did, would be too late by now. Besides, when folk sleep untimely, in the light of day, there are questions asked. I learned that long since. I have a plan more direct, and 'tis already in operation. The herbs I have administered will do no harm. Nay, they are beneficent medicine, and potent. They have taken their first effect already, and the upshot is no more than this, that the woman will not stir from Shottery this twenty-four hours. What's more, Meg will go under no suspicion. 'Twill all be blamed on green apples or hard gooseberries, for she took both to her dinner last night."

Shakespeare's laugh was sudden and explosive. The mowers, crossing the stubble to resume their work, looked back over their shoulders at him, but he paid no heed.

"Meg, this is the most resourceful stratagem in history. Bocace himself hath none better. Bless thee, thou art translated. I pronounce thee neither witch nor bawd, but the good fairy of Shottery. Will Shakespeare shall ever stand thy debtor. So this afternoon I shall keep rendezvous with Mistress Anne alone? That's the purport of thine errand?"

"Alone? Fie, Master Will. No virtuous maid walks abroad alone. I shall keep my mistress company."

"But not too close, Meg. Nay, I can trust thee. Hast stood apart, out of sight and hearing, before now."

"It may so hap," Meg retorted, "I shall remember an old obligation, and visit a friend I have, a good gossip, lives in Sanctuary Lane. And it may so hap I shall be so much intent upon this visit and conversation, it shall escape my mind Mistress Anne is no longer with me. And thus if she wanders afield beyond Lime Close, and there meets with a young gentleman we both wot of, I shall know nothing of it."

"This is meat and drink to me, Meg. Would I could reward thee better than with these poor words."

"I want no moneys of thee, Master Will. And there's the proof I am no bawd, spite of a free-spoken tongue. What I do, I do for love of my pretty Nan, for the truth is, she doth dote upon thee."

"And I upon her."

"A pair of turtle-doves! But hark ye, an I am a turn-away nurse, not seeing what I choose not to see, 'tis upon reason. Thou'lt not offend her, Master Will? Thou'lt curb thy longing? 'Tis a sweet maid, and a virtuous. Thou'lt do her no wrong?"

The young man was insulted, and drew himself up with braced thighs and shoulders as he answered: "I tell thee now, I do love thy mistress in all honour. My love for her is fenced with reverence."

"Ah, sweetly spoken. And I have seen for myself, by the scarlet flag that flies so sudden in thy cheek, thou'rt innocent as she. Yet I must remember thou'rt a man. And come to that, she's female. The fevers of close company are apt to dissolve the finest protestations."

"My most earnest desire, Meg, and I give thee my word on it, the word of a Shakespeare, ay, and of an Arden too, is to marry thy mistress. Did it rest with me, as thou knowest, we had been wedded ere this. But equally thou knowest I am but a minor, and my father's affairs lack prosperity at this present."

Old Meg sighed for sympathy. "That's ever the way of it

with the gentles. Money's the foundation they build their marriages upon. Nan's dowry is no building stone, either. 'Tis but a pebble. And thou'rt so young, not nineteen years yet. I have forgot what is the feeling of having but nineteen years in this world. Still, I remember I was better found in wisdom than thou, and no maid, I fear me."

She paused, remembering that Anne was twenty-seven, though few would guess it. If pretty Nan did not make a match of it soon she would die an old maid, doomed to lead apes in hell. An ill future for any female, and for one so sweet and comely as Anne 'twould be a foul calamity. Her mother dead, and her father too, this past year, and what did uncle or aunt, proud and mean, care for a poor maid fast in love, without hope of marriage? This was a wrong that cried to heaven for redress.

"The Hathaways," exclaimed Will mournfully, "refuse consent. They will not so much as have me within their doors."

"I know it full well," said Meg. "Else why am I here?" But she spoke absently, her mind busy with a project.

"As for my father, he's waist-deep in his own troubles, and looks sour at me for that I clutter his house with my unwanted presence."

"They'll not consent, quotha! But there's a way, Master Will, to make parents all eager to consent."

"Would I knew it."

"Go to. Thou'rt not so maidenly thou canst not make a guess. List to the blood in thy veins, and thou'lt get the answer. Nay, now! Fire-faced, again? But what's amiss? Thou'd think no shame were it done in a lawful marriage-bed. Troth, 'tis as sweet an encounter under the woodland boughs or under the stars. I pledge thee my word for that."

"I am not made for such treachery, Meg."

"Treachery! Treachery, quotha! Nay, an thou shouldst repudiate my Nan afterward, that would be treachery. But if I put a spark in thy secret hot thoughts to enkindle them,

'tis because I trust thee. The maid will weep, I doubt not.
'Tis the way of maids. But tears can be dried. And 'tis a
remedy beyond compare for mending the stubborn will of
unconsenting parents. Go to! I have tarried here overlong
and said overmuch, perchance. Forget my words. Let them
be as they were never spoken. And yet, Will Shakespeare, thou
art a fool if thou dost forget. Look for my mistress in Sanctuary Lane, by the Salmon Jowl, at three o' the clock. The
flower blooms but once. Opportunity knocks, and having
knocked and had no answer, flies away. There's wisdom for
youth. There's a riddle, and he's a dolt who cannot unriddle
it. Farewell."

"Commend me to thy mistress."

He lingered by the stile, and when at last he turned away
and began the footpath journey back to Stratford, he went
thoughtfully, and only quickened his pace when he remembered
that at best he would be late for dinner. His father gave him a
sour welcome, for the family had done with the neck of mutton
when he arrived, and the dish taken to the kitchen for the
servants. Will declared he had no stomach for meat, and would
be well content with apples and bread and cheese.

"Even so," John Shakespeare retorted, "thou'lt eat more
than thou'st earned. A sorry balance in my accompt books,
and then thou comest late and with an ill face."

Gilbert and Joan looked sorry for their elder brother under
reproof, but the sharp words excited them. They sat silent, with
bright, observant eyes. Young Dick, and Edmund, scarce able
to feed himself, were frightened. They dared not look up from
their trenchers.

"I'll prentice thee, and that right soon," John Shakespeare went on, stamping his feet noisily among the rushes
under the table. "Had I done my duty, thou were bound
years since."

Mistress Shakespeare intervened at that. She was older than
her forty years, perpetually disturbed by household cares, for,
as she often reminded her husband, she had been bred to expect

a lady's idleness. Her hands, though roughened front and back, were still slender, and her face, for all it had sagged out of its youthful freshness, was proud and thin.

"Leave Will alone, my goodman. The boy's not in health. Hath reached a troublesome age for those with gentle blood in their veins. Perchance the heat o' the day hath turned his stomach."

"Shouldst have been at work in the shop then, not gadding in the sun."

"Nay, Will doth all the work thou canst find for him. 'Tis no fault of his the work's to seek these days."

"The fault is mine then?" her husband roared, and morsels of wet bread spluttered from his lips.

"Now John, have a care. Eat delicately. The head of the house should set an ensample."

"Head of the house! The hindquarters more like, for anyone who pleases to kick. Insulted by my son, and then again insulted by my wife! I'll not bear it."

But the image he had evoked to picture his humiliation delighted his fancy. His wrath rumbled away, and he left the table, declaring he had affairs toward. The whole family, except perhaps little Edmund, for whom all his elders were unpredictable mysteries, knew that within a few minutes John Shakespeare would be asleep in his bed upstairs.

To Will it was incredible that anyone should wish to slumber during the daylight hours. He supposed his father must be getting old. Poor man, there could be little for him to look forward to except a godly death, and one in such a plight could be forgiven a few lightning flashes of ill-temper. He was not a hard man. He could not sustain his rages, and at a pinch they could always be turned aside with a jest. He would awake refreshed and in good humour. But before then his eldest son must be out and away.

So Will fetched water from the rainwater cask in the garden at the Back, which abutted (a fact he refused to admit in his thoughts and ignored if it were mentioned in conversation) on the Gild Pits. Then he went indoors to wash and to pick his teeth clean, to make his doublet tidy and comb his hair to order. That done, he contemplated himself in the hand-mirror awhile, and was pleased with the soft translucency of his complexion, with the rise and smooth planing of his temples, with the shape and the brightness of the eyes staring so gravely back at him from the mirror, although he could have wished them any colour but hazel, which was not a colour at all, but a mixture, a nullification. Blue would have pleased him better, his mother's clear Arden blue; or else his father's ox-eye brown. He tried to persuade himself that the line of his jaw and his chin was growing firmer, as beseemed a man, and that the fine down on his cheeks had acquired a sturdier growth. The red tones in his hair, however, delighted him: they were uncommon. His hair was fine and had a gloss like chestnuts new spilled from the husk. Nan had been pleased to commend it.

"At the mirror again, Will." His mother's voice, tender under the acerbity, disturbed him. "None who saw thee now would believe I have but one girl child alive."

Will turned quickly away. "There's a pestilent odour from the gutter outside," he complained.

"It offends thy nose, doth it? But thy father heeds nothing of it. We have had trouble with the Corporation before, on that same count. I must put him in mind of it. Or stay, Will. There's a matter thou couldst attend to."

"I will, I will."

"I doubt it," his mother muttered as she went out to the kitchen. "Like father, like son, all projects and no decisions. And this is what I am brought to, a cleanser of stinking gutters. I, an Arden!"

"Nay," Will called after her. "Fear not. I shall speak with the man myself."

But his mother did not hear, and before he was ten yards from the door the smell was out of his nostrils and the promise out of his thoughts. His step quickened, although he knew he was over-early and would have to wait by the field called the Salmon Jole for the coming of Anne.

She was the mistress of his heart, and they were troth-plighted, but in secret. When he told that scheming old lewdstress, Meg, that he reverenced Anne, he spoke truth. Yet not the whole truth, and Meg knew it. There was desire in him, as well as reverence. And, desire once consummated, reverence could go a-begging. That was what people said. That was the privy pith of young men's braggart talk and old men's snickerings under ale-house windows. That was the burden of old gossips' chatter. Man, masculine man, was the besieger, all eager to storm the breach, and the maid who wished for the commendation of the world held off the assault with fair words till she made terms of honour. The rules of the tourney were well understanded, and opinion had it that the vanquished could plead for no clemency. Such was the theory of it, but the practice otherwise: full many a bride came to the bride-bed with the chill of maidenhood already taken off her flesh.

But Nan and I, he argued with himself as he walked towards the town boundaries, are not of that easy sort. She is timid, and hath a proper pride. I have made no verbal test of her modesty: nay, were I bold-tongued, she'd fly me as I had the leprosy written white on hand and brow. That I am assured of. Yet old Meg is ever dropping lewd canticles into her ears, at least when she is in company with me; and Nan, though she chides, doth it with an absent air. Perchance I wrong her even thus to admit such speculations into my mind? 'Tis vile to think of Nan so. What am I then? Her true lover and suitor, or some idle gallant, with blood of fire and heart of ice, set to filch that the value of which he is not able to assay? Do I adore my Nan, and hope to live honourable in her esteem? Ay, that I do. But do I also lust after her body's beauties? If lust be cruel, reckless, violent, then I do not lust, and purity dwells yet in my heart. But if lust be this consumption of desire within me, this imagining by day and night of all of Nan mine eyes have seen and all they have not yet seen, these ecstasies of pain and unfulfillment—then 'tis true I lust after her. If lust be outrage, Tarquin's way of love, then am I free from it. And if lust be the rightful name for what burns in my heart, then fair is foully named, and all's confusion.

My desire is to marry Nan, and I am persuaded her protestations are sincere, and she would be my wife. What's ill with that? What offence to the law? We are not kindred, neither, so where is sweet religion harmed? Where lies the obstacle, save in my poverty, my youthful years, and the unfeeling opposition of parents? And all that, says old Meg, can be removed if I do but let loose desire, overbear my pretty Nan's opposition, and get her with child. Likely 'tis true. Hathaway, Shakespeare and Arden, there's this between them: they're peacock-proud, and would swallow the blackest draught ere they'd stomach scandal.

Meg's a cunning beldame. She is devoted to Nan. And that being so, would she have hazarded her advice to me this noonday, but that she knows my love is not lustful but true? Go to, Will Shakespeare, thou'rt a fool an thou forget! So said Meg. Meg hath made my opportunity for this very day. Shall I be, in sooth, a fool if I let it slip? Is it, in truth, a service I do my Nan, gaining inviolable leasehold upon our future marriage, if I do storm her virgin citadel? Nay, storm is no word. An I have her, I'll have her with soft words, endearments and gentle embracings, I'll have her yielding free admittance or not at all. But such a beguiling, dependent on the loving trust she hath put in me, coming in maidenly faith to rendezvous this afternoon, would be fouler treachery than force. Yet is it treachery if my further intent be marriage? Meg chuckles, and blinks her antique eyes at me, and holds me an idiot to use the word treachery. Would all this were as simple to me as to Meg's autumnal mind.

Out upon it, fool! Think on the legions of men that have jumped, lusty and glad, into the lists from which thou drawest back, all lax and pale with introspection; men by thousands and tens of thousands that have leaped and never stopped for a second thought. Yet other men are not I, and other women not Anne Hathaway. She loves me now; will she hate me afterward? That I could not bear. Meg says no. And Meg is old in wisdom. Or in sin? Moreover, after her crabbed fashion, Meg loves Nan. I could call a curse on my parentage, that hath fixed me before this dilemma. An I were a gentleman in substance, as I am by heritage, not tormented by lack of property, not bound within the petty scope of a town no one hath heard report of, there'd be none of this. I'd marry Nan, and live happily, in high romance.

Perplexed by such indecisive meditations, he made his way to Sanctuary Lane, and waited by the field called, from its shape, the Salmon Jowl—the Tail was beyond. And when, twelve minutes late, Anne appeared, walking slow to keep pace with Meg Candler, he still did not know what his intent was, if he would let pass the presented opportunity or take Meg's counsel. His thoughts abashed him, rising in tides of guilt as soon as he came forward to greet Anne, and saw her smiling a frank welcome. Meg watched him blush, and her scrutiny made his cheeks sting the more.

"Here I turn aside," the old woman announced. "I have employment for my tongue, with a gossip will tell me many a story, I warrant. And if haply, my chucks, ye do not follow me, that's an ill chance. See ye are returned here by five o' the clock, and I'll observe nothing and remember nothing. Yonder's the door. Knock once. All welcome guests knock but once, Master Will. Thou takest my meaning?"

She turned away, teetering to herself in her thin old voice.

"Meg's a stiff-kneed old mischief-monger," said Will as he walked on at Anne's side.

"Is it mischief to leave us alone?" Anne asked. "Nay, 'tis sweet mischief, and I cannot find it in my heart to reprove her."

Will's side glance was swift and startled. Had Meg been whispering in Nan's ear too? But the calm candour of those blue eyes rebuked him. I am but a rogue to foster such lewd thoughts, he reflected. I have already dishonoured in my mind the love between Nan and me. I am not worthy so much as to walk by her side, as I do now. She must never know what a turmoil of corrupt imaginations creeps in my brain, at times, like maggots.

"Where do we go?" he asked.

"Where it pleaseth thee, Will, so there is shade from the sun and refuge from curious eyes. I put my reputation to hazard, thus to walk the road in thy company, with Meg away."

"Shalt not repent this trustfulness. Look. We'll go to the greenwood on yonder bank of the river. The path is hedged and shaded, and 'tis not probable, though not beyond possibility, we shall be seen by any."

They turned under the high wall of the Mill Lane till they came to the narrow wooden bridge, railed on one side, which spanned the river above the mill pool and the broad shallows of the fishing grounds. Anne kept her head averted from the church and the town as they crossed the river: there well might be, she said, malicious eyes in the mill peeping out to observe who used the bridge.

Will laughed. "Millers' men," he declared, "are gossips, I doubt not. But they're not idle at this time o' day. They'll have their arms deep in their sacks, never fear.

"Better they see not my face, for all that."

"Unfortunate miller's men," said Will. "Their loss is grievous."

"Nay, an thou mockest me, I'll return to Meg this instant."

But she knew that he was tender and earnest, that he adored her, that not for ten seconds could he keep his loving eyes from her face. They left the bridge and took to the footpath which, sheltered by tall hedges, diverged from the black mud margins of the river and wound steeply up to a wooded knoll.

It was a difficult and cautious task to walk along the high-ridged ruts in the lane, baked dry and hard by the sun, and

Anne, lifting her green kirtle in one hand, complained that her ankles twisted and turned at every other step.

"I'll carry thee then."

She smiled, and said she was no boneless, famine-fleshed mouse of a woman, to be lifted without thought; yet perchance he might give her his hand, the better to maintain her balance on these high-heeled shoes.

"My hand and my heart are always thine."

"Gallantly spoken. Nay, Will, I do love thee for thy pretty speeches—so thou dost not rehearse them with other maids. I confess I have tremors at times, the words fall so pat and customary from thy tongue."

"Thou knowest," he began.

"Ay, I know. But give me thy hand."

When he had her hand in his, however, small and firm and warm, a little damp, answering his clasp timidly but without pretences, he was not content. He must needs come to a halt then, facing her, his shoes scrabbling for foothold in the ruts while he put his arms round her, one hand holding her against his breast, the other tight on her waist, drawing her in to him till her face tilted up and his kisses came swift and hot on her lips.

When she drew away at last, her cheeks were scarlet and she closed her eyes against him.

"Hast hurt me, Will. Nay, I am not angry."

He was trembling from head to foot, and his thoughts were a riot, dazing him.

"We must on," he said.

She put her hand in his again, but went with her eyes downcast, and so, without another word, each locked in a secret meditation on the throbbing blood borders of which desire was eager, apprehensive and hopeful, they walked side by side through the scented afternoon heat of the lane, till it levelled at the top of the knoll. Thirty yards beneath them the Avon flowed, sun-gilded over the muddy slow surface. They could see it between the branch spreads, leafed red and tawny among the green, of the beeches and oaks rooted in the bank, and the lower, thicker clusterings of the bramble and elderbush undergrowth. On the other side of the path the knoll rose higher and steeper, cool shadowed by tall young trees whose mossy roots arched out of the earth and were interspersed with beds of bracken.

"Canst climb yonder, with my hand to help?" Will asked.

She gave him a startled glance, a timid enquiry of the eyes, and at once he urged: "An we stay here on the path, whoever comes by will see us. There we shall be hid from every eye."

And so it was he who discovered the secrecy of that greenwood bower, hung between the purling river and the upland cornfields. It was he who decided, she who acquiesced; he who led the way up, pausing, with feet braced against roots and stones, to stretch back and hand his sweet Nan over the dry sliddery grass and moss, till they stood breast-high among the burnished bracken fronds, and panted and laughed. It was he who swept a half-dozen stems flat with his foot, and bade her sit in the clearing he had made. She sank to the ground with the green kirtle spreading around, the high heels which had so troubled her thrust into the turf, her hands clasped about her knees. Swift and easy he sat himself beside her, but a foot away, and it was he who began to talk.

"Nan," he said, "this is beyond endurance."

"To be with me here?"

"Not to be with thee always. To be compelled to let day after day, slow, empty days, go by and never to kindle my eyes on thee, never to speak, never to hear thee speak."

"But we have this moment now. 'Tis poor courtesy, Will, to sit with sullen face now we are together."

He looked up to where, overhead, the bracken fronds stirred against the sky, itself canopied with leaves and branches. The privacy of this bower, so swiftly found, so remote from the world, excited and terrified him.

"Ay," he admitted, "we have an hour now."

"Almost two hours."

"But I want a lifetime, Nan. My lifetime and thine. And all I get is soured-cream looks."

"Not from me, Will."

"O, my sweet! Not from thee, 'tis true."

"Would it were in my power to order our days otherwise. But there, 'tis not. Let's make no more complaint. Let us smile and talk, for presently we must part, and the minutes move apace."

"Time makes a fool of love."

She leaned towards him tenderly, and at once he had a premonition that cause was already charged with effect, that all his fearful resolutions to be cool and reverential with her were already void within him.

"Must not be sad," she whispered. "Come, I'll comfort thee."

She drew his head down on her shoulder, and presently he turned and lay in her lap, till she could feel his young, taut weight across her flanks, and the warmth of her body was communicated to him, secret, sweet, delicious, through the thin stuff of his doublet.

"Art sorry," she asked, "we went walking the mists by the Bank Croft that May morning?"

"It was the most glorious deed in my life," he whispered back. "Not that there's any other glory, now I reflect upon it, in my short chronicles. He wrote ill-poesy, was an idle fellow, but he saw Anne Hathaway and loved her. That's all the mason will have to inscribe over my tomb."

"'Tis not ill poesy, and thou'rt forbid to say so. And thou'rt not an idle fellow."

"Well, my mistress is kind. Charity tempers her judgment. But the rest of the inscription? Hast any quarrel with that? Is't true? Do I love thee?"

"Thou sayest."

"But is it true?"

"As true as most lovers' protestations, I make no doubt."

"More true. More true by far. And not because my merit

surpasses that of other men in love, but because it is Nan I adore. 'Twas not in nature that I should see thee and refrain from loving thee. I could demonstrate that as a proposition in logic, were I not . . ."

"Wert thou not! What art thou not?"

"Not willing to lay waste the precious time. O Nan, wilt thou wed with me? Wilt thou in sooth?"

"I have said it."

"Then say it again."

"Very well. I say it again."

The ardour of his eyes disconcerted her. She bent over him and with her fingers gently closed the lids, and held them closed. He smiled submissively, but soon asked: "When shall we marry, Nan? When?"

"That's more than I can say."

"Ay. God's curse on our ill-fortune."

She frowned over him, letting him open his eyes again while her fingers played with his hair.

"Must not speak curses," she chided.

"What else to do?"

"Nay, if employment is thine only lack, thou couldst kiss me."

She trembled at the swift strength of his arms coming up to embrace her, but in a moment her lips were yielding and responding warm to his, he had twisted his head and shoulders out of her lap, and she was lying full length under the bracken stems, caught close in his embrace. He could see the sweat now started on her brow under the dishevellment of her golden hair; he could see that her face was changed, smoothed into a languor; the eyes lidded against him; the lips, as if his kisses had crumpled them, soft and damp, with a faint rash mantling along the edges. And close against his arms and his body he could feel the ardent stir of her breast. He was astounded. His mind paused on the brink of achievement, bewildered by this transformation of his cool and dainty Nan.

The lashes lying long and dark over her eyes flickered for a moment. She moved her arms as if to thrust him away. But her eyes did not open, and when he tightened his clasp about her she murmured his name three times, almost moaning the syllables against the hot invasion of his kisses.

And so it was done, as Meg had foreseen it. And afterwards Nan wept, as Meg had also foreseen. But Meg had not known, or had not disclosed it, this abject shame, this ingrowing frost of remorse which possessed Will Shakespeare but a few moments after he had made Nan Hathaway a woman, and known himself a man.

He tried to murmur something of his contrition to her, but she seemed not to hear. She wept softly, without intermission. The tears flowed down her face, till it was stained and swollen. When he went to her side, to comfort her with kisses, he thought she would strike him, but abruptly her weeping ceased. She came close into his arms, and whispered: "Will, thou'lt wed me? Thou'st promised."

He bent his head to acknowledge the plighting, and kissed her again, sober now, earnest, a little frightened.

IV

THE FIRST gale of autumn was blowing. It had risen in the night and wakened him several times. Now on this clouded, sunless forenoon it was still blustering down the curve of Henley Street. Lying fully dressed on the bed that his sister Joan, silently reproachful, had tidied two hours since, he listened with a perverse satisfaction to the vehemence of the wind on the walls and the roof. It thudded against the leaded windows, and came into the room in thin cold penetrations so that he could feel his skin quiver and contract before the draught. It shook the heavy thatching on the roof beams over his head. It made the trees in the garden at the Back, overlooking the Gild Pits, sway and creak: the grass there was strewn with unquiet leaves torn away in the night, and one branch of the oak, lichened green down to the jagged yellow of the fracture, lay against the fence, twitching, heaving up as the wind tormented it, sinking again with every momentary lull. Sometimes a gust would bring with it a bombardment of raindrops ringing hard and peremptory on the window panes.

The whole house was dark and uneasy, full of strange noises: and he preferred it so. The destructive gale sorted with his humour. He lay stretched in arrogant, secretly shamefaced idleness, and thought of himself, Will Shakespeare, as a living tomb of aborted hopes and ambitions, twenty-two years old, married, the father of a family of three, and of no profit to himself, to his wife, to his babes, to his father, to the world. Even Hamnet Sadler, godfather to the twins, his ancient friend, though he spoke no reproaches, looked at him these days with bewildered eyes. Depend upon it, Hamnet, in his heart reckoned Will Shakespeare a useless fellow, of less value in the world than a cold fish: for a fish, though it stink when you keep it overlong, may be cleaned and cooked, an you seize the opportunity, and so eaten. A fish is good Friday fare, but Will Shakespeare is no man's meat any day of the week.

Yet, he reflected, there's always a reservation. His thoughts already had acquired the sensual urgency, compact of hot enjoyment and sour derision, which often overtook them since that afternoon he had taken Meg's counsel in the greenwood above the Avon banks. More frequently and more willingly his mind had filled with these throbbing images—though in sober recollection they abased him—since he had sunk into this lethargy of hopelessness. Bawdry had been his refuge, his sanctuary from the reproachful inquisitions of friends and family, and now he sped his thoughts into those unholy cloisters. No man's meat he might be, but still meat for Nan any night and every night. Were other women like his wife, a breed of hypocrites, doffing modesty with their clothing, one person in daylight and another between the sheets?

Nay, Nan was not immodest. No unseemly words came from her lips. She babbled sugar; she sighed; she kept silence. She was good. The evil was in him, but she never called him to account for it. All Stratford admired at her loyalty to a worthless husband who earned less than his own bread. But then Stratford did not know the reason for Nan's devotion. Nan made Will her precious treasure, and valued him dear, for the pith that was in him, the bedwork which alone mitigated and excused his idleness. Nan was a good mother, a decent housewife, calm-faced, busy-handed, beyond reproach. Who but Will Shakespeare knew that other Nan who never refused what was offered her, who would not await upon the offering, who was tireless in the hot response? Yet in the morning she would be up betimes, cool-lipped, steady-eyed, even in voice, discreet in gesture. She was two people, one all female flesh, and the other all housewife. But I, thought Will, I cannot leave behind me in the bedchamber all remembrance of things done there. My mind clings to the past and leaps to the future.

Before that first encounter with Anne in the bracken he had
been an innocent, a boy who dreamed of love as gracious
gestures, high-sounding phrases, reverential services. That
was no more. Anne—and yet she was a maid when he had her;
and she was a faithful wife yet; she put no horns on his forehead—Anne had unchained a legion of lusty devils in his
blood. What had he stirred in her for return? Nothing
beyond her control. She could quit the bed with the morning
light and go about her tasks as if codpieces were meaningless
ornaments, as if the flesh beneath her farthingale were marble
cold, as if men and women had but a vegetable power of
engendering. All Stratford despised Will Shakespeare and was
compassionate towards Anne: yet Anne had the better of their
bargain. She took benefit of his nocturnal service, and yet
poised herself, like a monument, upon the pedestal of modest
reputation. I cannot resist her, was his conclusion, so sharp
and bitter that almost he could hear the unspoken words
reverberate in his ears. I am kept like a stallion for stud. An I
do not something desperate, and soon, I shall have a family to
be counted by the dozen about my ears, and all a charge on
the parish.

He jerked himself upright on the bed, and, moving his legs
over the side till his feet touched the floor, he stood up, stretching his body, bending his arms, enlarging his chest, stiffening
his shoulders till the blades almost met in his back. The
action relieved the aching desolation of his mind. He told
himself he would now go downstairs and find work to do. But
at once he remembered there was little employment in his
father's business these days.

His sister Joan, with his mother and his wife, did the work
of the house, the cooking and cleaning, the care of the children,
and much of the fetching and carrying. There was one manservant, a porter, and John Shakespeare had no apprentices
now. He and Gilbert could do all the dressing and shaping
of leather, all the sewing of gloves, all the buying (little of it)
and all the selling (there was even less of that). Gilbert was

industrious, and had his father's approval. To Will, who should have been the succeeding pillar of the household, the accounts were entrusted. He disdained the work, but did it well, for he could write fair and clear, when he took trouble, both in the old and in the new Italian style. To enter the books occupied but an hour or two a day, and it was melancholy work: the debts grew no smaller.

Contemplating that sad record every day, Will had formed a philosophy, a philosophy in the abstract, inutile as yet, removed from all apparent expectation of his future. This philosophy had so far neither flower nor fruit: it was no more than a root, and the root was the idea of security. The adventures of the mind were always open to be blasted by poverty. They could proceed only from the safety of the body, and that depended upon money and property. Will held himself to be wronged by destiny, in that he was born of gentle blood, inapt to a burgess's life, and yet denied even the gross comfort, the freedom from care about pence, which a burgess's son should inherit. He could not bring himself to take an interest in hides and gloves, to fawn on buyers, as Gilbert did, he admitted, with no ill grace. And without that mercantile assiduity, there seemed to be no escape from Stratford, from poverty, from the shame of his wife and his family dependent on his father already over-burdened. I know the root I need, he told himself: but where to find it and how to plant it, there's the rub.

He opened the door and walked through into the next room—there were no corridors or galleries as in a big house. Here, in the canopied bed, he and all his brothers and sisters had been born. And here beside the bed was his little Susan, three years old, playing with her dolls. There in the double-cot —Gilbert had made it, for Gilbert was clever with his hands— the twins were sleeping, eighteen months old. There was no other room in the house free for them. He bent over the cot for a moment. Hamnet—named after Hamnet Sadler—had his father's hair: it had darkened since he was born, and was soft and silky, glossy, chestnut brown, a little damp as it curved over the smooth forehead. It was a sorry inheritance, Will considered. The boy smiled in his sleep, and silently his father bade him smile while he might: an he were another such as Will Shakespeare, life with all its favours would prove but a jade, ever receding as he advanced towards it. Judith had her father's eyes, and in the plump infancy of her face it was impossible to guess to what kind of womanhood she would grow. And her eyes were lidded now. But they were dark-lashed, like Nan's, and her hair had not changed hue as Hamnet's had. It was corn-gold, like Nan's. I'll wish thee a better husband, he whispered.

Susan, kirtled to her feet in a green velvet which once had been her mother's best, looked up from her dolls as he came across to her. She was gold-haired and blue-eyed, too. She tilted back her head for his kiss, and then rubbed her face softly against his short beard. This was an experience she always enjoyed. But almost at once she said: "Do not disturb me, now, dear father. I have much to do. Hast thou no employment?"

She began to rearrange the little wooden dolls with their painted faces and hands. The thin childish voice was quite without reproof, but the words startled him. He turned away to the head of the rear staircase, unlatched the gate, latched it behind him again, and went slowly down the stairs. Susan was but three years old, yet already she noticed her father's idleness. Better for them, he thought sourly, I had never been born, or had been gelded ere I set eyes on Nan.

In the front room his father was at work with shears, shaping a buff jerkin. As he lifted his eyes to greet his elder son they darkened for a moment, but almost at once they were glinting and merry again. His hair had bleached from brown to grey this last year or two, but his cheeks were still round and red. He might curse Will at times in the privacy of his own house, but he was determined still to maintain before all his friends that the boy had parts, would find himself yet, and—to grow to a point—that no Shakespeare was less than the equal of any in Stratford under the degree of knight.

John Shakespeare was a man who blossomed in prosperity and was plainly taken aback that his affairs should not go so well of late. He liked his food and his ale, his friends around him in a tavern, his family around him at home. Solitude withered him. He enjoyed his own jests. He had a mind to keep jesting through this period of debts and difficulties, protracted now beyond all belief, in the certainty that jesting would presently distil all that incommoded him! "The rose will bloom again," he was fond of saying. "Wait on the season, and the frosts will pass." Will was fond of him, and took his occasional hard words with patience. My father and I, Will reflected, are of a piece. We are not apt to this world, nor the next neither. He believes he is born to trade in leather, but he lacks cunning. Others deceive him as soon as they provoke him to the laugh, and that's no unconscionable task. But he does not understand he is no match for rogues within the law. Whereas I know I cannot deal with Stratford on Stratford's terms.

"How now, Will?" John Shakespeare exclaimed.

"Well, passing well, in body. In spirit, no such matter."

"The wind and the rain, do they o'ercast thee? Never heed them, Will. They'll pass. The sun will shine again."

"The wind and the rain have not oppressed my spirit, good father."

"Ay. When thou wert but a little boy, head to my knee, thou wouldst brave the storm, and cry joy to the thunder stroke and the lightning flash. Hast marrow in thy bones. Wast never a craven. None can say that."

"Perchance I should turn soldier. Perchance it were better so."

"Soldier, lad? Nay, what are soldiers? Chaff and dust. Hired to rattle a sword awhile, and then litter a ditch. Hard times are about us, son, but think no more o' that. No Shakespeare was ever a soldier."

"But an officer. One to lead his men to the assault, to win honour in the grim face of peril."

"They die like the rest, Will."

"We must all die, late or soon."

"Now what gall's in thy blood, to talk thus melancholic of soldiering and dying! A soldier's but a rogue dressed up to flatter silly wenches. And dying? There's time enough for that. Look on me. My hair is grey, but the flesh lies firm and close to my bones yet. I'll not think on death. Have I endured so much and shall I not inherit the reward of my endurance? There's a better time coming, Will, and I am resolved to see it and live far into it. As for thee, thou'rt young, thou'rt——"

"A thing of naught! Husband, father, and an unwanted guest in mine own father's house."

"Unwanted? Who said that? Give me his name and I'll crown him with rue."

"None said it, father. None but the voice I always hear, mine own conscience."

"Needst a purge. That's where thy troubles lies. A pill will set all right."

"Ay, but a pill no apothecary hath yet blended. A pill to extinguish hope, remorse, ambition, self-love, desire, all of life that's in Will Shakespeare."

And he walked away, his father gazing after him, shears in hand, head wagging, mouth open.

"A was always," John Shakespeare murmured at last, "of a disposition not to be comprehended. A yet a's not simple, neither. Hath a wit sharp and quick as Toledo steel. But what's to come of it all?"

Will was out of earshot now, in the kitchen, where his mother was preparing the dinner. She looked at him with gentle eyes. Plague upon them! Everyone in the house worked but he, and everyone was kind to him. Their kindness was the measure of their disappointment. He was a disease within doors, and the only remedy they saw was to pretend it was not there, to make a show that all was health.

He picked up a knife and rattled it on the table, trying to keep time with the patterings of the rain against the windows.

"Where's Joan?" he asked.

"Gone to market," his mother told him.

"Ill weather for that. And Gilbert?"

"Away to Charlecote to take measures for gloves."

"What! Does old Lousy Lucy trade with us now? I had thought none but London gloves were good enow for his dainty fingers. And let Gilbert take heed lest he come home o'errun with vermin."

"Have done, Will. Even though Sir Thomas used thee ill concerning the matter of his deer."

"I stole none o' them. Moreover, an I had, they are not enclosed. Save and except on a deer park, which he hath not at Charlecote, the offence is no more than trespass. I am not ignorant in the law, like Lousy Lucy. Three luces, that's three louses."

His mother paused, lifting her flour-covered hands from the dish. "Will, I'll not have it. The gentleman was doubtless mistaken, but that's past. And now he doth trade with thy father. 'Tis not for thee to complain, or to make play with his name, which is ancient and honourable."

"Are there then pedigrees among louses?"

"Peace. Forget and forgive. I like not a vengeful son."

"Nay, I've taken no vengeance. Beyond a few verses. And they are forgotten now, and so forgiven. They have escaped my own memory. No matter. They were indifferent bad."

"What's become of thy poesy, Will?"

"Why? Dost care for poesy? I never suspected it."

"That's not true. I always told thee poesy was a fitting accomplishment for a gentleman."

"But I lack the estate of a gentleman, mother. And verses earn no bread. Therefore, I make verses no more. True! I read thy thoughts. I forsake poesy and yet I earn no bread. Mea culpa. I think upon it night and day. But when thinking shall beget the lusty child action, that's more than I can tell. So Gilbert's to Charlecote?"

"We did not judge it an errand to thy taste, Will."

"And well judged. I'd rather measure Lucy for a shroud than a pair of gloves."

"Wilt never forget an injury?"

"Ay, when I have occupation for my mind."

Thereupon he forsook speech for meditation. It was true that the faculty of making verses had deserted him, but not because he considered it unprofitable. He rhymed no more because no rhymes sprang in his mind these days. The virtue was gone out of him. He was blasted within. He had no hope that it would ever return, and he consoled himself with the thought that nothing he had ever written came within holloing distance of the brave, golden visions which, wordless, first inspired him to net them in words. All slipped through the mesh. He had been sick of a fever of poesy, and now he was left with the shivering fits, the gripe, and the black bile in his throat. Perchance his father was in the right of it. Perchance he would soon wake from this despondent lethargy and find himself no poet, no gentleman, no figure in the wide world, but a merchant of Stratford, with every thought pinned to bills and costs and profits. Ignominious destiny!

Joan at Rother Market. Gilbert at Charlecote. Young Dick and Edmund at school. His father in the next room, and his mother here, roughening her Arden hands at kitchen work. His babes asleep upstairs, and Susan quiet with her dolls. The whole household was accounted for, and but for the wind and the rain the place would be tolerably quiet, fit for a man to cherish his own dismal thoughts in. But stay! He had forgot Nan, and that was passing strange. A man's thoughts should not overleap his wife, save in the sensual expectation of night-time.

"Where's Nan?" he asked.

"She went to feed the babes. 'Tis time for their nourishment."

"I saw them a minute since, when they slept."

"'Tis time, nevertheless. Nan's a good mother."

"Ay, and a good wife. The fault is all in me."

His mother offered no contradiction. He was astonished and hurt. So she too, although she would not give him a hard word, held him in contempt. If I were to die tomorrow, he thought, who would mourn me long or honestly? Nan, mayhap? But she would marry again, if any would wed a widow without dower. Nay, Nan would find a lover. She had been slow tinder, but, once alight, she burned. She was not apt, now, for sleeping alone. Ay, but sleep alone she must, or ere long she would be big with child again. We drift, he cried within himself. We are borne along on a flooding trust in providence, and providence supplies children to those who couple by night. We are three mouths too many already. More there must not be. An I were adult in mind as in body, an I were responsible, I would forsake Nan's bed. 'Tis the least I can do for her and for my father's fortunes. But where to remove my sleeping place? Already Dick and Edmund must needs lie on pallets downstairs—because I over-clutter the house with my brood.

Then suddenly he felt himself taut with resolve. To leave Stratford seemed no longer an incredible vision sustained since boyhood but kept beyond realisation: no more a dream, a desire, a prospect dimmed by distance. It had become his immediate duty. Nan would miss him o' nights, but perchance usage would temper the heat of her blood. She would have her children, and the mother should overmaster the wife in her. Susan would remember him a month or two: no more. The scope of time was needle-narrow to a three year old. Hamnet and Judith were but babes. He would do them no wrong. And who else in all Stratford would regret his going?

Anne would not at first believe him. Then she wept, and implored him not to go.

"Why?" she demanded again and again. "It is foolish. It is dangerous. Men lose their lives in London."

"They lose them everywhere."

"Art disappointed in me, Will? Am I not a good wife? Do I not cherish thee? Have I not borne thee children? Wherein do I fall short in my love towards them or towards thee?"

"The answer to all these questions, as thou knowest, is plain. 'Tis I who am insufficient. 'Tis I who have failed. And the only remedy is that I take myself away forthwith."

"Because we lack a little money?" She threw the words, in angry repudiation at him. "Time will mend that. Trade will better itself."

"But I am not apt for trade."

Startled, she lifted her hands from her face.

"And how," she asked, "wilt earn money in London, if not by trade?"

"I shall find a means. In London there is wealth. Some share of it must be mine. I am not the first to leave the poverty of a little town for the opportunities of London. Consider Dick Field. He prospers."

"Ay, but he was apprenticed to a printer's shop while he was yet a boy. Thou'rt a man, and with no trade to thy fingers."

"I can read, and I can write. I have made myself ere this useful at an attorney's desk."

"Ay, Will, but here in Stratford thou hast a father, thou'rt known. In London thou wilt be——"

"A dog without a name. That's thy thought, Nan. Well, 'tis a hazard doth not appall me. Doubtless I am indifferent idle, and if I continue here I shall worsen. I fear it. I know it. But I possess a talent, of no value in Stratford, yet London may pay me well for the use of it."

"Will, dost think to turn printed poet?"

He saw her tear-laden eyes glisten, and a smile, both sharp and tender, begin to curve the corner of her mouth.

"Money is not to be earned by poets," he retorted. "I need no instruction in that. Poesy is a pastime, an adornment for those who need not swink for bread."

"Then what wilt thou do in London? How shall it go with me, deserted, not knowing where my husband is, whether he be stabbed and robbed, or whether he starve?"

"I'll not starve. And I may be reached by letter at Dick Field's house. I shall visit him when I arrive. He will direct me where I may find employment. To the playhouses, perchance."

"Nay, Will, that's not respectable. The playhouses! The homes of riot and harlotry, for ever in trouble with authority, frequented by masterless men, snatch-purses and women of the town."

"How dost know all this?" he demanded angrily. "Hast ever been to London?"

"I have ears. I can catch the common report. Besides, I have seen the strolling players here in Stratford, toss-pots who must ever swagger down the middle of the street, and nasty pipe-voiced boys. Loud mouths, thirsty throats, and so poor, for all the forests of feathers in their hats, that any good housewife locks her doors when they're about. I should be shamed to confess I had a husband one of such a scurvy crew."

"I have not yet said I had it in mind to join a cry of players. I did but consider the project, as I might consider any possible employment. Perchance I turn soldier. Or secretary. Or steward to a great house. Who knows? Time and fortune will reveal."

But Anne was embittered. "I have been married to thee, Will, these three years. Time enough to learn to read thy mind. Thou'rt set on proving thyself a poet."

"It is so long since I made verses, I have forgot the very trick of it."

"But thou'lt start again in London."

"This is unreasonable," he told her. "Why dost show thyself so adamant against poesy? Wast well pleased when I would scribe my love for thee in verses, before we wedded."

"They were pretty verses, Will, and they flattered me. That I have never denied. Poesy is a delicate accomplishment in a lover."

"But when a man is grown to be husband and father, poetry is unfitting, 'tis no more than a child's play? I should stay in Stratford, turn all my thoughts to mercantile endeavours? That's thy meaning, is it not?"

"'Tis thy duty to stay," she told him.

"Eating my father's bread? Watching my wife and my children subsist upon his charity?"

"Time will mend all that."

"Time can do his repairs as well, and better, in London. No, Nan, I must go."

"'Tis thy duty to stay," she repeated.

But he caught up the word 'duty,' mouthing it over and over again. And at last he said: "My duty is to provide for wife and children. All are agreed upon that. I cannot perform it here in Stratford. In London there may be another story to be told. Besides, duty hath manifold meanings. I am idle by nature. I have been slothful. I have wasted my time here and shamed all whose name I bear. But now is the occasion ripe to be plucked. I must go."

She came into his arms, shaken with tears and reproaches. "Thou'lt never come back, I know it. I know it here in my heart."

He was pitiful but still determined.

"This is nonsense, Nan. I am to be reached through Dick Field. London is not so far as the Indies. Three days' journey. I shall return, and thou'lt welcome me, for I'll come back with plunder. Now that my mind is no more indecisive, I feel a power stir within me again. Never fear. I shall return."

"Ay," she murmured. "Yet I hate to let thee go. Thou'rt but a boy still, with lessons to learn. Thou'lt come back. I believe thee."

And when, resigned at last, she kissed him, he knew that already she saw him trudging home, weary and dispirited, from a London failure, to be a little man of Stratford again, a counter of pence, a dull householder, to church on Sundays, to the market on market days, and home to bed betimes every night. She grudged him from her side: she feared gossips: she feared to be a wife unhusbanded, a mother of fatherless children. But confidently she expected his speedy and penitent return. Astonished at such certitude, and resentful, he made a vow then and there, but kept it secret to himself, that she should not see him again till he came back in triumph.

Book Two

SCARLET AND WHITE

V

THE DAY was sultry beyond comfort, with a savage heat more apt to August and the Indies than to June and Southwark. Even in the shadows thrown across the narrow streets by the overhanging houses the air was close and oppressive. The threat of undischarged thunder brooded over London, and made the hair brittle, crackling under fingers ruffled wearily through it. Tempers were short, with no play or reserve left to them. The skin seemed to shrivel on the flesh, for there had been no rain for more than a week, and the streets were foul with the grit and dust thrown up by carriage wheels and horses' hooves and the incessant foot traffic of those who, hot or cold, had to go about their business. Cooks refused to stand in front of their fires. Gentlemen hied to their tailors for lighter clothing. Those who could make a jest of it spoke of fat men who died merely from the effort of trussing the points of their hose. There was a tale of a woman with three chins, who wiped them all away along with her sweat, and left herself only an upper lip.

People complained that although they were not over-nice, and understood that a great metropolis could not be kept like a lady's tiring chamber, the stenches from the drains and the refuse piled in the streets were become intolerable. They made dire prophecies to each other, saying that the Commonwealth had survived the Spanish peril of '88, with its Armada alarums, only to be like to perish in this sweltering summer of 1592. And the worst was to come. What would July and August bring, if this were June? The plague, for a surety, and if circumstance unfolded itself thus wise, the plague of previous years would be but a dwarf, a minimus by comparison.

Despite the heat there was chaffering aplenty in St. Paul's

Churchyard among the mercers', stationers' and booksellers' shops grouped round the pinnacled nave and square tower of the great cathedral, reputed to cover three acres and a half. Robert Greene, a well-built man with long hair as red and fantastical as his beard, did not linger there after he had made sure his own pamphlet, 'A Disputation Between a He Conny-Catcher and a She Conny-Catcher' was well displayed in a shop hard by the West door. He had taken his fee for the book and there was no more to be gained from it. The bookseller complained that it roused not such a demand as its three predecessors, all likewise devoted to the exposure of thieves and cheats about the town, their ways of taking purses, manipulating cards and dice, and holding the amorous citizen, in fear for his reputation, to ransom after he had gone to bed with some chance-met doxy. The conny-catchers liked not these pamphlets: they had issued threats against Robert Greene, and one evening three of them (giving his account of the affair in the 'Disputation,' Greene had put the number at fifteen) fell upon him with cudgels in Ludgate, as he sat at supper, and came near to despatching him out of this life. But he had survived, and although one bookseller forswore him, another was eager to print, and to pay for, his next venture, already promised, which was to be the life of Ned Browne, a notable cutpurse, who choked out his life at the end of a rope hung from a window, in France, for robbing a church.

Greene was of a mind to start to write the tale of this Ned Browne the same evening, for he worked, when he did work, fast and relentless: but the heat plagued him now, and he resolved to pass a few minutes savouring the cool shade within the Cathedral. There was no piety in this impulse: he mocked religion, and Paul's, save when divine service was being held, was no place for the devout. Calling his henchman, Ball—a ruffian known in all the taverns and bagnios between Wapping and Westminster as Cutting Ball—to follow close, Greene made his way into the church, disdaining the chorister boys who lingered by the door to exact, after the ancient custom, a small tax on all who visited Paul's with spurs on their heels.

Under the high vault of the nave, with the sunshine streaming through the stained windows, all was noise and animation, as hundreds of men and women paraded up and down the rush-strewn floor. The fine gentlemen with their lace-edged cloaks and multiple ruffs, for ever adjusting, sweeping off and replacing their feathered hats, and fidgeting with their gold-hilted, velvet-scabbarded swords, were of the most ostentatious, commonly known as Paul's men, or Paul's walkers: for here they resorted most days of the week, to stroll, to show themselves, and their finery, to make assignations, to stare at all personable and young women, and in loud voices to display their wit. Besides these there were a few ladies; a few merchants' wives, some of them pretty and, to judge from their smiles and their titterings to each other, sportive; and many young trulls and old bawds ready to ply their trade. There were other men not fashionable but wishing to be thought so, wearing boots for want of stockings, saluting their betters familiarly that they might impress their companions, and ever prepared to swap up a roguish bargain with a promise of gain in it. There were poets seeking a patron; sober-faced puritans meditating the time away before the preaching at Paul's Cross began, and scowling their righteous disapproval all around them; country gentlemen come to town and scarce able to keep their mouths shut for astonishment at what they saw: scholars carrying their scholar's garb more seemly than Greene, who never wearied of impressing upon his ruffian friends that he was Master of Arts of both universities: serving-men waiting to be hired for a twelvemonth period; priests and sea-captains: merchants seeking profitable commerce; colliers come straight from their barges, with hands and faces soiled black; horse-dealers, and the horse-thieves who called themselves, in their own cant, priggers: Italians and French and Spaniard visitors: Moors and negroes with heads wound about with cotton cloth; and here and there, jostling among the motley throng, went the conny-catchers, quick-eyed for an unguarded purse or a brown country face apt to be led away to drink, to gaming, or to a trugging house where robbery was easily done.

These last were well known to Robert Greene, and he to them. His pamphleteering had turned many old friends into enemies, for he himself, though professedly a scholar and a penman, deriving his revenue from the playhouses and the booksellers, had not in the past refused, when opportunity offered, to cozen a simpleton: and his man, Ball, the Cutter, was known still to take a purse upon occasion, in daylight by stealth and speed, at the point of a dagger in the dark. Yet Greene must needs write pamphlets to tell all the world the wiles and devices of his fellows, which was regarded as the basest treachery. He should be well acquainted with that which he inveighed against most sharply, the cross-biting law, for he himself, with his mistress, Ball's sister, had more than once profited from the cross-bite. This was a means of enrichment ancient but simple: the wench invites a fool with a purse into her room and when she has the fee put away and they lie in the act, who bursts into the room but the cross-biter or apple-squire, good Master Greene, shouting that the wench is his lawful wife, swearing fire and sword upon the adulterer, and not to be appeased from calling the Constable save by all the monies in the poor fool's purse. Greene as a competitor could be tolerated by the conny-catchers: but Greene the bewrayer of secrets was an abomination to them. They glared at him now as he strolled up and down Paul's, edged themselves close to him and cursed him under their breath, watching Ball's dagger hand the while. It would not be long, one of them muttered, ere Greene paid all his debts with his blood.

A little of this was more than enough. With the Cutter to clear the way, Greene pushed his way into the open air again, and thanked his stars for his henchman's devotion. The fellow doubtless had murder on his conscience—if conscience were not a tricksy invention of the priests. An his wits were as quick displayed as his knife, his fortune were made at Court: but his brain was a pudding, soaked in ale, sadly sunken, and past use.

No matter for that. Cutting Ball acknowledged but one religion, and his god was Robin Greene, who fed him and gave him to drink. Ball made it easy for his master to walk the streets despite the press of base cits, apprentices, serving men, messengers and all varieties of womanflesh. A look from Ball, a large, unwashed hand dropped on the dagger-hilt at his belt, and a quarrel died before it was born; mine host bustled with the respect and promptness due to one who waits upon a gentleman: mine host forgot to present his accompt. Debts dissolved where Ball thrust in his ugly visage, and officers of the law, charged with the arrest of Robert Greene, Master of Arts, turned away and would not recognise their quarry. The fellow earned his keep, and he would be the last in the world to admit that Robert Greene was no longer the man he had been. And perchance Ball was in the right of it: perchance these disquiets were but the ill-gotten bastards of a passing melancholia, and that itself engendered by this untimely heat.

"To the Bankside," said Greene. "I have a thirst prodigious. To the Bankside, and there we rest and refresh ourselves."

They crossed by London bridge, sixty feet high above the river which deafened their ears as it roared under the arches. Nearly a thousand feet from shore to shore, this wooden bridge was one of the marvels of London town, and men travelled far to see it. Greene had oft admired before it when first he came from his native Norwich, but now his eye was staled. He scarce glanced at the pin-makers' shops with which most of the structure was overbuilt, or at the tower at the Southwark end, where hundreds of heads, old and new, worn to a skull, leather-brown or still pallid and blood-stained, the heads of felons, heretics and traitors, were impaled on wooden rods. Ball would have lingered to stare at the Paris

Gardens, hard by the Rose playhouse, where bears and bulls mingled their noises with the howls of kennelled dogs kept to bait them. But Greene was weary of the heat.

Arrived at the Bankside tavern, where his reckoning was high, unpaid, but not probable to be brought to his notice, Greene dropped his big body into a chair, sprawled his elbows on the dirty table, and called for two cups of canaries.

"And bring me a mirror, too," he called sharply after the host, who, dismayed at his appearance, trembling every time he glanced at Ball, now let his mouth gape open.

"What a plague ails you? Have you never heard of a mirror?" Greene roared at him. "Shall I send the Cutter to make you dispatch? Or belike you hold me not a proper man to regard himself in the glass?"

"Nay, Master Greene, a proper man, a proper man indeed. A very handsome man, as all the ladies know."

"Ay, and know to their cost. Then speed! A mirror and two cups of canaries."

"At once, Master Greene."

Mine host scuttled out of sight.

"Shall I slash the rogue across the knuckles when he beings the wine?"

"Nay, good Cutter, for then he might spill all, and that would be pity."

"But there's more wine beyond, casked. I have seen it."

"No matter. Keep thy knife in its sheath. Blood is blood and wine is wine, whatever the prating clerics would have the plebs believe. I like them not mixed."

The host brought the tankards and a small hand-mirror, velvet-framed, which he laid on the table, and hurried quickly again out of sight.

The two men drank, pledging each other silently, and then Greene took up the mirror and began to examine his reflected appearance.

"'Tis poxy dark within doors," he complained. "The sun burns in the open street like the hell they imagine to terrify children with, but here's as dark and obscure as the soul thou dost not possess, Cutter. But what of that? I can see enow."

He stared at the image of his broad, handsome face, pallid, running with sweat, the flesh puffed and darkened under the eyes, pouted round the loose lips.

"Time was when I could run and ride in the sun with no such discomposure. I am stricken in health, Cutter. My body betrays me. My victuals make me retch oftimes, and the wine goes strangely sour to my stomach."

"The heat, master. Blame all on the heat."

"So my mind keeps faith with me, I'll not complain. And is there aught amiss with my mind? Answer me fairly, Cutter, as thou valuest mine esteem."

"Naught amiss."

"Am I not still Robert Greene, Robin to my familiars, Master of Arts of both universities, a figure in the town; Robin Greene who devised Orlando Furioso and got himself rewarded by the Queen's players, and the Lord's Admiral's men, to boot, twice over for one and the same play?"

"Yea. 'Tis so. And a merry prank that was."

"And are not my books demanded by the multitude faster than the printer can rip them from the press?"

"'Tis so."

"And 'tis well."

He fell then to combing his long fox-red beard, untrimmed, which drooped to a point over his chest.

"I am a man of pith yet, as thy sister knows. The world is full of thieves and cogging rascals. They would deny me the reward of my labour. The conny-catchers hate me because I have deciphered their cant and their thieving lays in sundry pamphlets. Pox on 'em. A man must live. And what do I get for the labours of my pen, beyond a belly-pinching pittance? Yet who can work as I can? Who else can make beginning, middle and end of a book within twenty-four hours? The mercantile wretches know it. They fawn on Robin Greene with their money in their hands, outstretched, clamouring haste. Only the miserable players look me cool and hold their distance. But they'll come creeping back, spaniels that they are. Thieves and cozening rascals, every man of them! But we'll outthieve them and outcozen them, Cutter. What say'st thou?"

"Marry, I say—pox on 'em all."

"I'll drink to that. Pox on 'em all."

Cutting Ball started and cursed as a hand reached from behind him and clasped round the cup. But he grinned when he saw his sister's red cheeks and bold black eyes.

"Was ever a thirsty wench," he muttered.

And Greene, his arm round the young woman's waist, said: "Here doxy, drop thy haunches next mine. We've mingled closer than that, have we not? And shall again?" Raising his voice, he called: "Host! More canaries, and speed the drawing of it." Then to his mistress: "And how's my son? How fares my little Fortunatus in this knavish world?"

"Why, passing wet in his body, for he cannot yet control his humours, but in his throat, passing dry. Hath a dusty inheritance."

"The wench shows wit. A sparkles at one end, and at t'other she burns. A rare wench!"

But Greene's good humour soon passed. He drank and drank again, and the sweat began to start on the pallid lax flesh of his nostrils and dribble down the furrows of his cheeks into his red beard.

"Men marvel," he said, "that I, a scholar, consort with such as thee. But where's the marvel? Are other scholars so lively that none will forsake their company? Do scholars praise a man that excels them? Do they put money in his purse? Not so. And think not I am shamed to be reputed thy friend, wench. 'Tis true, thou'rt a whore. Peace! I doubt not thy fidelity since I took thee to bed, charged thee with child, and set my mark upon thee. What's a whore that any should despise her? Bawdry is the natural state of man. An I love thee, 'tis because thou'rt whorish. And I have gone a whoring also."

"How now!" exclaimed Ball, his stupid face spread with bewilderment. "What means this? A man, a proper man, such as thou, may be a whoremaster, but not a whore. Else all's confusion and I know not my right foot from the left."

"Have I not written dramatic pieces for the players to perform? And not in privacy, before ladies and gentlemen, but performed in the public playhouses, where the groundlings stand and sweat at a privilege price of two pennies a man? I have put out my talents to hire before the populace. What apter name for that than whoring? And, like many a poor wench before me, I am ill-rewarded for my endeavour. They like not Robert Greene and his works in the playhouses now. They have new favourites."

"Shakespeare!"

"Ay, Shakespeare—Shakescene—Shakeshift, whatever his baseborn name be. A mere player without education, sprung from chaffering stock in some village where doubtless he slept with the cattle. The other day I stopped him at the Rose playhouse, and asked him if the straw and the burrs were still clinging in his hair. But the fellow's not to be provoked. He turned me away with a smile and a jest."

"Would I had been there," Ball growled. "I have a way of removing smiles. But that damned money-gathering Henslowe hath commanded against my admittance to his playhouse."

"What's the world come to," Greene continued mournfully, "when gentlemen are less esteemed than hireling players? Treachery and ingratitude surround us. For who created the playhouses? Answer me that. Was it Henslowe or Burbage or the like? They're but merchants seeking profit, and were there no plays to traffic in they'd deal in corn or cloth or bagnios. Was it the players? Without lines to speak, they're but dumb beasts. Who created the theatres then? I'll tell thee. It was scholars such as myself, instructed and wit-sharpened at the universities. Before we took pity on the players, they had naught but dull moralities to offer the populace. 'Twas I created the theatre, I, and Nashe, Peele, Lodge and Tom Kyd: he's neither from Oxford nor Cambridge, but that's nor here nor there. Ay, and Kit Marlowe, too."

"Kit's a trusty blade," Ball murmured, and his sister ran her fingers soothingly through Greene's damp hair and then rubbed her cheek against his beard.

But he was not to be comforted.

"Marlowe is in favour with his ' Jew of Malta ', and his ' Edward II '. Well, they are worthy plays. No man in his responsible senses would compare them with my ' Orlando '. But they have workmanship. There's no bilious jealousy or yellow hatred in Robin Greene. Green for freshness! Even when Henslowe comes creeping to me with his long face, complaining that the people like not my ' Friar Bacon ' as they like Marlowe's ' Jew ', I utter no word against Marlowe. Kit's my friend. But Henslowe, and that ranter, Ned Alleyn—he's set to marry Henslowe's daughter, I hear, and hath used her as a wife before this, I'll warrant. I know his stealthy ways: he plans to inherit the company and the playhouse by way of the bed."

"Yet he hath a sweet voice, and deep," said the woman at Greene's side. "A gives me rare pleasure when he struts to the front stage, and spreads his arms, and roars out Tamburlaine's will upon his jades of Asia."

Greene looked at her furiously for a moment, and then lifted his arm from the table and struck her, back-handed, across the face.

"Jades of Asia!" he cried. "Thou'rt a Bankside jade thyself. Keep thy hot eyes away from Ned Alleyn, and Kit Marlowe, from every man but thy master. And what's thy master's name?"

The woman wept.

"Answer, wench! Name the master of thy flesh, the man who got young Fortunatus upon thee, the only man with right of entry to thy secret parts? His name?"

"Robin Greene. I meant no harm," the woman sobbed.

"And see thou doest none. An thou cuckold me, though only with thine eyes, I'll——"

"Nay, I'll do it for thee," broke in Ball. "She is my sister but thy woman, and I am the instrument of thy vengeance. Host! More canaries!" he shouted. "The heat dries us up. More canaries!"

Another draught of wine and Greene became fuddled. His thoughts went indignantly back to the owner of the Rose theatre, Philip Henslowe.

"The man came to me," he complained, "with a tale that fashion had changed, that tragedy and poetry were out of favour. He needed a comedy, he said, to make the people laugh. He besought me to write him a comedy, for he said—and it was the only word of truth he spake—I was a man of the most diverse parts, and could adorn whatever I chose to essay. A comedy Henslowe wanted, not a thing of fine wit, to please the Court, but something broad and rumbustious, to tickle the fat ribs of burgesses. And I wrote him ' Friar Bacon and Friar Bungay '. Lord, how that man delighted in the script when I took it to him. He could not pause to catch breath for praising me. Yet now, because the yard is but half full and he's scant of his twopenny toll and his shillings for seats, he gives me ill-looks, and the piece is not put on but once in twenty days."

"Henslowe's a rogue," Ball declared tipsily. "Say but the word and I slit his face to mark him for life."

"I should never have heeded him. I should have written another ' Orlando '. Comedy's to no man's taste these days. I offered to provide another tragedy, but Henslowe would give me neither yea nor nay. Said he must consult with Alleyn. And Alleyn is full of his darling Will Shakespeare. Why's that? I'll tell thee. 'Tis because this lackey Shakespeare writes grandiloquent speeches for Alleyn to mouth forth. Alleyn's love-struck with the sound of his own voice. There's no judgment left in the world, else even the prentices would not flock to see this Shakeshift's fustian. What's it called? 'Harry the Sixth' ?"

"I went once," said Ball. "Before Henslowe's ruffians had orders to shut me out. But I could not wait till the end. No! God's teeth, no! I am a patient man, but I could not endure to the end. 'Tis sorry stuff, and I marvel at its success."

He put an arm across his sister's shoulders and began to weep into her wine. Dazed with drink, they heard but did not comprehend what Greene said as he lengthened his complaint: "Sorry stuff it is. And stolen, too. Stolen from me, from Kit Marlowe, from all the villain's betters. The man's an ape. He hath no learning of his own, so must thieve from others. Will Shakespeare! What a world, when a mere player can set up as wit and poet! The man's an ape. Would even attempt to pass himself as a gentleman. Nice in his clothes and his deportment. Speaks you fair. Smiles in your face, with treachery in his heart. Bows to the ladies, kisses hands, and crosses the street to avoid a stench. I tell thee, Shakespeare hath not only stolen my wit, my fame, my money, he despises me."

"Out upon him," muttered Cutting Ball, uncertain whether his animosity was required against Henslowe, Shakespeare or Alleyn.

But they all sat up when the darkening street outside became noisy with shouts and the sound of running feet. The host came timorously out of his parlour.

"What's to do?" Greene enquired, and then added roughly: "Go, host. Ask questions. Discover and disclose! Make speed!"

The tavern keeper came back in a minute or two, breathless and agitated, but anxious to comfort himself and his guests.

"'Tis overpast us now, good Master Greene, though I doubt there'll be damage done elsewhere. But we have 'scaped in this street, praise God."

"Praise God for nothing, till thou'rt sure he exists."

The host gazed at him with open mouth, appalled by this

blasphemy. Small wonder folk said certain gentlemen had truck with the devil.

"Well?" Greene demanded. "That's not the end of thy tale. Give us the why and wherefore of this uproar."

"The prentices make trouble again. It seems the Knight Marshall's men arrested a serving man and put him in the Marshalsea. That was five days since. I heard of it, for it is said they used themselves arrogantly, and did affright a good-wife, not implicated in the matter, and her child."

"But today? Leave the chronicles of the past."

"Well, sir, the Knight Marshall's men have brought no charge against the servant they hold in arrest, and the round-cap apprentices of Southwark are wrathful. Wherefore they have besieged the Marshalsea, creating a riot. The Knight Marshall's men drew swords, but were like to have been over-powered, but for the arrival of the Lord Mayor's men. Or so I was told. The fighting is not done yet."

"Another prentice's riot," exclaimed Cutting Ball. "And I not there. There's purses to be taken in a riot, and a little cut and slash keeps a man's hand in trim."

The host backed away at these words. He wished Master Greene, with his henchman and his doxy, had never made acquaintance with his tavern. They paid no reckoning: they earned the place an ill-name, and drove away good customers who did not omit to pay for what they ate and drank.

"I am surprised," said Greene, sobered a little now, "that so many prentices were allowed to assemble. Their notorious habits are known."

"Why, sir, they were very cunning. They went to a new play at the Rose this afternoon, and proceeded afterwards, singing and shouting, a throng of them, to the Marshalsea."

"At the Rose! They assembled at the Rose? Is this the truth, host?"

"Why, sir, 'tis on every man's tongue."

"Then bring more canaries. This calls for joy."

Cutting Ball stared at his master.

"Dost not understand, Cutter? A riot proceeding from the Rose: 'tis certain now that playhouse will be shut down. And that will hurt Henslowe and Alleyn where alone they are vulnerable—in the purse. And there's an end to Shakespeare and his ' Harry the Sixth'. My word on it, the ape hath ended his brief reign. Next season Robin Greene will waken the town with a new tragedy. And Marlowe too—I'll have word with him. He'll furbish another. There'll be no room left for Shakespeare. The upstart is blasted in the bud. He'll be heard of no more. Host, you have brought good news. I'll praise your wine from Eastcheap to Westminster—but fetch it now, fetch it in quantity, and fetch it with a smile. Robert Greene, Master of Arts, would pledge his host. There's an honour for thee, there's a tale to boast of to thy grandchildren."

HE TURNED the corner and saw the river again at the end of the street, and then as he came nearer, the tall flat sides of the playhouse reared above him. A painted sign on a post behind the wooden fence denoted it: The Rose Playhouse. Proprietor: Mr. Philip Henslowe.

The porter produced a deferential greeting, for although his was a new face on the Bankside, and his name was never printed large among the list of players in the bills, Master Shakespeare had waxed important, had turned author and writ a piece which pleased both the gentleman and the groundlings. Master Alleyn had been asking for him, this same forenoon, and last season Master Alleyn (who knew his own worth, if any man did!) was for ever closeted with this Master Shakespeare, beseeching him for longer and more heroic declamations. And the head and source of all employment, Master Henslowe himself, would step aside to greet this Shakespeare courteously, and, speaking with him, would oft-times lean on his shoulder—which was no light weight for a young man to bear. But that was a jest not to be cracked in public. Sufficient for a gatekeeper who wished to retain his office to observe, to take note who grew in favour, and to direct his behaviour accordingly.

"Good day to you, Master Shakespeare," therefore observed the porter, splitting his dark face with a smile of blackened teeth and sore gums. And he added: "The Rose will be glad to see you back again, sir."

"And I—I am glad to be back," said Shakespeare, stepping inside.

"I heard you did not make the tour with the company, sir?"

"No. I have been at my house in Warwickshire."

Was he a country gentleman, then? All sorts wrote for the playhouses these days, and this one's manner had more breeding than most.

"All well there, sir, I trust?"

"All's well that ends well, and here am I returned for work, and that's a good ending to a summer of plague and plaguey rumours."

"Ah, sir, the wars in France and the wars in Spain and the wars on the seas, they have us sore vexed. Yet the realm is quiet in itself, sir, like my health. Troubles without, but sound within. Thanks to the good Queen. Although, again, there are Jesuites, they tell us, everywhere, disguised." The old man threw a quick enquiring glance to see if this country gentleman, this poet, this favourite of Master Henslowe, were yet another in sympathy with the Old Faith: but he learned nothing from the hazel eyes and the comely mouth smiling serenely at him.

"And the plague in London. Forget not that."

"Ay, sir, the plague. And the summer heat not gone from us yet. No need to cross the seas to meet with death. There's many taken from the Bankside and from Shoreditch since you were away. Death's a fell sergeant, and strict in his arrest."

The playwright, not tall, but comely in build, bravely apparelled in grey and crimson, looked at him with a new interest, and repeated this last sentence aloud. They were a strange lot, these makers of plays, stranger and wilder than the players, and a man who'd devil-porter it at the Rose could resign himself to an unquiet life. This one, this Shakespeare, was better than most of them: he drank, but was never seen other than sober: he jested, but never ranted in his cups: he frequented the company of the boisterous, and was well-liked, but was never in trouble for debt or riot or wenching. And it made him the more strange, that he was not of the kin of black Marlowe or red Greene. Red Greene: a memorable name for the rascal.

"Master Shakespeare, hast heard the news concerning Master Greene?"

"No. What is it?"

"The poor gentleman is dead."

"It grieves me to hear that. Not that I had his intimate acquaintance, but I esteemed his art. When did this happen?"

"But four days since. At a shoemaker's house in Dowgate across the river. He had been sick these several months."

"Did he die o' the plague?"

"Nay, sir, but near as nastily. He fell sick of a surfeit of pickled herring and rhenish wine. Well, sir, you will have heard how he would eat and drink. Moderation was not within the compass of his ability. But he died penitent, and made a godly end, rest his soul. Or so I am informed."

"Thanks, and here's for thy pains."

This was a gentleman indeed: a playhouse doorkeeper did not expect largesse from players and poets. They were more like to borrow.

"I'll enquire further," said Shakespeare. "Is Master Henslowe within?"

"No, sir. Yet he hath been here this day, and will come again, I doubt not. But you'll find Master Alleyn within."

Shakespeare walked down the paved path across the grass and into the wooden theatre itself. It was built three stories high, and although the exterior walls were flat sided, the galleries within were run on a curve round the greater part of a circle, overlooking the open yard, for the plan of the new playhouses was developed from the inns where theatrical performances had formerly been given. In this yard the poorer folk, the groundlings, and especially the apprentices on their holidays, woollen-capped, with canvas or fustian doublets and leather girdles, according to the statute, stood close-packed, coarsely fragrant, and noisy. A wooden platform projected into the yard, raised three feet above the ground level. At its extremity, on the front stage, the principal actor would stand alone to pronounce such soliloquies and exhortations as he could compel the author to write for him. The front stage at the Rose was Ned Alleyn's stamping ground. Here his eyeballs rolled white, his arms flailed the air, and here he would send his bass voice reverberating protracted syllables over the yard and round the railed galleries. Here, too, the chief comedian, Will Kemp, would come to droll for laughter and applause when tragedy gave place temporarily to the comic, or when, the play proper at an end, the groundlings demanded their customary twenty minutes of fooling, known as the Jig.

The rear portion of this platform, flanked by pillars supporting a sloping roof, was the middle stage, where the main action of the play was shewn. Two doors, on either side, admitted to the middle stage from a corridor, and this corridor, opening on to the back of the platform, was then curtained across to form a recess known as the rear stage. And above that was a small railed gallery which could also be used by the players to represent battlements; the towers of Troy; or a balcony for a lady's tryst with her lover; or for musicians when the play demanded a song or a serenade.

Staring down on the stage from the second tier of gallery seats, to which the price of admission during a performance was one shilling, Shakespeare concluded appreciatively that the theatre was a marvellous ingenious device, an instrument apt to his hand.

It gave him no less than four stages, with all the necessary exits and entrances, by which to keep his creatures in a turmoil, leading them into a ravel of misunderstandings and out again; shifting the attention of the multitude from one city to another, from shipboard to land, into this house, then into another; and then again out to the streets for a chance encounter. With such riches of resource at hand, who would beggar himself to keep to the one time, the one place, the one group of persons, following the stiff Senecan fashion? All within a few hours of daylight (and unless the sky were thick-clouded there was never need of the pitch-stinking torches and candle-lamps to light a stage open to the heavens) a man with a gift for making plays could range the whole world, rifle history and fable, present to the eye and the ear what else could not be garnered from a hundred books. He could so devise his lines that the players were informed with his fancy, and the spectators, gentle and simple, responded to his touch like the keys of the virginals: a martial foray stirs their blood, and as soldiers depart, taking their dead with them, a door opens at the opposite side; eyes wander there at once; and the mood is changed, to high romantic love, to polite discussions, to noble grief, to the pranks of clowns and waiting-women, to whatever your playwriter's fancy called for. This playhouse was an instrument a god might welcome with thanks, finding it ready to his hand.

Just now it was an instrument in disuse, and, leaning over the gallery rails, Will Shakespeare savoured for a few moments the unusual silence of the theatre emptied of spectators, of players disputatious or earnest in rehearsal, even of a carpenter to cut a board or drive a noisy nail. He had never before known such tranquillity within these walls; he was not like to experience it soon again, for the new season was due to begin, old plays would be taken from stock, and new plays be called for and published (before they were rehearsed, even before the authors had completed writing) as welcome news among the multitude for whom the playhouse was the choice, the exciting, the prime and characteristic entertainment of the age. By tomorrow the company—Lord Strange's Men— would be assembled here, clamorous with tales of the summer tour in the country and their private expectations of the London season.

But here and now the Rose was dusty, empty and silent. It needed Will Shakespeare to breathe life into it! Wiser not say so much to Alleyn. Alleyn could speak you fair when he wished his lines amended or lengthened: and amendment with him most often meant increase, for the fellow was sustained upon applause as any other man on meat and drink. And yet he did not stint himself at table, neither. Alleyn could be courteous upon occasion, but brooked no question of his dignity. Alleyn, in Alleyn's eyes, filled the stage, front, middle and rear: the rest of the company were but furniture to extenuate a possible bleakness; furniture and intermissions to divert the spectators whiles Alleyn rested and gathered his powers for a fresh assault upon the echoes. As for the poet, the deviser of plays, what was he, in Alleyn's eyes, but the merchant who supplied goods at demand, the menial who furnished coals and logs for Alleyn's fire? Alleyn—it could not be denied—was the flaw in this rare jewel, the playhouse.

Alleyn must needs be accepted. Perfection is always not yet. Better the playhouse with Alleyn, than Stratford without the playhouse. The dreary time of indigence, when he went quick-eyed about London like a cur begging and filching food, was now behind him: lost years, better forgotten. Dick Field, the printer, had helped him within his poor ability, and made him the acquaintance of a player or two. But he had come to the playhouse the meanest of servitors, ready to fold costumes, to fetch and carry, to wait upon commands, in return for a few pence and a meal on occasion. Hungry and ill-clad, he had counted it then a privilege merely to stand obscure on the borders of this brave new world, the playhouse, sprung so sudden from inn-yard performances and vagabonding travels to a fixed habitation, no small profit, and the favour of the London populace, gentle and simple. Scarcely now could he recognise himself as the young countryman, all timid and agape to be in the company, near enough to lay hands upon, of applauded actors and poets, who would retire to his hard pallet o' nights exhausted with the day's doings and yet so enthralled that he might not sleep till all was enacted again and again in his mind.

Those first fresh exultations lasted not so long. Although he could not credit that he would ever come in sight of a play-house without a stir in his blood, he had soon enough lost the marvelling aspect of a stranger in that world, exchanging it for the ready acceptances of familiarity. First he had trooped it in a band of half-a-dozen nameless hirelings, to and fro across and behind the stage, all stalwart swagger and slow martial port whiles they were in view of the spectators, all scuttering haste, cloaked by the curtains of the rearmost corridor, as they sped back to the entrance to keep in progress the seeming endless march of a stage army. Later he was suffered to speak a line or two—and told to amend the country broadness of his vowel sounds. Soon he was conning small parts, under Alleyn's and Henslowe's tutoring care, and could boast himself a player: not a principal, and not one with a holding in the company, entitled to draw his share of the profits, but still—a player. Thenceforward, out of the monies earned by his hired services he was able to remit to Anne in Stratford, and deem himself a man again, upon whom his wife and children in some sort were dependent.

Meanwhile, when it became known he was clerkly by inclination and not only read books but could write a fair hand, he was employed first to copy scrips, and later to cobble them into more modern shapes. With his eyes and ears open, and his mind, ever quick, nourished upon every syllable spoken in his presence, he speedily learned the crafts and customary subtleties of the playhouse; learned that a dramatical piece is something more complex than so many verses to be declaimed: learned that a poet's characters must be cut, tailor-wise, to fit the players at his disposal, and that a player cannot exceed the bounds, the oft-times narrow bounds, of the voice, the body and the nature God gave him; learned that your playhouse onlookers are niggards of their patience and fickle as April weather, so that they must needs be swiftly diverted, now with heroical speeches, now with the gathering of conspiracies, now with the tenderness of love, and anon all for laughter, to which the shortest and surest path is bawdry. Thus, out of copying and acting and the furbishing of old plays to meet the moods of changed times, he schooled himself in playmaker's cunning, and in the course of this instruction discovered new worlds in his own mind.

Success fetched in its boon fellow, prosperity, and for some years now he was able to send home such monies as amply clothed and lodged and fed Anne and her children, and made his father exclaim astonishment. He who not so long since had quitted Stratford, secretly and with the shame of failure heavy upon him, abandoning his family to his father's care, had but lately returned there: and Stratford had welcomed him at more than his own estimation. It had been pleasant to be home again; to hear the Warwickshire speech (ringing a little rough, broad, uncouth now, after London's sharper syllables); to walk and talk with Susan, now near on ten year old; to find his baby twins grown into school children; to be no more the disdain of Stratford citizens but a successful gentleman from London, with mother, father and wife proud of him to the bursting point of arrogance. The earning of money was the foundation of all respect in this world: he had been right in that early philosophy of his. He was another man, now that London had crowned him with success.

And Anne had changed, too. So sweet, so loving tender, and no more reproachful that he had taken himself from her: but so much older. Nearly nine years was the measure of his advantage over her in age. With old Meg Candler whispering in his ear, he had recked naught of that. But Meg was dead, and Nan was old. A man should not have a wife whose years visibly left him in arrear. It made a chaos in the heart, it instilled secret reproaches into all good resolves. The fault was his, not Nan's. Yet he could not conceal from her, who was in nothing quick of apprehension, the span that time and the ventures of his mind widened between them. Nan spoke no reproaches, but he arraigned himself. And even so, he could not feign that which his heart no longer felt. His marriage was all error from first to last. Best leave it behind in Stratford, comforting his conscience with the tally of the money he had despatched, and would despatch, there. Best put Stratford and Nan out of mind, and turn to the playhouse. Best make haste now and seek out Ned Alleyn, for courtesy and for the diligent furtherance of the fortunes of Will Shakespeare.

But it was Alleyn who found him first, coming quietly into the balcony, and then loudly slapping him upon the shoulder—one of his Tamburlaine gestures.

"Well met, Will Shakespeare. Let me see thee, man."

Shakespeare turned and gave greeting, but Alleyn paid no attention to his words.

"Thou'rt brown with the rustic sun. Didst well to fly the plague."

"Thanks, Alleyn. And how's the world with thee?"

"A little the worse for work, but that's no news. They could not have too much of me, on the tour. Never a performance without Edward Alleyn. I was weary before the end. And since then, no rest. The new season must be prepared long in advance. But I will not complain. I shall die in harness."

But not yet awhile, thought Shakespeare, noting that the actor had put on flesh. Alleyn was not tall but heavily built, thick in the arm and the thigh, with broad clumsy hands. Taking his physical handicaps into consideration, Alleyn did marvellous well. He was not so good a player as he esteemed himself, but for all that, passing good. His voice was the foundation of his success, rich and ripe, resonant with suggestions of nobility which many professed to find absent from his nature. His voice could make poor verse sound good, and good verse seem magnificent. His voice was impressive even when he was but finding fault, behind the stage, with some detail of the accounts. His body was too thick set, too ponderous in movement, for the tragic and heroic gestures he forced it to. He sweated when he came off stage, exhausted with the violence of his gestures, but the concentration of his vanity, in which there was no chink for humour to penetrate, made his lambent eyes, set under heavy brows over a broad, bold nose and a thick beard, glitter and darken and roll, so that all attention left surplus by the thundering voice was fixed on his eyes. He is a basilisk endowed with powers of speech, Shakespeare thought: he has magic in tongue and eye, else surely he would be laughed off the stage. No matter: here was the embodiment of a tyrant king, a hero, a tempestuous villain spurring to disaster.

"What news?" Alleyn demanded. "That play we spoke of, before thy departure, another history piece, is't ready?"

"The play of Richard the Third? I have the fair copy at my lodging."

"Then fetch it, man. Fetch it. I am all eagerness."

"I believe the part will please thee, Alleyn. Yet there are some subtleties will need consideration."

"Subtleties? Ay, subtleties, that's what I need. To make plain what another man could not convey—save in riddles—that's Edward Alleyn's destiny."

But I fear, was Shakespeare's private complaint, subtlety's beyond thy range. And he was disturbed by a remote view of himself as a false flatterer, giving this roaring tragedian the soothing words he needed to swell his self-esteem, and all to keep the peace, and to foster the fortunes of Will Shakespeare.

"Shalt see. I'll fetch the scrip tomorrow."

"Is there a death in it?" Alleyn demanded eagerly.

"Ay, deaths aplenty."

The player rubbed his big plump hands.

"And lamentations properly writ in round blank verse?"

"Even so. Scenes of battle, too. Little children slain. Treachery to move the heart, and a royal usurpation."

"I begin to like the piece already. Fetch it to me today. At once. 'Tis not far to thy lodging? Nay, I'll come with thee, and now."

I have him in the mood of appetite. He sees himself already as Richard. His carping spirit is turned aside before he has read a word. I have learned to play this big-voiced fish; and, learning, I have lost another portion of my innocency.

To escape from this reflection, as they walked down the stairs and prepared to quit the playhouse, Shakespeare asked: "Hast heard that poor Robert Greene is dead?"

"He's none the poorer for being dead."

"But the playhouse will miss him sorely."

Alleyn would not admit this. "Greene had passed his best. Was never the equal of Marlow. Come to that, and let's make no bones about it, Will Shakespeare, he was thine inferior, too. And hated to acknowledge it."

"Nay, that I never claimed. From Greene I learned much."

"No. From Greene thou tookst a little and made it much. Have done. The man served his turn. He was somewhat of a ruffian, for all the scholarship he would never let us forget. He was without the blessing of moderation. He laid waste his powers, and the penalty for that cannot be abrogated. Greene is dead. No more of him. My intent is all to scan thy new devised Richard. Yet give heed: I expect much."

"Pledge thee my word," said Shakespeare, "'tis a part to sunder the soul from the body, to make the eyes start from the head, the flesh to twitch on the bones. And think me not immodest when I say there's thunderous music in the lines."

"If this be true, Will, my name is not Alleyn if I do not make thy reputation known from one end of the kingdom to the other, this coming season. I have prophecies concerning it leaping in my mind already. Hitherto I have been but a young man, but now I feel maturity upon me. Give me the requisite lines to speak, and I'll speak them so the far-off hills shall quiver. Nay, there's a notion for thee. There's a free gift. Canst weave that into verses and insert it where best it fits."

"I will remember."

But Shakespeare, while he played the plunging, greedy vanity of this actor (and disdained himself for doing it), was still thinking of Robert Greene, and resenting the cold indifference Alleyn had displayed towards a man who had furnished him with some of his most successful parts.

Alleyn is Alleyn's god, he thought, and in that religion most devout. Were it Will Shakespeare lying dead today, he would speak of me in just such a manner. Greene's fault is that, being dead, he can write no more for Alleyn. Therefore, a pox on the fellow. He's useless. Put him out of mind. But Shakespeare is alive, Shakespeare can write, indeed Shakespeare hath written for Alleyn to con, rehearse, and declaim. Therefore keep Shakespeare in mind, and stroke him soft with fair speeches—till he, too, has served his turn.

Arrived at his lodging, he took Alleyn upstairs, called for wine, unlocked a box, and produced a bundle of written parchments tied with ribbon.

"Here is the play. Take good care of it, pray, for there is no other copy as yet."

"If this," said Alleyn, "excel thy ' Harry the Sixth,' it shall be treasured, I warrant thee. Have no fear."

He sipped the wine and began to unfasten the ribbon round the manuscript.

"I am impatient. I must take a quick survey, a glance here and there."

"No haste, good Alleyn. Sit here and read from first to last. I am eager to have thy opinion. But pray thee, let me absent myself awhile. I have business near at hand. That done, I'll return, in hope to hear that I have not disappointed thine expectation."

And so down the stairs and out, in the certain knowledge that Alleyn would want amendments here, finer epithets there, a prologue perchance, and always more room for Ned Alleyn to strut the front stage and lift and sink and lift his voice again. Let him first read the scrip through in solitude: it would be intolerable to stay at hand and listen to pointless comments as the reading progressed. There would be enough of requests, suggestions, doubts and complaints, well buttered with easy praise, when the reading was finished. Meanwhile, an hour had to be filled, and suddenly, thinking of Greene and his lamentable end, Shakespeare resolved to make his way to Dowgate. It was surely Dowgate the porter at the playhouse had mentioned, breaking the news that Greene was dead? And in a shoemaker's house. To walk, to stand, to stare in Dowgate would be a fitting idle occupation for an idle hour.

It was not difficult to discover the shoemaker's house, small dirty and tumbledown, for people passing by frequently halted, and looked at the door and the windows, and when they talked the name of Robert Greene was on their lips. Perhaps there was no matter for astonishment in that: Greene's plays had, till the last year, stood high in favour, and his pamphlets on the tricks of pimps and snatch-purses were bought and read by such of the gentlefolk as did not disdain an interest in the more sordid ways of the town. Moreover, Greene was a man of defiance; a man who set out to affront the eyes and ears of his fellows; shameless in pride and dissolute living; known for his red beard and his braggart blasphemies. His name kept company, in whispered gossipings, with that of Kit Marlowe and Walter Raleigh, for some held that these three professed there was no God, and religion naught but a conny-catching device of thieves who called themselves priests: others had it that they were all three sold to the devil.

Robert Greene had never scrupled to hurl his dissolute living in the faces of sober citizens: he was known to mis-quote scripture to bawdy and impious ends. He walked ever in danger of arrest, always quitting an old lodging—with the reckoning unpaid—for a new, in the dead of night, so that no man knew where to find him, save in a tavern or at the play-house. And there he was not to be apprehended, for he had in attendance a ruffian named Ball, a cut-throat—till Ball was lately hanged at Tyburn. Greene had been a man extravagant in his speech and in his wrath, a wine-bibber, a roisterer, a whoremaster and a getter of bastards. His evil reputation lingered after him, here among the nodding and whispering passers-by of Dowgate. Yet he was a man richly gifted, a servant of the playhouse, with wit at command, and diverse in his abilities.

Determined not to return to his lodging till Alleyn had had time to read the whole of the new play, Shakespeare crossed the road and, walking under the eaves, was just passing the shoe-maker's shop—the faded signboard gave the name as Isam—

when the door opened and a woman in a lace cap looked out. Shakespeare stopped to give her passage, but he was misunderstood, for the woman opened the door wide and said: "You will have come about poor Master Greene? Yes, sir, this is the house where he died. I can show you the very bed where he breathed his last in this world."

Yielding to the impulse, Shakespeare stepped through the doorway, into a dark room fusty with stale smells of food and soiled clothing.

"Ah, sir, the place is like a cathedral church or a monster show, since it happened. Two, three and on to a dozen coming to enquire and to look every hour. I confess, I had not known Master Greene was so high in fame. Were you his friend, sir?"

"No. That I could not claim. Yet we had some small acquaintance."

He remembered the last time they had met, when Greene, testy with wine, had plainly sought occasion for a quarrel. Probably the poor fellow knew not what he was doing, and intended no offence. What reason for dispute lay between them?

"I also," he explained, "write pieces for the theatre. It diverts my leisure. My name is Shakespeare."

"Shakespeare!"

The shoemaker's wife—for who else could she be?—sounded the name like a cry of astonishment, and her glance flew quick and wary to his face.

"I have heard your name on his lips, sir, not long before he made an end."

"And what report made he of me?"

"Nay, sir, that's more than I can remember. A did not always talk clear, in his pain. That's to be understood. But a was another man before the end. Died penitent. Come up— be careful on the stairs, they are old and worn, as I am—and I will show you where he died."

Breathing heavily as she led the way, the shoemaker's wife

nevertheless did not stop talking. "Such a many visitors in so few days this house hath never known. I was looking for Doctor Harvey when I oped the door and saw you there, sir. He promised he would return. And there's printers, too, have taken away all the papers they could lay finger on. I trust I did right, permitting them. They paid me monies, for poor Master Greene was ten pounds in my husband's debt, I'd have you know. And though he charged his wife, whom he'd ill-used, as he confessed, with the tears on his face like rain coming from the conduits of a palace, though he charged his wife to repay my husband, who's to know she hath the ability? I have neighbours who tell me I should not have let Master Greene's papers go to the printers so cheap, but money's hard to refuse when you need it."

Quietly Shakespeare thrust a finger into his purse, to make sure he had loose coins there; this woman would expect a recompense for her trouble when he left. By her own account, and judging from the way the words fell quick and fluid from her tongue, she had already played guide to many visitors, and doubtless taken toll of them all. Greene was discharging his last debt in vicarious fashion, after his death.

"Well, sir, here's the room. Here's where the poor creature lay, changed in body and soul. For he was sick a many weeks of a surfeit. 'Twas always his weakness, to eat and drink beyond capacity. Pickled herrings and rhenish wine, it was, destroyed him. He swelled, sir. 'Twas pitiful to behold. But it turned his thoughts away from his impieties. He was all tears and penitence, never swearing, but beseeching God to forgive him his sins, and they were grievous. He swelled sir, like a dog that's taken from the river after many days. It hurt the heart to see him."

Shakespeare looked down at the narrow, tattered pallet bed, and then round the little low-ceilinged room, with a broken chair, dirty rushes on the floor, and an empty box as its only furniture. So this was where Robert Greene, red-beard master of arts, had crept to die, bloated like a drowned dog. A dog's death it was, save that a dog could not call upon God in its last misery.

"A was so poor, sir. We are poor, here in this house, for my husband's trade prospers not, and it was our last ten pounds went to provide food and medicines for good Master Greene. Yet he was the poorer. Had but the one shirt, and while that was a-washing, he would fain borrow from my husband. To speak truth, and in trust you keep the confidence, for I have told it to none but Doctor Harvey—do you know Doctor Harvey, sir? Doctor Gabriel Harvey?"

"Methinks the name is not new in my ears, but I cannot remember that he and I have met."

"He's from Cambridge, sir. Perchance that is why you know him not. It seems Master Greene had given Doctor Harvey cause for offence, and he came seeking him in Dowgate, filled with wrath. But when he arrived, Master Greene was already dead. He was buried next morning, for the days are hot. But as I was telling you, sir, Doctor Harvey, though he came in anger, yet when he heard how the poor gentleman died, stricken so sore with pain, yet godly in penitence, he was moved to tears."

"But what was it you told only to Doctor Harvey?"

"Ah, sir, that's not to be repeated, for they say we should never speak ill of the dead. And I tell you, sir, only because I know from your face, and from this our brief converse, you have a kind heart and will understand. When I took Master Greene in, sick already, he was lousy. Nay, I know that a louse or two is nor here nor there. Even at the Court, they say, delicate skins are sometimes mottled by the creatures. But poor Master Greene! The louses ran through his clothing like armies. A rare task I had of it, a rare slaughter. He was far gone, already, when he came to me. And then he grew worse day by day. He would strive to work, to continue his writing, for by writing, he said, he could always earn money. But the pain would stop him short. Yet he kept strength till near the end, and even the night before he died he moved to his chair, and back again, holding to my arm, and groaning. Then the swelling crept from his belly up to his face, and under his shirt we could see the flesh rising over his heart. He knew he was to die, then, and took to his prayers. But not always could he speak Christian sense. Sometimes a cried pitifully, and only for a penny pot of malmsey wine. A babbled in brief portions, of this and of that, of his wife, of poesy, of his ill-got child, and of flowering fields. And so he died."

I am as cold in the blood as Ned Alleyn, Shakespeare arraigned himself in the privacy of his thoughts. Here I stand, listening to a tale of death, the tale of such a death as may yet be mine own, for I too serve the playhouse with scrips as Robert Green did: and I am not moved, for him or for myself. Or if I be moved, then the emotion is dwindled within me, it touches me not at the quick, for there I feel only the excitement of garnering stuff for a playhouse death scene. He babbled of flowering fields with his last breath! ' Flowering fields ' is clumsy on the tongue. Flowering meadows. No, green fields. Green fields for Robert Greene. He babbled of green fields. That's better.

"And next morning, sir, before they took him to burial, I went out and procured bay leaves. For by that time the visitors were thronging the house, and it was borne upon me that a great man had died under my unworthy roof. I wove the bay leaves into a garland, and bound them round his head, and so he was buried, God rest his soul. Four shillings his winding sheet cost me."

Mistress Isam had told her tale so often that she never halted for a word now, and she took the offering he dropped into her hand, as he went, with an equal facility.

Back at his own lodging, Shakespeare found Alleyn thumbing over the pages of the new play.

"I have seen where Greene died, and talked with the woman who tended his last wants. Say rather, she talked with me."

"Still turning thy thoughts to Greene? The man's dead, and there an end."

"And there an end? Art so sure? Alleyn, give me wine. That house hath the stench of death and disease, and I feel it lingering about me still."

"But," the actor demanded, "he did not die of plague?"

"Of a surfeit. Yet the house stinks. Alleyn, I like not death."

"Who doth?"

"Some embrace it joyfully, of their own will. There was a maid, when I was a boy, at Tiddington——. Alleyn, dost fear death?"

"Verily. But my time is not yet come, I trust. Nor thine. Empty thy thoughts of death and Robin Greene. He's gone. Was never fit company for those in good repute."

"He died penitent."

"He had much to do penance for. Come, drink up. I would talk of thy new piece."

"Ay," said Shakespeare, "willingly. Richard the Third. How doth it like thee?"

"Excellently well. There are speeches here that already resound in my ears. Hast surpassed thyself, Will Shakespeare. Hast justified all my early hopes, all my earnest commendations to Henslowe."

"For the which I have not yet done thanking thee," said Shakespeare smoothly.

"This now, where Richard, still Duke of Gloucester, holds forth to Buckingham. This is majestical." He read, enouncing the lines with sonorous emphasis, rolling the syllables round his mouth before he trumpeted them out:

> "If not to answer, you might haply think
>   Tongue-tied ambition, not replying, yielded
> To bear the golden yoke of sovereignty,
> Which fondly you would here impose on me."

Nay, thought Shakespeare, that's but journeyman work, and jerks in the movement. But Alleyn ever loved sound above sense, and brass sound above silver.

Aloud he said: "There's always a new pleasure to hear my own words from thy lips, Alleyn. They are like unborn children till thou playest midwife."

"Wait till I have them by heart, wait till the playhouse is thronged, with every man-jack silent, attentive, and I in full voice, holding them captive to art. With this new help of thine, Will Shakespeare, I'll fetch all London to the Rose. Beshrew me if I do not. And there's poetry here, to boot. Where's the line about tears like pearls?"

Shakespeare came over to help him find the place, and read:

"The liquid drops of tears which you have shed
  Shall come again, transformed to orient pearls."

"That's it," the tragedian exclaimed. "But thou'rt too swift in thy discourse, and yet again, thou'rt too laggard at the climax." And he repeated the lines, expanding the vowel sound in ' tears ', and making a long pause before beginning the last phrase with an eruptive ' transformed '.

This fellow sees all that's writ merely as a machine to put into operation his frenetic tricks, his stops and starts, his revolutions of the eye-balls, the monotonous thunder of his voice. Yet he is the player the populace loves, and I made the piece for him: 'tis all the worse for that.

Alleyn was turning over pages again, muttering to himself, and Shakespeare's reverie continued its secret course of dissatisfaction. Yesterday, even this morning, I liked my Richard the Third well enow, and when it is rehearsed, and staged, and praised, when I am pointed out in the street as its only begetter, I shall be pleased. Yet, already, I feel it no part of me. Is this to be always so? Always to conceive and bring forth in hot delight, and then to gaze on the child of my travail with lack-lustre eyes of disappointment? Alleyn thinks he hath the length and breadth of Will Shakespeare clipped in those written scrolls, but he's mistaken. That's part of my servitude to him, to

Henslowe, to the playhouse, like the playing of minor parts in my own and other men's plays, which I trust I shall do no more.

There's a worth, a secret treasure, a pith of poesy and philosophy, locked in Will Shakespeare which no man yet hath dreamed on, which I have not yet been able to release in words. I am slow to develop my strength. Nigh thirty years old, and what I write hath no better quality than what I thought and felt ten years since. The ceaseless traffic twixt my heart and my brain now in this present year of 1592: that bodiless notion, superb but lacking shape, purpose and delineation, which visited me but half an hour since, when I looked at the bed on which Robert Greene died, and heard tell of a chaplet of bay leaves, a pot of malmsey and—what was it? a babble of flowery fields? No, green fields! Green fields for Robert Greene! Must another ten years pass me by before I can catch all this in a net of words?

Heroes and kings that die majestical, with their own tongues for funeral trumpets, they sort well with the fashion, and I can furnish them to feed the vanity of Ned Alleyn, twice and thrice in a playhouse year. But the compass of life is not bounded in heroic verses. The loud voice deafens the delicate ear of apprehension. There's humour, and there's wit: Alleyn lacks both, and contemns them. Put them together with tragedy, and the one emphasises the other's quality. An I had a rascal like Greene, yet not too like him, clapped in a piece of drama, I could make the people to laugh at him in life and weep over him in death. That would be a task to distil pleasure from. And why not? Death comes no softer to a rogue than to a warrior king.

But these are visions. I know too much, and can do too little. I know how a good player should comport himself: but I am indifferent dull upon the stage myself. I know all Alleyn's faults, so that he would draw sword on me an he could read my thoughts: but I can neither remedy his excesses and defects, in his person or my own, nor equal his merits. I am a man inwardly beset with visions, and could weep my eyes sore when I seek to copy them in words and find that all I value escapes my pen. And, when I put vaulting ambition aside, I fear it will always be so. Alleyn's notion is the truer: the whole breadth and width and depth and length of Will Shakespeare is contained in that poor scrip which he dotes upon and I— though I would perish ere I let him know it—despise. Yet it hath points of virtue.

"Ah," said Alleyn, not looking up, "'tis a brave piece. 'Twill be the talk of the town. 'Twill make thy fame. Yet there are one or two items, trifles, mere trifles, I would have amended."

This was known before, this was to be prophesied, this was inevitable!

"Here in the early part," Alleyn continued, "Gloucester hath little to do, and less to say. That will not please the people."

"But the end, the climax, that's all Richard's. Then he has the stage, front, middle and rear, all for his own. I took special care of that."

"True. Else there would be no play. Think not I demand undue attention. No man in the company works more diligently, on stage and off, than I. I am wearied with toil, and if I demand more speeches and longer speeches in these early scenes, I know full well I add to my burden, already heavy. But we are servants of the playhouse, all of us, great and small. We must make sacrifices, and I am certain Henslowe will agree with me: Gloucester's part must be extended."

"Soft you, pray," said Shakespeare. "There is a subtlety in my device. 'Tis true, the people will not see or hear overmuch of you as Gloucester in the first scenes. I admit the indictment. But 'twas not done by indifference or want of skill. 'Twas done to an end."

"And that end?"

"To whet the appetite. Thou art Edward Alleyn. Every mother's son who comes to the playhouse knows that, and knows that the character portrayed by Edward Alleyn must be the principal part in the play."

"True."

"Therefore he looks for you, he prepares himself to listen. This appetite is not denied, but 'tis tickled to the point of eager expectation, until Gloucester's tragedy is all prepared; and then there's Alleyn fixed in the public eye, holding the whole playhouse in thraldom."

The actor pondered this solemnly. "I perceive the point of thy device. 'Tis pretty! 'Tis skilful! To provoke the appetite before satisfying it. Yes, it is a new subtlety. And yet, I have fears. I have doubts. Custom is not easily or lightly to be overthrown."

"I'll tell thee what I'll do. I'll write a new exhortation for Gloucester, long and heroic. And it shall open the play. It shall be my very best. It shall be jewelled with poetry. I promise thee."

"To open the play? That's a brave idea. That might well put all to right."

Shakespeare was quick to follow up his advantage. "Consider how this device works. Why do the people come to the playhouse? For to see and hear Edward Alleyn. Very well. No sooner is the play announced to begin, than they'll see him and hear him, at the full height of his glory, for I have promised thee the opening speech shall be of my best. Then for a while the people are teased, as a man by a lightsome maid who first she will and then she won't. But in the end she doth, and all the more enjoyment for the uncertain delay. The people have their Alleyn in small rations for a while, and every time he quits the stage they are left clamouring for more; till the tragedy is all in train, and Alleyn, Gloucester, Richard, gives his full art without pause or stint."

"Thou'rt a man of parts, Will Shakespeare. I always said so. Remember that. Alleyn was thy sponsor at the Rose from the first. This scene, before the battle, where Richard is visited by the ghosts, wait till thou seest what I make of this long speech which concludes it."

"And the ending? How do you find that?"

"The best part I ever had. This makes a page boy of Tamburlaine. The lines are sounding in my head already."

And Alleyn, springing from his seat, began to stride about the room, roaring:

> "I think there be six Richmonds in the field;
> Five have I slain to-day instead of him.
> A horse! a horse! my kingdom for a horse!"

VII

SOUTHAMPTON HOUSE, fronting on Holborn, was large and impressive, ancient in its original structure and here and there, in its amendments, annexes and renovations, exquisite according to the new Italian manner. It had pediments, and pillars, and stone busts of Virgil and Plato and Cæsar set in niches in the wall, like the saints of the Old Faith. A man might be well aware, in the cloisters of his own mind, that the blood in his veins was gentle, moreover that he was a figure of some note in London, and yet know that his London was Bankside and Shoreditch, a playhouse London which stopped short at the guarded gates of such mansions as this Southampton House. A man might feel himself full value in wisdom and experience for the advantage of years he held over a handsome young Earl, and take pride in not bending the knee too full before the soft spoken, gracious patronage of a youth who was doubtless but another nobleman anxious to surround himself with poets, as a vain beauty with her mirrors. And yet the bold demeanour was cracked and shivered from within by the knowledge that here the youth might enter without let or question, master of all, while the elder man, freighted with howsomuch poetry, must bide his time, marked a venturer in great houses, and not stir a foot beyond where he was bid. A man might carry locked in his bosom a dozen palaces larger than this, peopled with kings and cæsars and great ladies, whole worlds of imperial stones to make even an earl cry astonishment and joy: and yet, when such a man comes to call at Southampton House in Holborn he is stiff in the tongue, uncertain of his limbs, dumbfoundered, ill at ease.

One leaf of the tall wooden gate, under the stone archway, stood open. The porter demanded—neither rude nor courteous —the visitor's name and his business.

"My name is William Shakespeare, of which you may have heard report."

The porter's visage admitted no knowledge. This surly rogue would never, it seemed, expend a twopence on the play-house. Perchance he was a Brownist, one of these disapproving puritans who would turn religion all to melancholy, and prayed that merry men might choke over their cakes and ale. Yet that was unlikely, for the Earl's father had held to the Old Faith: there would be no puritans here, and that was as well, considering the tenour of the poem he had brought.

He tried again. "My lord, your master, bade me wait upon him."

"Appointed he the hour and the day?"

"Nay. I was to come at my leisure. That was the order of our arrangement."

"There are many come flaunting here upon such terms. My lord's a courteous gentleman, but folk will strain his idle words to their own purpose."

Shakespeare's wrath broke about the porter's ears.

"How now, fellow? Season this presumption awhile. Because I respect the usages of courtesy with you, do you think I am debased to your degree? Have you not eyes nor ears to sort a gentleman from a throng of suppliant knaves? Go to. Send my name to your master, and have me shewn to a waiting chamber. And despatch!"

The porter cringed. This stranger must be from the country, for one who kept watch at the gate of Southampton House learned the name of every gentleman of note in London, and assuredly there was no Shakefist among them. Plague on it, what was the name? Shakesomething or another. He came afoot, and that was misleading. But customs change, and other gentlemen, impatient, would appear these days without waiting for horse or escort. There were loudmouths, pretencers and roisterers aplenty in town, who would affront the devil himself with their arrogance: but a man who dare spill his anger at the doors of Southampton House must be sure of himself and sure of his welcome, a gentleman born. Doubtless he came from the country: that would explain all.

"Nay, sir, be not wroth with me. I intended no offence. This duty of mine, sir, keeping the gate against the importunate, the villainous and the needy, is no easy duty, sir, I do assure you. An I admit those who should not be admitted, I suffer for it."

A sorry world, in which a man must needs lose temper before a menial would do him service. More softly, but still with some impatience, Shakespeare said: "No more! Conduct me where I may wait upon his lordship."

"That's more than I dare do, sir. My office is to keep guard. An I stir foot from here I lose my bread, and that's a prospect I would not contemplate. But I'll have your wishes observed."

He walked to the inner wall of the great archway and reached up to pull a rope there. Overhead a bell clanged loud, again and again. Presently a manservant appeared from a door in the courtyard.

"Conduct this gentleman at once," said the porter, "to Master Hollis. He will impart to you his name and the occasion of his appearance."

Master Hollis, doubtless, would be the steward, the overlord of the servants. And so, thought Shakespeare, he was at last within the walls of Southampton House, after much parleying, but how much nearer to the young earl's interest and his own preferment he could not guess.

He would not allow himself to inspect, like a yeoman come to town, the high walls of the courtyard across which, with the manservant in respectful attandance, he walked. The house was indeed a palace; he gathered a swift impression of size and grandeur. The Holborn front, itself four times as large as his father's house in Henley Street, was, he perceived now, but a gatehouse. The main buildings were hid behind, grouped round this flagged courtyard. Their walls were studded thick with windows, some of them curved forward, and to see the roof tops and the chimneys one would doubtless need to set one's head back on the neck: he would do no such thing. A house such as this was a small town in itself, and a stranger could easily lose his way among so many rooms and halls and corridors and passages. But honour demanded that Will Shakespeare should walk as though all his life had been spent in palaces and manors.

The servant went ahead, opened a door—how did 'the fellow remember to distinguish one door from another among so many?—conducted him down a corridor, and into a panelled room, where a bright fire was burning. Excellent hospitality which provided such a fire, for once within doors, although the early spring sunshine gilded the air outside, the stone walls struck chill on the flesh. The room was furnished with a large table, and several cushioned settles. Two gentlemen were already waiting there, talking in low voices. They glanced up as he entered, but he did not recognise them, nor they him, it appeared, for they fell to talking again.

"Will it please you," said the servant, "inform me of your name and your business?"

"I wait upon my lord at his bidding, and my name is William Shakespeare."

"I will inform Master Hollis at once."

One of the talking gentlemen, rather swarthy, black haired and brown-eyed, appeared to take notice of the new-comer now. But he continued his conversation, speaking so low that the words could not be distinguished one from another.

Shakespeare warmed his hands at the fire, and then walked over to the mullioned window of clear glass which gave direct on to the courtyard. He watched several men and women, grooms, body-servants, cooks, doubtless, come and go, and then turned as he heard himself addressed in a mellow voice oddly accented.

"Crave your pardon, sir," said the dark-haired man, "and take no offence if I am in error. I could not but overhear your

name, and I would ask whether you are that same William
Shakespeare who devises plays for the Rose Theatre?"

Gratified, Shakespeare bowed.

"I am he."

"Right glad to make your acquaintance, sir. I have lately
seen your tragedy of King Richard, and much admired it. My
own name, which will not be known to you, I fear, is Florio,
John Florio. I am in his lordship's service, his secretary, sometime his tutor."

"Give you good day, Master Florio."

"The name, as you may guess, is Italian. Such is my
parenthood. I, also, write a little. Nothing that I would
mention in the same breath as your noble verses. In truth,
I am translating into the English tongue the opera of a certain
Montaigne, Comte Michel de Montaigne. A labour of love,
for there's wisdon richly stored. Yet to find precise equivalents
between French and English is a task for Tantalus. Perchance,
sir, you know the writings of Montaigne?"

"By repute, but no more than that. I am but an indifferent
poor scholar. I can but make shift with the French tongue. In
truth, even my mother English comes but unwillingly under
my domination."

"Nay now, Master Shakespeare. This modesty is unworthy.
A man should know his own abilities, and feel no shame to
acknowledge them. I have heard your verses spoken by Alleyn.
They have a noble ring. They lift English almost to the
height of the Latin and the Greek. Nay, listen to my prating.
That's the way the pedants talk. I'll not be discreet, Master
Shakespeare. In my heart, I think our English may yet out-
dazzle the ancient tongues. 'Tis but an opinion, yet I hold it.
What say'st thou?"

Shakespeare looked at the eager, yet shrewd face of the man
who spoke so quickly and surely, and yet with a faint foreign
intonation, of the English tongue.

"That is my opinion, too. I have not such command of
Latin and Greek that I can make strict comparison. Yet I'll

confess: an I had an equal facility in all three tongues, I would still choose to write in English."

"Bravely spoken. Master Shakespeare, give me no answer if the question is froward—yet I must needs put it. My lord, who betimes gives me his confidence in problems of letters, hath spoken of you, always in commendation, and I believe he did mention a poem, a long poem in the heroic manner. Not a piece for the playhouse, but a poem to be printed. Is this news true?"

"Ay. The poem is writ, complete. An you will keep confidence, Master Florio, I will confess I have a fair copy here."

"And you have come to consult with my lord concerning it?"

Shakespeare nodded.

"Excellent. These are brave tidings. My lord will be delighted."

"That's as may be. The verses please me now, but to-morrow, next week, next month, who can tell?"

"They will please the Earl. My word on it. Was it your intention to offer them, in a suitable epistle, to my lord? Do I ask too many, and too pressing, questions?"

Shakespeare gave Florio a quick glance. He was Italian, and Italians were by notoriety cunning, double-dealers, smiling only to betray. But here was a man all openness and eagerness: and he had penetrated to the heart of the matter, already: there was no further use in concealment.

"I am flattered by your interest in my affairs, good Master Florio. Were my poem to find his lordship's favour, it is true I had hoped to offer it by dedication on its printing."

"Excellent, excellent. I'll not ask to see the scrip. My lord must be first in the field. But tell me, what is the theme?"

"'Tis nothing new. A narrative and a lamentation upon the story of hot Venus and reluctant Adonis. 'Tis made by stanzas, rhymed, and that was difficult. I fear it speaks of intemperate love somewhat intemperately."

"'Twill not displease my lord on that score. Is but a boy, for here in England, where the fogs so often obscure the sun, maturity comes late. Is but a boy. And yet his thoughts are hot. As for his deeds, I know nothing."

Or else, what you know, you'll not disclose, thought Shakespeare. The reports he had garnered of the young Earl of Southampton were to the point then: this new exercise in verse, this task he had set himself, to discover if he could rival Kit Marlowe—whose Hero and Leander was bravely done—in print as well as in the theatre, might well meet with approbation. A man who would earn his bread by writing needed a patron, and a patron with power at Court. Southampton had spoken courteous words the other day, coming from the Lords' Room at the Rose to the players' tiring house. An his thoughts were indeed warmed with desire, ' Venus and Adonis ' should come apt to them.

"But I trust," Florio went on, "you do not intend to forsake the playhouse? You perceive I am not of those arrogant scholars who hold it in abhorrence, as vulgar."

"The playhouse"—these words were spoken with a solemn authority, of which the comely-faced poet was all unaware— "may well prove the beacon-mark, the sign by which this our age may be set apart from all that have preceded it. Nay, I'll not desert the playhouse. But this last year it hath almost deserted me. It hath become the plague house."

"A pretty exchange of words, and marvellous apt! The playhouse becomes the plague house. So thinks authority. As soon as death stinks in the city, the order goes forth: close down the playhouses."

"And closed they have been: the season cut short to a mere cold weather stretch between December and February. And so, Master Florio, I have employed this undesired leisure writing a poem of hot blood to warm my cold fingers."

"Neat and pat. Neat and pat. You talk, sir, as you write. My lord will be grateful for your acquaintance, will accept your dedication—and you know what goes with that?"

Ay, thought Shakespeare, and sore I need money.

The door behind them opened, not suddenly or loudly, but

with a deliberate dignity, it seemed to Shakespeare, as he turned and saw a tall man, with a silver-topped staff as high as himself, enter the room.

"Master Hollis," Florio whispered.

The steward was richly clad in a black doublet and round hose, slashed open to shew purple silk beneath. He was thin in the shank and the arm, holding himself painfully erect, hollow-cheeked, frigid-eyed. When he spoke his voice was round and deep, deliberate and slow as his gait, and creamed with the importance of his office.

He ignored Florio and Shakespeare, and addressed himself to the other gentleman waiting on the settle by the window, who at once sprang to his feet.

"My lord bade me give you his kind wishes, sir, and earnest commendation, but he must ask your forgiveness this day. Affairs of moment yield him no leisure, and he would thank you, sir, either to call again at your convenience or to put your petition into writing, when he assures you it shall have his early and close attention."

The visitor stood for a moment, frowning. Shakespeare could see that he was tempted to speak, and to speak angrily, but he turned away and then, drawing on his gloves, was content to say: "Give your master my service, and tell him I will write."

The steward looked to be offended, perhaps at the phrase "your master." He drew himself still higher, it seemed, with his arm thrown wide to the top of his staff and the lace ruff cocking up under his thin arrogant chin, as the other man hurried out of the room.

"There goes one who'll do the Wriothesley name no kind service," Florio observed. "Master Hollis, thou shouldst temper the wind to the naked ribs of humiliation."

"I spoke him fair words, as I was bid."

"But how didst thou speak them? Like the angel turning poor Adam out of paradise."

"The fellow is of small importance."

"His skin is no thicker for that. And tomorrow, next year, who knows, he may be no longer a Master Nonentity; he may have it in his power to do thee injury. A little gentleness, Master Hollis, costs nothing and may yield large profits."

"When I have need of your admonitions, Master Secretary, I'll come ask for them."

"Not so. Hast the need, but thou'lt not ask. Let be. Here, Master Hollis, is one who waits upon my lord by my lord's desire. He is Master William Shakespeare."

"I am informed upon the matter. It shall be attended to."

"But despatch, Master Hollis. Even though my counsel be unasked, let me say that my lord will be displeased an he discover Master Shakespeare has waited here this half hour."

"Better leave me to manage my own office."

And the steward, cold, serious and tall, went out.

"He is part of the Wriothesley inheritance," Florio explained. "My lord cannot abide him, but my lady, my lord's mother, insists that Hollis remains."

"He entertains the onlooker against his own will. One would think he dressed his backbone, as well as his lace, with Dutch starch."

Suddenly Florio exclaimed: "Chettle! That is the name, is't not? Chettle was in the right of it."

"Do you know the man?"

"Not I."

"He is jack of all trades. Writes books, devises plays, cuts verses to fit any shape, like a tailor, plays tinker to other men's plays. Nay, I have patched and mended myself: 'tis useful prentice work. Henry Chettle is a passing good fellow. Why did you speak his name?"

"I had in mind what he wrote about you, Master Shakespeare, in his latest book. What is it called?"

"'Kindheart's Dream'."

And at once Shakespeare was inwardly seeing the passage printed in the copy that Chettle had sent him, damp and fragrant from the press. 'I am as sorry as if the original fault had been my fault, because myself have seen his demeanour no less civil than he excellent in the quality he professes; besides, divers of worship have reported his uprightness of dealing, which argues his honesty, and his facetious grace in writing that approves his art.' This praise was adequate reparation for the scandal.

"That's the name," said Florio. "Chettle hath described you fair."

"I bear him no ill-will. And, I swear, none towards Greene, wherever his soul be now."

"Greene was a dissolute rogue."

"Yet he wrote well, Master Florio. And his death was pitiful. I returned to London but a few days after, and I saw where he died, in penury but repentant. I mourned him truly."

'But he was your enemy and made base accusations against your good name?"

"That I did not know, till Chettle had his last scrip printed, his 'Groat's-worth of Wit'."

"Is it so? I had understood that you and Greene were sworn enemies."

"I scarce exchanged a hundred words with him. But hark you, Master Florio: be just to Greene. He did me an ill-service, and though all's set to rights now, I doubt not there are those will long remember his accusations against me. Evil persists like a weed: good repute needs constant tending. But Greene, when he wrote of me, was a man sour in disappointment. His last piece for the theatre lacked success: his sins were heavy on him: and he was stricken with the disease that soon fetched him to his death. A man in such a condition is given to disordered judgments. He is not to be held culpable for all he does. Nay, I doubt not, had Greene lived, he would have struck from what he had writ in haste and pain all that I had, afterward, to complain against."

"You are sure it was not done by Nashe, and passed off as Greene's to catch pennies while Greene and his lamentable end were on every man's tongue? I have heard that whispered abroad."

"Nashe hath denied it," said Shakespeare, "and Chettle, too, who took away the scrips from Greene's lodging after he died. I believe them. The sole author was Greene, but I tell you, I hold him not to blame for it. If God may forgive his grievous misdoings, I may overlook this last small offence."

Chettle was right, Florio decided privately; this William Shakespeare was a very pattern of courtesy and gentleness. For Greene had written furiously, to warn his fellow writers, nearly all of whom, like himself, had schooled their wits at the universities, against this new-comer from the country, this obscure player turned, against all precedent and expectation, against nature itself, a maker of plays. Greene saw Shakespeare as a rival, dangerous, swiftly successful; and jealousy made him believe that such success could spring only from theft. "An upstart crow, beautified with our feathers," he had written, inferring that Shakespeare stole other writers' notions, stories and phrases. Greene had called Shakespeare a wolf— or was it a ravening lion? or a tiger?—some beast of prey dissembling his true nature under the humility of a player who takes to the stage only to learn the elements of a trade. He had called him a bombasting Johanes factotum, and a Shake-scene. And here was this Shakespeare, with his tragedy of King Richard the talk of the town, and a new poem locked in his satchel, speaking kindly of red beard Greene, who doubtless was frying his hatred and lecheries in hell, and in no case to render thanks. This Shakespeare would appreciate the sage conclusions of Count Montaigne.

Florio put this last reflection into speech, and Shakespeare replied that it would pleasure him much to be honoured with the reading of the new translation as it progressed.

"I might aid you there again," said Florio. "There's more work writ today than comes to the printer's hands. Sonnets, now, after the fashion of my own Italian Petrarch. The newest mode in poesy. They circulate about the court this last year.

And it comes to my mind I have in my room a translation, by one Bartholomew Yonge, of a pretty tale from the Spanish, or it may be the Portuguese. It is called Diano Enamorata. 'Tis not a new tale, nor a new Englishing of it. The theme is love, but not tragic. You should write comedy, Master Shakespeare. We need good comedies in the playhouse. This is a tale of a lady whose true love abandons her, wherefore she pursues him in the habit of a page, and is not recognised. Would it interest you to read?"

"Why, surely. This device of the lady in men's clothing is ancient. But then there are no new stories. All's old wood, and must leaf again in the mind. And it is true, I would wish to escape a while from the chronicles of kings and battles. Henslowe and Alleyn are all for holding to what has yielded profit in the past, but I would fain venture away. Master Florio, I shall be grateful if you will loan me the English scroll of this tale."

"Surely. And at once. My lord, I know, will be wroth an Hollis hath not informed him you are in attendance here. But perchance it is true, and my lord cannot free himself. You did not advise us of your coming?"

"No. I deemed that would be presumption. The Earl hath spoken with me only once in the playhouse."

"Well, an you jib not at waiting, to fill time I'll fetch the Spanish tale, and be with you anon."

Not every Italian, then, was bred after Machiavelli, Shakespeare reflected, left in solitude for the first time since he presented himself at the gate of Southampton House. This Florio had poison neither in his ring nor in his tongue. He loved the playhouse, too, and made no shame of his love. Full many a scholar affected to see only lewdness in the theatres, as if their Ovid and Terence texts were nicely modest. And many an English born writer would have displayed jealousy and suspicion towards another writer competing for patronage.

Haply the secret was hid in that word display: being Italian, which to some was the equivalent of a dissembler, Florio perchance did not display what he truly felt. Jealousy, suspicion, hatred might be there, hid by these ready—too ready?—professions of friendship. Haply Master Secretary's poison had been withheld awhile, and was now, under the pretext of fetching the Spanish tale, being subtly distilled into my lord's ear, so that he should greet with suspicion a new suppliant who might rival Florio? It had been wiser to say naught about the Venus poem: wiser to give the first news of it direct to my lord himself. Well, it was done, and past mending. To throw the dice so soon, without long and indecisive meditation, was not the common Shakespearean way: no worse for that. The change was pleasant. Nothing to do now but wait in this warm and handsome room, idle and at ease, until my lord or one of his men came to announce which way the future would direct itself.

An Florio be honest, Southampton will read the poem, accept it—would be a fool to decline such an offering!—and so Will Shakespeare breaks on London town as a printed poet, to be taken into reckoning with Chapman, with Lyly, with Spenser, even with Marlowe, Marlin, Morley, Marley. It is strange that one man should put his name through such a parade of variations. A little latitude in spelling is any gentleman's privilege, but Christopher Marloe (as he printed it on his ' Hero and Leander ', a poem which the new ' Venus ' should rival) gives himself enough names for the muster-roll of a regiment. Under the rant and the braggadacio, he must be subject to indecisions, perchance as variable and unsure as I am, who sometimes spell Shakespeare with two e's, sometimes with one, sometimes with none, and again I never know whether to put in the a, or leave it out. No matter: 'tis no common name, and comes easy to the recognition. Yet it would be well to fix upon one form, and hold to that. I must consider it. I have been considering it this many a year. What I must do is to bring consideration to an end, and know my own mind.

Shall I ever know my own mind? Is it ever constant from one day to the next? Is there a Will Shakespeare who persists

from the past to the present, on whom I may depend to sponsor
my future? Am I, in verity, that same who span romantical
poems to Nan Hathaway and thought the sky like to flame in
rapture when she permitted me to kiss her cheek? Nay, that
young Will Shakespeare had never dared to man a women,
as I, or someone with my likeness and name, did that September afternoon on the banks of Avon.

Yet if it were not I, how comes it I have the memory so
sharp in my mind, and have turned it to poetry in this ' Venus
and Adonis' lying snugly rolled at my hip? For Nan is Venus,
though I be no Adonis. Grant it that Nan was a maid till
then, yet she had the years of me: there was knowledge in her
blood. I thought to woo her to my desire. I thought old Meg
had launched the project. Yet was Meg prompted by Nan?
That's a question I shall never put answer to. All I know is,
Nan was ready-ripe for the encounter. 'Twas she took me, not
I her. She's the Venus of my poem. Nay, she was. For where
is that Nan now? Displaced, transformed, and Mistress
Shakespeare, that was Nan Hathaway, is now a mother of
children, a sober housewife of Stratford town, and so chill
and overcast, so wintry in her desire, that she never misses her
husband absent from his bed the year round in London.

And that husband—go to, he's not the Will Shakespeare
which Stratford knew. He is become a paragon, a nonsuch, for
the flesh he inhabits is ever cold also. There's ink in his veins
in place of blood. His mistresses are got from books and have
no substance but in copied parts for boys to con and speak in
shrill voice upon the stage. He is an unquiet spirit, for ever
shifting his guise beyond recognition, a stranger to himself,
making his own mouth gape bewilderment. He is every sort of
man; godly and blasphemous; mercantile and prophetic by
turns; a poet and yet strict in a bargain; nice in his manners
save when he chooses to haunt ale-houses; whirling between
lofty visions and saucy jests.

Every sort of man in one; and something of the woman
in him too. Yet what does he know of women, save that he

has got children on his wife, and dropped kisses on several
mouths not his wife's—and found the kisses sour ere they
were fair returned? It is possible to clap lips to lips, ay and to
march in for the full surrender, and still to know naught of
what passes in a woman's heart. Behold a barren bitter
wisdom, that doth no more than fix the frontier of ignorance!
Even so, it is more than most men learn. And yet one of these
myriad Will Shakespeares which torment me with their
sudden metamorphoses is, I'll swear, a woman, or close cousin
to the female kind.

This random meditation, this maze of inward scrutinies,
in which I have lost my way long since, hath Will Shakespeare
writ all over its confused geography. There's neither daylight nor symmetry here: first I bemoan that I know not any
woman except after the flesh, not even Nan. And she's not
Venus, either: I have wronged her yet again, and it shames
me! And then, proclaiming my ignorance, I deafen myself
with vainglory, if it be vainglory to judge that one of my host
of Will Shakespeares is cousin to a woman, and ergo—for
that was the purpose of the vaunt—by instinct knows womankind from the inside out. God gave me mild eyes and smooth
temples but to mislead my fellows, for within this tumult I
call a mind, all's frenzy, fog, riot, and endless uncertainty.

A clatter of hooves in the courtyard interrupted his
' random meditation ': He turned towards the window, and,
perceiving the shadow shape of horse and rider a few yards
away, moved closer till he could peer through one of the small
panes, between the lozenge leads, and see clearly what was
toward.

Through the window pane, horseshoes could be heard
stamping on flagged stones, and even the metallic chime of
harness; lips could be seen to part in speech and in smiles;
but never a word penetrated the glass. It was as if he had come
late to the theatre, knowing neither the play nor the players,
and were watching an inset piece deftly mimed in dumb-show:
he lacked knowledge of the purport; his response was all

speculation, guess and surmise; but how bravely his eye was taken, how his heart turned away from its own dismal inquisition to admire this gallant player.

It was no codling youth, he saw now, who had drawn rein, sitting small and slender and imperious on the white Barbary mare. It was a woman, scarlet-breeched and high-booted, as ladies of the Court sometimes garbed themselves for hunting and for country excursions. Doubtless she had ridden in from Mary-le-bone fields, or the foxglove meadows by the Reading road, beyond the hamlet of Charing. She wore a doublet of white sarcenet, wide-striped with scarlet. A long cloak hung from her shoulders, falling back over the mare's crupper. Her hair was caught up, knit with silken strings, under her feathered velvet hat; but peering intently, he could see that her hair was gold, exchanging glitter for glitter with the sunshine. A mask, made of the same black velvet as the hat pulled aslant on her head, hid eyes and brows: of her face all that was visible to him was the straight white ridge of the nose; the curl of the nostrils; the smooth, thin cheeks; the peep of the ears under the gold hair; the proud yet soft turn of the chin; the column of the throat emerging from the lace collar turned over the top of the scarlet and white doublet; and the mobility of her wide mouth as she spoke, and smiled, listened, and spoke again. Scarlet and white in her habit, she was scarlet and white in her countenance, for like all town-dwelling ladies she had guarded her complexion from the darkening stroke of the sun, and her lips—though they were soft and delicately formed and swift in their varieties, tender, petulant, eager, mocking, disdainful and meditative by turns—were doubtless scarlet more by art than by nature.

He watched her as he might have watched a skilful player miming in a dumb-show, yet her every movement, every word she spoke unheard by him, seemed to be without premeditation, uncalculated in origin and in effect, free, untutored, the first and natural expression of what next sprang up in her mind. A tall young man, richly dressed, hatted and cloaked, was standing by her horse's head, one hand on the bridle. The lady looked down at him: he looked up to her. His back was to the window, and he kept it so, although the mare sometimes fidgeted and with dainty steps swung this way and that. It was such an arrangement as might have been contrived upon the stage, to turn a boy player enacting some great lady at a rendezvous full face towards the lords among the audience, so that the lines he spoke might achieve their full emphasis. A boy player to take the part of a lady garbed like a boy, a page, a young prince? The device was not new, but there were plentiful riches still stored in it.

The lady was amused by something said by the gentleman in the cloak. She threw back her head and laughed: she was a lady confident of herself, not preening her way through tight-drawn niceties of behaviour. And yet she was modest; even the boldest gestures of her masculine guise kept faith with maidenly reserve. Now she had grown earnest. She leaned forward a little in the saddle, and her face, so much of it as the velvet mask revealed, was changed, turned all to anxious enquiry.

But what was this? Smiling now, the bridle rein looped over one wrist, she drew off first a gauntlet glove, and then a ring from one finger of the ungloved hand. She held the ring out and down: the stone, ruby or cornelian, winked in the sunshine. The man in the cloak took the ring, releasing the bridle, and the horse curvetted a yard or two away. The gentleman bent his head to examine the ring. Was this a first and secret plighting of troth? Did great gentlemen and ladies exchange their love tokens thus publicly in a courtyard? The man in the cloak turned towards the window, the better to examine the ring, and Shakespeare's body jerked with surprise as he recognised the young Earl of Southampton. A further astonishment took him then, for he felt a tide of jealousy, both hot and chill, tear impetuously through his blood, throbbing in temples and veins. It was a jealousy sprung immediate from fear lest this lady in her scarlet and white bravery be pledged, not to Will Shakespeare, player and poet, but to a nobleman whom Shakespeare could not hope to rival, whose patronage he must beg for.

Nor fear nor jealousy was well-founded. Almost at once Southampton returned the ring, and the lady slipped it carelessly back on her finger. There was no drama in this dumbshow: it was but a casual, polite encounter, a question idly asked and indifferently answered by the momentary exhibition of a ring. No love vowed; no cause for envy therefore. And what a fool am I, thought Shakespeare, past my youth though not past foolishness, to mistake a storm in the blood for true love: to spy on a lady through a window glass and imagine into her—whose name I know not, nor the colour of her eyes, nor the sound of her voice—all manner of virtues I would delight to honour? Out upon it! An I saw her skirted like a woman, viewed her eyes without a mask, heard what small beer her conversation draws, she would be but another female, and so no excuse for day-dreaming!

The Earl stood back now, with hat doffed, bowing. The mare, obedient to bridle and spur, wheeled away. The lady raised her hand, gloved again, to return the salute, and rode off towards the gateway. As Southampton turned, Shakespeare drew sharply back from the window, but not before he had seen Florio, a scroll in his hand, overtaking his master. So the Italian secretary had spoken truth: he was indeed fetching the Spanish tale. And it was a tale of a lady in love pretending to be a page, perchance a tale of a lady in scarlet and white? Her name! Imperative to know her name! Florio would tell him!

The door opened and Southampton, uncloaked now, courteous, yet idly magnificent in his gracious assurance, came into the room.

"Master Shakespeare, I owe you many apologies. But truly it was not in my capacity to come to your earlier. Even now I was detained upon my way."

Now why the dickens should a man who, in his private

thoughts, knew that he had powers to confront the whole world and reduce it to a rapture of admiration, stammer and stare because a young Earl chose to speak fair words concerning a new poem offered him?

When he saw from Florio's friendly eyes that it was time to withdraw, he was glad to go, glad to escape into the ease of being Will Shakespeare alone with his own mind. The world of great houses and great lords enchanted him, now he had seen it near, as it had enchanted him when he dreamed of it from afar! but it made him secretly shy; it lamed his manners. He was slow to digest a new experience, and slow to adapt himself. Time and usage would remedy that. My lord had spoken fair, and if he had pledged himself to nothing, that was not to be expected till the poem were read and reflected upon. If Southampton accepted it, Florio would give counsel over the drafting of the epistle of dedication. Well, there was a fashion for such things, and doubtless he could fit phrases to the mode.

Suddenly he stopped dead on the crowded pavements of Holborn, and heeded not the remonstrances of the citizens he incommoded in their progress. He had forgotten to ask Florio the name of the lady who had offered her ring for Southampton's inspection. Nay, he had found no occasion to question Florio: they had not been alone for a moment, and to ask the lady's name in Southampton's presence would be uncourtly. He considered for a moment whether he should turn back and ask for Florio at the gate. Better not to show himself again so quickly. He would see Florio within a few days. He would not soon forget the lady. Yet he wished he knew her name. She must have a name. Until he knew it, he would call her The Lady in Scarlet and White.

VIII

THE MONTH of May, which should have been a sequence of triumphs, proved itself all shock, disaster and dubiety. Young Burbage, who was like to prove a player of rare merit, was quick to point out that none of these misfortunes touched Will Shakespeare nearly. What was Christopher Marlowe to him, or he to Marlowe? Rivals they might be, for the laurels of London poesy, and rivals, too, for admiration in the playhouse. Yet there was room for two, and more than two, stars in the London galaxy: and the orbit of Marlowe, or Marlin, or Marley, hardly impinged on his own. Their names might flow together on men's tongues, but they rarely met. He could praise Marlowe's art (he overpraised it, said Dick Burbage) in all sincerity, though he liked not the man, with his black-avised swagger, his loud lewd mouth, his reckless arrogance. Marlowe, for his part, affected hardly to be aware of the existence of William Shakespeare.

Marlowe offered outrage to religion and decency. Folk muttered against him, and marvelled that the State permitted such a breather of fiery impieties to go freely about and affront sober citizens. Even those who most delighted in his 'Tamburlaine' play, his 'Edward II' and his 'Jew of Malta,' shook their heads over the author's behaviour.

"The man who bestrides Pegasus," said Shakespeare to Burbage, "is not asked to temper his pace to the gait of a bean-fed palfrey. All's explosive within Marlowe's breast: some of it must out."

To which Burbage, trained to the caution of a man of affairs by his father's long experience in building and administering The Theatre, and discreet beyond his twenty-four years, answered: "Grant that Marlowe hath a mettlesome talent, but who's in command? He or Pegasus?"

The common opinion clearly was that Marlowe was due for a downfall. He would come to a sudden and miserable end, like Robert Greene. Those who saw in the playhouses naught but licensed bawdry anticipated for Marlowe reproof, imprisonment, even hanging, drawing and quartering, and were not sorry. If Jesuits, witches and Brownist puritans were to be put out of the way, as being dangerous to the State, why not this boasting blasphemer?

"Is it not possible," Shakespeare asked, "to send him warning in time? A word spoken now, a friendly counsel of moderation, might save him from God knows what calamity."

Burbage shook his head.

"Kit Marlowe never listened to good counsel yet. And he's swift in quarrel. Take advice, Will: leave Marlowe alone, or else thou'llt be lucky to escape without drawing sword. The man is dangerous."

He paused and then, choosing his words slowly, added: "And trouble not thy mind with fears for Marlowe's safety. All is other than it seems to the sight. He goes not without protection."

Shakespeare looked at the broad, thick-featured, yet mobile face of the young player, but got no further enlightenment from it.

"Something thou knowest, and wilt not disclose. Why not?"

"Nay, I know nothing. I pick up a hint here, a surmise there. And what I do not know, I cannot disclose. The sum of what I will say is this: consider Kit Marlowe, his impious oaths, his mockery of scripture, his vices publicly shewn. Were he another man, he would have paid penalty for all this long since. Is't not so? Very well. There's a reason. What that reason is I do not know. Nor thou. Best not to enquire. Those who meddle in the inmost affairs of state oft get their fingers burned, ay, and more than their fingers."

So there was the spot the secret lay hid beneath. A man all virtue in his private life might play the villain on the stage to utmost conviction. A man, all subtlety within, might there-

fore assume a part compact of crudities and childish boastful-
ness, the better to conceal some secret purpose. Yet the loud
voice, the brag, the resounding phrase, surely these were the
essence of Kit Marlowe? They roared through his plays. They
could not be feigned. But Burbage was in the right: it were
wiser not to speak of such matters; wiser still not to think of
them.

The first weeks of May were the sweet of the year; the air
was soft and, even in the city, fragrant with blossom scents,
a-chime with singing birds. The ladies and gentlemen went
gay in their summer apparel. ' Venus and Adonis ' was
printed now, printed by Richard Field who had left Stratford
in 'seventy-nine. It was to be had from the bookshop of John
Harrison, at the sign of the White Greyhound in Paul's Churchyard, and already was much in favour. Kindly comments came
to Shakespeare every day from ladies and gentlemen, direct or
by report. Doubtless that was because my lord of Southampton had been pleased to accept the dedication, and to allow his
name to be set in the forefront. The epistle was over-dutiful,
perhaps, yet where obeisance was demanded, best make it full
low and sweeping. Will Shakespeare no longer read in the little
volume every day, glowing to think that this, "the first heir
of my invention" was permanently crystalled in print. In
truth, the poem seemed to him now as "unpolished" as,
conventionally humble, the epistle declared it to be: unpolished,
stale in every phrase, and in substance crude. Would he might
print his plays: but, as Henslowe and Alleyn demonstrated,
a play in print was certain to be stolen by other companies.
The acting scrips were kept under lock and key, and no player
permitted to hold a copy of more than his own lines. But times
would change, and when he had writ other and better plays, as
he surely would, doubtless custom would permit their printing.
Meanwhile, he was Will Shakespeare, a figure in the City of
London, a new poet installed under the canopy of Henry
Wriothesley, Earl of Southampton.

At Southampton House he was always welcome now.

The old Countess, against whose dowager dominion the young Earl fretted, commended him. She had even begged his influence with her son, whom she desired to see married. The youth valued his freedom yet awhile. Almost Will Shakespeare had burst out in laughter full in the Countess's face, for was it credible that he, married and saddled with children, in his first youth, should advise a twenty-year old to follow his rash example? Yet he had held his tongue, and had promised to write sonnets of good counsel, fourteen line poems after the Italian manner. Sonnets were new in fashion, and passed from hand to hand about the Court: some tricked in fine conceits; some ponderous; some that throbbed with the passion of carnal love.

No more of such love for Will Shakespeare. Among the fair words spoken of ' Venus and Adonis ' had been a few reproofs, from people in high places disturbed by the naked imagining of some of the stanzas. People's minds were crowded market places: there was room only for one or two ideas to be attached to a poet's name. Greene had been marked for his knowledge of thieving. Marlowe was noted a blasphemer. He, Will Shakespeare, must take care that guilty amour was not the tag tied to his name. A new poem would set the balance true, a poem commending innocence. The Countess had suggested the old story of Tarquin and Lucrece. It might serve. Meantime, he had undertaken to write sonnets to persuade her son into matrimony. The task was begun: and a task it had proved. They were stiff in the joints, these sonnets. He could supple them here and there, ere he produced fair copies, but they would never waken his pride. To say to a poet: Here's a theme, a theme not near your heart, perchance, but a theme you are bidden to, so produce me a dozen sonnets— it was as if you were to say to him: Here's a wench, not wise nor witty nor beautiful, and you do not love her, but no matter: bed her at once, couple and engender. The task could be performed, was half-performed, but the performance must needs lack spirit.

Lo! in the orient when the gracious light
Lifts up his burning head . . .

It was stiff-jointed stuff. A line or two had quality:

When I consider everything that grows
Holds in perfection but a little moment . . .

But all in all, the sonnets were poor. The one about the widow's wet eyes was so bad it offended the ear like a counterfeit coin rung on the table. And endeavour would not mend it. The Countess wanted her sonnets, and wanted them quickly. She'd not know good from bad. Nor the young Earl, neither. They had poetry to command, and that would satisfy them. A horse? Send for the groom. Food and wine? Send for the butler. Sonnets? Send for Will Shakespeare. Yet, with a purpose not imposed but lifting itself from within the mind, these new sonnet devices might be turned to catch a thought, a mood, a meditation which else might slip back, unworded, into oblivion.

His mind teemed. At any waking moment the narrow fane behind his temples was athrong with perceptions, fancies, jests and incipient dramas; aspirations, desires, remorse, hope; snatches of song; words leaping to link into garland phrases and swinging into tune like bridle bells; memories and visions; the awareness of others and the awareness of himself; instruments of action which were also instruments of recording: and out of this motley confusion, so rich and so various, restless and ever-changing, now exultant, now bewildered and dissatisfied, he was compelled, in bounden duty, to select and shape to his purpose the constituent elements of plays and poems. Here was wealth out-dazzling the wealth of the Indies, but not so easily to be worked into gold ingots, stamped coins and faceted jewels. In his mind all was flux and instability, and his clutching fingers, dipping feverishly, always let slip the more precious treasures. That which glittered so brave in his mind was at once diminished and abstracted of colour when he sought to pen it in words.

Were all poets thus perplexed? Had Marlowe bigger, bolder, louder tyrants striding through his brain than ever he caged on paper for Ned Alleyn to con and deliver? Was Greene's death-bed malice the product of this same anger against his own inability to put forth more than a moiety of the pageant in his mind? Was Kyd able in his reveries to slay by thousands where in his plays he could strew corses only by the dozen? It must not continue so. As a man matured, he would surely learn to dominate his own creativeness. 'Richard III,' the 'Shrew', the 'Errors' comedy, and 'Andronicus,' these had all been praised by lettered judges and earned their plaudits on the stage: only their sire and author, Will Shakespeare, knew them for what they were, poor, botched copies of the original visions. But hereafter this gulf should be spanned. There should be new plays, and better.

This Spanish tale commended by John Florio might furnish a first deliverance. Felix and Felismena—the names would not do. But the maid bringing the letter from her mistress's lover—there is an egg to hatch there. And the lady in guise of a page: suppose that were played not so much for saucy comedy as for sweet sincerity? Conceive a lady who puts her modesty to hazard, knowing all the perils, and yet daring them: for why? For that she loves. Sufficient reason! A lady breeched and doubleted in scarlet and white.

Now why the plague must Florio be sent to Titchfield, so that I have not seen him from that day of the courtyard dumb-show to this? Had I asked him the next morning, or even within the se'nnight, he had remembered and told me her name. Now, on his return, can I make enquiry in our conversation? Dost remember our first meeting at Southampton House, I say. Ay, I remember it, says Florio. There was a lady rode into the courtyard and spoke awhile with my lord. Ay, says Florio, many a lady speaks with my lord. Describe her, Florio bids me. She had gold hair? So has many another.

She was masked? It is a custom among ladies riding abroad? She was clad in scarlet and white? Why, any tailor will render such garments. Thus Florio could not disclose her name. For Will Shakespeare, who never spoke with her, or even heard her voice, of whose existence she was unaware, she remained no more than: the Lady in Scarlet and White. She was but a picture seen in dumb-show colloquy through a window pane; a picture animate in graceful motion; a picture to stir a poet's heart to the semblance of love; a picture already fading in memory.

Early in May the London gossips were murmuring questions about messages scrawled by night on churchyard walls, messages that threatened the Flemish exiles, accusing these strangers of crime and of endangering the lives of peaceful citizens. Commissioners were empowered to seek out the authors of these libels, and given powers of household search. On the eleventh of May Shakespeare heard that Thomas Kyd, a deviser of plays best known for his 'Spanish Tragedy' (not only still in demand at the Rose playhouse but printed as a book) was arrested after his lodging had been searched. Rumour named him as the author of the churchyard libels against the Flemings. Doubtless he had not undertaken such a temerarious venture without reward, and it was said he would be put to the torture in Bridewell to discover who had employed him.

That day Shakespeare was aware of folk pointing secretly at him as he passed in the street, nodding their heads, and whispering together. The godly, and those who, not aspiring to any notable godliness, yet prided themselves that they were sound in behaviour, strict in their affairs, honest citizens, even those who regarded the Flemings as competitive intruders and had, before the establishment of the Commission, commended the nocturnal libels: such folk were saying that Kyd served the playhouses, the playhouses were a disorderly shame to a great city, and all connected with them ranked no better than rogues and vagabonds. Will Shakespeare, aware of this, went carefully and quietly about his ways.

The next day matters were not mended. They had grown worse, for it was now to be heard on every hand that, whether Kyd were the libeller or not, among his papers had been found a discourse which openly and abominably denied the divinity of Jesus Christ. As he proceeded on foot that afternoon to the Rose playhouse, Shakespeare heard a voice shout after him, calling him a blaspheming, bawdy playhouse dog. He turned quickly and saw curious and hostile faces staring at him, but which of these passers-by had abused him he could not determine. Better avoid a brawl. And it might be wise to change his lodging tomorrow.

As he walked on he felt a soft impact on his shoulders and knew that some ill-wisher had flung a clod of mud after him. The loan of a brush at the theatre would remedy that, but the insult was not so easily removed from his memory. This was the penalty of poetising in the reign of Queen Elizabeth: to be called a dog and a blasphemer, in the streets, by the stinking, treacherous mob; to have one's velvet sullied by mud flung, as like as not, from the hand of some gaping idiot who but a week since had stood in his own sweat among the groundlings and cried applause to verses writ by the gentleman he now assaulted. To be a poet was to expose one's vitals, and to rank oneself with wine-bibbers, pimps, brawlers and bawds. To serve the playhouse was to serve other men's pleasure and be subject to their contumely, when the mood changed, like any greasy drab in the stews. A curse on Kyd for dabbling his inky fingers in illicit doctrines. Let the cobbler stick to his last, and leave parsons to nibble their way through the creamy cheese of theology.

His indignation cooled a little before he reached the playhouse and Alleyn's room there. He put his complaint and his fears temperately, but with urgency. Alleyn, weary after the performance, and doffing the robes of Machiavel—as Henslowe's son-in-law he was privileged to avoid the common tiring room—shared his perturbation.

"Will," he said, "we suffer as pioneers. We are gentlemen

born, and therefore suspect for that we mix with players. We subserve the ends of art. But who's to give us credit for that? And in truth our society is vulgar. Thinkest thou I rejoice to be known as the companion of such as Will Kemp whose very breath is bawdy? The public mind is fickle. The State but tolerates the playhouse. We must walk delicately. We must in nothing offend. Already I have ordered that no pieces by Kyd or by Marlowe are to be put on at the Rose."

"Kyd, I understand," said Shakespeare. "But wherefore is Marlowe's work struck out of the list?"

"Hast not heard? All this pother concerns a blasphemous disputation found in Kyd's room, which is alleged to gainsay the divinity of Our Lord. And now Kyd, under examination, swears it was writ by Marlowe and left there by him two years agone."

Yet Burbage had surmised that Marlowe was secretly in the State service: in bald words, not to be spoken aloud, Marlowe was a spy employed by Cecil upon State affairs. Here was more than the eye could detect, here were irreconcilables twined together to make mystification. Shakespeare said nothing beyond thanking Alleyn for his news and agreeing that the less they were seen in public for a few days the better. They talked of other matters, but when they parted Alleyn suggested that, unless opinion swung their way, it might be well to close the playhouse till other news, of a victory in France, or a witch-taking or some such succulent matter, diverted attention.

On the eighteenth of May it was known that Christopher Marlowe had been ordered to appear before the Council and give account of himself, and was to attend daily as required until released from the obligation. All the little, excitable, emotional world of the theatre foamed in a turmoil of uncertainty. Livelihoods were at stake. Suspicion replaced popularity. Tongues were put on guard. No man dare speak the fears that beset him. The playhouses were now matched in gossip not merely with loose speech and riotous living, but with impiety, with the bold intellectual attack upon religion which, many said, emanated like a poisonous mist from the Court itself, from Walter Raleigh and his friends.

But at the end of the month Marlowe was dead, and not by judgment of men. His end had been horrible, by all accounts, and clearly was devised by God as a punishment for his blasphemies and as a warning to all tempted to follow his evil ways. The man who held Christ to be a deceiver, the Bible a hornbook for gulls, and Moses with his tablets a conjurer, was slain by his own dagger in an inn at Deptford. One named Ingram or Frizer (it was hard to come by the right name) was held for his death, but the common bruit was that Marlowe, known to be quick-tempered, had provoked a quarrel and drawn on the other man first. There were witnesses who would attest all this at the trial which must follow. Some said the quarrel was about a woman; others over the reckoning, for Marlowe and his companions had eaten and drunk well. Whatever the cause, he was dead, his dagger, held in his own hand— Ingram or Frizer wrestling with him for it—run through his eye. If that were the truth, it was false gossip which said he blasphemed to the end, roaring terrible oaths through all his agony. A man pierced through the eye to the brain died on the instant. The truth would be known when the crowner's inquisition was complete, and when Frizer or Ingram stood his trial.

But young Burbage, who would not speak of the matter till he had Shakespeare closeted in privacy, thought otherwise.

"We shall not know the inward of this affair," he said, "for many a year. We are like die in our old age no wiser. For hark 'ee, Will, not Kit Marlowe alone but this Frizer was Walsingham's man, which is to say now Cecil's man."

"Dost mean that Cecil had Marlowe put out of the way?"

"Nay, that's more than I'll let myself guess at. I'll only say this: servants with secrets to disclose have so been removed before today."

Shakespeare considered. If Marlowe were indeed a spy,

and if he let his ranting atheism, instead of furnishing a useful cloak for his secret service, get out of hand, so that he became a public scandal and must needs be arraigned before the Privy Council, his masters might well be glad to see him dead, and any incautious testimony he might make in tavern or street silenced for ever. A quarrel in an inn, with none but Walsingham's agents at hand to observe, a quarrel ending fatally: it looked all too convenient. Here was cause for Will Shakespeare to tremble, thinking that Kit Marlowe, the only poet and make-play he called, in his heart, his peer, should perish like a rat in a drain. Tamburlaine, Faustus, the Jew, unhappy Edward, Hero and Leander—and all that might have succeeded them—quenched by a brawl and a dagger-thrust. The instinct of the past few days was already bloodily justified: let the play-cobbler stick to his last and meddle not with prelates and ministers of state.

"Depend upon it, Will," said Burbage, "we'll hear no more of the end of Kit Marlowe."

"But Frizer must stand his trial?"

"Frizer will be pardoned, and the pardon issued so quietly none will remark it."

"Yet a man like Marlowe, befriended by Raleigh, his work esteemed in high quarters—such a man cannot perish, and no questions asked?"

"Who will put his own reputation to hazard by soliciting to know more than is vouchsafed about the death of a man whose life was a scandal of blasphemy? Shall I do it? Not I. And thou? An thou takest my advice, Will Shakespeare, thou'lt keep silence. Depend upon it, Marlowe, with whatever knowledge he was privy to, is buried deeper than the Spaniards' galleons of eighty-eight rotting under the sea."

The silence between them protracted painfully, until Burbage briskly said: "Enough of this. Out of ill-fortune cometh good for those who dare to take it."

"Thy meaning, at a guess, is that there'll be no question of closing the playhouses, lest the mob lack diversion, and lest any link a closed theatre with the decease of one better dead?"

"Near enough. But that's not all. Look around thee, Will. Look at the host of playhouse poets, thy fellows. Is not the assembly notably diminished of late? Greene dead. Kyd, suspect, and already past his best production. And now Marlowe dead, too. The path is cleared. London is thine oyster, Will Shakespeare. Or art thou content to end thy days turning long speeches for Ned Alleyn to mouth and thunder?"

So that was the reason for this visit? He had not been without premonition. Dick Burbage's professions of friendship were honest, but they had a purpose. Dick's father was owner of The Theatre in Shoreditch: had indeed built it, the first of the independent playhouses, and made it the home of the Lord Chamberlain's men. Dick was a rising actor, fast perfecting his craft. It was known that he considered himself Alleyn's superior. He and his father were not always well disposed towards Alleyn, nor Alleyn to them. Dick Burbage believed in himself and his future. It seemed he believed also in Will Shakespeare and in Will Shakespeare's future. He was half-declared already. He was bidding for Shakespeare's scrips, offering to take him away from the necessity to write plays to fit Alleyn's requirements—and that was a bondage indeed. To be free from Alleyn's solemnities: the prospect was pleasing. But to sell the scrips of plays yielded small profits. Now, were my Lord Southampton to make good that promise and gift his poet a hundred pounds, as beyond doubt he would do upon delivery and dedication of the Lucrece poem, the poet might purchase a sharer's interest in the company. And because he would furnish the plays, his division of profits should be the greater. This called for bargaining.

Player and poet looked at each other across the table with the cautious eyes of those engaged in affairs concerning money, and each read in the other's eyes the same confident claim: We are the coming men, and London is our oyster!

IX

FLORIO'S SPANISH tale became 'The Two Gentlemen of Verona', and was writ, rehearsed and performed. Felix, renamed Proteus, was given a friend more staunch than himself: all lovers must have friends also in love; it diverts and yet balances the play. And for the heroine, she was absolved from the Spaniard's awkward title of Felismena and christened anew, Julia. Will Shakespeare, having made her, was more than a little in love with Julia.

This Julia was hardly to be found in Bartholomew Yonge's English rendering of the Spanish. She was a creature of his mind, not comparable with any woman in the flesh known to him, except the Lady in Scarlet and White; and her he had seen only for a few minutes, through a window pane. For a month or so afterward, whenever he went to Southampton House he looked to meet her again; but she never appeared. He had not asked Florio, now returned, for her name, either. And that was passing strange. Sometimes, when he remembered her in the night, he resolved to put the question to Florio; but always he let slip the opportunity. And when he began to adapt the play of 'the Two Gentlemen', the Lady in Scarlet and White quitted his mind; she became absorbed into this pen and ink Julia.

How came Julia to be so charming, so wayward before she plighted troth to Proteus, so steadfast when she followed him to Milan, garbed as a page, and overheard his faithless wooing of Sylvia? Who was Julia but a phantom engendered between his desire for love and his fancy? The poetry she spoke was not hers, but Will Shakespeare's:

> The current that with gentle murmur glides,
> Thou knowest, being stopp'd, impatiently doth rage;

But when his fair course is not hindered,
He makes sweet music with th'enamell'd stones,
Giving a gentle kiss to every sedge
He overtaketh in his pilgrimage.

This was the late fruit of a boyhood spent by Avonside.
Yet many another lad and lass lived by a river and learned
to treasure its varied moods, without bringing forth verses
to catch memory in a crystal goblet of words. Memory,
observation, dream and desire, night fears, laborious indecisions, fancy, tales of battle and treachery; all were turned
to verses within him like milk clotting to cream in the churn.
The expense of spirit necessary for that manufacture was
labour as heavy as dairy drudgery, too: and never quite at
command. This faculty of poesy was a visiting in the mind:
he could invite it, wrestling like the man in the scriptures with
a dread and dazzling angel, but never order either the coming
or the issue of the conflict.

And Julia was more than a voice to speak his poetry, to
which, by precept and ensample, he must tune the speech of an
empty-pated boy-player. Julia was a woman other women
could recognise as blood-kin; eager for the letter from her
Proteus; too proud to admit that eagerness; and supple-
minded to glide through a dozen devices to recover the frag-
ments she had torn and scattered on the ground. That early
scene enchanted the whole playhouse, stilled even the twopenny mob to silence. He had made a woman, chaste and yet
free-spoken; trifling when love was secure to her; steadfast
when confronted with wrong; a woman so credible that he,
who had played Pygmalion to her Galatea, was tender now to
the core of his heart with love for her.

There was drama in these concealments, open to the
spectators, shut against all the players but one; and drama—
here was discovery, here was the swelling future of the playhouse!—consisted in more than outward action: drama was
a bright light which could be made to turn inward, to illum-

inate the secret recesses of the heart, and move them that
watched and listened to tears and to awe. As when this
darling Julia, passing as a page, is sent by her deceived and
deceiving lover, Proteus, to carry loving messages to the
Sylvia who wants him not, to carry to Sylvia a ring given him
by his trusting Julia. Consider how Julia the page, required
by Sylvia to report on Julia the woman, depicts herself with
subtle indirectness, revealing to the playhouse far more than
any purport Sylvia may take from the words:

> She hath been fairer, madam, than she is.
> When she did think my master lov'd her well,
> She, in my judgment, was as fair as you;
> But since she did neglect her looking-glass
> And threw her sun-expelling mask away——

"Her sun-expelling mask": the words pointed Julia's origin,
for such a mask the Lady in Scarlet and White had worn that
day in the courtyard at Southampton House. But this was
nonsense, for of that masked lady he knew nothing. A glimpse
of her in dumb-show, and then no more. An ever he met her
again, and heard her speak, like as not she'd prove flat-voiced,
a chronicler of dull nothings, a female not fit to compare with
his Julia who spoke poetry and revealed a heart so true and
gracious that any man might be honoured to stand in her
presence. He fell to fretting helplessly over the last scenes of
the play, which were all action, surprises, confrontations,
and tidy-making ends for the plot, among which machinery
Julia perished. She remained on the stage only to clutter it,
a player with a name, but neither poetry nor life in her. The
last scenes were all Will Shakespeare, journeyman of the
theatre, who could get this player on and that player off, make
clear what must be explained and so bring all to a feat conclusion. The Will Shakespeare in whose mind sprang up brave
worlds bravely peopled had no part in these last scenes, and
though journeyman Shakespeare might stroll about and

politely, modestly, accept compliments on this new play, the other Shakespeare was not so to be deceived and satisfied.

'The Two Gentlemen' at least brought him fresh confidences from Southampton. The young Earl was still in no marrying mood: life was a jewel to dangle from his wrist, and he would enjoy it as well when its lustre was clouded as when it glittered under the light. There was no stability in this Henry Wriothesley, although on all public occasions he could conduct himself with courtesy and grace, smiling upon flatterers and importunate alike, confident that naught could happen but for his entertainment. This exquisite and polished front for the world was, Will Shakespeare had already learned, a defensive instrument inherited. Those who never need take thought for the next provision of food and drink—the richest food, the finest wine; those for whom the attendance of servitors, the immediate achievement of every wish, the furnishing of clean linen and soft napery, was as customary as the breathing of common air: such privileged beings possessed of right the grand, the courteous, the all-conquering manner. Others might envy and admire, from near or far; but to emulate was impossible without that firm basis, a childhood spent as heir to a great house. Others must bend, charmed against their will, shamed of the resentment croaking secretly at the back of the mind, to the condescensions, so winning, so unaware of their condescension, of this young Earl.

To be thwarted, to feel a desire and not to achieve it, was a new experience for Southampton. Since he grew tall enough to deem himself a man, he had not often been baffled in any ploy he set his mind to, even for an hour's diversion. At first, refusal or evasion made him petulant. There were those who, with due deference, warned him that when he ventured more nearly into the Court, he must study to acquire diplomacy: the Queen, vainer and more peremptory than in her youth, would volley harsh words at a lip pulled thick and rebellious in her presence. Let not Southampton model himself too close on his friend, Essex. Gloriana would not stomach a tithe from another man of what she was amused by in that indulged gallant. And even Essex might take a step too froward. South-ampton listened, and affected to be undisturbed. The Court was no venturing ground for him, he declared. He would put in his attendance there, as required in duty: but further than that was not his interest. Hawking and hunting, the management of household and estate, the playhouse, the furtherance of learning and poesy, friendship, the clash of wit, and love, these would plentifully employ his time.

Nevertheless it was to be observed that upon the rare occasions when his will was baulked, when inclement weather forbade a projected expedition, when sickness kept absent a friend summoned to his side, Southampton employed a new method in receiving the ill news. Sulking no more, he would fall into a melancholy, wistful and soft-spoken. Thus he turned disappointment into a pleasure, and fancied that he the better understood the sad moods of sad poetry. And so he came, gently complaining, to his poet, his frere, his own Will Shakespeare; a slender young noble, a little disordered—by design—in his rich dress; with his long hair ravelled over the smooth pallor of his brow; sombre-eyed; by fits feverish and reckless or pale and chill.

"Will," he said, "what shall I do, for I cannot sleep o' nights?"

"I am no physician, but I am told the remedy is to exercise the body. Your lordship should weary himself on horseback. Then sleep will return."

"The sight of a horse, these days, sickens me. And call me not lordship. We are alone, and I am Harry Wriothesley, a man as human as thyself. More human, for thou under-standest womankind, and I do not."

Shakespeare took this, as intended, to be a complimentary reference to the success of 'The Two Gentlemen.'

"So, it is women again?"

"Not women, Will. A woman."

He's young and sensual, thought Shakespeare, half in

scorn and half in compassion. This was an old penalty laid upon riches and high degree, that so many women should offer for a lordly bed that the master thereof staled and lost appetite. Southampton already had hurled his way in and out of a dozen or more amorous encounters, sometimes in the ruff of ribaldry, jesting before and after, sometimes all eager to sustain the note of lofty passion. In none of these affairs, Shakespeare judged, was his heart touched: lust and vanity prompted him first here, then there, and as soon as the crude energy was spent, he was all for hawking again, or books, or visiting the playhouses. But now he had another female in mind: she'd be a fortunate lass if her reign extended beyond the end of the month.

"Tell me about her. Doth she not please thee?"

"Ay, too well. 'Tis I do not please her."

"That cannot be."

"Nevertheless, it is true!" said Southampton earnestly. "She'll converse with me, and dine with me, but not alone. And as for love, why, she'll not suffer me to mention the name."

"Is she married then?"

"Not she. Nor, so my observers report, hath she engaged her heart to any man. Her good name is beyond calumny."

"That's no ill commendation."

"The devil of it is, Will, she's impregnably chaste. Nay, I would not have her otherwise, with other men. But for me—surely chastity should not be an absolute virtue? The purpose of chastity is to guard treasure not for its owner but for one other's enjoyment. Will, she's as far above the rest of woman-flesh, as rare and as lovely—I dream of her by day and by night, and yet it is not dreaming, for I cannot sleep. See how my eyes are red-margined with lack of sleep. I am sick with love, Will."

"Hath the lady seen thee in this plight?"

"Indeed yes."

"And no pity?"

"No pity."

"Then depend upon it, her heart is cold as stone. Unless thou wouldst offer to wed her? But perchance her degree is not suitable?"

"It would pass. My lady mother would tell me I might have done better for myself, but the lady is a lady, and my mother would accept her gladly. Yet marriage, Will! I am young yet, and marriage is a desperate remedy. It shuts love in a cage, and there poor love wilts and dies."

Here is for me to utter wise reproofs, to counsel all the state and social virtues of marriage, thought Shakespeare: but, remembering his own wife, half-forgot in Stratford, he said nothing.

"An she would listen a moment, an she would let me but begin to woo her," Southampton complained, "I would melt that coldness which seizes her heart."

"Doth she refuse you admittance to her society?"

"Why, no. And there's the plague of it. I can see her at her father's house, at other houses, at the Court: but always with a company around. I plan occasions to speak a word with her alone. I whisper. I have even been fool enough to send her letters, Will: not signed, but she knoweth whence they come. And withal I am no further in my suit. The woman will be the death of me. Look! I have lost flesh. My eyes are dull. My wits are wandering. Will, thou'rt wise in womancraft. Explain to me. How can she be so cruel?"

"I should need more information, as well as more skill, to do that."

"Nay," Southampton broke in. "I intended no discourtesy. It was by oversight I have not told thee her name. She is— but this is strict in confidence, Will."

"I understand."

Southampton then named the lady, and, watching his friend's eyes, realised that the name meant nothing to Shakespeare.

"Very well," he declared, "thou shalt meet her. She hath

a wit. She loves poetry. She will be more glad to see thee than
to see me. I'll arrange it. And when thou hast set eyes upon
her, Will, thou'lt understand my plight. Farewell. I'll appoint
time and place."

The forlorn lover made off, and Shakespeare was left
thinking: So! Thou'lt appoint time and place, and it is for me
to wait on thy bidding.

He shrugged his shoulders, but by the time he was making
his way out of Southampton House into the bustle of Holborn,
he was the courteous, calm Will Shakespeare again, successful
maker of plays, poet under distinguished patronage, a sharer in
the Lord Chamberlain's company performing at Burbage's
Theatre in Shoreditch: a man not so young as he had been,
but a man of substance and a man with a future.

He was stripped naked of all these consolations, stripped
to a heart all open to wounds and unsatisfied desires, when,
a few days later, he was ushered in to be presented to Southampton's new lady love. She wore a gown now in place of the
doublet striped scarlet and white, and she was not masked:
but at once he recognised her, and recognised her again for
the only true original of his Julia. And if he had made that
Julia, out of an old story and new verses, to expend his love
upon, then that resource was already outworn: here was
the authentic and living aim for his desires. Nor could he slide
away from pain, from jealousy, from humiliation as he had
done when she was but a diminishing memory of a brief
dumb-show in his mind: for all that her mobile silent lips, her
gestures, the rapid alternations of expression in her face, seen
through a window-pane, had quickened in his fancy, was
brought to pass in reality now that he heard her speak. This
was a lady quick and rich in mind, as lovely within as without:
no chronicler of stale small beer.

For some minutes he was unaware what he said and what
was said to him, his heart being so tumultuous with joy,
astonishment and humility, and all his senses dazed by the
close disclosure of her gold hair glittering in its braids, fine and

exquisite, her blue eyes opened wide to his gaze, now soft, now bright with laughter, her lips, her throat, her hands, her whole and composite verity here within a yard or two of his reverent observation. Then, grinding forth from the back of his brain, came the reproof: Will Shakespeare, thou'rt a man of thirty summers: cease to blush and stammer like a boy!

The fever cooled in him abruptly. He could return comment for comment now. Thrusting wit before him like a rapier, he was secure for the moment, invulnerable.

"Is she not beautiful?" Southampton exclaimed, using all the freedom in speech of a nobleman whose mood dictates the behaviour of those around him. "Is it to be wondered at that I am stricken with love for her? Come, Will, endorse my suit. Thou'rt sage and expert of woman's beauty. Speak out. My lady will not jib at a compliment."

"That's to assume a compliment is coming," said the lady. "And is Master Shakespeare in sooth a judge of women fit for the devotion of men?"

"Not so. 'Tis my lord's fancy that because I have made a piece or two for the playhouse, I must needs be a Marco Polo in the world of love."

"And are you not? Better hold back your compliments: an you have no means of comparison, your praise is naught to me. 'Tis overlong in the preparation. When it comes, it will be white-haired and rheumy-eyed."

"Cry your pardon, madam. The truth is, my wits are put to rout. I have seen many lovely ladies, and perchance a poet is quicker and surer than other men in his response to beauty. I have seen many lovely ladies—though I have not, as my lord fancies, any near experience."

"Near experience!" exclaimed Southampton, with a laugh. "Delicately phrased, Will. Near experience! That's good."

"His lordship," said the lady, paying him no heed, looking only at Shakespeare, "is headstrong even in his thoughts. He comes to the point, at least in his desires, at once. Not like you,

Master Shakespeare. I still wait for a compliment, even a little one."

"Mistress, conceits and comparisons are poor offerings. I would not put before you what other men may offer. I will say only this: I am a poet of some repute, not wont to be meek, not wont to seek for words. You see me ravelled and helpless in my own astounded wits. Other men, I doubt not, have been reduced to the same pass, being admitted for the first time to your presence. My plight is singular only in this: today is not the first occasion I have set eyes upon you."

The lady nodded, to show that the confession pleased her. But Southampton turned to Shakespeare in surprise. "How now? When I told thee who was the cruel mistress of my love, and named her, thou gavest me the blank face of ignorance. Was this feigning, Will? I thought better of thee than that."

"No feigning. I saw the lady some months since. At Southampton House, in the courtyard, one morning in May. I never knew her name till now." He turned to her to continue his explanation. "I saw you, madam, through a window, while I waited. You rode in on a Barbary mare, and you were booted and hosed like a man. Your doublet was white, barred broad with scarlet. Your collar was white lace, your cap of black velvet, and you were masked also in black velvet. You had a ring: that same you wear now. You took it from your finger to shew to my lord here."

"I believe I remember the day," said Southampton.

"I remember it well. But my lord"—she spoke mischief with mischievous eyes—"did not at that time imagine himself in love with me. I was then but a girl—whose growth to womanhood was no such matter, one my lord had seen between times ever since she was a small child, and he a page. One female among many, and not worth his lordship's notice."

"Nay, this is unjust." Southampton's expostulation was splutter-voiced, hot-faced. "Perchance I did not then understand the way of my own heart, but I believe I have loved you ever since—ever since I was old enough for love."

"Indeed. I am honoured. But if gossip speaks true, I stand not alone in your lordship's regard. I have had fore-runners. Perchance I have companions now? Perchance I shall have successors?"

"Will! Now thou seest what a hardened heart lies hid be-neath this fair exterior. Thou hast heard how she mocks me. Come to my aid, good Will. Plead for me."

The lady laughed, her arms thrown wide in her chair, her head tilting back till all the white splendour of her throat was revealed. But in a moment she was speaking kindly to Shakespeare.

"Could you do such a service, Master Shakespeare? And would you? Nay, I'll not press for an answer. And so you remembered me, although I am now without doublet, hose, boots, belt, spurs, hat and mask."

"You had a cloak, a white cloak, also," he reminded her. "And gloves of brown neats leather, embroidered on the long cuffs."

"Stop, prithee. There seems to be nothing thou didst not observe." A vein throbbed in his temple as he noted that she had begun to use the familiar ' thou ' towards him.

"I went to see ' The Two Gentlemen of Verona ' at the Rose, Master Shakespeare. And it liked me well. My best thanks for the entertainment. And now that I have it in mind, thou hast put a woman in that play who wears breeches and doublet. What is her name?"

"Julia."

"Julia. Why so. I like thy Julia, Master Shakespeare."

"I like her also. Nay, like is a cold word."

"Left alone, it may enkindle a warmer."

Southampton broke in: "There's enlightenment here. Will sees you, mounted, through a window pane, and the next thing he has writ his play about Julia who turns page for love. Confess now, Will Shakespeare: did'st not take the idea from what you peeped at through a window in my house?"

"I'll confess, but if I am to confess truly, the lady turns page in the Spanish story from which I made the play. John Florio gave it to me."

"See. His lordship is disappointed. He would fain have been proud to own a passion towards a lady who is put by a poet to playhouse employment. This was a churlish sincerity of thine, Master Shakespeare."

"Then I am sorry for it."

"Nevertheless," said the lady softly, "though she be no cousin to me, I like thy Julia."

It was plain to him then, with Southampton standing by, too young, too coarse in grain to understand what was toward, that this lady knew that he had loved her ever since he looked out through the window of that waiting-room in Southampton House. And she was treating him tenderly.

"I'll make other Julias, and better, for your pleasure," he declared. "I am as yet but half the poet I shall be. You shall see plays from Will Shakespeare the like of which the world has not dreamed on."

"Thou art not modest then? These are words to climb the sky."

"Ah," said Southampton, "Will's a rare fellow. He honours my early judgment."

Turning away, the Earl did not observe the resentful stare which Shakespeare gave him. The lady did. She smiled, and then she nodded.

What kind of a lady was this? The lady was of this kind: not to be swayed or deceived by Southampton's patrician wooing; not offended neither; gracious to one below her in degree, a poet, a pen-man dependent on patronage; easy and familiar with him; secretly stealing his secret—that he loved her—but not disclosing it; wing-witted; gentle in her mockery of Southampton's dishonourable suit, but staunchly possessing her maiden modesty; and intimating, with a glance, with a smile perished ere it was born, that she and a poet were at one in comprehension, while a great Earl stood excluded from their privy understanding.

She was still unmarried, and not to be taken by force or treachery; no prey for this codling noble with all his wide-jawed appetite, now frustrate, turned to sighs and oaths. The management of men came within her natural inheritance: she needed no schooling in that craft. She was cunning to with-draw the favours of her lips behind a swordplay of words, and ever as she eluded she found amusement in the pursuit and the escape. She was beyond range of Southampton's clutching mind as sure as she evaded his arms. Yet she was not cruel. Nor was she cold: her thoughts were engaged with love, but love shaped and coloured to her own interpretation. Did not vanity and crude desire make Southampton obtuse, he could learn much from her merely by the inclination of an ear. She was teaching him now: though he were unable to profit from the lesson, another could, even a disregarded poet called in, upon a lord's lordly whim, to stand idly by at an obstinate courtship.

"It would be wise," she said to Southampton, "to forsake this love which brings you only woe. It is but a form of mad-ness, and deserves the dark house and the whip."

"Yet lovers," said Shakespeare, "are not punished as mad-men are."

"There is a reason for that."

"Give it me, pray."

"I'll give you two reasons: choose either. Love cannot be cured. Contrary to that, my lord hath oft been possessed by love and restored to health. Ergo, love can be cured: or else my lord was never in love, and merely fancies or feigns the passion."

"The first reason, mistress, is half destroyed already. Proceed to the second?"

"Love is a madness all too common. 'Tis more infectious than the plague, though not so deadly. Therefore those that would whip to cure are mad with love themselves."

"I am not mad," Southampton declared. "I am but sorely tried by this fair cruelty."

"Thou'rt but half mad," the lady told him. "There's insufficient conviction in thy protestations of love."

"How? What more can I do to gain credence for my passion?"

"Why, a lover, a true lover, is a man distracted. Or so I am told: I have no experience. He hath a lean cheek, which thou hast not. His eyes are dull with want of sleep: thine are light as ever I saw them."

"No more! I do protest, this wrongs me. Will here will testify. Thine own observation will testify. I have lost flesh in thy behalf."

"What, in the wars?"

"Jest not. I have lost flesh, I tell thee. And mine eyelids ache after nights without sleep, calling on thy cruel name."

"Thine eyelids ache because thy fingers rub them. Fie! Too much reading of fantastical romances puts notions under thy pate. Learning the signs-manual of a true lover, thou dost counterfeit them, to impress me, who am not impressed, and to impress thyself, who may well be. And that's not the sum of thy defects in the part of an unfortunate lover."

"Why, what else?"

"Thy beard should be untidy and overgrown."

"And so it is."

"A moiety. Each day I see thy beard disordered just so far. And the next day precisely the same disorder. Oh, 'tis done with art, I grant thee. But so much careful calculation is no mark of a lover. And then, thine apparel. I look for a lover by these signs: the unbuttoned sleeve, the untied shoe, the loose gartering of the hose, the desolate abstraction which forgets the whole world for love's sweet sake. But thou'rt as punctillious in thine array as ever man was. Go to, Southampton: what love thou hast is all at the service of thyself."

"This is intolerable! The woman hath no eyes."

"Upon that point," said Shakespeare, "the strictest courtesy cannot make me agree."

"Thank you, Master Shakespeare. It is a comfort to know that one out of two men can observe that I have eyes."

"You sport with me," the Earl protested. "And you sport unjustly. For look, is not my ruff all in disarray?"

"Even so. As if it had been done before the mirror. And now fare you well. I may stay no longer. Forgive me that I smile when you come as a lover. As a friend you are welcome."

"A friend!" exclaimed Southampton when they were out of the room. "That's all the change I get from her. Mockeries clinked before me like a rain of halfpence. But is she not lovely, Will? Is she not a nonpareil? Is she not booty worth an arduous siege?"

Shakespeare nodded, his thoughts elsewhere.

"I am not easily daunted," the young Earl continued. "I have known hopes as seeming short of promise turn all to fulfilment. I am not to be turned away by jests, nor coldness neither. Women are giddy, swift to change. I'll have her yet."

You are crying your wares in the wrong market, thought Shakespeare. But he kept his opinion to himself.

X

Day after day went by, and he spent them for the most part, rocking between indecisions, wondering if he dare press the occasion and, unsponsored by Southampton, visit the lady who surely knew that he loved her, and loved her as Southampton could not? Again his thoughts were raging against circumstance, which had ushered him into the world with Arden blood (but what were the Ardens here in London?), with all the impulses and requirements of a gentleman, yet bereft of arms, property, estate; a poet come from the country; a servant of the playhouse. Were it otherwise, he had been at the lady's gate this and every day. As it was, he span himself into melancholic moods, deeper and deeper, and put off decision, until Southampton sent and bade him call again.

He went light-hearted, perceiving here an opportunity for another meeting with the lady. Southampton greeted him, brisk and gay, and in the first moment all his hopes (which must never show in his face) were strewn in ruin. Southampton announced himself a triumphant lover.

"Rejoice with me, Will. I have clipped my mistress in my arms, between sheets. And shall again. She's a woman and therefore to be won: was not this what I told thee?"

Shakespeare could not remember the youth uttering the phrase before; but it was a good phrase, treasureable. He would remember it, if only for the wound it gave him.

Others came to disturb their colloquy. They spoke no more of the lady although now and again Southampton gave him a privy smile, a smile, thought Shakespeare, too fat and lickerish for so young a face. Sick in heart, he made his excuses as soon as he might, and hurried away.

A month and a month and another month went by, and he did not see the lady again. He did not see Southampton either: first the Earl was all webbed like a spider in his affairs which, being interpreted, doubtless meant that he lay abed, day and night, with his new mistress. And then he journeyed to Titchfield, and on to the Welsh marches to stay with my lord of Essex. Doubtless the lady went with him. These creatures of the Court were all decorum on the formal occasion, but otherwise shameless in their amours. Shakespeare hoped he might never see either of them again. Nothing was left to him but poetry. For Southampton, young, proud, stupid, the world, its action and its rewards: for himself a spectator's seat on the rim of the world, and in place of action and reward the diversion of mending a broken heart with verses.

He had the skill to know the lady's worth; to read her mind; to treasure her beauty. Was Southampton his peer in this accomplishment? Nevertheless, to Southampton the lady had given herself. Why? Her mouth had spoken the words of a great lady being courteous to a poet, but with her eyes she was woman to his man, excluding Southampton, blind to this their troth-plighting. It was true. She had pledged herself to him, not carnally, or after the common amorous sort: sweeter and rarer than that, the pledge her eyes had given him. And now she was Southampton's slut. A pox on them both! If perfidy had odours, the wench stank like the Fleet conduits at midsummer. Doubtless she was a creature constant only to the present moment: having Will Shakespeare in her presence, she knew his worth and her own, and the world seemed but a bauble to her. But, Will Shakespeare gone away, the world swells again around her, and in that world Southampton is a great noble, a curled, jewelled and perfumed noble, and she but a female made to fall on her back. And so, treachery's done. A pox on them both!

His misery turned him to sonnet making. He wrote:

> Tir'd with all these, for restful death I cry,
> As to behold desert a beggar born,
> And needy nothing trimm'd in jollity,

And purest faith unhappily forsworn,
And gilded honour shamefully misplac'd,
And maiden virtue rudely strumpeted . . .

He wrote another poem of abnegation.

Farewell! thou art too dear for my possessing,
And like enough thou know'st thy estimate:
The charter of thy worth gives thee releasing.

It went dead thereafter, until the final couplet, the bitterness of which he tasted over and over again till the syllables rang in his ears night and day, like the funeral bell of all his hopes:

Thus have I had thee, as a dream doth flatter,
In sleep a king, but, waking, no such matter.

Sonnet making was unprofitable: therefore, while the mood lasted, he loved it the more. Day after day he kept his own dismal company, and every night added another fair copy to the store of manuscripts locked in the little brass-bound cabinet at his lodging. On some of the manuscripts he noted the date of composition, at top or foot: some he numbered in sequence. When, if ever, he were delivered from these shivering fits of jealousy he would set them all out in an order, the good, the bad, the hot and the cold sonnets, and those which had a live line or two stirring among the dead drywood. God knew what they had in common, these exercises he had set his wits to; these that were experiments; and these he was now writing, the pen jerking across the paper, while sweat dribbled chill down his heated brow, and his blood ached. Poesy had become a medicine, a purge for all his frenzies of dispossessed love. He distilled the poisons of his brain into sounding phrases, and then, sniffing the essence of them again, was cured: or if not cured, calmed; calmed by the gratified vanity of the poet in awe before his own achievement. Neither Southampton nor his wanton was fit for the company of Will Shakespeare who could strike such splendours out of his humiliation:

> When in disgrace with fortune and men's eyes
> I all alone beweep my outcast state,
> And trouble deaf heaven with my bootless cries,
> And look upon myself, and curse my fate,
> Wishing me like to one more rich in hope,
> Featur'd like him, like him with friends possess'd,
> Desiring this man's art, and that man's scope,
> With what I most enjoy contented least;
> Yet in these thoughts myself almost despising,
> Haply I think on thee—and then my state,
> Like to the lark at break of day arising
> From sullen earth, sings hymns at heaven's gate;
> > For thy sweet love remember'd such wealth brings
> > That then I scorn to change my state with kings.

For 'kings' read 'earls', and all's plain as a kitchen wench's face after her Easter bath. He addressed his thoughts to one who had been The Lady in Scarlet and White and was now Southampton's mistress. Proudly he told her he did not envy him the possession of her bed, nor herself possessed in it: I am, his thoughts declared, superior to you both even in this my outcast misfortune, for I have the memory of those brief moments when, no word directly spoken, I was your true lover: and besides, I have the nightingale's consolation: I use a wounded heart to tune my tongue.

One morning he took all the sonnet manuscripts out of the cabinet and read them through with jaundiced eyes. The first seventeen, writ at the Countess's request, enjoining Southampton to marry and perpetuate the Wriothesley succession, marched heavy in his ear, like weary ploughmen's boots: what else to expect from such commanded exercises? Poetry began with "Shall I compare thee to a Summer's day":

and that was addressed to a vision, to a memory of a lady breeched and hosed, seen through a window pane. Taken in sequence, without a key to the changing interpretations of "I" and "thou", the sonnets were as muddled as an army put to rout. So much the better. While they stood thus disordered and unexplained, they kept his privacy. He had opened his heart only to admit the world into a maze. Maliciously, to make confusion yet more confused, he set himself, this morning when his head ached and there was no spring of poetry in him, to add a few more sonnets addressed to Southampton. And to spite himself, to quicken his own pain, to gibe at all his fair dreams and memories, he made the theme of these stiff-syllabled sonnets the friendship between Southampton and himself. This friendship he assumed to be near perfection, to be equally given and taken—if Southampton were an earl, Shakespeare, nine years older, could address him as "Boy!"—and let the blame for disaster fall on the woman.

> Take all my loves, my love, yea, take them all;
> What hast thou then more than thou hadst before?

And again:

> That thou hast her, it is not all my grief,
> And yet it may be said I lov'd her dearly;
> That she hath thee, is of my wailing chief,
> A loss in love that touches me more nearly.

When they were finished, all but the last couplet to this last sonnet, he read them through, and felt abased. They came no nearer to poetry than Tyburn tree to Hounsditch, and their insincerity, although he had willed it, sickened him, roaring reproaches through eye and ear. But throw them into the cabinet with the others! Will Shakespeare was in the fashion, had turned sonneteer, but in secret: the cabinet should hold the full record of his heart in these dismal days, and nothing that he penned, in joy or misery, should be omitted. The cabinet should be a microcosm of modern life in which hope and despair, virtue and profligacy, truth and pretence, knock elbows and lie together, pock-marked jowl by rosy cheek.

But before the third week of Southampton's absence he felt able to emerge into his playhouse world again. To those who asked, he said that he had been sick, but was now recovered. Pressed, he declared he had been cured by a dream, and the dream he would turn into a play: the writing would be swift, for the dream had been romantic and tragical, sprung from an old Italian tale, and his mind was even now afire with the poetry for it. This was true: he had found a way of escape from the pains of jealousy. He put Southampton out of his mind by refusing to think of what had happened. He would write of love, young love, true love, tender love, as if it could never be betrayed from within. The tragedy must strike from others, from the old, corrupt world. Southampton had no place in this: but the lady could not be kept out. From Julia she became Juliet. She stayed pure as when he had spoken with her, but not in her lightsome mood. His heart was heavy, so Juliet must be a heroine with scarce a jest, and doomed. Thus, in a dream transformed to a play, a poet might compensate his heart for the wrongs done to it.

Southampton had no part in the scheme: yet, just as Shakespeare was conning Arthur Brooke's long, lame poem, thirty years old and more now, just as he was beginning to see it shaped to a play, came news from Titchfield of a quarrel between families, for all the world like the feud between Montagues and Capulets. No lovers here, but two brothers on either side. Sir Charles and Sir Henry Danvers were intimates of Southampton. And close by Titchfield lived the Longs, another Henry and his brother Sir Walter. There were brawls between serving men, insolences in the street, embittered letters. At Cosham, some Hampshire village, Sir Charles Danvers must needs break in upon the Longs at dinner with other gentlemen. Cudgels, swords and pistols were brandished in the affray.

Sir Henry Danvers slew his adversary, Henry Long, some said with a pistol shot; others, with a dagger, almost by chance, as Long thrust himself between drawn swords to call peace. The dagger ending was the more dramatic: so should Mercutio perish in the play.

Southampton stayed on at Titchfield, sheltering his friends, the Danvers. Presently rumour had it that he had conveyed them to France and safety. Rumour also said that Southampton would have to account for his defiance to the State: the Queen's subjects could not be assaulted and done to death, and none pay for it. That was as might be. Kit Marlowe had been slain in the Deptford tavern, and, as Dick Burbage prophesied, no more was heard of that. Southampton was powerful, and the powerful have friends everywhere. He who is powerful may succour a murderer; may obtain a mistress where he pleases, snatching her, if the whim takes him, from under the nose of his own devoted poet, who must still smile and crook the knee in his verse. But Southampton would not shew his face at Court yet awhile. London would not see him. Very well then: let him rot among his Hampshire beeves. Will Shakespeare, ill-used, was yet able to make a play that would live when Henry Wriothesley should be forgot.

Southampton had, however unwittingly, done this service at least to his devoted poet: his minion murderer, Danvers, furnished the notion for Mercutio's death. That duel should glitter upon the stage. And if Mercutio must die so soon, let his wit shine the more brightly while he lived. These young men of fashion, darlings of the Court, curled and dainty, who conceived they had but to bend a finger to take any woman to their bed, who rollicked at their own jests, commanded sonnets as they ordered from their tailors, and marvelled at the sparkle of their own speech—they should learn from Will Shakespeare how to deliver wit and poetry. There should be bawdry too, to tickle their apprehensions, but bawdry dainty as filigree lace. In Mercutio they should see the ensample of their kind. In a month, in a week, Mercutio should become their idol, their glass of fashion; every mincing man of them should ape Mercutio and strive so to look, so to jest, so to speak of fairyland, so to die, brave and bright of tongue. Would they could all die as swift, arrogant apes that they were!

Brooke's fable would serve his purpose, but it must be cleansed. Its essence was tragic, and Brooke lacked the perception to know the value of what he handled. Here was true love, young and clean, brought to disaster not merely by mischance, but because it flowered in a dunghill world. Let Mercutio speak naughtiness of codpieces and medlars, but Romeo (a name sweeter to the ear than Romeus) be other than Brooke made him. Take off the stains of random lustfulness, and leave a young man all sworn to love and loveliness, tender in heart, steadfast. So with Juliet. Brooke made her a " wily wench," inconstant, apt for lies and deceit. That could be done: there were such women aplenty, and one now couched with Southampton, at this same moment. Let that go. Here was a play to reproach the gross and unfaithful. Here was a play to make a certain lady (for whatever her faults, she was not slow of apprehension) understand how poor a bargain she had made, forsaking Will Shakespeare for a popinjay. Let Juliet be Julia of ' The Two Gentlemen ', but set in another key, richer in poetry and womanliness. And let her be young, as young as fourteen: only such youth could verify such purity of passion. Past fourteen they all go rank.

Brooke's friar must be changed too: tragedy demands dignity from those who stand within its shadow. But the lickerish old Nurse, let her be lickerish still, the better to point the contrast with Juliet. Meg Candler, long since dead in Stratford, would waken again in his memory to make a lip-smacking old Nurse. He put her lines in, quick and unhesitating, and never gave a thought to Anne who became his wife because old Meg had found a stratagem. Once the play was started in his mind, it grew like a lusty child: and all was intermingled pain and joy till he was delivered of it.

Within six weeks it was complete, every line amended in fair copy to his satisfaction. Burbage who, now that he was sure of Shakespeare's services for The Theatre, did not commonly waste flattery upon him, went about exclaiming his high hopes. The parts were copied speedily, the complete scrip locked away: rehearsals progressed from the first stumbling readings to the hot excitements, misunderstandings, broken tempers and impatience of the day before performance.

Then the play took the Town. Day after day it was performed, and those that had not seen this new ' Romeo and Juliet ' and could not talk of it, went shame-faced. The ladies and gentlemen of London, and many fetched up by gossip from the country, thronged to see it. James Burbage boasted of his Will Shakespeare as if the poet were his own son. He was welcome now at the Inns of Court, and the gentlemen there kept silence and listened respectfully when Shakespeare opened his mouth. Noblemen drew rein in the street and kept great entourages waiting while they spoke fair words to the poet of the age. He was invited to this house and that, and given honourable place at table. And as he had guessed, the young men of fashion went Mercutio mad. Many of them had whole periods of his speech by heart. Lovers wrote to their mistresses of balconies and tombs and signed themselves ' Romeo '. And Southampton was insolent enough to send, in a secretary's writing, with his own sprawling signature at the foot, a letter to his ' good Will ', rejoicing in the play's success and announcing that he would be graciously pleased to come see and hear for himself as soon as he returned to town.

Shakespeare took this calmly, all except Southampton's letter, which he tore to pieces. So much and so often he had dreamed of success, and now it had come he was pleased, but his heart unmoved. Sometimes, waking in the night, he feared that ' Romeo and Juliet ' marked the end of his ability, that he had writ all the fire out of himself in one play. His mind was slack now; neither verse nor fable stirred there. And if he were exhausted, if all the rest of his life must go barren, he knew how soon those who stayed now to flatter him would hurry off to ridicule. He felt no more the agonies of envy and jealousy, no more the empty-handed outward clutch of desire. His heart was cold; and a poet in whose heart neither anger, desire nor affection moves can make no poetry. Yet there was a bitter peace in this exhaustion.

The peace ended one afternoon at the playhouse: ended in an instant, between the stop and start of the hand of a clock. It was after a performance: the last of the crowd was noisily making its way out-doors again, and he was resting in Burbage's room. A messenger arrived and gave him a lady's name.

"Is my lord of Southampton with her?" he asked.

"Why no, sir. The lady come accompanied, but his lordship was not among them. Her companions have gone. She waits alone."

And the messenger gave him a lewd and covert look.

So she had left Southampton in Titchfield, and she desired to see Will Shakespeare alone? How now, lechery? Ever ripe for a new venture? He was half in mind to send a rude refusal, but the words halted on his lips.

"I'll come," he said.

The balcony running round the stage and the centre yard of the playhouse was partitioned into rooms which were hired for the length of a performance to parties of gentles: ladies came to the playhouse, masked against the stares and comments of strangers. Sometimes a nobleman would reserve a room, and then forget or disdain to make an appearance: unless he were one of the very great, Henslowe saw to it that he paid the fee. Sometimes a number of servants would be sent to occupy the seats. There were also one or two who insisted that any room they occupied should be equipped with running curtains for the open side which faced the stage and the mass of townspeople and apprentices standing close-packed in the yard. The curtains, half-drawn, afforded privacy. Sometimes, if part of the performance did not please, the curtains would be drawn right across, and behind them the party would divert itself with its own conversation, till one, peeping through, reported that there was now better entertainment on the stage. Whenever this happened Henslowe would be ill-tempered for days afterward, and would give orders that the next application for a room from the offenders should be refused.

In such a room, but uncurtained, the lady now received Will Shakespeare.

He stood in the open doorway, and bowed low, and said: "Mistress, you commanded my presence?"

"Then the message was ill-delivered. I sent a request."

"A request from you is a command."

"Such courtesy!" The lady feigned to breathe a sigh. "Yet it hath a chill upon it, as if you were displeased. And yet again, Master Shakespeare, it is I should have the privilege of displeasure. You have not shewn yourself to me since the day my lord of Southampton presented you, and that is some time since."

"It will be three months to a day tomorrow."

She laughed and put down her mask. He could see the deep, dark, brilliant blue of her eyes now. He had kept her, a treasure, in his mind, and struck poetry out of the recollection of but two meetings: and yet he had forgotten how lovely she was. What he must not forget, also, was that she had since become Southampton's trull.

"So you have counted the days? Master Shakespeare—nay, we are alone and I'll make bold to call you Will. We were friends once, if only the half of an hour. You kept count of the days, and you tell me so? Southampton spoke truth when he said you were skilled in the craft of pleasing women. Such compliments, thrown out blank and unsmiling, wing to their mark more sure than sonnets which compare an eyebrow to the arch of heaven."

"I can write sonnets also."

"Is that a promise for the future, or a boast of what's already achieved?"

Wounded, he struck to wound: "I have written sonnets, at his lady mother's behest, to urge my lord Southampton into marriage."

The implication he intended was a rebuke to this woman, Southampton's mistress. But she received it all calm and oblivious. "'Twill need more than verses to force that one to the altar. Have you not heard he stands to forfeit much, five thousand pounds they say, because he does not accede to the match arranged for him with the lady Elizabeth de Vere?"

This Shakespeare received as a vaunt, as if she had said: Southampton prefers to lose all these monies rather than forsake my bed even for the brief formality of a wedding night. He marvelled at her composed shamelessness.

"I have heard of your sonnets," she went on.

"They are poor things. Merchandise ordered and delivered."

"But I have heard also, Will Shakespeare, that thou hast writ other sonnets, and wilt not shew them abroad. Or so says rumour."

"Rumour's a lying jade. I have kept close counsel with pen and paper of late, but that was when this play of mine was in the making."

"Ah! 'Romeo and Juliet'! I have forgot my manners. For what other reason did I desire this colloquy but to tell thee, face to face, how excellent I found thy play. No matter. Others are shrewder in judgment than I. Yet I thought it would be churlish, as we were friends once, to depart without rendering thanks."

"I am glad my efforts gave you pleasure, good mistress."

"Will, what's this vexation between us? I am not commonly slow to anger. Ask my friends if you believe me not. But with thee I am patient, so patient I marvel at it. Have I not rid myself of company thus to parley here with thee alone? Have I not, after this three months short of a day, sought thee out, putting aside maiden modesty and such considerations of rank as the world holds me titled to? Art not admitted to the familiarity of my friendship? Have I not even now used thy name Will? And in return I get 'you' and 'good mistress', and am affronted with this blank stare. Wherein lies my offence?"

"The offence is all in me. Say that I am distraught, my wits gone abegging, and taken my manners with them."

"That's no answer that I'll accept. Where's my offence? Evade the question no more."

"The offence," he said, "if offence be the right name, for I have no just cause of complaint, the offence is Southampton."

She knitted her brows over that.

"This is beyond knowledge and comprehension. Hath Southampton quarrelled with thee?"

"Dost think," he asked, bitter and sharp, "it would enter the noble head of a great earl to consider a playhouse poet his rival?"

There was, he could see now, no pretending in her astonishment.

"I do not understand," she said slowly. "Thou hast me lost in perplexities. I lack some key of significant information. Perchance, had I seen Southampton of late and talked with him, I should understand the better."

"But were you not," he cried, "even lately at Titchfield?"

"I have never been there. Will, I fear thou'st been a fool. Better tell me all."

So, shamed and sick, he told of Southampton's triumphant boast and, barely, quickly, glossing it over, of his own jealous misery.

"And I thought thee wiser than other men," the lady cried, "because thou canst make such plays as move the heart. Thou'rt a fool and a child. And even so, foolish and childlike, wherefore believe me light and apt for such as Southampton? Doth all thy knowledge of hearts run into verses? Is none left over for thy daily needs? Southampton! Dost not know that boy is vainglorious and fickle as the wind in April? Did he name me in his boast?"

"Now I think on't, he did not. But a few days before, in

thy presence and out of it, his discourse was all of his love towards thee. And then he came prancing in, debonair and combed high like a cock, to tell of victory."

"Fool! A few days is time enough and to spare for such as Southampton to find another female target for what he calls his love. I do not blame him: he's as God made him. But as for thee, Will Shakespeare! To catch at an idle word, and believe the worst, it is an old device in plays: but keep it out of thy privy life. Nay, I believe thee. Thou'rt no rascal. Thou'rt but a fool and I'd do well to box thine ears and put thee out of mind."

"It is true. I am a fool, confounded and abased. Yet I am happier now than I have been this many a month."

"Because thou hast found me still chaste? Is chastity so great a matter that it can turn a poet in one delirious moment all from sullenness to joy?"

"Chastity is an intrusive name. I would not be over-familiar. Say rather, I rejoice to find thee heart-free."

"Heart-free? Vacant of tenancy, vacant for thy love, Will Shakespeare? There's timidity on thy lips, but the purport of thy words is bold enough."

She paused, and they looked long at each other: the poet sober-suited in russet cloth, bare-headed, a slender figure yet compact, pale-faced under the chestnut sweep of his hair, high-templed, with his hazel eyes hopeful and entreating; the lady, unmasked, bright-eyed, quick-eyed, magnificent in green silk and lace, the blood tumultuous in her cheeks. A rash adventure, a defiance of all that the degrees and order of society enjoined upon them, held them both poised on the swift in-takings of their breath as they faced each other in the little room overlooking the deserted stage.

The lady was keyed to a mood of rare candour: she had slipped the leash of her normal self: her wits were all lively, daring, experimental. Then suddenly she shook her head: her eyes widened and softened: and Shakespeare knew that these rash new hopes of his were already frustrate.

"Will," she said, "art saying in thine own roundabout fashion, thou lovest me?"

"Even so."

"Then do not. Do not say it! Do not feel it! It is an illusion. It can come to naught. Let us be good friends. I am not compact of the elements to make any man a mistress."

"I do not love in such wise."

"Indeed?" she said, light and cruel. "Yet I have heard thou'rt married and the father of children?"

"I had forgot."

"So! Married and childed, and the man forgets! The more easily he will forget me when another diversion turns his mind."

"That," Shakespeare protested, bitter and earnest, "is not true, as thou knowest."

"Time will disclose which of us hath the better judgment. And if time reveals me any man in the world steadfast in love, I'll get me to a nunnery and take vows."

"That would be a poor reward for my devotion."

"Thou canst jest again? Good. That's my Will that I like and esteem."

"Ay. Like and esteem, as a lady treats her clown. I am a hired jester. I make comedies to flit an hour away, and for that alone am I esteemed."

"Now wherefore this complaint? Wouldst have all, the whole wealth of the world? Is it not sufficient to possess such power of poetry? Think on the rest of the world, Will, that lacks all thou hast, and put envy away. It becomes thee not. Besides, thou'rt no jester now. This 'Romeo and Juliet' is not comedy. It surpasseth all thou'st done. Dost not need me to tell thee that."

"Wouldst have me satisfied," he demanded, "to make love in words scrawled on paper, and in mine own person have none of it? Have I, writing lines for Juliet, writ them, all unknowing, for myself? 'Oh, I have bought the mansion of a love, but not possessed it'."

"Poor Will! But this Juliet furnishes the answer to all thine outraged questions. Whence came she, if not from thy knowledge of love? I am not the first woman thou'st cast longing eyes upon. And I'll not be the last."

"Not the first: that I confess to. But the last, though all my protestations earn but mockery, I'll say it. I have it in me to be faithful. I am not of Southampton's breed."

"True. But the difference is not where thine imagination places it. The difference is this: thou'rt a poet. Thou canst make Juliets."

"Yet I cannot make a Juliet alone," he cried. "She and Julia, I got them both on thee. And did not," he added coarsely, "tarry for thy consent. 'Twas a rape. Yet the outcome is fair. Admit it. Juliet and Julia, they are fair daughters."

"In such a manner, Will, I am thine for the taking whenever thy mind turns to it. And because of that thou hast from me, not love, which cannot be given if it give not itself, but my fond affection. Be content with that. If it be less than was looked for, it is not nothing."

"Let be," he said. "There's wisdom in womankind, though you would not think it to hear many of them at their tattle. Doubtless I should bring thee naught but garlands of disappointment, were I thy lover. The very word is presumptuous, and I owe thanks thou hast not scorned me for letting my thoughts o'erleap into speech."

"Peace, man. This is no way to parle with me. We are alone. What's said now between us will not be witnessed or remarked. Therefore let it be frank. An I withhold my love, 'tis not by reason of the world, not because thou'rt of one degree and I of another."

"No? Or is it that thou'lt not admit such a reason? Is it because thy pride must find a false, a substitute reason for refusal, to make a better appearance before thy heart? No more of this. Reasons and motives are shadows in the night, never seen in shape and substance. Truly, mistress, I thank thee for much courtesy. Thou'st broke my heart, but done it gently. And behold another reason why my love cannot cease upon this refusal. Thou'rt gentle: therefore I must needs continue to love thee."

"Nay, I have a sharp tongue. I can make gentlemen to stammer and trip foot over foot in anguish of humiliation. I can turn maids and matrons to red-eared anger and lip-biting. Those that hold me intimate fear my tongue."

"And yet thou usest me gently. The more I must therefore love thee."

"The more fool thou, good Will. And now I must away. I have stayed too long."

"A word first. This our conversation is frank, without reserve: I have thy word for it. Then answer me one question. Now that I have disclosed my heart and the desire in it, art thou quite indifferent? Doth it mean nothing to thee that Will Shakespeare pays tribute with his love? Even though thou wilt not accept the offering, art not glad it was offered?"

"Nay, this is indeed presumption! Such questions deserve no answer."

"Then this thy sincerity is feigned and incomplete."

"Will, I'll give thee answer, and a truthful one. For thine offering of love, though I may not accept it, yes, I am glad. Glad and proud."

"Ah!"

"That's for myself. I am a woman and vain. Yet being a woman, I have a heart open to compassion. And for thee, Will Shakespeare, with all the splendour in thy mind to entertain thee and yet maundering around for a woman no better than another to waste it upon, for thee I am sorry. And now, farewell. Do not so long neglect me again. Be kind and fetch me those other sonnets, I am sure thou'st written. Fear not. I'll read with understanding. Remember, thou'rt always welcome at my father's house—as a friend."

He bowed, kissed her hand, and then turned to open the door.

"Better thou dost not accompany me further. O, and yes,

Will. Another precept for thine education. When next thou hearest ill reports of me, with Southampton or another, remember thine own words: Rumour is a lying jade."

So she left him smiling upon the thought that when all was done and said she was not invulnerable. She had been hurt, and was unable to conceal her resentment that he had believed her capable of yielding to Southampton. But soon the smile faded from his face. She was tender with him; she would give him friendship; but she did not love him. He need cherish no hope for the future because for this woman he could unpack no more of his heart's treasury. She was rare and delicate in sensibility: in her was a full and authentic response to his poetry: but his poetry was not enough. So young and yet so wise she was, to feel the full impact of Will Shakespeare the poet, and to know that all the shocks and ecstasies his poetry roused in her heart did not sum up to love for Will Shakespeare the man.

Book Three

DARK WOMAN

XI

WILL SHAKESPEARE saw his lady again, as often as he could trust himself to visit her without offending decorum and without putting his heart to intolerable pain: for she led him now along the easy bridle ways of friendship. He did not even discover to her the new name he put upon her in his thoughts—'dear Lady Disdain'. Upon occasion, he met her in other houses. He saw her when he was in attendance, wearing the Lord Chamberlain's livery, for commanded performances at Court. Never again—but once —were they closeted in privacy, and never—but once—did she speak to him openly as she had done that late afternoon in the playhouse.

This solitary exception of frankness, forced by her own contrivance, was brief and at first unhappy. She put into his hands a new published book, and bade him read. He looked back to the title page: 'Willobie his Avisa.'

"No," he said, "I have not read or heard of this."

"Read now. You will hear enough anon."

He read at the page she had left open:

H. W. being suddenly infected with the contagion of a fantastical fit, at the first sight of A., pineth a while in secret grief, at length not able any longer to endure the burning heat of so fervent a humour, bewrayeth the secrecy of his disease unto his familiar friend W.S. who not long before had tried the courtesy of the like passion, and was now newly recovered of the like infection; yet finding his friend let blood in the same vein, he took pleasure for a time to see him bleed, and instead of stopping the issue, he enlargeth the wound, with the sharp razor of a willing conceit, persuading him that he thought it a matter very easy to be compassed, and no doubt with pain, diligence and some cost in time to be obtained.

Shakespeare looked up. "Who's the author of this?" he demanded.

"There's no name given."

"I can enquire. But scurrilous books oftimes come to the printer's hands through several agents, and their origin is not easily to be traced."

"Will!" The single, familiar syllable rang sweet in his ears again, after such frequent public usage of 'sir' and 'Master Shakespeare'. "Will, answer me on your soul, as you value it. You have not talked of me treacherously?"

"On my soul, no."

"Nor idly, by inadvertence?"

"No. Thy name, and what hath passed between us, so little as it is, I have not confided to any."

"I too have been discreet."

"This," he exclaimed, looking contemptuously at the little book, "is malice missing the mark. The periods are vilely composed, but let that go. 'Twill do no harm."

"Thou takest it lightly, Will. I cannot. There's no pleasure for me, to see myself lampooned in print, and under the figure of a stork-legged, stupid letter A, to boot."

"None will join thy reputation with this. Think: the start of this fable hath some ground in truth. H.W.: Henry Wriothesley; that's Southampton. Divers will guess so far as that. And guess that W.S.—"his familiar friend"—stands for William Shakespeare. It is true Southampton once confided in me that he wasted away for love of a lady, and that lady was thyself. But the rest of the tale wanders from fact: it is malicious, but malicious against only myself. Someone unnamed likes me not. That's no news."

"But this woman called A? And the fellow makes her an innkeeper's wife!"

So that's where the sting went home, thought Shakespeare.

Aloud he said: "Have no fear. How many women, inn-keeper's wives a dozen among them, I'll warrant, have stirred Southampton's tongue to boasting? I make no doubt rumour will interpret this female letter A. by names aplenty: but thy name will not be among them. Didst not tell me Southampton's fickle fancy had turned elsewhere within a day or two after he had come to me, all piteous, complaining of thy cruelty? Did I not blunder shamefully, because I credited him with at least a se'enight of constancy?"

"Ah, Will, there's always comfort to be had from thee. My good friend. Here, take the book. I would not ever see it again. Burn it."

And so she slipped from him, back to the company, and he never after heard from her lips his intimate name of Will.

He held long to his grudge against Southampton, and was uneasy, deeming himself churlish. With the young Earl's gift of a hundred pounds, bounty for the dedication of the ' Lucrece ' poem, he had purchased himself a holding in the playhouse company, and upon that most of his present pro-sperity was founded. Yet a hundred pounds is not sufficient to buy a man's soul, or even his friendship. From the word ' friendship ' his thoughts jibbed, as a horse at a barking dog that ever runs in the way. For he must acknowledge that in time past, and not so long past, he had been glad of South-ampton's kindly interest, and in return had professed a devo-tion far exceeding his true feelings. He had indeed writ sonnets to the Earl, sonnets not to be concealed, for they were kept and copied at Southampton House, and many had read them. Pen and ink monuments of insincerity! All too durable reminders of shame! Whenever he thought of them his traitorous face, ever revealing his emotions in tides of come-and-go blood, burned till the flesh ached on the bones.

He was snared in a sad complexity of motives, passions, regrets, putting himself under obligation to a young noble he could not naturally like, and repaying that obligation with written professions which now abased him. Southampton was not of his kind. Yet he was sensual also, a lewdster in his thoughts, as Southampton in the act. He stood in no case to claim superiority. In truth, his grudge against the Earl was no matter of monies burdening his conscience: monies could be repaid. Nor yet was it the withdrawal of a delicate mind from lewd society: Will Shakespeare's mind was bawdy as well as fanciful, and he did not disdain to keep company with men whose fleshly inclinations left Southampton far behind. Were a taste for wenching to bar friendship, there would be few in London a man might sit to table with. His grudge against Southampton was that the fellow had intruded, all casual and magnificent, into a blossoming bower of affection, and laid it all in ruins. Between the Lady in Scarlet and White and Will Shakespeare all misunderstanding was overpast now, all explanations given and accepted. But where there had been the hope and potentiality of love only the cool secondaries of friendship remained. As a poet he triumphed, doubtless: as a lover he had suffered courteous defeat. And he ascribed his woes all to Southampton.

Sometimes he imagined counter-assaults, hot words, rash deeds, for he had the malice to scheme revenges in his mind. Next he thought it best to pose magnanimous, to see himself, with power to strike, witholding the blow. And again he fretted that he had taken Southampton's bounty, crooked the knee in words, and so dare not now, for fear of his own shame, offer insult. Fortunately the Earl, it seemed, no longer desired his poet's company: either he was busied with his own affairs or he had wearied of the patronage of letters. Yet he lingered in Will Shakespeare's mind, a festering sore of hatred and resentment: until on a day one came with a report that Southampton had been publicly reproved by a lady, and at the Court, for using the name of Will Shakespeare lightly.

"A goodly poet," the Earl had said. "He is my man."

"He is not," exclaimed the lady.

"You are mistaken," said the Earl. "And there is no excuse, for you have spoken with him in my presence."

"Master Shakespeare," the lady replied—all this came to the poet by immediate report, from one who liked not the Earl nor his ways—"is no man's man. And if my lord conceives that a word of praise and a purse of coins yields him the right to lord it over a poet who will be remembered when none will know one Earl of Southampton from the next, his error is grievous. Time will prove which is the other's man."

These words, the observer reported, she spoke with a proud chill air, and although my lord would fain laugh and turn away, he was much abashed, and the Queen herself, who disapproved his amours, commended the lady and called her the picture of justified disdain.

So, Will Shakespeare thought, she kept her word. Refusing love, she maintained herself his champion. It was after this he named her in his thoughts not always the Lady In Scarlet and White, but, sometimes, his dear Lady Disdain. Concerning Southampton he troubled no more, judging himself rid of all burdens of gratitude, and trusting also that the Earl had passed, once for ever, out of his life.

Yielding him nothing of herself but what was made common to many, the lady none the less served him well as year after year went by, and new plays added to his fame and fortune. She was Titania in 'A Midsummer Night's Dream', which he wrote quickly, snatching the nuptials of Theseus and Hippolyta from Chaucer, the interchange of lovers from his own 'Comedy of Errors', lately revived for the Revels at Gray's Inn, and the fairy lore from his Stratford boyhood. She even contributed something to the making of Nick Bottom the weaver, and his rude mechanical comrades, for, herself city bred and knowing little of country ways, she delighted in Will Shakespeare's improvised renderings of rustic speech, and told him that, put into a play, they would delight Londoners, ever ready to find countrymen slow-witted and ridiculous.

The notion of Bottom and the play presented before Theseus he picked, a seedling to plant in his own fancy, out of Tom

Nashe's tale, 'The Unfortunate Traveller,' which he held to be unexcelled among English prose writings. Nashe, writing as the rascally Jack Wilton, told of a number of German scholars making themselves ridiculous by presenting an ill-considered entertainment before the Duke of Saxony. After a speech by "a bursten belly inkhorn orator", full of mis-meanings and mispronounced words—"Mechanical men they call us, and not amiss"—a comedy was "so filthily acted, so leathernly set forth, as would have moved laughter in Heraclitus." One of the players "trod the stage so hard with his feet that I thought verily he had resolved to do the Car-penter that set it up some utter shame." Another "flung his arms like cudgels at a pear tree." Yet another "did nothing but wink and make faces." Taking a start from this, and casting back to his own memories of rustic masques and revels in Warwickshire, it was not difficult for Will Shakespeare to invent the rude antics he needed to add body to his Midsummer Dream.

With his pen striving to keep pace with the crowding fancies of his mind, he soon forgot the occasion for which the play was commanded. It was to be done as part of the festivities at the wedding of the Earl of Derby to that Lady Elizabeth Vere whom Southampton had, after much pro-crastination, refused to marry, and been fined for the refusal.

Henslowe and Alleyn continued the principal rivals of the Lord Chamberlain's men, who flourished although the Theatre building was now in bad repair, and the Burbages, father and son, perplexed to know what to do for the future. That did not hinder young Burbage, given the lines and the hint by Shakespeare, from strutting the stage in mockery of all the acting excesses of Alleyn, and in Alleyn's Tamburlaine voice roaring out Nick Bottom's lines: "Yet my chief humour is for a tyrant. I could play Ercles rarely, or a part to tear a cat in, to make all split." And again: "Let me play the lion too. I will roar, that I will do any man's heart good to hear me; I will roar, that I will make the duke say, 'Let him roar again, let him roar again.'" Dick Burbage had his Alleyn off pat, the straddling of the legs, the stiff waving of the arms, the rolling of the eye-balls, and the deep, monotonous thunder of the voice lengthening all the open vowels. The crowd laughed, knowing that Alleyn's tricks were being parodied, and those whose lives were spent around the playhouse knew also that here was mild, indirect but inescapable reproof to Alleyn for his overweening vanity which made him so ready to swallow up a whole play in his own part. Alleyn, it was said, took the news of Burbage's buffoonery sorely, talked of insults and reprisals, and called the playwright an ingrate.

Yet there was no malice in this Will Shakespeare: he had escaped from Alleyn as any man of spirit would fly a servitude, and if, from liberty, he looked back to laugh, many another would have struck to wound. He laughed daintily as well as broad through his rustics. His Oberon, his Titania and the spritely Puck spoke tuneable verses which the finer spirited gentry did not disdain to catch and record on the slate tablets at their belts that they might learn them off by rote, and speak them again to impress their friends. The Athenian nuptials and the trooping of the benedictory fairies through the palace (timed in the subsequent public performances to fall pat with the coming of dusk, so that the soft-marching players wove moving mazes of torch-lights on the stage): these were much admired. The boys about the streets caught the tune of it for their whistling; and many of their elders could sing the words of Oberon's inductive stanza:

> Through the house give glimmering light
> By the dead and drowsy fire;
> Every elf and fairy sprite
> Hop as light as bird from brier
> And this ditty after me
> Sing and dance it trippingly.

He evaded his Lady Disdain in 'Richard II.'; in 'King

John '; and in the two plays about Henry IV. which brought him trouble, for the young Lord Cobham, with no marrow in his bones and no liking for laughter, took offence that his forebear, a Lollard martyr, should be presented on the stage as a fat, cowardly, bawdy rascal: so Sir John Oldcastle had to become Sir John Falstaff. Yet if Cobham complained, the populace loved the white-haired, swaggering bag of guts, with his attendant humourists, Bardolph and Pistol. They could not have too much of them. And, as Alleyn's vanity still yielded good sport, he and his favourite plays at the Rose Theatre were mocked again:

> These be good humours, indeed! Shall pack-horses,
> And hollow pamper'd jades of Asia,
> Which cannot go but thirty miles a day,
> Compare with Caesars, and with Cannibals,
> And Trojan Greeks? nay, rather damn them with
> King Cerberus; and let the welkin roar.

Will Shakespeare acquired a reputation anew: the man was as various as the weather. First a chronicler, a dramatiser of Holinshed's records of English history: next a poet of love: then again a deviser of Courtly comedies, shaped to perfection and pearly bright with wit. Again, all lorn with tragic love and poetry which ached along the heart, in ' Romeo and Juliet ': and now rumbustious, the creator of swag-belly Falstaff at whose antics, it was said, the Queen herself laughed till the tears channelled through the scarlet paint on her cheeks.

For himself, Shakespeare enjoyed his success, and no less keenly that he took it calm and sober. He was become, beyond all question, the poet and playwright of the age. He had expected no less, and came into his heritage as unperturbed as a young noble for whom title, privilege and wealth had always been predestinate. Which part of his achievement he esteemed most precious he kept privy to his own thoughts:

the printed poems, the first historical plays, he seldom thought of, as little as he sent his recollection harking back to the last years between his first departure from Stratford and his advent as cobbler of plays to Henslowe at the Rose. The comedies pleased him only in parts; a scene here, a run of lines there, and those heroines, Julia, Titania, Portia, who pictured, yet never completely pictured, the Lady in Scarlet and White who had become, in his inward contemplations, his Lady Disdain. He had done enough to dazzle the town, and to ensure himself a refuge from poverty and its humiliations. He had not yet attained the mastery, and the occasion for mastery, which would enable him to plumb his own heart for its richest treasure and display what he found there in words. The Will Shakespeare who wrote was still several years younger than the Will Shakespeare who observed his own thoughts and actions and the events of the world as they happened. Experience, with him, had still to be left cellared in the mind to mature. That of his work which still seemed to him wholly good was no more than ' Romeo and Juliet ', and certain of the sonnets, a long but inconsequent sequence by now, shewn to the lady who would be but his friend, and by her to a few intimates: for there was no reader, as she said when she sought his permission, who could find a way through all those I's and thou's and thee's, for ever changing their values, and be sure at any moment precisely what his comprehension grasped.

And just now, if opinion fixed on Shakespeare chiefly as the maker of Sir John Falstaff, let opinion have its way, till mood and occasion struck fire in him and he could provide a new diversion. But Falstaff, having stolen, besides purses, the better part of two plays to himself, had become more liability than asset. The knight could not continue in his prime: and to let him falter and stale would, the mob being fickle and always ready to bite where once it kissed, reduce past achievement to discredit. Falstaff must die: he must die, for safety's sake, at the beginning, not the end, of the next play; and all by report, without an appearance on the stage.

So in 'Henry V.' (a piece all patriotism and heroics, by request of both Burbages, who had a shrewd eye for the political weather of the moment, when armies were in train for Ireland and the Low Countries) the Hostess came to give account of his ending, a brief chronicle shaped both for laughter and for tears. Falstaff repented his sins before he died, as Robert Greene had repented, years before; and at long last wanton memory yielded back to Shakespeare that phrase spoken by the shoemaker's wife in Dowgate: like Greene, Falstaff with his last breath "babbled of green fields." His nose, too, was "as sharp as a pen." Whence that image came who could say? Everyone who had seen death invade a failing body knew that often the flesh thinned visibly on the bones: but why "sharp as a pen"? Because Will Shakespeare was a writer and had the tools of his trade in mind? Or because Robert Greene had been a writer also, and had died? The elements that went to compact this Falstaff, even in his unseen death, were diverse and mysterious in their origin. Even Will Shakespeare, who bore him, nurtured him and now killed him, could not render close account of his creation. No cause for wonder there: what could a woman big with child report of the enlarging life within her womb, beyond a tally of pains, sickness, and little astounding leaps rising ever nearer to her heart? Falstaff was dead. Robert Greene was dead. The upstart crow lived and flourished, and, if he too must die, ere that time came he had work to do beyond the scope of Greene or fat Sir John.

But if the best was yet to come for Will Shakespeare, the best, it seemed to many, was already past for England. The summer of 1594 had been ruined with untimely rainstorms which Titania had commemorated:

> Therefore the winds, piping to us in vain,
> As in revenge, have suck'd up from the sea
> Contagious fogs; which, falling in the land,
> Have every pelting river made so proud
> That they have overborne their continents:

The ox hath therefore stretch'd his yoke in vain,
The ploughman lost his sweat, and the green corn
Hath rotted ere his youth attain'd a beard:
The fold stands empty in the drowned field,
And crows are fatted with the murrion flock.

It was lightsome verse, fluting to its own various and gently wayward measure, not marching clank-foot to the tabor beat. Well for Shakespeare that out of the great disaster he could strike such poesy. The consequent ills for poor people were not soon to be forgotten. Because the crops failed, prices rose high the following summer. Again and again in June riots broke, in the City, in Billingsgate, and on Tower Hill. July brought martial law, and towards the end of the month five prentices were hanged, at the place where they had been arrested, for making protest, and their bodies cut down, still breathing, for the executioners to quarter. Compared with these unhappy youths, thought Shakespeare, he had small right to grumble because the playhouses were closed, by order of the Council, from the 26th of June. They remained shut for two months.

Many, however, were more concerned with the twelve months to follow September 6th, for on that day the Queen entered the ninth, the grand, the most dangerous, climacteric year of her life, in which the mystical numbers seven and nine, by multiplication, were united. On the 6th day of September she became sixty-two years old, which was a great age for anyone, and not all the dye in her hair, nor all the unguents, paints and powders stained on to her wrinkled cheeks, could conceal this astrological fact from her subjects. Her eighth climacteric had brought the Spaniards' invading Armada: the mercy of God blowing in the providential wind had averted that disaster. But, men wondered, privily and among trusted intimates, what greater evils would her sixty-third year unloose upon her realm? And what was the chance that at her age she might survive the star-borne perils?

Moreover, Elizabeth was unwed, past wedding and bedding, though none dare hint it in her presence: certainly past child-bearing. She was old, she had reached the most hazardous years of her long life, and the Crown was without heir apparent. Would England, after this long Elizabethan reign of prosperity and order, see the bloody, battling days of York and Lancaster come again with civil disaffection, brother all eager to shed brother's blood, and the supreme power no better than a bauble for the most villainous rascal with the most reckless hand to snatch for his own? Or would she fall, like a ripe medlar, into the lap of the Stuarts of northern, barbarous Scotland, her ancient enemy? Some whispered that, rather than let circumstance bring forth such calamities, it were better now to discipline a Queen, doubtless good, but mind-palsied by age and so beset with vanity that she would not consider the succession: better (to out with it) the Council select some likely nobleman, such as the Earl of Essex, and nominate him now England's heir and coming monarch. But the Queen was not dead yet. Some said she was in love, an old woman's dotard love, with Essex: it was plain she indulged him as she indulged no other. Yet when she was given a copy of a new book, called 'A Conference About the next Succession to the Crown of England,' and read with her failing, angry eyes the foolish dedication to Essex, her wrath was terrible. For some time Essex walked small and quiet, the royal displeasure dark over his head.

Abroad, the French alliance was failing. Henry of Navarre, now Henry the Fourth, expected more help from England than the Queen was prepared to give, and upbraided Sir Henry Unton, in open audience, scornfully. The Spaniards prepared a new invasion, and although a fleet and a force of sixty thousand men-at-arms was prepared for the defence of the English shore, it seemed that all the miseries foretold in the stars were relentlessly coming to pass.

Early in April news arrived that the garrison of Calais was invested and the town like to fall. The Queen tarried to drive a bargain for what she should get in return for succour, but on Good Friday six thousand men were started on the march to Dover, where Essex and Lord Charles Howard waited to take them to raise the siege. Next day the gossips were dismayed to learn that, according to the newest estimates, Calais could no longer hold out, and the levies had therefore been dispersed to their homes again. The more malicious or more humorous among these gossips found consolation in telling each other the story of the Bishop of St. David's who, preaching on the Good Friday, with the Queen and the ladies and gentlemen of the Court as his congregation, was bold enough, or stupid enough, to announce for his text: " O teach us to number our days that we may incline our hearts unto wisdom." He discoursed on the mystical numbers and the grand climacteric, and even offered prayers of his own devising as suitable for a Queen at an age " when the senses begin to fail, the strength to diminish, yea, all the powers of the body daily to decay." The Queen's eyes, said those near enough to watch her through the sermon, were not yet so dim that they could not flash fire. She muttered to herself throughout the unasked prayers made in her name, and afterwards sent for the Bishop and told him he would do well to keep his arithmetical talent for his own entertainment.

On Easter Monday the authorities again changed their minds, and the levies were ordered to assemble once more. This time they marched as far as Dover. But two days later the citizens of London were bidding each other keep silence while they listened to the thunder roll of cannon, far off but awesome. On the 16th it was known that Calais had fallen, even while the relieving force at Dover was embarking. Many said that the French had played traitor, preferring to lose the city to the Spaniards, through whom they might hope to make peace with the Pope, rather than to the English, who had held it so long, and were now heretics.

Yet the Queen survived her year of alarms unharmed, and with her realm uninvaded. For Will Shakespeare, though his plays continued successful, the twelve months brought calamity, but not till they were near elapsed. He was working that summer of 1596 on the play of King John, but working under distraction, and he liked it not so well. He had a quarrel with a Justice of the Peace in Southwark, William Gardiner, and his son-in-law, Wayte, and was threatened with a law suit. And at the beginning of August ill news came to him from Stratford. He rode there post, but arrived too late. Hamnet, his son, but eleven years old, was already dead of a sudden fever.

The funeral preparations were all advanced: he had to lose temper with the black-suited, sepulchre men to have the coffin lid unscrewed, and then he was left for only ten minutes to look on the white, waxy face, muslin-shrouded, of his only son. Left alone in the room—the room where he himself had been born—with this little corpse of a boy almost unknown to him, he was aware at first chiefly of shame and silence and the blood pounding in his own temples. To get life, to burst another human soul upon the world: to desert the child, with his sisters and his mother: to be known to this boy principally as a name whence arrived monies from London, and only at far-spaced intervals as a father, a stranger garbed and neat-bearded Londonwise, who came, gave sweetmeats, talked a little, smiled a little, and was gone: this was an ignoble and insufficient fatherhood. And now the boy was dead, dead ere life had peeped more than an eye half-open upon him, dead with all promise closed behind these whited temples (arched and domed like his father's, in shape like the shoulders of a fiddle), these grey, cold lips, these coin-weighted eyelids. Forgive me, my son, for I have used thee ill: the entreaty, humble and unspoken, shuddered through his mind as he bent over the coffin. Anne, his wife, coming softly into the room, was startled to see tears on her husband's face: her husband, who had once been her lover, young Will, was now almost as strange to her as a brown Indian fetched from America and to be viewed for a penny in a raree show at Rother Market.

The boy was buried hard by the Parish Church, where two of Will's sisters, dead in infancy, already lay. The funeral over, the father recovered his composure. He could face this narrow world of Stratford again in which he had once been a scapegrace youth and was now a man of substance, a man with the mark of London fame upon him, a man with whom the most prospering burgesses were proud to be seen in converse. He could receive their condolences with calm and seemly courtesy now. Hamnet was dead: no more of little Hamnet. Let that grief lie close in his heart. Do I seem hard to all these enquiring eyes, he wondered? I think I am not so, but I cannot be judge upon mine own plea. Perchance he was in his heart an obdurate man? Perchance he traded, with plays and poetry, too much in fanciful emotions to feel the pangs, quick and unquestioned, which others felt? Whatever the cause, he could not now make long and open lamentation for his dead son: and when he returned to London he would, he knew, busy himself with further plays he had in mind, and in them none of death and mourning. Yet the boy had not died and left his father the same man. With that change, with that agony in his heart which he could not and would not yet comfort, he must some time keep a tryst.

He stayed a few days in Stratford. Hamnet Sadler, godfather to the dead boy, came to comfort him. Hamnet had grown fat by now, and was portentous in his speech, full of polysyllabic wisdom. Will, for all his friendship, grew impatient, until he saw he could no longer take this stout burgess seriously, and then he began to treasure, where formerly he had resented, the voluble stream of wise saws and modern instances.

He talked with his father, an old man now, gratified that this son had confounded all the Stratford prophets of woe, and yet unwilling to admit that Will, being famed in London, was any marvel in Stratford. He talked with his mother, too, and with both of them together concerning the old-standing application for a grant of arms to the Shakespeare family.

His mother was anxious to have the Arden arms impaled thereon for Will, although, she said, and wept to say it, there was little to look for now Will had no male heir. But John Shakespeare roughly told her she had other sons with the power of engendering, and then was sorry for his rudeness, and kissed her to take the smart of his words away. In their old age they were sweet as wrinkled apples left in the sun, and Will loved them.

He loved Anne too, but remotely, feeling no virtue drawn from himself by that gentle affection. It was as if she had never been his wife, this woman so many years older than himself. He fretted no more against the tie of his marriage: Anne had borne Hamnet, who was now dead, and Judith, Hamnet's twin, and Susan, now thirteen years old. He talked to Anne mostly of the children, forbearing to ask questions about Hamnet's sickness and suffering, to save himself, as well as her, from further hurt. He was happiest of all walking and playing and gravely discussing with Susan and Judith, his little maids, elbow high and heart high, big-eyed with awe at their brother's death, but too young to feel sorrow deep and long. Susan was already brisk and quick-tongued, apt to sudden explosions of laughter, which rang like her father's in his merry moods; just as Hamnet, with his father's brow and his father's eye, had been a quiet treasurer of sights and sounds and phrases. Little Judith, gold-haired, already began to show the candid temples, the open gaze, the soft-lipped smiles which had been Anne Hathaway's in youth. He walked with them in the buttercup meadows by the river, and told them (what he had half forgot himself) how he first met with their mother by chance when he and she were lost in a September mist. He took the children across the Clopton bridge, and held them up to peep over the wall above the last arch on the London side, where they could see for themselves how a straw or a twig, borne on the current, passed swiftly towards an outthrust of the bank, whirled for a while in an eddy there, and then was sucked back, almost as swift, under the same arch.

"When I was a little tiny boy," he said, "I marked that, and never after forgot it. I put it into a poem once."

Then he paused, remembering that the poem was 'Lucrece', a thing indifferent bad, low in his estimation now, and connected besides with Southampton, whose fair front concealed an ill-favoured spirit, and whose lavish friendship had not persisted. Southampton, besides, brought to mind a lady whose love he would never have, a lady not his wife, and not the mother of these his dear daughters.

Putting away such thoughts, inapt for a father bent all on kindness towards his living children to still his unquiet conscience concerning the dead, he told them: "There it is, a river current coming and going under the same arch of the bridge, and that's an oddity the Thames cannot match."

But Susan and Judith were eager to be told the marvels of London, and all the way home they kept him busy with questions about Nonsuch palace and Westminster and Richmond, about soldiers and the Court, and the Queen and the Queen's barge, and what kind of kirtles and headdresses the great ladies wore.

XII

LONDON, when Shakespeare returned to it, was all triumph and rejoicing. Calais had gone, but the French alliance was solemnly renewed: and Essex with his expedition was returned from the successful expedition on Cadiz. The Spanish pride had been curbed again, and a great ransom exacted. Then the Queen's life passed smoothly out of its climacteric year, and the realm of England could go quietly upon its business without foreboding.

All the young gentlemen about the town transformed themselves in the mode of the expeditionaries of my lord of Essex's command: they wore swelling bombast sleeves and breeches stuffed with hair, and hats of high block and broad brim; they were proud of their moustaches twisted to fine points and spread wide, their spade beards newly dyed; many of them carried a love lock hanging behind the left ear, and bound at the end with a knot of silk ribbon to match the rosettes on their shoes. They were stout stiff blades, or gave themselves out to be, and the young housewives of London, ever preferring the lively to the discreet, tittered and opened their eyes when they passed, while the puritans, with texts of scripture embroidered on their white shirts, shuddered and looked away.

One of these fine gentlemen, and one authentically returned from Cadiz, where he had comported himself well, was said to be a poet of uncommon parts, by name Jack Donne. A copy of verses in a scrivener's hand, reputed to be from his pen, came into Shakespeare's possession, and he was impressed by them:

> I long to talk with some old lover's ghost,
> Who died before the god of love was born:

I cannot think that he, who then lov'd most,
  Sunk so low, as to love one which did scorn.
But since this god produc'd a destiny,
And that vice-nature, custom, lets it be;
  I must love her, that loves not me.

Here was a theme close to his own heart, ancient under scrutiny, but not yet exorcised of its anguish; and this new poet expressed it harshly but well. Shakespeare had half a mind to seek him out and strike an acquaintance. Then one day, jostling among the throng up Lombard Street under the signs of the money-lenders and coin-changers, just as he came abreast of the great gilt grasshopper that marked the house of Sir Thomas Gresham, a swaggering piratical fellow, a veritable Mounseer Magnifico, came swinging past and with a careless buffet of his shoulder sent Shakespeare reeling to the gutter.

"Hold there! Hold, I say!" he called. People turned their heads, and one spoke to the grand gentleman still thrusting ahead. He halted then, and waited with straddling legs and derisive smile.

As Shakespeare came up he saw that the man had an ugly face, dark complexioned, with a splay nose, little eyes, and a wide, wet mouth.

"Well, sirrah," the fellow demanded. "What wouldst have with me?"

"A word of contrition, a sign of courtesy and regret."

"And for what?"

"For an ill usage I am not customed to, and not minded to stomach. Are you in such haste, sir, that you must needs jostle a stranger from the path and stay not to ask pardon?"

"It is not my way to truckle to any, strangers or not," said the swarthy man. "An you are not satisfied with that reply, and so you be a gentleman, I shall be pleased to meet you where you will. My name is Donne. John Donne. What do you stare at, sir."

"Why," said Shakespeare with a laugh, "I had wished to make your acquaintance, Master Donne, but not after this fashion. We are two of a trade, for I am told you make poetry. My name is Shakespeare. You may have heard of me."

The soft wide lips split in a grin. "I have heard of you, sir, and seen your pieces in the playhouse. Well, poets must not quarrel upon such small occasions. I am sorry it was your shoulder I pushed against, Master Shakespeare. Will that suffice to make amends?"

"Amply. And perchance a pint of wine would foster our better acquaintance?"

"I thank you," said Donne, gruff and curt. "At present I am in haste. We must meet again, but for now, farewell."

And he was gone in the crowd.

Donne by name, and dun by complexion, Shakespeare thought: for the man was dark-skinned, and scowled at all around him as he made his way through the press. A poet he was, past cavil, but he had been one of Marlowe's and Robert Greene's misfortunate tribe, doomed to poverty and a pestiferous end, were he not descended on his mother's side from Heywood, the writer of epigrams, and inherited a goodly estate from his father. Upon further enquiry, Shakespeare learned that the life of this Jack Donne consorted with his appearance: he roistered much about the town, was abroad by night full oft, chambered with cutpurses and conny-catchers, frequented trugging houses, railed at women even while he had them, and ranked wantoness above virtue. He boasted his proficiency in work done abed and conceived himself a lover surpassing all others in the attributes of a man. Yet if the verses were his, and were to be trusted, there was one woman would not yield. Shakespeare was not disposed, on that score, to feel compassionate towards this dark and surly Donne, and avoided any further occasion to meet him.

He saw his lady again, and she was kind to him. He told her of Hamnet's death, but would not speak of his own grief.

She put out her hand and clasped it over his for a moment, the first intimacy she had yielded him since, in anger and anxiety, she had thrust the copy of the Willobie book under his eyes. All she said was: "I am sorry for it," but he felt the compassionate beat and sympathy of blood from her. Yet she did not love him, would not love him, could not love him. There were others present (there always were when he saw her now) and they all talked light, jesting nonsense. Only when they parted she said to him, softly so that none should overhear: "See, was I not wise to take decision for us both? Thou'st made thy life, and must endure it, good and ill, and there I may not intrude."

Sometimes he felt that she was indeed wiser than he, that this severance was better for them both, even though he beat out his heart against the sustainment of her decision, like a bird, such as he had often seen in his Stratford boyhood, limed in a bush and fluttering helplessly. Yet, even as the bird must struggle till its strength be exhausted, so must he go on loving this lady in vain, and cherish his love which doubtless was the purer because it could find no expression save in poetry. He thought of the sensual urges of his blood, unleashed so unexpectedly by poor Nan, now living sober matronwise on the banks of Avon. They had not troubled him of late: chastity of life came easier now. Yet he wrote bawdry, playing for the loud laugh, and between times he was ashamed. He sent his lady, a few days later, a neat-written copy of a new sonnet, all humility and resignation:

> Alas! 'tis true I have gone here and there,
> And made myself a motley to the view,
> Gor'd mine own thoughts, sold cheap what is most dear.
> Made old offences of affections new;
> Most true it is that I have look'd on truth
> Askance and strangely; but, by all above,
> These blenches gave my heart another youth,
> And worse essays prov'd thee my best of love.

Now all is done, save what shall have no end:
Mine appetite I never more will grind
On newer proof, to try an older friend,
A god in love, to whom I am confin'd.
Then give me welcome, next my heaven the best,
Even to thy pure and most loving breast.

He kept back another, telling himself that two of the lines displeased him and needed amendment. This was a mortise-jointing between the public acclamation of the Queen's sixty-third birthday safely attained and passed, and his own pride in his art. His lady had refused a prentice poet, with the laurels still green and new-set on his brow: that, he implied, was understandable; but to continue with refusal when the poet was become established, master of his craft, master of himself, and everywhere applauded, called for more justification. He kept the sonnet from her until the Shakespeare grant of arms was accomplished, and then he made a fair copy in his own hand of the manifest signed by the Garter King of Arms.

"To all and singular Noble and Gentilmen . . . Wherefore being solicited and by credible report informed, That John Shakespeare of Stratford uppon Avon, in the counte of War-wike, whose parentes & late grandfather for his faithfull & valeant service was advanced & rewarded by the most prudent prince King Henry the seventh of famous memorie, sithence which tyme they have continewed in those partes being of good reputacon & credit, and that the said John hath maryed the daughter & one of the heyres of Robert Arden of Wilmcoote in the said Counte esquire, and for the encourage-ment of his posterite to whom these achivmentes by the auncyent custome of the Lawes of Arms maye descend. I the Said Garter king of Arms have assigned, graunted, and by these presentes confirmed: This shield or Cote of Arms, viz. Gould, on a Bend Sables, a Speare of the first steeled argent. And for his creast or cognizaunce a falcon his winges displayed Argent standing on a wrethe of his coullers: supporting a speare Gould steeled as aforesaid set uppon a helmett with mantelles & tasselles as hath ben accustomed."

And so, Will Shakespeare thought, she would know that he, born a gentleman, was now recognised in his right by the State and by his peers. He sealed the letter and stamped the wax with the new ring he had, in his confidence, ordered months earlier. The delayed sonnet (not a word of it altered, after all, since the third day after he had, hot and tense, set to drafting it) was proud, apart from a phrase of conventional, unmeaning modesty near the end. In it he addressed his lady not as his friend, which he did in his moods of resignation, and also, mischief-moved, so that chance readers (for sonnets were apt to be copied and handed round) might confuse her with the earlier apostrophes to Southampton: he spoke roundly and forthright his love for her, and told her that his art, serving his devotion, would make her immortal.

> Not mine own fears, nor the prophetic soul
> Of the wide world dreaming on things to come,
> Can yet the lease of my true love control,
> Suppos'd as forfeit to a confin'd doom.
> The mortal moon hath her eclipse endur'd,
> And the sad augurs mock their own presage;
> Incertainties now crown themselves assur'd,
> And peace proclaims olives of endless age.
> Now with the drops of this most balmy time
> My love looks fresh, and Death to me subscribes,
> Since, spite of him, I'll live in this poor rime,
> While he insults o'er dull and speechless tribes:
> And thou in this shalt find thy monument,
> When tyrants' crests and tombs of brass are spent.

Some years were to pass before, remembering this first use of his signet ring, he was able to laugh at the strange juxtaposition of a sonnet, concluding with a contemptuous reference to " tyrants crests," and his father's grant of arms, folded and sealed and sent to a lady who would have the poetry but not the poet. By that time he was no longer young, and older than his years: he had writ himself out of the creative fever and out of vanity, and yet, to the end, though he could smile as at foolishness, he took pleasure in the respect of others and still delighted to see the shield and helmet surmounted by the spear-shaking falcon.

In February 1597, James Burbage died, leaving The Theatre to his son, Cuthbert, and the Blackfriars playhouse to Dick. Dick was distressed over this inheritance, which was like to be useless. The playhouse at Blackfriars was excellent, if small, and moreover roofed. Dick's father had lately converted it, expending much money thereon, after it had served as fencing school and lodging house. But before a play could be staged, the neighbouring householders, including Lord Hunsdon, petitioned the privy council, alleging that their peace would be disturbed by the throng of lewdsters and vagrants who would attend the performances. They alleged the noise of drums and trumpets upon the stage must be heard in the church, and even in the midst of divine service. And they did not scruple to urge that the players sought refuge in the liberties outside the City only because the Lord Mayor, aware of the unruliness in which they lived, had banished them. So the playhouse in Blackfriars was built, finished and ready, and yet perforce stood empty and unused.

The Earl of Essex was already losing the gilt from his Cadiz reputation. He quarrelled openly with the all-powerful Lord Burleigh and his crook-back son, Sir Robert Cecil. He was reputed to have debauched a nobleman's wife, and one in the confidence of Her Majesty. The Queen was turned quite against him, and had not forgot her late quarrel with the Lord Treasurer, who had argued against her decision that Essex should not profit from the Cadiz ransoms. And yet again, it was whispered that the Queen's displeasure with

Lady Mary Howard was rooted in jealousy: for that the Lady Mary possessed a velvet habit, powdered with gold and pearls, surpassing any in the royal wardrobe, and flaunted it to take my lord of Essex's eye. Whereat (it was said) the Queen sent one day and had the Lady Mary's habit brought to her, and donned it, and showed herself to her ladies, asking their opinion: at which the Lady Mary spoke and said it was too short for Her Majesty, and ill-becoming.

In the summer another sea expedition was prepared, none knew for what destination. There were many privy meetings, and the Queen oft in a rage. But it was known that Essex was to command, whether as reward or punishment none could say. The victuals provided were said to be stinking rotten, and the men pressed for service the poorest sort of lame and diseased vagrants. And when, in July, the ships did set sail, they were driven into Plymouth a few days later by a tempest.

At this time Will Shakespeare was as busy with varied projects as a juggler at a fair tossing and catching oranges. He was first creating and then killing Falstaff, and troubling his mind between times with the first shoots and shapings of very different plays, still striving to catch in a crystal of lines the wit and charm of his Lady Disdain. A printer, one John Danter, had issued a quarto volume of the text of ' Romeo and Juliet ', not registering it in the customary fashion. Burbage was vexed by this, for a play was the property not of its author but of the company he sold it to, and until it had run a full course in popular esteem and attendances were weakened at its revivals, the company kept the complete script locked from sight.

Danter's text was full of errors, and had plainly been compiled from the memory of one or more players out to make a little money on the side. The product was vile: lines were omitted, put in the wrong place, cut without ear for the metre, and prose printed as verse, verse as prose. Will Shakespeare was furious that such a botched version should be presented to readers as his work, and, after long arguments, persuaded

Burbage and the other sharers in the company that, as such printers' thefts were becoming more common every day, it would be better if he were allowed, as his plays exhausted their first popularity, to let a reputable printer have access to the company's full text. Yet even these texts, transcribed in haste, much-handled, amended during rehearsals and after, were difficult for the printer to follow. Always he resolved to make all corrections himself, to demand proofs before the printing of the book, and read them with care: always, when the time came, he was too busy with other matters, and left the work to another. Thus he saw fifteen of his plays published in the next few years, some by consent, some by theft, none of them as he would have wished. He told himself that when creative urgency died in him, when he was no longer brainridden with new plays in the making, when, in brief, he was a little older, a little wealthier and at leisure, he would take time to go back over the whole body of his work, correct and emend and improve, and send it out printed fair and seemly to the world. But at present he was busy, and could spare time only to curse the printers as their ill-copied books came into his hands.

He was living now in the ward of St. Helen's, Bishopsgate, and in May he took leave to visit Stratford again, where he hoped to make a profit from a store of malt, ten quarters of it, bought in his name. While he stayed, he saw an attorney, and completed the purchase, for sixty pounds, of the house called New Place, built by Sir Hugh Clopton, on the corner of Chapel Street and Walker's Street, facing the Gild Chapel. It was a large house of ten rooms, with a walled garden. Will Shakespeare had long known it as it stood empty and falling into disrepair: the brickwork between the timbers did not hold so well as clay and wattle. It seemed to him now that all Stratford must recognise his success, with his grant of arms and this property to his name. The Shakespeare motto, displayed beneath the gold-and-black shield, was: Non Sanz Droict, and not without right was he establishing himself again in the town of his birth. William Underhill of Idlicote, a lawyer, had bought the house from Bott, young Clopton's agent, and let it long stand empty. Underhill had been poisoned by his son, Fulke, and, this being discovered, the attorney's deeds were void, for a felon could not inherit from his victim. But another son, Hercules Underhill, quickly obtained authority and so New Place became the property of William Shakespeare. Will remembered passing comment on the house to Hamnet Sadler one day as they went, youth arm in arm with youth, down the mudded lane to the Bank Croft in the mists. Hamnet could come now and see his friend, with London fame and London manners aureate upon him, ordering the masons as they started to make the dwelling habitable again. The garden was in fact two gardens, and there were fruit trees in the orchard, a bricked well, and a pair of barns which needed a little timbering. Here he would make him a peaceful refuge for when he should tire of London.

But that was not yet. The theatre called him. He kissed mother, father, wife and the two children left to him, and hurried back to Bishopsgate. He found the playhouses again closed down, all because a rash young fellow, one Jonson, had finished a play, 'The Isle of Dogs,' started by Nashe; beginning, middle and end, it was held to be seditious, satirical of the times, and highly slanderous. It was done by Lord Pembroke's men at the Swan, and outraged authority. Not only did the Council ordain that no plays should be publicly given within three miles of the City of London till the season of All-hallows, they commanded the magistrates to see to it that the playhouse structures, stage, galleries and privy rooms, be bodily plucked down.

This was disaster, and Burbage and his brother Cuthbert for a few days were men hard to recognise, so downcast they were and full of foreboding. The common woe even made them civil to Henslowe and Alleyn of the Admiral's men at the Rose, who, it was said, had contracted for Jonson's services, as make-play and as player, and were paying his upkeep in

the Marshalsea prison to which he had been committed, along
with Gabriel Spencer and the Irishman, Robert Shaa. Nashe,
who had started the play and the mischief, was too old in the
ways of the world: he had seen much crime and vagabondage
and, it was said, had been reduced to such a shift that once,
with his friend, Lusher, they had but the one pair of breeches
between them and took turns, day and day about, the one to
be abed and the other to go forth and cozen enough money
to fill both their bellies. Nashe, scenting in good time the wind
of chastisement raised by 'The Isle of Dogs' play, 'scaped
arrest by taking himself out of London swift and fleet. It was
said he lay at Yarmouth, feeding on red herrings, and liked
the lenten fare passing well.

Presently it appeared that the Council's edict was not to
be fully enforced: there would be no performances till summer
was ended, but the playhouses were to stand undamaged. Dick
Burbage smiled again, though not at Alleyn. Meanwhile,
Jonson, with his two companions, lay in the Marshalsea. Will
Shakespeare, his worst fears at rest, conceived the idea that
he would visit this new make-play in his prison, commiserate
with him on his unfortunate first essay in the London playhouse, and perchance offer him some useful advice. He took
with him his friend, Michael Drayton, the poet, like himself
a Warwickshire man.

The prison was cold: even in the summer heat the thick
stone walls made all within dark and chilly. It stank: they
expected no less. Men died of gaol fevers here easy as flies in
a frost. Yet they did not see the inner chamber, where the
worst malefactors, or such as were held dangerous to the
State, lay and rotted on straw fouled with their own ordure.
No more than the effluvium of that inner part of the Marshalsea, wafted from a gated corridor, troubled them, as they
passed by, but it was enough to sicken Drayton, who had
lived dainty in the household of Sir William Goodere; and
Shakespeare, a gentleman to the tip of his nose, blenched. He
dubbed himself a fool, for attempting to body forth his delicate

visions in the playhouse, whose servants must lie under a curse. Greene had died, swollen like a drowned dog, debt-ridden, and lousy; Marlowe, stabbed treacherously after a tavern brawl; and George Peele more lately, of a pox if gossip were true. And now this Ben Jonson, eight years younger than himself, a mere fledgling pet, was cabined among these unsavoury stenches. He felt moved to compassion for Jonson.

The gaoler ushered them into a room about fourteen feet by ten, stone in walls, floor and ceiling. The stone dripped water. A small window, iron-barred, set high in one wall, afforded the only natural illumination. Nine prisoners were here, five of them dicing by rush-light. The others lay about on sacks of straw. They all looked up as the two visitors entered, and then quickly returned to their dice or their sullen meditations.

Shakespeare recognised Spencer and Shaa among the dicers: perchance one of the other three was Jonson?

"My name is Shakespeare," he said, "and with me here is Master Michael Drayton. We come to speak with Master Benjamin Jonson."

A thickset man, with a short beard and tumbled brown hair, said: "Your leave for a moment, gentlemen." He rattled the dice in the cup, threw, dropped a glance to the floor, cursed, and then got to his feet and came towards them. His eyes were small and blue and sharp under brows heavily fleshed though scant of hairs.

"Why this is honour," he exclaimed, his voice broad and deliberate in its enunciation. "I have long desired your acquaintance, Master Shakespeare. Divers of your plays which I have seen performed have won my admiration, and that's not lightly or loosely yielded. And yet they are not, in every aspect, faultless or equal in merit. I should want honesty to let you conceive amiss. But there's a subject for long discussion. It will keep. And you, too, Master Drayton. Your poems have the stamp of ancient authority and symmetry upon them. I take it kindly you should visit me thus in my momentary misfortune."

Why, thought Shakespeare, here's a prentice to the trade will outface his masters! He was amused by this Jonson's assurance. They sat facing each other, each planted on a short, three-legged stool.

"I am sorry," he said, while Drayton, ill at ease in his blue velvet and his fine cambric ruff, stared distastefully round the crowded cell, "I have not seen your ' Isle of Dogs ' piece. I was in the country, about my affairs, when it was performed."

"You have missed little."

"Yet it provoked an uproar. The playhouses are all empty and idle because of you, Master Jonson."

"They shall be full and loud with applause yet, and also because of me."

"Hast no small conceit, young man," said Drayton. He smiled as he said the words to take away offence, and patted his red hair with his long bony fingers.

"Why, a man must needs know his own merits. Knowledge begins at home. I have been thoroughly schooled. At Westminster the good dominus Camden enriched me well with Latin and Greek. No offence, Master Shakespeare, but the playhouse stands in need of scholarship, and scholarship is Ben Jonson."

Shakespeare asked him: "It is thine opinion then that art can be inculcated?"

"Why certainly. Yet not every pupil hath the ability to profit by his lessons. You, Master Shakespeare, have worked marvels out of much fancy and but little knowledge. Mistake me not. I do not underestimate your worth. I but consider how much greater it had been had you received a full education."

"Well, this is indulgent, at least. You have heard the Council relents, and the playhouse buildings are not to be pulled down?"

"I had never expected otherwise. This vile incarceration will not last long. The State strikes blindly, like the thunder-stroke of Zeus. And yet the State is not blind, nor stupid, neither, though but yesterday it sent two spies in here, feigning to my fellow-prisoners and to make report on my conversation. But I denounced them for what they were. A poor device. The State will presently take note of my abilities, for I am a man of parts. I have done the State some service."

"So had Kit Marlowe."

Jonson took his meaning. "I spoke not of such employments as his. I have soldiered. I served as a volunteer in the Low Countries."

"Indeed. Crave your pardon, Master Jonson, but it would not surprise me if that experience proved more fertile for a maker of plays than hic haec hocs learned at school.

Jonson took this in good part. He plucked at his short beard and his small eyes were reflective as he answered: "Say you so? I had not considered it. Perchance I ought so to have considered it? And if the wars provide theme and substance, for I am a man of sharp observation, and find amusement in the conduct of my fellow creatures, each after his humour, then these days I spend in the Marshalsea, they also may not be wholly wasted."

"Even so. And depend upon it, we'll talk and consult with sundry to further your release, as best we may. I begin to turn to your own opinion, Master Jonson: London and the playhouse hath need of you."

The burly young man, for all his vanity, could not disguise his pleasure in this commendation.

When they were outside again, Drayton exclaimed: "That's a good quittance. The light of day and the clean air are welcome after such malodorous darkness. Come, Will, let's find wine to take the taste of prison air out of our throats. But why the dickens didst thou flatter this upsprung young fellow? He stands over-tall in his own esteem already."

"Nay, he's but putting on a brave front among dismal misfortunes. Would I believed my own spirit might stay so undaunted in the Marshalsea. Besides, I was an upsprung young fellow myself once, and not so long ago."

"But what hath he done? Had he a tally of books and plays behind him, his vaunts were easier to understand."

"Ay, when the work's done and praise given and taken, modesty's easy to wear. It is while a man feels his worth, his future, still pent in his own mind, not yet demonstrated to the world, that he must needs utter cock-crows at all his acquaintance."

"Thou understandest this Ben Jonson well," said Drayton. "And yet I'll swear, he believes he knows thee, mind and heart and soul, the better."

"That may be. And yet I like him for that he offers no easy flattery. He is an honest young man."

"I believe," Drayton conceded, "even he would be well pleased to hear that commendation from thy lips. Go to. We'll admit Ben Jonson to the worshipfull company of poets, penmen and make-plays, not for his writing, which is yet to be proved, but because Will Shakespeare, having seen him but once, and then in prison, declares him an honest man."

For Will Shakespeare, the days and the months racing to mark the completion of the century were never unoccupied. He acted no more, and was glad of it. Did destiny not call him to greater ends, he was confident he could show Burbage, Alleyn, Kemp, and the rest of them a skill and resource in acting, both tragic and comical, which would widen their eyes. He knew he was deemed but a competent player, and he had never been given a principal part, even in his own plays. That, he told himself, was because his energy was distracted, his mind, most of the time, set upon other business. But there: sufficient to be the poet of the age, and as he could not take the centre and front of the stage, he would quit it, and waste no regrets.

Burbage called ever for new plays, and whiles the play-house seasons lasted, with private performances at the Court and in great houses between times, Shakespeare was busy from morning to night. Such leisure as he found was called upon by his many friends for feasting, merry excursions and endless talk, comment and dispute. This new-comer, Ben Jonson, released now from the Marshalsea, was proving his ability to make good his vaunts. He was a rare companion, too, never lost for arguments and instances over the wine. His wit struck slow, like a great beetle-hammer, but hard. He would make his mark on the Town. Some there were astonished that Will Shakespeare should so freely welcome a rival: some muttered that as Lyly had given place to Marlowe, and Marlowe to Shakespeare, so might Shakespeare see himself supplanted by Jonson. But Ben and he could laugh together over such prophecies. "Hast a long start, Will," said Ben. "I'll give thee a hard run, and make thy lungs burst yet." Privately they knew themselves too different in purpose and in method to come into close competition.

Ben could never refrain from arguing, and yet his argument had point: perfection comes not so easy in art, and perchance that which is faultless beyond cavil may never

achieve high stature. This Ben would not admit, but he failed
to demonstrate perfection except in the ancients, and was
taken aback to be reminded that they too had been mortal
men. "Perfection," Will told him once, "hath something of
the stillness of death upon it. Error comes with the intake
of breath. And there is a beauty not prescribed in Aristotle,
nor in Seneca neither, sprung from error." But Ben had theories
and was resolved to shape his work by them. He was writing
a comedy to satirise the plentiful follies of mankind. He
called it ' Every Man In His Humour.' It had many merits,
although Shakespeare thought his young friend Ben saw
people mathematically, as this man a compound of one, two
and three qualities, and another made up from the fourth and
fifth qualities. Ben distilled the abstract essence of human
behaviour into its component parts, and then gave to each a
name and called upon a stage player to body it forth. Well,
every man must work with such tools as his workshop, his
mind, provided: and, though young Ben was never chary of
advice to others, Will Shakespeare would but smile and en-
courage him, and never speak his full mind.

His full mind was indeed a strange and uncharted world
to himself: small wonder that he could report such a tiny
portion of it to others in speech or even in his plays. His full
mind, ever complex and involute, grew secretly dark these
days: to let his introspections wander in it was to send a mole
burrowing into the deep, dark earth. His full mind was
shadowed now with thoughts of death. Since he had seen his
small son, coffined and pale-lipped, it was as if the knowledge
of death crept cold in his own flesh. And death was but one,
the conclusive—if it were conclusive—evil of evils, which by
its dread surcease at last gave respite to the turmoil of ambition, envy, lust, treachery and hatred. Keep innocency, the
scripture advised. But how to do it, in a world where men
plotted one against another, where war, under its swashing
front of gallantry, stalked intent on rapine, the making of
widows and orphans, the satiation of greed and vanity: a

world where lamed and blinded soldiers, used up in the wars, whined through the streets, begging bread, whiles fat captains (the like of that Oldcastle of his, rechristened Falstaff, but not so neat in wit) fed their guts, bullied and cheated? And the fat captains were but little lice in this lousy world, suffered to prosper in a small way whiles foolish great gentlemen, jewelled and rich in estate, set their fashionable wits to scheme which new bed they might crawl into the coming night: and wise great gentleman, only a few of them, all told, and not often in the news, held the domination of all and profited by the wars, the expeditions, the trades, and even the amours, they planned for others to perish in.

The world was magotty rotten, and doubtless would stink worse yet: and yet it was more complex than Ben Jonson dreamed on. Its evil, so vast in its expansion, could never be extracted, even as an idea for the mind to inspect. All was complexity and subtlety: not one man, not one action, one speech, not one phrase spoken by one man, could you select and say: "This is wholly evil." It occurred to him then that, though innocence was likely the sole privilege of children, and that perchance because they lack as yet the ability to do ill, it was possible to find here and there a deed or a word which was good and naught but good. And so, it might be, the devil had not the supreme dominion in the world. But his booty was rich enough.

Such considerations as these occupied the dark inward and abysm of his mind, and yet he was a happy man; a busy man; a man of much consequence in the playhouse world and honoured even in great houses; a man of many friendships. His brow was smooth, his eyes clear and calm, and he smiled readily. Nor would any guess the tenour of his privy thoughts from the plays he devised and saw staged that year. These were ' Much Ado About Nothing ' and ' As You Like It.' He invented the titles in contempt of himself, for these comedies danced in the light of the noonday sun, like wanton flies which have no care. He gave ' As You Like It ' a sylvan setting, in a forest that never was and never will be, though he called it, after his own Warwickshire woodlands, and after his mother's maiden name, Arden.

The origin and the centre of these plays was his lady, for whose love he had no longer any hope, to whose friendship he thus paid tribute, holding dear what he must needs anguish over because it was less than he desired. She was Beatrice in 'Much Ado', and he made Benedick address her outright as "my dear Lady Disdain." Benedick's protestation was his own, still enchanted even in resentment: "I stood like a man at a mark, with a whole army shooting at me. She speaks poniards, and every word stabs: if her breath were as terrible as her terminations, there were no living near her; she would infect to the north star." His lady, personated upon the stage by a boy-player who earned praise from those that could not guess the original, became more tender as Rosalind, still mischievous, but gentler in her mischief. This was because she had up-braided him for making Beatrice so sharp of tongue: useless to disguise in her presence whence he drew these heroines. "Your Beatrice," she had told him, "is little better than your nasty Shrew. And she raileth too hard and too oft against love. You make her say she would rather hear her dog bark than a man swear love to her. An you must put me on the stage, my friend, do me justice. I am sweeter-tongued and softer-hearted than that."

He admitted the impeachment, but, unrelenting, she added: "'Tis not love I demur to: only thy love, good Master Shakespeare."

Having dealt the wound, of course she must pour balm in it, and of course he must make amends in his next play, and so Rosalind, caparisoned like a man, had no doublet and hose in her disposition. Rosalind—this was a daydream desire with no correspondence in reality—was all compassion for her Orlando at first sight, feared for him in the wrestling match, and, being told from Celia that Orlando returned her love, babbled out eager questions: "What did he when thou sawest him? What said he? How looked he? Wherein went he? What makes he here? Did he ask for me? Where remains he? How parted he with thee, and when shalt thou see him again? Answer me in one word."

It was pretty, it was neat, it charmed and brought laughter in the playhouse: but it was not his lady's way with Will Shakespeare. He gave Rosalind a category of a lover's significant marks to speak—lean cheek, sunken eyes, neglected beard, ungartered hose, unbuttoned sleeves—as he remembered his lady enumerating them to Southampton's disfavour. Always he brought away from a meeting with her treasures of speech, to be remembered and shaped anew for these heroines of his who were all incomplete and faulty portraits of her. And in 'As You Like It' he made her, as Rosalind, speak in her own reproof, when Rosalind admonished Phebe, disdainful of her shepherd's devotion: "Down on your knees, And thank Heaven, fasting, for a good man's love." She smiled when she came to the playhouse and heard the words spoken on the stage. She understood, but was not moved to alter her heart towards him: although she said afterwards, when they had a moment to speak with each other, the rest of the company talking loud of sundry matters: "Friend! thou'rt marvellous patient with me. Better to loose thy wrath about mine ears, and so put me out of mind."

The great world was still unquiet, and the Court much perturbed by ill news from Ireland, for the rebels there grew hydra-headed, and as fast as they were put to the sword and their miserable hovels burned about their heads, they sprang up again in hordes. Sir Henry Bagnal marched a force out of Armagh to relieve a fort sorely beset, and it was put to rout in the bogland, more than half the men and fifteen captains slain or wounded, and the rest scattered. Such a disaster to English arms had not befallen since the Queen ascended the throne, and men said openly that Ireland might be writ off the roll of Her Majesty's dominions. Then Cecil, even Cecil, even the omnipotent Lord Burleigh, at last proved mortal, in his seventy-ninth year: the pall, the drums and the sad-mouthed bugles of his funeral procession made the young men of London to gape, for they had not seen or imagined such magnificent pomps; whiles they that were older in years marked it as another sign of the decline of a century ageing to its end, the last years of a period overblown. For in Spain King Philip, who had wedded Mary, sister to Elizabeth, and Queen before her, lay dying. It was said he kept in front of his fading eyes the leaden shirt in which his corse was to be encased, and that corse was putrefying ere the breath was out of it: the stench of his sores sickened even the physicians. Her great assistant dead, her ancient enemy dying, Elizabeth yet continued vigorous, keen-eyed under her wig.

In Burleigh's funeral retinue went red-beard Essex, and none could say whether the grief clouding his face and making him forgetful of his customary doffings, bowings and smilings to the populace were for dead Burleigh or for his own fortunes in eclipse. The Queen would have none of him, and still frowned at mention of his name. He was not permitted to show himself at Court. Nor was Southampton, his friend and henchman, in better favour. Southampton's desires had ceased their giddy whirlings at last, and fixed themselves upon one woman's face and form. She was Mistress Elizabeth Vernon, and cousin to my lord of Essex. Yet, though he stayed faithful, continence was not to Southampton's taste: scandal had found much employment, linking his name with that of Mistress Vernon, and now it was known she was big-bellied, seven months gone with child, and the Queen furious upon the matter. Next, all was open and to be freely spoken of. Southampton had returned, and wedded his mistress, whereat the Queen was in no way appeased. She commanded the new-made wife to be imprisoned in the Fleet, and Southampton, who had returned to Paris, to make all speed to London, on his allegiance, to hold himself at Her Majesty's disposal, but not to shew face at Court till he be bid.

And Ben Jonson was in dire trouble again. For one so

young he had an ill talent to find out mischief and embrace it. His play, ' Every Man In His Humour,' was completed and staged the September after his release from the Marshalsea, and made a success. His braggart Signior Bobadilla, whose courage wilted at prospect of the bastinado, was well-liked, and spoken of as first cousin to Shakespeare's Falstaff; some said he was more directly derived, as son from father. But Jonson, who had begun with Henslowe and Alleyn of the Admiral's men, was by them expected to continue in their service. Indeed, Alleyn looked to him to repair the defection of William Shakespeare, and to outshine him. Instead, Jonson must needs take his play to Burbage and the Lord Chamberlain's company, then making shift at the Curtain playhouse in Shoreditch, where who but Will Shakespeare was present to commend his talents ere ever the script was read. And so at the Curtain ' Every Man In His Humour ' was staged, and Burbage delighted to see its reception, and count the money taken.

Pleasure at the success of his new play swelled Ben Jonson's pride, and he went about returning smiles to smiling fortune, and commending himself for his wisdom in forsaking Alleyn and the Admiral's men for Burbage and the Chamberlain's. Alleyn was furious, and one of his players, Gabriel Spencer, who had been immured in the Marshalsea with Jonson, took it upon himself to prosecute the quarrel. He lay in wait as Jonson left the Curtain, gave him testy words, and in the up-shot challenged him to fight forthwith in the Hoxton Fields. Jonson, having soldiered in the Low Countries and multiplied his exploits there in words a many times since, durst not refuse. They fell upon each other, and Jonson (for which insufficiency he was afterwards much ashamed) found himself wielding a sword ten inches shorter than his adversary's: he soon was pinked in the arm. Haply Spencer had been content with this, but not Ben Jonson, for, swearing, as he later reported, most horribly, he renewed his attack and ran his enemy through the right side, leaving him dead on the grass.

He was apprehended, and brought to trial a month later,

very penitent and sober in mood by now, but, as ever, ready to justify himself and his actions with no lack of words. It was plain, however, that Spencer had taken the aggressive part, and the two swords, one long, one short, were put in as evidence. Ben was allowed to plead benefit of clergy, and so scaped with forfeiture of his goods, which at that time was a very small loss. Alleyn still inveighed against him, and, having heard of his step-father's trade, to which Ben had been unwillingly apprenticed and from which he had run off to the wars, would not refer to him but as "that bricklayer".

Meanwhile, Shakespeare expended money in order to benefit himself the more in the future. Already drawing part of the profits earned by the company, he now became a 'house-keeper', owner of a tenth share in a new playhouse, the Globe, which was substantially the old structure of The Theatre in Shoreditch. It was a strange, and, strictly regarded, a lawless venture in its origin, though not unjust. Dick Burbage's brother, Cuthbert, to whom old James Burbage had by his will left The Theatre, had come into conflict with Giles Allen, who owned the land whereon the playhouse stood. The lease, drawn up in 'seventy-six, provided that the building should continue as the property of James Burbage, his heirs, successors and assigns, upon condition that it be removed before the date of expiry. Giles Allen proved fair-spoken but a great dallier and putter-off of decisions. He promised much with his mouth, but had little mind to set pen to paper and sign his name. Depending upon his promises, Cuthbert Burbage allowed the lease to expire and when at last, in response to frequent requests, Allen had a new lease drafted, Cuthbert found its provisions intolerable. And in the face of his protests, Allen bade him go elsewhere an he thought he would be better convenienced.

Cuthbert consulted with his brother, Dick. The Lord Chamberlain's men were performing under disabilities, and with much complaining, at the Curtain, waiting upon such time as they could return to The Theatre, which they all regarded as their proper and rightful home. Now it seemed they could not have it again except upon such terms as would mulct them heavily of their profits. They cursed and complained. Their discussions began in the morning, abated for the duration of a performance, continued into the night, and were begun again next morning. Dick Burbage roundly called his brother a fool for letting the old lease run out before he had another signed and sealed, and Will Shakespeare had much ado in reconciling them.

The problem appeared to be barren of solution until Allen resolved it by greedily tempting their forbearance yet again. For Cuthbert came post-haste one evening to say he had a report, of dependable authority, to the effect that Allen proposed to tear down the timbers of The Theatre, stage, tiring-houses, galleries and all, and use or sell them to his own advantage, which he was entitled to do by warrant of the old expired lease. His soft-spoken promises to Cuthbert were not, in the view of the law, to be held against him to prevent this.

When they were weary of cursing, the Burbages, Shakespeare, Heminges, Phillips, Kemp and Pope at last came to a resolution: item, they would have a new playhouse, on the Bankside, hard by Henslowe's the Rose, where a garden now stood in Maiden Lane; item, it should be called the Globe; item, the money necessary for this venture should be found between them; item, a lease of the land should be taken forthwith, valid as from Christmas Day; item, the new playhouse should be for the greater part the old one, which was and always had been Burbage property.

Christmas was a season of hard frost, of winds that nipped inside the sleeves and set the flesh shivering and shrinking upon the bones. Two days later the sky darkened and snow fell heavy and soft all night, so that in the morning it lay everywhere some inches deep, and London woke to a rarer daylight, glittering back from the snow, and a silence in which the children's voices, shouting delight, rang pure and clear like bells. The city was transformed to new shapes, and the undisturbed snow revealed faint blue tints. Familiar colours were changed: against the snow the howling, unhappy seagulls looked grey: clumsy, splay-legged starlings became sooty black, and the speckled breasts of the thrushes shewed gold and green. The river was now quite frozen over, and the more venturous were already essaying to cross to the Middlesex bank afoot, trudging through the snow which lay, a long, thick carpet, over the ice. If the frost held, the gossips said, London would again see the grand spectacle of a fair, with booths and rings and shows in pavilions, pitched upon the frozen bosom of the Thames.

But Shakespeare and his partners had other affairs to turn their minds to. They mustered a party of ten, all girt and sworded, with Dick Burbage to command and one Peter Street, a master carpenter, to oversee the work. Besides these they had a considerable number of strong and resolute workmen, equipped with pikes and axes, which might be employed as well for offence as for labour. Burbage led the way to Shoreditch and the disused building erected by his father and named by him The Theatre. Asking leave of no man, and not announcing their purpose, they posted themselves around the playhouse, whiles the master carpenter proceeded to order the workmen to take down, using due care, the whole timber structure, walls, roofs, doors and fittings. The men's breaths steamed visible on the frosty air. As fast as the playhouse parts were stripped away, the carpenter set his several marks upon them, and they were loaded on to carts, chocked and chained against the snow, and drawn away to the Bankside.

The roofs came off: the walls were hauled down one by one: the tall proud playhouse diminished slowly to a few piles of timber in the snow. The strokes of hammers and axes, the sharp cracks of timbers wrenched away, sounded clear on the snow-chilled air. The men laughed and shouted to each other as they worked. And James Burbage's widow, mother of Cuthbert and Dick, looked on from an upper window, and smiled approval while her maid-servants below warmed ale for the labourers. The common sort, drawn thither by the commotion, gaped for awhile, and presently cheered; some of them were pleased to aid the loading of the carts, and some went off to haul on the wheels where the snow lay thickest or the road went uphill. Giles Allen did not appear, but several of his men came and protested loud, saying their master would seek redress at law: but they were intimidated as soon as the players put hand to sword-hilt. Night fell before the demolition was complete, and the last loads despatched. The workmen, marching off with their faces glowing red in the light of the pitched torches, sang Christmas songs as they went.

"It shall go hard with us," said Shakespeare, "if Allen hath recourse to law concerning this."

"Never fear," Dick Burbage replied.

"Thou'rt always confident. But right in justice is not always right in law."

Burbage laughed. "Even so. I put my trust in this, that Allen hates to part with a penny piece and the law is a great user up of monies. When he returns and finds the playhouse gone from his land, he will make much moan, and growl like a bear at a baiting. But we possess at last that which is ours by right, and I'll wager we hear no more of Allen. Thus begins another venture. Soon we shall see a new century, and a new life for thee, Will, and for me also."

A new century, thought Shakespeare: doth a man find a new spirit in his flesh when the tally of one hundred years is complete, and another begun? Doth the mind put on fresh thought at such an era, as the body is given new-bought garments for Eastertide? Or was it that, crossing foot into another century, a poet might at last find, explore, and report, that which had long been locked within him? Dick Burbage wanted new plays for the new Globe: whence they came, and how, he neither cared nor could understand. No matter: he should have them.

IN THE new Globe playhouse Master William Shakespeare had his own room, with his name painted on the door. It was one more sign of his importance, and it afforded him some of the privacy he now desired inordinately and beyond the measure needed for his writing. His comedy, ' What You Will ' (he had first intended to call it ' Twelfth Night ', and might yet restore that title: one name was as good as another) completed its first performance, and was as roundly acclaimed as any of its predecessors. The Londoners loved their Shakespeare, and, surfeiting on him, like Duke Orsino upon music the food of love, yet suffered no loss of appetite.

The play ended in a tumult, the assembly shouting and clapping hands to signify their approval, calling for the players to gather upon the stage again and again; and Shakespeare must show himself at the front of one of the lord's rooms in the lower gallery, and bow, and smile, and smile and bow, till he judged the moment of climax had come and so withdrew lest he overstay this gratifying acclamation. Thereafter, to the tiring-rooms where Burbage, still red-faced and buskinned as Sir Toby Belch, and the rest of the company, pressed round him, loud in gratulations, the while fashionable gentles came thronging in by twos and threes, eager to commend the players, and more eager to exchange courtesies with Master Shakespeare himself. A triumph so outstanding called for celebration, and the company forthwith began to plan a festival of wine and food and talk at the Falcon tavern nearby. Some young lords, anxious to be thought patrons of poetry at small expense, took up the project. Doubtless they would pay the reckoning. And as some of the players suspected that the host at the Falcon could make the chalk walk on the board to augment their debts, the lords might well pay for more than the night saw consumed. But Shakespeare, although he had made his Sir Toby reprove Malvolio for seeking to scant others of their cakes and ale, was by nature temperate: he knew that the evening would be boisterous with jests and songs, the Carman's Whistle, Friar Fox-Tail, Watkin's Ale, and such. Everyone would acclaim his fellows as delectable brave boys, till the night ended in drunkenness, sick or quarrelsome or maudlin; wherefore Will Shakespeare excused himself. His reasons for this abstention being demanded, he said he was in pain. Dick Burbage, who had heard him make this plea before, upon similar occasions, winked a heavy eyelid, but did not attempt to dissuade him.

And so, while the playhouse was still crowded and noisy, Shakespeare made for his own privy room, locked the door behind him, and sat in his chair to relish solitude and silence. He was weary in body and spirit, as always when a play, so long in the making, so troublesome in the presentation, was at last brought to display upon the stage. For a time his thoughts knocked clumsily against each other in shapeless disquiet: too many people had spoken too many words in his ear this past half-hour. But presently his mind smoothed into a retrospection: the chime and pulse of his own verses sounded again in his memory, and his lidded eyes recalled the bright sequences of scene after scene lately enacted upon the stage.

Always the embers of creation, still glowing in his mind, tempted him to deem his latest work his best, but this time, in ' Twelfth Night ', or ' What You Will ', a calmer judgement told him he had climbed to the summit: this was a comedy he would never better, were it only that in Viola he had at last crystalled the full perfection of his lady, and because— though neither the rabble nor the gilded lords so courteous would perceive it—this was a comedy for tears as well as for laughter. He had given them light-hearts aplenty; Mercutio, Beatrice and Benedick, Falstaff (but he died piteous), Nick

Bottom, Dogberry, Lance and Gobbo. Even here they had
Sir Toby Belch, Maria and Aguecheek. And perchance they
thought Malvolio wholly ridiculous? Perchance he was?
Malvolio had begun as that long-legged, stiff-faced steward
at Southampton House, who would not accept John Florio's
reproof. (Florio's Englishing of Montaigne's discourses proceeded apace, and made good reading: rich learning enriched
by belief withheld.) But the geniture of this Malvolio was
crossed by considerations of an imposter, one John Darrell,
lately brought to trial for his false claims to exorcise evil
spirits. From that, by inversion, Malvolio must be given
yellow hose and held to be mad, possessed, and so incarcerated
and mocked. But whether these misfortunes left him still a
proper target for scoffing was not so sure. Arnim, the new
clown who had replaced Will Kemp, and had a more delicate
wit, was ready, as Feste, to wring the observers' hearts, in
the prison scene, for pity: but the fellow who played Malvolio
had it not in his capacity to reverse his appeal. He roared out
from behind the bars like a stricken animal, like the boy im-
personating the calf and its killer behind a curtain in the old
heartless parlour game which Shakespeare could remember
playing long ago in Stratford to the delight of his boyhood
friends and the admiration of his elders. Malvolio was neither
fool nor victim: something of each, and not one nor the
other wholly. For a man who writes plays must something
invent, something abstract from older plays or books, and
something adapt to the forms, the dispositions and the voices
of the players in his company.

Will Kemp, Cavaliero Kemp as he loved to call himself,
had lately quarrelled with Burbage and quitted the company.
Always proud of his sprightly bearing and his lightsome heels,
he had undertaken (so report had it) to dance a morrice all the
way from London to Norwich, with his bells that he called
his trill-lillies, strapped between knee and ankle: all for a
wager or a vaunt. He would find it hard going on that road,
with the mud, thick and thin, wearying his thews. Kemp was

an excellent clown within his degree, but in his opinion of himself overweening. He held by the old clown's privilege of improvising his lines, which might serve for the jig at the end, but, interposed, lengthened the play, set the other players, waiting to take turn on the stage, in a fume of fury, and disordered the balance. Kemp's wit had outlived its freshness, as Burbage, standing upon no terms of courtesy (but he had been much provoked) did not hesitate to tell him. It went mechanically, dependent on pauses filled with a grin and a naughty rolling eye, and amendments to what was stated immediately before: as he would say a certain man had the port of a gentleman—but for his knees which gaped apart like those of a prick-louse tailor. It was easy to write speeches for Kemp, an the fellow would keep faith with the scrip given him. He must always improvise, however, and, asked to utter a word strange to his old-fashioned mind, he would complain to the groundlings against it as an unchristian foreigner in the language. And notably he lacked discretion, and presumed upon his privilege: he oft would call those that listened to him a pack of beetle-heads and clod-pates, which failed to amuse. He was a coarse fellow, and overfond of tippling and hanging about the bear-baitings. Not Burbage alone had suffered his insults, for he had, frequently in private and once openly (that once was more than sufficient) glanced at William Shakespeare himself under the base and detestable verbal guise of ' Shakerags.' Kemp was gone, and no call to waste pity upon him.

Because Kemp had left the Chamberlain's men, and Arnim promised to better him, Feste could be void of the rough and tumble of Gobbo and Touchstone, and to him could be left the conclusion of the new play, the singing of that song, without meaning but all sweet sadness:

> When that I was and a little tiny boy,
> With hey, ho, the wind and the rain;
> A foolish thing was but a toy,
> For the rain it raineth every day.

Only one part in this comedy had not been writ to fit the shape of a player's mind, and that was Viola. She was his last tribute, a catching-up and a firm knitting of a dear memory, already fading and intermingled with his own previous renderings, with Julia, Beatrice, Titania and Rosalind: for the lady who would not love Will Shakespeare had now found another to love, a country gentleman, and was gone to dwell in far-off Northumberland. For the last time she was named again for the stage, breeched and doubleted as he had seen her first, through a window-pane: and, for irony, given the line to speak: "Lady, you are the cruellest she alive." Out upon her: she had married, and gone to live in the foggy north. Better to love a dream than a woman who prefers another man and takes herself a hundred leagues away. Yet Viola was fair, the best of his word-begotten women, queen of them all. She lacked only the gay upspring of joy from the heart, if that were a lack.

His spirit was heavier now in his flesh, and his flesh not so young as it had been. The coming year would begin a new century, and make him thirty-six years old, at which age a man had passed beyond the midway of his utmost expectation; the green of life behind him; only the sere and yellow to come. At thirty-six a man who spoke of love, save as a diversion for younger men, went in fear lest he be called an old lecher and stand reproved for not conforming the ways of his mind to his failing flesh. At thirty-six experience was something tucked away, old memories to be conned over but not added to. All suddenly this dullness of the middle-age of man had come upon him. But a little while ago he consorted with young gaiety as an equal, sharing its jests and its reckless, make-shift philosophy: 'He who will not when he may, When he will he shall have nay.' Perchance of late years he had, all unawares, played the clown, and his companions, the young gentlemen of the Inns of Court, the Paul's men, and those who aped his own Mercutio, secretly stood aghast to see one of such ripe years skip in his mind and speech to emulate a colt? Perchance they bruited his behaviour among themselves, some shaking their heads for pity, and some laughing to see Will Shakespeare wear the motley of a youth he no longer possessed. At thirty-six a man should be grave; substantial; free from excess in all things; neither exalted by triumph nor abased by adversity; preserving his inward balance and decorum of face, gesture and speech, whatever joy or suffering fortune brought to him.

Even such a man as this he was resolved to be henceforward, and it should shew in his plays, too. This 'Twelfth Night' was comedy, but comedy freighted with sadness, with that awareness unsuspected by the young, awareness of the dread of death, of the last and all-consuming ordeal which is life's total and not-to-be-evaded inheritance. It was a play threaded upon songs, and songs older and wiser in accent than those, hitherto his favourites for tuneable delights, in 'A Midsummer Night's Dream.' "Come away, come away, death," Arnim in his cap and bells sang, his voice cracked and plaintive. Even "Oh mistress mine, where are you roaming?" flowered from melancholy rooted deep, not feigned and easy forgot as were the plaints of authentical young lovers. The comedy was gay as a man past the midway of life achieves gaiety, with death, disaster, and despair, doubtless remote but ever whispering in his ear, and drawing nearer. The comedy was a good comedy and good poetry too; but the poetry was melancholic in its music: like the strain commended by Orsino, it had a dying fall, intermittently sustained and voiced full at the end, in Arnim's song about the little boy and the wind and the rain.

What else could the world expect from a man no longer young, a man aware of the maggot of remorse in his brain, for that his son was dead, dead ere his stray-away father could make his intimate acquaintance? Hamnet was dead, his son, his only son, and grief for that would not be quiet in the mind. And now Burbage, careless, unheedful, intending no hurt, must needs renew the ache by fetching up from the company's box of oft-acted and half-forgotten scripts, this old play.

"Toss over these leaves, good Will," Burbage had said. "The fable is tragical and strong, but barbaric. It made some diversion years ago, and Tom Kyd furbished it again. The times are sombre: an thou couldst re-write, we might hit the taste of London town again."

Looking down at the tattered, yellowing manuscript Will had seen, writ large over the front page in the angular old English style, the title: 'The Revenge of Hamlet, Prince of Denmark.' The name Hamlet was but a variation of Hamnet, which he had given to his son to commemorate his friendship with Hamnet Sadler of Stratford. He had heard of this play long since, and forgotten it again. Still with his thoughts fixed upon his dead son, resentful and dismal, he began to turn over the pages. It was crude stuff and Kyd had done little to improve it: but the story had interest. A king murdered, and supplanted by his brother not only upon the throne but in the royal bed: his son (more proper that way, rather than a father surviving his heir) suspects the treachery, seeks evidence, and is visited by his father's ghost. Do men believe in ghosts these modern days? They say King James of Scotland, son of Mary Stuart beheaded at Fotheringay, puts credit in all manner of apparitions, and is hot to have witches burned by the hundred and thousand. And he is like to inherit the crown of England when the Queen dies, as at last she must!

This Danish Hamnet—no, his name must be Hamlet—is all distraught with grief and suspicion, and ill-uses the lady to whom his troth is pledged, Ofelia, so that she ends her life in a river. And that, byr Lady, was passing strange! For was there not, long since, another maid drowned in a river, and that river the Avon, when Will Shakespeare was but a fourteen-year-old? And was not her name Hamlet? Kate Hamlet? She went to fill a pail with water, and was taken dead from the river, under the willow boughs. A boy had planned to write her elegy.

She had come to his mind again when he stood by the Avon, on the Bank Croft, in the morning mists, a few minutes ere he made his first strange encounter with Mistress Anne Hathaway. Anne became his wife, and mother of little Hamnet, who was dead now, while Will Shakespeare lived and, for his profession's sake, conned an old play about a Danish Hamlet or Hamnet, and meditated upon the whirligigs of time as they fetched in their revenges.

Intrusive on his thoughts came a loud knocking on the door of his room. He shuddered, he knew not why, but would not attend. The playhouse must be empty now: the company gone to roister at the Falcon; the spectators dispersed. He was entitled to be left in peace.

Again a hand knocked on the door, a quick, sustained, peremptory rattling.

"Go away," he called.

There was a scuffle of feet, a whispering outside. The handle was turned this way and that.

Then again, came the loud knocking, the third assault, composed this time of three strokes, spaced apart, deliberate. Knock! Little Hamnet is dead. Knock! Poor Kate Hamlet is dead. Knock! And the Prince of Denmark is dead, long, long ago.

He fetched himself painfully out of the depths of his meditation, shifted back his chair from the table, and exclaimed: "Who's there? In the devil's name who's there?" Without waiting for answer, he went to the door and turned the key.

All this banging and clattering heralded no one more momentous than a smooth-faced and silver-haired man; plump; sumptuous in his apparel; one given to tittering at lewdness. Will Shakespeare knew him, from a dozen or more casual encounters, as Peter Fender, a merchant in trade with France and the Low Countries, and yet, being the sole inheritor of his father's riches, rather a gentleman of the newer sort, not welcomed among great nobles or at Court but conversant with all gossip and scandal alleged to emanate from high places.

"God ye gode'en, Master Shakespeare," said this visitor. "Do I intrude? Were you asleep?" He skipped over the threshold as he spoke, a heavily built man with thin shanks, neat wrists, white, well-tended fingers, too frolicsome in movement, voice and gesture to keep the dignity proper to his age and apparel. Within the room now, he looked round and exclaimed: "Nay, you cannot have been asleep, when I knocked. That straight-backed settle was made neither for slumber nor for love. And the table's for work. That's plain. This is an austere room, a puritan's room. Or a monk's cell, good Master Shakespeare. I talk too much? I always do. I know it, as I know all my faults. 'Tis my only virtue, that I know my faults. Nay, not quite my only virtue, for I have a kind heart, a heart that bleeds for others, as you shall presently discover. But first I must crave pardon for this disturbance."

"I had thought," said Shakespeare, "the playhouse empty by this time."

"Why so it is, but for you and me, and a serving-man or two. I waited, and waited long, for your appearance by the gate, and then when you did not come, I persuaded a fellow to shew the way to your room."

"I left word that my solitude should not be broken."

"Now you are wrathful? And I am the cause of it?"

With mingled anxiety and delight Peter Fender stood swaying his body, his hands twisting tight over each other, his little eyes in his plump face peering now at Shakespeare, now away, then back again. "Tis true, I undid your preparations for peace with a small expenditure of money. In brief, I bribed my way to the door of your room. I was presumptuous. I said to myself: Peter I said, Master Shakespeare is alone in his room. Were it any other man, one might suspect that his loneliness included a woman. But not Master Shakespeare, whose fame is sweet on everyone's mouth, who keeps nor mistress nor drab. If he be alone, Peter Fender, I said, haply he is at work? And yet, I said again: To-day saw the first performance of his new comedy—and 'tis a pretty piece, good Master Shakespeare, a pretty piece: 'twill storm the town. To resume, I said also to myself, in reproof: To-day it cannot be that he works, with new laurels but freshly set on his brow. Therefore I overcame timidity, and, by way of a little harmless bribe, made my way hither."

Shakespeare's anger, sprung from jangled nerves, was dissolved by now. His furies were rare and brief, always apt to be diverted by some new imagination stirring in his mind; and this fat-bodied, lively-legged Peter Fender was rich and strange in his loquacity, grotesque as he maypole-danced in words round the purpose of this his visit. In the presence of such as avoided the stamps of common usage in their behaviour, were they villainous as Beelzebub himself, Will Shakespeare must always be softened, smiling, secretly observant, and grateful for what he could see and hear and so treasure for his own use.

"I was at work, Master Fender," he said now. "But not on paper."

"What? Another piece afoot already? Thy mind, a superb mind, a mind in a thousand, in ten thousand, nay, in a million, already conceives and feels the first pangs of travail? And I come blunder-footed to distract you? Truly I am sorry for it."

"There's naught to repent. I had come to such a pass I doubt I could do more this day. The mind will work at no man's bidding, but when the mood takes it."

"Which means you are set to depart?"

Shakespeare nodded.

"Excellent, excellent! Now let me forestall your excuses. You were invited by the company and sundry young nobles to a feast of celebration, and you refused? But you refused not because you were sworn to another engagement? You said you were sick? Ask not how I came by these informations. I confess I am a parlous corrupter of servants when I have a purpose in hand. You said you were sick, Master Shakespeare, but now you admit you have been at work since: moreover, my own eyes, delighting in your manly and noble countenance, tell me that you are not sick. Therefore, come dine with me forthwith?"

"Why, this is kind, good Master Fender, but——"

"But me no buts. I am not so thoughtless as I sound. Well I know you are weary after such a day, and I do not purpose to confront you with a great company. I will be honest. I should magnify myself, and boast it everywhere, an I could invite my friends to sit at my table with the famed Master Shakespeare: but that is too much. I offer you a simple supper, and yet 'tis well-cooked and nicely furnished, conveyance thither and back to your lodging afterwards—the coach waits even now—and the quiet society of myself and my niece. She is but a child yet, and when we have supped, an it please you, she shall entertain us upon the virginals. The music shall soothe your weariness. There's the project. Is it to your mood?"

A comedical fellow this, thought Shakespeare, to spill such a deal of words, to corrupt serving men, and to come knocking upon a door like a Constable seeking a murderer, and all that he might invite a man to supper. But Peter Fender, lifting his chin high above his lawn ruff the better to scratch his fat throat with a pointed finger nail, and glancing entreatingly between scratches, was too rich in his unaware absurdity to be refused.

As soon as the poet nodded, Fender acclaimed him, cried that he was ever a gracious gentleman, and now they must make speed. With that, he bustled his guest out of the room.

The coach jolted them over cobble stones and ruts, led them across the plank pathway of London bridge, with the traitors' heads on the ends of the poles frised like gargoyles against the star-clustered sky, and so to a house in Gracious Street. It was something less than a mansion but large, comfortable, and, as presently appeared, well appointed. Shakespeare's host drew back with a bow and a flourished arm to yield precedence, and then skipped ahead, talking rapidly the while of his new tapestries from Ypres, to lead the way to a room, plentifully lighted with tallow candles set in bronze coronas suspended from the ceiling. Here a table was already spread and set for supper.

"We'll fall to within a few minutes," he promised. "Meanwhile, a little wine? Sack? Canaries? Claret?"

Politely Shakespeare refused. He had now fallen to an inward speculation. He was come here upon a whim, for wantoness of purpose and to hear more of this Peter Fender's discourses: but why had the man invited him? For the pure gratification of being able to boast tomorrow that Will Shakespeare had sat to table in his house? There were such hosts, but as Fender himself, a fellow subtle in his foolishness, had indicated, a man whose hospitality was designed to further his own prestige would have gathered a company together. Haply Fender, hearing that the Lord Chamberlain's players prospered, and Shakespeare with them, planned to induce him to put monies into some enterprise? If the wind blew in that quarter, it would blow in vain. Yet that could not be the reason: Fender, by reputation, and the size and furnishing of this house bespoke it, was a substantial merchant and not like to be interested in small investments. Moreover, if gossip spoke truth, he was a second generation man, apt to leave the conduct of his affairs to others and to spend his time and money in the pursuits of a gentleman. Perchance it was all for pure devotion? Perchance he did indeed so love the plays of Will Shakespeare that to eat with him and talk with him was an honour?

"I cannot serve you on gold plate," said Fender now, "such as you are accustomed to in the houses of the great lords, your patrons and friends."

"I have no patron."

"No offence, no offence in the world intended, Master Shakespeare. Doubtless I have been misinformed concerning my lord of Southampton."

"I was in his debt once. He hath been repaid long since. But continue. My interruption was unmannerly."

"Not so. Now what was I saying? Ah, yes. You will not sup off silver or gold tonight, but I have something very dainty to shew you. Ware from Delft, in the Low Countries, and ornamented most exquisitely."

"I shall examine it with care."

"And here it comes."

Two serving women brought in a roasted shoulder of mutton, spiced and aromatically dressed with sauces, and smaller dishes of stewed veal and pigs' petty toes, garnished with beans and carrots and minced cabbage.

"My niece is late," said Peter Fender. "'Tis a monstrous vexation. Women, women! For ever fidgeting about their toilet, a hair to be slid into place here, a ribbon gone astray there. Yet we must needs forgive them."

"She begins to prink at an early age." Then, seeing his host's round face broaden into an almost perfect circle of astonishment, Shakespeare added: "You said she was a child."

"Why, indeed, and so she is. But that's a manner of speaking. Still in the heyday of her blood. Yet she hath been married this five years. Nay, fear not. I keep my word. You and she and I: there shall be no more. I would not inflict her husband on you. Is a good man of business, and great in his revenues, but otherwise a paltry fellow. Greyer than I am, and shrunken with it. Time was when he was capon fat, but a sickness reduced him. Skin and bones, and a constant cough to rattle them. His throat bobs like an apple in the ale whenever he speaks. And he walks lame. A paltry fellow."

"Yet he may be offended, surely, not to be asked to keep his wife company? Or is it that he resides out of London, and his wife, your niece, visits your home awhile?"

"Nay, he lives but round the corner, and she with him. But he travels much, seeking trade, and when he's from home he entrusts his wife to her uncle's care. She is young and comely, and he's jealous. That's an old story. But where is she now? This is intolerable. She shall beg your pardon when she comes. And you will forgive her. Ah, but you will! She's a sweet wench, and dainty: Helena, that Faustus longed for, was a dish-clout to her. There are men aplenty would give an eye to change places with her husband."

"Now fie, good uncle. This is naughty talk."

Turning swiftly, Shakespeare saw a serving maid returned, carrying branched candlesticks of silver, broad based: over her shoulder, in the open doorway, a brown-skinned young woman stared at him with merry eyes. She had a wide mouth, widely smiling. As the servant moved away, to set the candlesticks on the table (all was in the newest fashion here), he saw swiftly that Fender's niece was black-haired. Yet he had spoken truly: she was comely; somewhat tall; somewhat broad in the shoulder in her crimson velvet gown, gold-laced; and she held herself supple and poised.

"I was but promising to chide thee, niece, for this delay. Master Shakespeare is an-hungered, and not customed to be kept waiting."

"Then I am sorry for it, sir, if the fault be mine."

She swept her gown wide as she sank in a curtsey, but her eyes mocked his.

"I am glad to make your acquaintance, Mistress—I fear me your uncle hath not told me your name."

"It seems he hath told you other things concerning me, less to the point, and, I daresay, unflattering."

"Nay, nay," cried Peter Fender. "That's a lie. I ever speak well of thee, sweet Nell, as thou knowest."

"There, sir," she said to Shakespeare, "you have heard my uncle use my name. Nell. That's for Helen, as haply you may have heard elsewhere."

"But I may not make so bold upon our first acquaintance. I intended to ask"—he paused to imply the reproof—"your husband's name."

"Tush," said Peter Fender. "Her husband's not here. He's in Milan. His name does not matter. Call her Nell, or if you jib at that, Helen will do. She'll not wince at it. You would not think it now, but she hath been in a flutter ever since I told her I might be fortunate enough to bring the famed Master Shakespeare home with me. Why, at mention of your name, sir, she fetched her breath as short as a new-ta'en sparrow. 'Tis a pretty villain."

"You would make me to blush, uncle, were I not certain Master Shakespeare knows how to interpret these your idle and false exaggerations."

"Ah, she's the prettier when she blushes."

"But now I am hungry. Let us sit and eat."

The discourse for some time was all with Fender, whose volubility was not incommoded by the pigs' toes and aromatic mutton he fed himself in rapid fingerfuls. He commended to his guest especially the novel vegetables, skinned and boiled, known as virginians. They cost much: two shillings a pound. But even more by their flavour were they to be distinguished from the similar, but now not uncommon, potatoes, which were more properly to be called sweet yams. Both, said the host, smiling and rolling his eyes, provoked to venery. He described, to flatter his guest and instruct his niece, the whole of the new comedy first performed in public that day, and Mistress Nell declared she must look out her mask and be escorted to the playhouse at the first opportunity.

Shakespeare took pains to be courteous, but, watching her covertly, reckoned her not to his taste. He had never cared for dark women, and this Mistress Nell had hair black as a raven's feather, so black that the candlelight discovered blue tints in it, as well as gold. Her brows were heavy, and black, almost meeting over her nose, which was passably neat. Even her eyes were not as he had imagined, dark brown, but black: bright, quick, as ready to smile as her wide scarlet mouth: but black. Her skin was brown as a hill stream in an autumnal spate. He did not admire such a dark-visaged comeliness: had never done so, and never would, and that not merely because the fashion was all for gold and corn-yellow hair. Besides, the wench was more than a thought too free in her manner: a woman need not be cribbed close in modesty, looking on every man she met as a Tarquin, but there was a trespass mark at the other extreme, and this dark woman exceeded bounds there. The young wives of old merchants were, by proverb, sportive: yet it was odd to see this one, guarded by a doting uncle, shooting her black glances and parading her pretty ways; she ate daintily but without the birdlike pickings and dartings which destroyed Peter Fender's dignity.

When the oranges were served, with Naples biscuits and marchpane, she begged to be excused, saying she would join them presently in the withdrawing room. No sooner was the door closed behind her than her uncle turned to his guest and demanded: "Now tell me, in honesty, is she not well-favoured?"

"You have not overpraised her."

"Say you so? That's good judgement. It warms me to hear that. They that cry down dark women have not seen my pretty Nell. A toothsome morsel. Mine own hair was black when I was younger, but I never had her eyes. It comes from my mother's side. We are Welsh in origin—like the Queen. But black, not red. Nor do we run to untimely virginity in our family. Black hair and hot blood. 'Tis a pleasing combination."

Now what sort of an uncle was this? Had he provided coach and supper and this privacy in order to pimp for his ebon-haired niece? But it would not make logic, not even chop-logic. This Peter Fender, and his niece also, to judge from her gown and her pearls, stood in no need of money. Then why the devil was the man commending her charms like an old bawd in Shoreditch, and announcing, in all but the blank, bare words, that her husband did not satisfy her abed?

Presently this curious host, goatish, it seemed, not in his own stead but vicariously for others, goatish even in the little skips and starts of his gait, indicated the way to the withdrawing room, which he called the long gallery. A gallery it was, not so large as in a great house, but balustraded with carved oak, and the walls panelled where they were not hung with the new Ypres tapestries. The designs worked upon these tapestries were, as might have been expected, amorous: Jupiter and Semele; Eros and Psyche; Venus and Mars; and again, Venus with Adonis—"as in your own verses, Master Shakespeare."

"Verses I have forgot long since," the poet declared, bluff and defensive.

Mistress Nell awaited them, sitting upon the silk cushions of one of the new fangled daybeds, a kind of extended seat with panelled ends leaning outwards, and long enough for three people to sit upon side by side or for one to recline at full length. Peter Fender conducted Shakespeare to this daybed and would have him admire the texture of the silk, the embroidery of the cushions, and the wool-filled pallet which was stretched from end to end.

"Some," he said, "make an outcry against daybeds, and declare we shall all be rotted with luxury. For my part, I prefer to be comfortable, and if our forebears sat stiff-backed against straight wood, the worse for them. As for Nell, she's a dove in the nest: she coos, of a verity she coos as she sinks upon the cushions. But rest you here and try the comfort of it for yourself."

A pimp, a bawd, a Pandarus of modern times, exclaimed Shakespeare's unspoken thoughts, watchful and suspicious. But before he could find an excuse and utter it, Mistress Nell stood up.

"Good nuncle," she said, "hast no eyes? Canst not see Master Shakespeare is bashful? But fear not, sir. The daybed is for your sole occupation. Beyond the name, there's naught about it to attaint the strictest virtue. See, I go to play the virginals. You may rest here alone, and listen or not as you please."

So she was not all forthcoming? She was not so obtuse that she did not mark the displeasure her uncle's smooth, chuckling persuasions aroused in him? He liked her better as she was now, with her full lips compressed, and a tint of red, natural red, showing in the brown over her cheek bones. Perchance his mind was foul (having produced much bawdry for the groundlings) and had misinterpreted what was no more than an easy Welsh hospitality?

Fender seated himself upon a cross-chair, built like a double-X: the fashion for them was just reviving after a century's disuse. "You favour music," he said. "I am sure of that, for you make such use of it in your plays, and include such loving and knowledgeable allusions."

"Music delights me," Shakespeare admitted. "But I cannot make it myself, with voice or instrument. Your niece will pleasure me greatly an she will play."

"There, pretty Nell. Do you hear? And pleasure it shall be, I promise you, sir. Nell hath a sweet voice, small but sweet. Not shrill neither: you shall hear. And she is wondrous skilful on the virginals."

She opened the instrument—it was of fine rosewood—and disclosed the keyboard with its row of polished jacks. Then she sat to the stool, drew it closer, spread her gown, and without nervousness or indecision began to play. Music was ever the surest way to bend Will Shakespeare to a compliant mood, and this was daintily, truly, and cunningly rendered. The melodies, gay and sad, ran soothingly through his mind as he lay back against the cushions and, holding himself at ease but very still, moved only his head so that, as in a dream, he noted the fine furnishing of this room; the two buffets, shelved and cupboarded, one of fine walnut wood, and one of ebony inlaid with silver; the panels and the tapestries; the oak presses; the chairs with hardly a stool among them; and all the cushions of silk. Truly this Peter Fender was a substantial fellow, a man of rich revenues! Presently, as he listened and recognised the dancing impetus of ' The Countess of Westmoreland's Delight ', he fell to watching the keyboard, and the slender brown fingers of Mistress Nell as they leaped and dropped, tickled and struck, and poised and struck again, upon the nimble jacks. Then he started as she began a new tune, and sang it in a voice full and clear, so deep as almost to be harsh, but not displeasing for that. The song was his own: 'It was a lover and his lass' from 'As you Like It.' When she had finished, she turned at last and, seeing him smiling, smiled back. Almost she would be beautiful, were she not black of hair and brow and eye.

But black she was, and no remedy for it. He thanked her, and declared he must go. Peter Fender, his legs jigging, his hands waving, protested in many words, the while his niece sat, turned upon her stool, and watched.

"Forgive me," said Shakespeare. "I have had an arduous day at the playhouse. 'Tis ever so upon a first performance, and I am full weary now. I offer a thousand thanks, but go I must."

Whereupon Fender became solicitous, and blamed himself, and then, glancing first at his niece and next at his guest, declared he would away to send for the coach to bear Master Shakespeare home.

Master Shakespeare nodded his head, murmured thanks, and, when his host was gone, could not prevent a yawn. Turning, he saw Mistress Nell regarding him.

"I am unmannerly beyond pardon," he exclaimed.

"No. The offence is with us. This was a most cruel hospitality my uncle forced upon you."

"I have ill repaid the entertainment. Forgive me now, good madam. Another time, when I am not consumed with sleep, I'll better deserve your kindness."

She made no reply to this, sitting with her black head cast down, unmoving, while second after long second ached by. But at last she said, as if out of this meditation she had decided a problem: "We must meet again. Or do you not wish it, sir?"

His vision of her as she sat before him, hands folded and eyes, widely opened now, turned full upon him, was blurred and unstable, for his mind was aswim with oncoming sleep and he rocked on his feet as he stood.

Reluctantly, very slowly, as if the words were charged with vast, indefinable purport, he answered: "Yes, it is what I would wish."

"You may call upon me here, and be safe in my uncle's discretion. Or you may send messages here. I shall receive them swift and safe." This she told him in a whisper, rough-voiced and sibilant, fetched all upon a single quick breath. So had Peter Fender spoke of her: "like a new ta'en sparrow." Or was it a sparrow-hawk, taking, not taken? No matter. She was staring at him again, and, jerking his body out of its lethargy, he asked sharply: "Why do you regard me so close and fierce? Such talents as I possess do not shew in my appearance."

"I have seen poets worse favoured."

"And younger, I doubt not?"

She mocked him with a laugh. "Younger too, and liked them no better for that. You are not old, Master Shakespeare. An you fancy you are old, I'll prove the error yet. I find you a proper man—to look at."

Her uncle came back, walking trippingly, to say the coach was waiting at the door. He glanced at them both, merrily and shrewdly, and rubbed his hands together.

"A pretty couple, i' faith. A pair of turtle doves. Nay, heed not my idle words. Leave all to time. Time is a great contriver of opportunities. Time will bring all desires to pass."

Sleepily Will Shakespeare bent over a brown hand, and kissed it, and so away.

DAY AFTER day went by and still he did not visit Peter Fender's house in Gracious Street, or as some called it, Gracechurch Street. Nor did he send messages there. When he woke, late, heavy eyed, despondent, on the morning after his first and only visit, he thought of Fender and the dark woman his niece, and concluded that he misliked them both. They thrust at a man too eagerly with their proffers of hospitality and friendship. He remembered that Mistress Nell, left alone with him for a few minutes, had made some sort of assignation. A hot wench, and some would deem her comely. More coming than comely. A foolish wench to appoint encounters with a man turned by sleep into a veritable staggering bob, a mooncalf of a man with falling shutters for eyelids. She could do better for herself than that. As for Will Shakespeare, an he sought a bedfellow, it would not be a merchant's wife with a roving eye and an ailing husband: and her hair should not be black. True, one lady had disdained him year by year, and then married and gone to suckle fools in the north country. But there were others, just as authentical ladies, with amber hair, honey hair, corn-gold hair, and Will Shakespeare, gentleman, with arms lawfully borne, need not go in lack of a mistress—save that it was his pleasure to do so.

Having thus avoided Gracious Street for a se'enight, and having put black Nell and that skipping pandar, her uncle, out of mind, he was astonished to find himself trembling one evening when, as he neared his lodging, he encountered a woman in a long cloak and, as she came under the light of a bracket lamp, saw the brown face and bright black eyes of Mistress Nell.

He stopped, doffed his hat, and bowed.

"Why," she exclaimed. "'Tis Master Shakespeare. What do you here?"

"A question easily answered. I lodge yonder. But what brings you to this part of the city, good madam, and alone?"

She answered in some confusion, breathing quickly and making swift amendments: "Why, nothing, Master Shakespeare. At least, I have been visiting a friend, a woman friend. Rather, I was about to make such a visit. But 'tis over late now. I must home."

She was a poor dissembler, he thought, and mismanaged her lies. Doubtless she was abroad upon some gallant occasion, and lingered even now for her lover's coming. He smiled at her, gently contemptuous, and then he remembered that this was the woman who, in her uncle's house, had appointed for him amorously to visit her. True, he had not come, but if the wench must pledge herself unasked to Will Shakespeare, she should keep faith. His lips set tight; his eyes grew sharp, observing her unease, the flutterings of her hands under the cloak, the way she glanced this way and that as she stood facing him. When he spoke, his voice was sharp with jealousy: "Good mistress, you must not travel the streets alone. You will surely encounter some offence. With your leave, I shall be your escort."

"No, thank you, sir. No, indeed. It is kind of you, but I shall be quite safe."

"Alone? Perchance you do not expect to be alone for long?"

"I do not take your meaning, Master Shakespeare."

"I think you do. But no matter. I will conduct you forthwith to your husband's house."

"My husband is still in foreign parts."

"Foolish man."

"Why so?"

"To leave his wife without escort, and with all these dark and dangerous streets to traverse."

"But I am not without escort now," she objected. "Master Shakespeare, I had it in mind that you and I were to have extended our acquaintance? Why did you not come nor send a messenger?"

"Madam, that same evening I parted from you, I was so overborne by sleep I knew not what I did or said."

Clinging to his arm as they went down the centre way of the roads, keeping clear of the dark alley entrances and the shadows thrown by the eaves, she glanced up at him, her eyes shrewd and bright under the hood of her cloak. "But you remembered," she said, "the next morning?"

"Not a word."

"You speak lies."

He felt no anger at this accusation. His laugh admitted its truth.

"Then why did you not come?" she pressed him.

He shrucked his shoulders. "Why does the wind blow now in the east, now in the southern quarter? I did not come —very well, if you must have a reason, I'll be blunt. It is because I like not dark women."

It was she who laughed now. "The reason is insufficient. Until thou'st set teeth to the fruit, canst not guess the taste. Besides, I have seen that in thine eyes makes nonsense of this calumny against dark women. Besides, again, there is only one dark woman in question, sirrah."

"And only one man for her?"

"Only one man."

"Wherefore, then, did I find thee unaccompanied in the street, hard by my own lodging, cloaked and waiting?"

She would not stop laughing then, rocking against him as she matched her shorter steps with his, until he halted suddenly, pulled her round to face him, and putting both hands on her arms above her elbows, shook her bodily.

"Enough, enough," she cried at last. "My hood is down, and all my hair is in disarray."

"An I set thee free, wilt tell the truth? All the truth?"

She nodded, still with laughter in her eyes and on her lips.

"Then here's the question. For whom wast waiting when I found thee?"

"For a man."

"Ay, but for what man?"

"For thee, Will Shakespeare."

Startled and angry, he stepped back from her.

"The truth was asked: the truth is given," she said. "Would'st not come to me: therefore I lay in wait, as thou saidst thyself, hard by thy lodging."

"Ay, in wait for another man. Else wherefore this discomposed air, these tremblings, these starting eyes, when I offered to bear thee company?"

She laughed. "For to deceive and for to rouse thy jealousy, in which I have been successful. Nor was I unsafe. My uncle waited round the corner. He will be home ahead of us now, preparing supper."

"What manner of wench art thou?" Shakespeare demanded.

"Why, female, like another."

"But wherefore doth the choice fall on me?"

Mischievously she beckoned him close to her again. "Hither. Bend thine ear and I will answer that question with a whisper. Wherefore do I desire thy company, good Will? That's what thou would'st know? Harken carefully, then, for I am not shameless, and this is strict between thee and me. The answer is—lust."

In this avowal he perceived something superb. Only bawds, and common punks among women confessed openly to desire, and their speech was the filthiest cant of the stews. But this Mistress Nell, black avised though she be, desired a man and was not to be turned from her desire by the considerations of modesty. He recognised the venturous courage of her declaration, and saluted it: in the open street, lighted only by the bracket lamps fixed to the walls and the glow spilled from windowpanes, he put his arms round her for the first time and his mouth to hers. Her lips were warm and damp, and, first yielding to his, came back responsive and invading to renew the kiss.

Short of the consummation, which would surely follow at no tedious interval, he had now transformed his state and was become a man with a kind mistress, apt and willing to fall upon her back when requested. If not a mistress, a doxy, then. In a mistress fidelity was looked for while the affair lasted. But this berry-brown, sloe-eyed Nell gave her secret away in that kiss: it was manning she needed, and if one were not there to fill the breach, another would serve. She would provide sport awhile. She asked no more, and would get no more.

If this venture were not so clean as the fancies with which Will Shakespeare had garlanded the public reputation of love, what would you? It is not in the nature of a man to remain constant to a wife older than himself, a mere memory of a wife far away in Stratford: or even to the memory of a mistress who never gave him so much as her lips, and had since wed another. Not that this was his first unchastity: only by comparison with other men was his record this ten years fresh and pure. Yet he was uncertain this Nell would prove a wench to be forgot by morning. What she had begun with that kiss was like to astound him yet. The more he strove to persuade himself he was a cold and finical gallant, intent upon the pleasure of an idle encounter, the more his mind was filled with apprehensions.

As they made their way by Bishopsgate to Gracious Street, he told himself it were unworthy to squander the word love on this hot-lipped, waggle-tailed doxy: she was to be put to use and, being enjoyed, she found there her sufficient reward. Well then, upon that understanding he could deal with her, and she should not disturb or distress any part of his life that he valued. If there were aught about her not to be compassed by a plain, round word, if there were anything to bring him to perturbation, it could only be the presence of the hovering, hand-rubbing, benevolent uncle. A wife with a disposition to creep between other sheets than her husband's was nothing untoward: but a wife with a wealthy uncle to play pandar for her, such was a rare commodity. Why the devil did not Peter Fender, an he were lecherous, busy himself with his own amours? It confounded nature that a man should be anxious to preside over the bedding, the illicit bedding, of his own sister's daughter? 'Twas but half a step from that to incest. The plague take Peter Fender and his smiles. A man may smile and smile and be a villain. But wherein did Fender stand to profit? What did he hope to gain? What did Nell hope to gain? Why, naught but pleasure: the whore's delight, and the satisfaction felt by him who, all for wantoness, brings clients to her bed. Featly answered. But what did Will Shakespeare hope to gain, walking back now to the house in Gracious Street? Why, pleasure also! For pleasure the cock crows, the lion roars, the stag lowers his antlers to the fight, and Will Shakespeare, most deject and wretched of poets, trots along in rut, all eager to bed with his new black doxy.

Pandarus awaited them, a-smile and a-bob. Pandarus supped with them, and talked of this and that, while his eyes slid over their faces: sometimes he patted his niece on the hand, and giggled to himself. Pandarus pressed hippocras upon his guest, good Master Shakespeare, declaring that the wine was not oversweetened, and spiced to make the blood dance. Pandarus declared he must go abroad in the night, to visit a friend, but he doubted not they would forgive his absence and find suitable employment for their time. Detecting Nell trilling a little sigh, he wagged a plump forefinger at her: "See how impatient it is, the naughty, pretty creature. Cannot wait for nuncle to be gone. But fear not. This ho-ho-ho will speedily change to ha-ha-ha." He intoned the ejaculations wickedly, mimicking first the langorous plaint of a damsel sick with love, and then the panting ecstasy of a woman possessed and satisfied by her lover. It was obscene. Will Shakespeare, his mind hot and confused with wine, desired to hate this Peter Fender: but he could only sit at table, and smile, and watch the fat rogue depart.

A maidservant came to clear the soiled dishes, and when they moved away, Shakespeare suggested that his hostess might make music again upon the virginals. She gave him no answer, but put her hand in his, and drew him through the long gallery, first to the right, and then to the left; up a stair; left again; and so into a room hung with painted cloths around the walls, softly carpeted, and furnished principally with a four-post bed, valanced and curtained with green embroidered silks.

"Wait here," she whispered. "I'll fetch candles."

"What need?" he asked, and made the two words carry a freight of importunate meaning.

She laughed as she answered: "Thou shalt see. I am proud and fear not the light."

As soon as she was gone, he chilled to a mood of fear and disgust, wondering at himself that he stood here, in a dark wanton's dark bedroom, waiting to begin a sordid encounter and mock all the high canticles of love he had cherished in dreams and celebrated in verses. Was it for this he had quitted wife and children in Stratford? Had he given five years of chaste devotion to his Lady and Scarlet and White, breaking up his heart in words and receiving not so much as a kiss for reward, in order to yield himself to this brown-fleshed Nell, with a pimping uncle who, like enough, was listening and chuckling in the next room? But the thought of those five long years enraged him now. His lady prized only his mind: she would keep him like a hived bee, for the honey yield of his poetry. She would not have him as other women desire their men, body to body abed. She would make of him an eunuch, a singing bird for her diversion. If that be the way of it, let her endure a lesson. What she turned from, another woman would gladly receive. Doubtless Nell cared nothing for his poetry, but she would joy to take service of his body. Call it lust or call it love, heap epithets upon it, as ignoble, degrading, nasty, infect with all the vices: such as it was, here was a venture ready to his hand. He had gone womanless too long. Now he would prove himself. He would not allow there was any misery in his mood. All seemed illusion except the fever in his blood and next, a moment later, the small sound beyond the door which set his heart in tumult. He heard the stiff rustle of her farthingale and then, with the candle flames lighting her face from below, making the brown all golden and fantasticating the forms of her features with upward shadows, Nell came towards him, her chopine shoes sibilating through the rushes strewn on the floor.

"Thou'rt trembling," she cried. "Art cold?"

"Nay, but"—he knew not why the words came tumbling unguarded from his tongue—"Nell, I must tell thee: for five years I have lived chaste."

"But why?"

"I am a poet."

Seeing she did not understand, he went on: "I earn my bread and my reputation out of the fancies of my mind. All that is Will Shakespeare to the world must be wrested out of my imagination. My mind must ever be kept toiling."

"Is this to say thou'rt craven? Dost not desire me?"

"Surely I do."

"Then what's amiss?"

"There was another woman," he explained.

"Still less a reason to live like an eunuch."

"She was not of thy sort, Nell."

"Is that thy way of calling me a whore?"

"Nay, take no offence."

"But tell me about this woman, Will. Didst love her very deep? Very sore? Dost love her even now?"

"Nay. I honour her, and always shall. But love—she never gave me so much as her lips to kiss."

"What, in five years? The miserly jade. And all that time thou'st lived chaste for her sake? Is this thy story, Will?"

"'Twill serve as a summary. But I have no complaint against this lady. That must be understood."

"What's her name?"

"Wouldst be pleased if I gave thy name to another?"

"Well answered. But how goes this thy explanation?"

He peered close at her serious face, and then added: "I

tremble because five years may have disordered my ability. Yet needst have no fear I am less than a man. I have married a wife and fathered children."

"Say you so? Yet I have heard of cuckolds, and willing cuckolds, to boot."

Quicker than he was aware of it, impulse lifted his hand from his side and sent it, open, to strike across her mouth and cheek.

The mark of his fingers showed, imprinted red upon the brown of her face, as she stood, unmoving, and stared at him.

"Thanks for this courtesy," she said at last.

"I am sorry I struck thee. I was sore provoked. Why must thou insult my wife and my children?"

"Why must thou make mention of them—to me, and here and now?"

He let the breath sigh out between his lips, and the tension from his muscles. "Softly, Nell, softly. Let us understand one another. I am a man unproven in thy sight. To reinforce argument, I say that I have begotten children. At which, thou must needs spit venom in my face."

"And I," she cried, "am treated as no lady was ever treated by a gentleman."

"Poor fool, dost not know that when two are met alone by candlelight, there's no gentility, only male and female. There, I have said I am sorry I struck thee, and I meant it. Thy suffering is less than mine."

"Why? And how?"

"Because there's but an infinitesmal, brief pain for thee, a little heat and pricking of the skin: and then no more. As for me, I am abased. I am William Shakespeare and I have been tricked into behaving like one of the common sort, whose amours begin in a brawl. Woman, thou hast used me ill."

"I'll use thee worse yet. Thou'rt stubborn with pride."

"Haply I was once. But proud no more—else I would not be here, a suppliant for thy bed."

She spread her gown around her as she drooped into a curtsey before him, and laughed to see his eyes burning upon the brown curving expansion of her breasts. He pulled her to her feet with little gentleness, and, his hands shifting and urgent upon the small of her back, visited her with hot kisses upon brows, cheeks, lips, throat, shoulders and bosom. He felt tall and strong, invested with the pride of a conqueror. But secret and small, burrowing remote in his mind like a blind worm, another idea was active, telling him that he was conquered not conquering, that evil had lifted up its head within him and rejoiced when he struck this woman, and was rejoicing again now that he held her, lax and drowsy-eyed, in his arms. Worms, however, must wait their time, must wait till death provides them a feast: meanwhile, let life cheer itself, proceeding from the timid five-year failures of chastity to this bold success.

The come and go of breath in her body, small, warm and firm-fleshed as she lay in his embrace, excited him further. But she was for dalliance still: she pulled away from his arms and, disdaining to snuff out the bedside candles, seated herself upon the quilted counterpane and would have him assist in her disrobing. She emerged at last, by way of hooks, buttons, tapes and laces fumbled at and impatiently torn, from the finery she left strewn about her feet, a naked woman with her black hair loose over her shoulders, a brown woman with firm, rose-pointed breasts which slid high when she stretched her arms and looked at him through the tangle of her hair and over the crook of her elbow. She ran the tender inward of her hands, quick and light, over her body, as if appreciating its loveliness; shivered for a moment; and turned and leaped under the feather-filled coverlets of the bed, drawing the sheets up to her chin.

"Haste," she said. "'Tis unmannerly to keep a lady waiting."

XVI

THEREAFTER his days were filled with new discoveries of this
dark woman. She was such a mistress, he told himself, as
few men could know; extravagant, shameless and resourceful
in her love; disdaining all timidity; wanton, passionate,
mocking, tender and cruel by turns; infinite in her changeful-
ness. She absorbed him, demanding the full expenditure of
his vitality, repaying it royally. He did not boast her abroad,
and hinted to none of his friends that his way of life was
transformed. There were times when, absent from her awhile,
he was filled with self-contempt, with forebodings, and with
the stupified amazement of one who beholds himself acting,
against will and judgement, in response to a compulsion which
fascinates by its very unloveliness. Nell was a wanton, in all
things the opposite of what he admired in a woman, down to
the damnable black hair and brown hues of her body: yet she
had but to beckon and he came to her. He would not allow his
mind to range her alongside his romantic mistress, his dear
Lady Disdain who had given him no more than her hand to kiss,
for whom he was but a fount of poetry, and who was now
wholly lost to him. But sometimes his memory cast back
nearly twenty-years, to a boy who had been Will Shakespeare,
who in Stratford had fallen in love with Nan Hathaway. That
boy had been astounded by all the heat and energy let loose in
him by Nan his wife. Yet Nan's desire (she was bereft of it now,
and that was as well) had been simple, rustic, wordless. This
dark woman, his new found mistress, transformed love from a
single word to a lexicon, a treatise, subtle, devious, boldly
experimental and inexhaustible.

She played woman to his man in a fashion he had heard of
but never experienced. She was not to be taken by storm, nor
did she lie inert waiting upon the event. She provoked him
to strange and venturous caresses, answered his kisses, and

kissed and caressed him in such manner as he had not known lay in female nature. She had a guidance and an order for desire, and put him in tutelage even as she whipped delight through his veins. He ascended by ecstasies of sensation through new and ever-changing experiences. He burned in a flame of fever and in that flame was consumed first the world beyond Gracious Street, then all beyond the dark room, and, as desire tapered to its fiercest aim, all beyond the dark bed softly yielding and creaking upon crossed ropes where, between sheets and feather coverlets, flesh coiled and glowed and intertwined, and Will Shakespeare was no more, nor had the woman, held and cleft against him, any name or likeness: here was only male and female, and a fire between them.

The playhouse and all the normal busy traffickings of his life became remote to him, vapoured over with unreality. Absent from Nell, his mind was sterile of invention: he waited impatiently upon the hours until the time came for their next meeting. Most often she stripped herself to her proud brown buff in her own bedroom at Peter Fender's house: but sometimes, mischievous and reckless, she would not have him come to her unless upon her uncle's new daybed, or stretched on a scatter of cushions strewn in front of the fire: then she would laugh silently when someone rattled the handle of the locked door. Peter Fender lurked about the house, smiled on them, rubbed his hands, and encouraged them with smooth and cryptic commendations. The very servants, who could not be ignorant, looked at Master Shakespeare with sly, glinting eyes. Nell would not admit him to her husband's house, and there he did not wish to go. Nor would she visit him in his own lodging. "Here is our best abode," she said, "in my uncle's house. Here is our secret kept close for us. Be thankful."

Thankful he was, and told himself, and her, he envied no prince or caesar. "Thou'rt a queen in bed," he assured her. "Cleopatra could not emulate thee." And she mocked him, but gently, asking when he had been Cleopatra's lover to make such comparisons. Most of his nights, for she was no niggard of herself, and often a good part of his days, were consumed in this frantic, various, insatiable love. He wrote naught but a few sonnets, and they were of a sort so new as to surprise himself:

> My Mistress' eyes are nothing like the Sun,
> Coral is far more red than her lips red,
> If snow be white, why then her breasts are dun:
> If hairs be wires, black wires grow on her head:

It was plain-speaking, without a tincture of sugar till the last couplet:

> And yet by heaven I think my love as rare,
> As any she beli'd with false compare.

These lines did not please her when he gave her a fair copy; but she locked them away in a wooden box she kept in her room. She affected to be unmoved, but that night she refused to bed with him, and when he asked the reason she said, cruelty agleam in her eyes, she must remember he was not so young as she, not so young as he had been, and it was for her to take care lest he exhaust himself in her service.

This was not the first time she had spoken of his age: it was a weapon she knew could wound, and she kept it in reserve to punish him when the fancy took her. Again, her mood would alter, and she would chain her arms about his neck; her eyes would grow all tender and pitiful in their black beauty; she would blame herself, and take back every hurtful word she had spoken. His heart would swell to find her so gentle, and then he would catch a glitter of watchfulness in those expanded black pupils, a hint of pretence in the parting of her lips. He could never be sure of her sincerity. While he was in her presence, he was never wholly at ease, never without a corner of timidity to flaw his confidence. Joy he had of her, but no peace, only what furious, blood-beating ecstasies dwelt in the furious moments of consummation. Returned to the solitude of his lodging, he felt soiled and bewildered, and wrote again, for sonnets were all the endeavour he was able to sustain these days:

> When my love swears that she is made of truth,
> I do believe her, though I know she lies,
> That she might think me some untutor'd youth,
> Unlearned in the world's false subtleties.
> Thus vainly thinking that she thinks me young,
> Although she knows my days are past the best,
> Simply I credit her false-speaking tongue. . . .

There was no comfort in these deceptions. He did not, and could not, trust her. Whenever she would not have him come to her, he suspected her with other men. He lay awake in his lodging through the long nights, imagining her sweating, lax-mouthed, naked of shame as of clothing, yielding to another all that she had yielded to him. He fevered himself with these shuddering fits of jealousy, and cursed the ignominy of such hatred as filled him, and the worse ignominy which followed, when cold daylight shewed at last, and his aching eyeballs stared at their own image in the looking-glass to observe there the sick dementia of a slave who lacked nothing to escape his slavery but the resolve to demand freedom. All the dignity and grace of being Will Shakespeare, the poet of the age, was taken from him now. He avoided his friends: he was remote in such conversations as were forced upon him: he produced no work but these complaining sonnets; and, feeling the virtue sucked from him, he was convinced he would write no more plays.

One evening, when she was kind, and he knew the reason for her kindness as he felt the hot, dry touch of her lips, he endeavoured to delay the sequence of their privy ceremonial.

"There's misprision betwixt thee and me," he said. "Thou dost not return what I offer in the same kind."

"How now? Art tired of me, Will Shakespeare? Wouldst have another bedfellow?"

"Let us not talk in this wise. I have told thee, and I will ever repeat it, not Cleopatra herself was more gamesome between the sheets."

"Then why complain, ingrate?"

"Listen, Nell. Thou givest me lust in marvellous degree. No man was ever better answered by woman. But my measure is not to be taken in lust. What I would have of thee is love. Only a little. But love is what I desire."

"So, wouldst be a puritan? And is there no lust for my body in thee, Will Shakespeare? Or have I dreamed these many nights?"

"'Tis true. I have desired thee much, desire thee much now, and shall again. But I love thee too. And thou—there's no love in thee, only feigning."

She laughed in his face. "An I do not satisfy thy requirements, canst ask elsewhere. Do I hold thee here? Do I implore thee never to forsake me?"

"An thou didst that, I might believe there was one spark of love in all the fires of thy lust. Dear my Nell, have done with fooling. Look me in the eyes and tell me true—dost love me or not?"

Smiling she said: "Behold, I am naked and in thine arms. Is't not an insult to ask if I love thee?"

"Nay, but tell me. An I heard it from thy lips, I were a happier man."

"What, so little to ensure happiness? All else I give thee, and thou'rt still disconsolate. Fret not thy heart, Will, on such vain toys. Come clip me, take me, and there's thine answer."

Thus she evaded, and gave him the royal bounty of her body in place of the confession of love he had asked. Yet he knew she could lie to him, swift and glib, and had she spoken the words he desired, he would not have been able to accept them in full confidence. The order of nature, as he and all men conceived it, was reversed: he did not possess her, but she him. He was her slave, or the slave of the passion she roused in him: and she went ever free, yielding so much of herself as she chose upon such occasions as pleased her. He asked for her love, and she gave him the acknowledged tokens of love, her lips, her arms, the burning target of her body: but whether the tokens were indwelt by any honest affection, whether it lay in her power to love him or any man, these were questions he could not answer.

One day she sent him word by Peter Fender that her husband had returned from his foreign journey, that she must keep to her own house for some weeks, and that her lover must not attempt to visit her or hold any communication with her.

"The man is less than a man," Fender whispered, "yet a master of jealousy. Or affects so to be, when he is at home. When he's away, it seems he entrusts Nell entirely to my keeping, and never a qualm. But fear not! A little care, a little abstention now, and the joyful occasions shall return. I'll bring thee word as soon as it is safe to see her again."

This news came to Will Shakespeare like an icy obstruction thrust across the hot tide of his desirous blood. At first he raged against the separation thus forced upon him, and was all for seeking out his dark woman and claiming her in despite of all the cuckold husbands in London town. Next, he grew bitter-lipped and narrow-eyed: he suspected her in league with her pandar uncle to betray him: he believed she had taken another lover, and feigned an excuse to rid herself of Will Shakespeare now he had spent his pith in her service. That evening, he lurked about her house and was not satisfied till he discovered it in full occupation, with men-servants and serving-maids at work. Presently he saw his mistress sally forth in company with an oldish, thin fellow, lame, yellow-faced and shrivel-faced, who must be her husband. Unseen in the eave-shadows of the house opposite, he watched them go, and cursed silently to think that such a man, with all the power of church and state to uphold his privilege, had lawful access to his Nell. Yet he was somewhat comforted to know that, in this matter at least, she had not lied nor conspired against him.

Not till he lay awake that evening, unable to sleep, fevered and dissatisfied, did he begin for the first time to take a reckoning of what this woman had done to him. He, Will Shakespeare, whose mind not so long since was a fair demesne of fancy, of the music of words, of sweet and pure imaginings, of wisdom and wit, a demesne not to be matched by any royal possessions, was now abased. He had become a slave; a slave to a roaring lust which consumed his days and his nights; to the servitude of a woman, black-haired, black-eyed, dun-complexioned, whose face and body went contrary to all he conceived as womanly beauty, and whose mind and spirit were for him ignoble; to a furtive adultery; to the deception of a husband with whom he had not spoken and to whom, instant upon his reappearance, he must give place; to the chuckling, whispering confidences of Peter Fender, a creature who pimped for his own niece, and all for the love of filthy deception and sportive harlotry.

Through the long night Shakespeare lay, turning upon his narrow bed, staring into the darkness at this vile image of himself. He rose at the first paling of the sky upon his windowpanes, weary and hot-eyed, but resolute. The dark woman should have no more of him. She should be put out of his life henceforward. He had recovered, wasted, from a fever: he would fight now to recapture his health. His adulterous mistress sent him word to absent himself awhile from the felicity of her bed, for that her husband had returned. There was no cause for complaint in that: it presented him with the opportunity for escape. He would forget her now: he would forget her in work, a sovereign remedy for disorders of the blood.

All that morning he read the scrip of an old play, 'Hamlet's Revenge,' a crude Danish story part rewritten by Tom Kyd, who was dead this five years: or was it six? Dick Burbage had given it to him, with a hopeful suggestion. But as the weeks went by it lay in his room untouched: he had wasted the powers of his mind in a riot of lustfulness. That was past now. He would make something of this play, something to astound the world. Out of mud fair lilies grow.

In the afternoon he presented himself at the Globe, grey-faced, with red-rimmed eyes, but more cheerful than his friends had seen him for many a week. To Burbage he announced, privily, that he had an idea or two about the play of Hamlet, and indeed was ready to start work at once upon a rewriting of it. Burbage at once began to see himself upon the stage in the part of the Prince of Denmark, and clapped his good Will upon the back, declaring that the sooner the scrip was ready the better.

"Nay," Shakespeare protested. "T'will take time, much time. A poet is not a gardener or a mason, who can turn his energy to one task if another be not opportune."

"Yet thou'st had the old play long in consideration."

"This is ever the way of it. I can never make a man who doth not write understand the methods and processes of writing. Some pieces may be done swift, to an order. But not the best. 'Tis like the getting of a child. Once it is conceived, the birth is inevitable, but not to be hurried, and not to be achieved without travail."

"See thou dost not keep me waiting nine months then," Burbage laughed at him.

"Nine years it may be, for I have a premonition this Hamlet means more to me than a source of revenue."

Burbage pulled a face at that, and Shakespeare went off.

Nevertheless he began to reorder and rewrite the play that same night, and, apart from necessary deep draughts of sleep, sometimes twelve or fourteen hours on end, and two evenings spent feasting with his friends (when he was unwontedly voluble, jesting and discoursing as if his heart were light as a pigeon's cast feather), he worked on the play, day after day, for a month and more. The drama was there ready to his hand: the fable began with the visitations of a ghost, the ghost of Hamlet's father, the rightful King of Denmark, murdered by his brother Claudius. This Claudius, moreover, had usurped the throne, which should have been Hamlet's, and married the widow of the man he had murdered. And of all this Hamlet, an innocent young man, knew nothing till the Ghost appeared and unfolded his story.

The drama was there already, and need only be shaped and sharpened to gain its full effect. But drama could reveal no more than its crudity in action, in assignations, murders, suicides: the inward force of drama came from the mind, and was to be expounded only in words. Words were potent and magical instruments, to the better usage of which Will Shakespeare had devoted his life: and yet words, pushed to the furthest point of mental enquiry, dulled the pregnant edges of their meanings, and were left—as what? As words, words, words! The very contemplation of them might sicken a man. To be a poet was to engage in an endless, formless, unsatisfying, in the end perhaps a futile struggle with the chaos which lay in the abysm of the mind. To take this old play of ' Hamlet ' and endeavour to understand all that was implicit in it, to put new, modern, subtler life into a stiff and antique tale —this was to grapple with clouds of darkness, to slither among illusions, to groan, a madman, in a whirl of smoky, volatile speculations. A damnable destiny, but let it be: in such a dark, unstable world should Prince Hamlet dwell. If the story demanded that he be an innocent upon whose flinching mind evil strikes blow after cruel blow, let him be a worthy antagonist: an innocent, but no simpleton. This Hamlet should body forth the mind turned inward upon itself; he should present the man of contemplation obsessed by men of action, and himself, in contemplative sort, seduced, yet not quite overcome, by all the easy allurements of violent action.

The Ghost fetched a clutter of problems trailing in with his sepulchral garments. No man in sober verity had ever seen a ghost; and yet no man, in the solitude and silence of the night, dare swear that spirits may not walk abroad. Witches were burned for calling up the dead by their black art: King James of Scotland, who was like soon to be King

James of England, harried old women by the hundred for such practices. Those that have died may well lie unquiet in their graves, and return to this earth to reprove the living. Haply they are but fanciful embodiments of uneasy conscience. Yet whiles their memory persists in the minds of the living, the dead are not to be enclosed, body in the grave and spirit in purgatory or paradise or oblivion. To put the question at its blankest, did not Robert Greene after he was buried, lousy and garlanded with bay leaves, strike at Will Shakespeare, calling him an upstart crow, beautified in other men's feathers? Was not the fate of Greene and Marlowe and Peele, all dying young and wretched, ever present in a living poet's mind, a warning and ensample, enjoining him to eschew the wanton riots of the playhouse life, to order his days discreetly, to accumulate monies against the future?

To come closer to the point, it was his own small son, Hamnet, dead so untimely yet preserved in a penitent memory, who had urged his father to take interest in this old play, and make it an instrument for the consideration of death, of conscience, of all the disasters flesh is heir to. Hamnet or Hamlet: the name, variously spelt, remained the same. For these reasons, Prince Hamlet should be a man at variance with himself, debating action past, present and to come, with his own conscience. But because conscience may not be presented to the eye and ear of the playhouse beholders, the Ghost should be retained from the old scrip. Yet it should not be a ghost after the playhouse customary way, a leather-hooded absurdity waggling up from the front stage. It should be majestical, kingly. It should wear armour and speak grave portents. It should be seen by the spectators, be seen by Hamlet and perhaps by some others upon the stage, but not by the guilty King and his Queen. And, the Ghost being in effect the conscience of Hamlet, with Hamlet alone should it have discourse.

The advantage of working over a play already complete was that he could concentrate at any moment upon such a tract of it as responded best to his mood, striking out a

colloquy here, inserting a new phrase or two there, and knitting
in whole passages of fine poetry, principally for Hamlet to
speak. The disadvantage lay in this: that as he thus amended
the text, the characters, being given new words to speak,
transformed themselves, and so transformed the tenour and
significance of the play. It became like an old costume, so
patched and darned with new cloths and threads, that none
could recognise it, and yet all could see it was not newly
tailored and of a piece. Each morning, when he woke, the
complex idea of Hamlet and his misfortunes had grown in
his mind, and as fast as he pieced in a new amendment it
started new notions, demanded further developments, and
roused his imagination to fresh activities. He worked with a
kind of ingrowing concentration of the mind. He used himself savagely, oblivious of all but the words forming in his
thoughts and the words he scribbled and scratched and cor-
rected on to paper; until, as the fury spent itself, attaining a
momentary imperfect satisfaction, he woke to awareness of his
own body again, and found himself sitting to the table in a
contorted attitude, wrists and ankles chilled, and cramps in
every muscle of his body.

One morning he realised, what he should have known from
the first, that this Prince Hamlet was such a man as he himself,
Will Shakespeare, had lately become. A poet may turn his
observation outward upon the world, noting the manners,
the virtues, the faults, the absurdities of other men, and use
much of what he thus garners profitably in his work: and
yet he can see in others no more than exists, though only as
seeds and mere potentials, within himself. Thus he peoples
his plays with creatures he has known, who are, at the same
times, creatures he might himself have been: and where his
sympathy penetrates closest, he creates in words and in action
figures imbued with the essence of himself. Romeo and a
dozen romantic lovers had been, in greater part, Will Shakespeare. Mercutio, aglitter with wit and bravery, was also
Will Shakespeare. Viola, Rosalind, Beatrice, Titania, even

they, close modelled upon a lady who once went breeched and doubleted in scarlet and white, were just so much of the lady as Will Shakespeare could perceive and respond to. Falstaff was Shakespeare stripped of poetry and nobility, sodden with brag and drink. Henry V. was Shakespeare an he had been born to soldiering and kingship. But all these Shakespeares were overpast, thrown aside now like a split and shrivelled snake-skin. The new, the true, the naked and unadmixtured Will Shakespeare was being manifest at last in Prince Hamlet, a man of speculative thoughts and protracted indecisions, in whom action was apt to spend itself untimely in a rage of words, a vapour of introspective doubts.

Yet Hamlet, being a creature circumscribed by the length and breadth of the stage, and the brief duration of a performance, could see good and evil only in crude shapes. Sufficient for him if he quiet the Ghost by avenging a death with a death: vengeance was Hamlet's good. And there lay the rift which split the play, for Hamlet being (by inheritance from the old play refurbished by Kyd) an instrument of punishment, was also (for that he presented the quintessential Will Shakespeare) a man of delicate mind and a nobility thrown out of balance by the inrushing awareness of evil around him. Between Hamlet peering into his own mind and Hamlet called to bloody action, there was not, and could not be, any reconciliation. Here lay a bottomless gulf: to stare into it was to lean over the brink of chaos, to sight the final, un-answered, perhaps unanswerable, question, which required the why and wherefore of existence. This Hamlet terrified the man who made him. This Hamlet had an energy within his words that could not be denied or aborted now: he was a spirit possessing the Shakespeare who, penning words to paper, day by day, created him; and naught that penman Shakespeare could do might arrest the progress of this Hamlet, impetuous through all his laggard dubiety.

The other persons in the play came easier. Gertrude, the Queen, was innocent of her first husband's murder by her second husband: that was clear in the old scrip, and could stand. Villainy centred in Claudius, and, to make Hamlet's hatred the fiercer, a scene should be written in, developed and adapted from a passage in ' The Unfortunate Traveller ' by poor Tom Nashe, now reported dead at Yarmouth. In that tale a certain Cutwolfe, desiring to revenge the death of his brother slain by one Esdras, pursued this Esdras and at last had him at his mercy. But to slay the body was not sufficient vengeance. Cutwolfe desired the damnation of his enemy's soul, and, under promise of mercy, compelled him to renounce God and his laws, to write a conveyance of his soul to the devil, and sign it, and pray that God might never have mercy upon him. These abominable blasphemies the craven Esdras performed in order to save his life, and then, as soon as the last culpable word was uttered, Cutwolfe shot him dead, sparing him not one second in which to repent.

As he lay waiting for sleep one night, Shakespeare remembered this fearful invention of Nashe's, and later he wakened with a clear perception of how, by a neat reversal, he could make use of it in his own ' Hamlet.' Let Claudius be discovered, not blaspheming, but in prayer and repenting his sins. Let Hamlet enter, in mind to kill him, and then stay his hand lest the murderer's soul, parted from the flesh at a penitent moment, be absolved from the damnation it had earned. So should Hamlet explain his abstention to himself. Most of them which saw such a scene enacted on the stage would shudder, and delight in shuddering. Such a cold, subtle, Italianate vengeance should please the multitude: and haply there might be one here or there who would discover a subtlety hid behind a subtlety, who would note what manner of indeterminate man this Hamlet was, and so perceive that, when he discoursed of a more terrible revenge to follow, he did but use the ingenuity of his mind to make his indecision plausible to himself.

The girl Ofelia was more troublesome: she had not overmuch to do with the action of the piece, and killed herself out of distress at Hamlet's unkindness. Will Shakespeare did not wish to be troubled overlong with Ofelia: he was in no mood to make another romantic heroine to add to the line of Julia, Rosalind, Portia, Beatrice, Titania and Viola. A dark woman had come to make nonsense of all his notions of women: he had escaped from her and was back at his work: let not his work now be concerned with women. Ofelia should die, as the fable demanded. She should be demented first, and then be drowned, as Kate Hamlet had been drowned long since, in the Avon, at Tiddington. Let her be drowned like Kate Hamlet:

> There is a willow grows aslant a brook,
> That shows his hoar leaves in the glassy stream;
> There with fantastic garlands did she come,
> Of crow-flowers, nettles, daisies, and long purples,
> That liberal shepherds give a grosser name,
> But our cold maids do dead men's fingers call them:
> There, on the pendent boughs her coronet weeds
> Clambering to hang, an envious sliver broke,
> When down her weedy trophies and herself
> Fell in the weeping brook.

This was all for sadness: so with the fight between Hamlet and Laertes in the grave: and, for further sadness, when Ofelia appears bereft of her wits, let her bring the flowers which are to tempt her steps (like Kate Hamlet's) to a watery death. "There's fennel for you, and columbines; there's rue for you; and here's some for me; we may call it herb of grace o' Sundays. O! you must wear your rue with a difference." This was the very accent of dejection and reason destroyed.

Her father, Corambis, had no character to bother about in the old scrip: he was but a device for furthering the plot. In the new play he should become an old fool, a tedious old fool, and talk, succinct but lengthily, advertising his wisdom on all sides. A little he might be drawn from Hamnet Sadler, in Stratford, whose burgess conversation was now all slow with saws and empty solemnities. And more, Ofelia's father might be drawn from Francis Bacon, whom the Earl of Essex sought vainly to advance to the high office of Attorney General. Bacon had but lately published a little book of essays, which would be excellent were they not tedious. It should not be difficult to catch the tight, trim, ponderous march of those wiseacre phrases, as thus:

> Neither a borrower, nor a lender be;
> For loan oft loses both itself and friend,
> And borrowing dulls the edge of husbandry.
> This above all: to thine own self be true,
> And it must follow, as the night the day,
> Thou canst not then be false to any man.

Here surely was the very content and form of old man's wisdom, of which the effect lies rather in the solemn delivery than the meaning of the words delivered. This was the essayist to the life. And, like as not, the most of them that heard it would not suspect the speech of being all hollow within. They would accept the white-haired pronouncements of Corambis with reverence.

Ofelia's family must suffer dire hurts from Hamlet's distraction: the girl to the river, the old man run through, behind the arras, and Laertes, baulked of his vengeance, slain with his own poisoned foil. Yet they must not be innocents: there are none innocent above fourteen year old. Corambis is a tedious old fool, and Hamlet shall say so. Yet an old fool may work mischief, so this one shall report Hamlet gone mad, and shall use his own daughter as a bait to throw in the Prince's path. Let Ofelia be a virgin, and foolish virgin-wise: and yet she is not innocent neither, for she lends herself to her father's stratagems, permits herself to be left alone to await Hamlet's coming, pretending to read in a book. Thus, when the Prince perceives the trick, for him she is henceforward no better than a whore. Again and again he chides her from his presence, bidding her remove to a nunnery, which is to say, to a brothel. "I have heard of your paintings too, well enough; God hath given you one face, and you make yourselves another: you jig, you amble, and you lisp, and nick-name God's creatures, and make your wantoness your ignorance." The wisdom of men, as the flesh grew older and tamer and ceased to plague the mind, was to eschew women and the temptations they paraded. Prince Hamlet was the quintessence of Will Shakespeare, and must speak his sober conclusions. Virtue was not in woman, nor constancy either: fraility's other name was woman. There was a phrase there, ready to be turned to trim a verse. No more of women in Will Shakespeare's life: no more of black-haired Nell. Henceforward, he shall pursue naught but wisdom and poesy.

XVII

ON AN evening in the late summer of the year which some
held to be the last of the old century and others the first of
the new, Will Shakespeare, in Watling Street, met by chance
his friend Michael Drayton. Of late they had not oft encountered, Shakespeare living close upon himself, grown
tristful, oblivious, eschewing company, and Drayton working
for Henslowe's rival company at the Rose playhouse. To cele-
brate the meeting, Drayton persuaded his friend to turn into
the short, narrow thoroughfare of Bread Street, that they
might sit and drink and talk in the Mermaid tavern there.

Williamson, the host, came forward to greet them, and
they felicitated him upon his recent escape from the penalties
of the Star Chamber.

"See," said Shakespeare, "what rewards virtue brings in
its train. Do you think that I or Master Drayton here, called
to account in your place, would go scot free? We are known
by the company we keep, branded invisibly with the harlotry
marks of the playhouse, and the Lord Chief Justice had
looked on us but once ere he pronounced a fine of a hundred
pounds."

The taverner took this for the pleasantry it was intended
to be. "There are few in such good repute as you and Master
Drayton, sir. Well conducted gentlemen both. Not like them
who near brought me to disaster that night. I had doubts
I should not have admitted them, but they were ferocious ere
ever they set cup to lip. I was afeared."

Michael Drayton, smoothing the fine red curls, a little
damped and darkened (for the night was hot) away from his
temples, said: "Tell us about this brawl, for the reports are
various and confuse each other."

"Why, sir, 'tis soon told. There came four gentlemen, late.
I'll name no names."

"Behold a good taverner's caution," Shakespeare cried. "The fellows near broke the place about mine host's head, they shed blood, they dashed down a fair reputation built up laborious this many a year—and their victim will name no names. They were but four gentlemen."

"I remember to have heard Sir Edward Baynham was one of them," said Drayton. "And, I daresay, the ringleader."

"That's as may be," Williamson countered, his rosy face dimpled with smiles. "I have said nor ay nor nay. Why, sirs, if one were to come and enquire had Master Shakespeare or Master Drayton supped at my table, do you think I should satisfy him, at least till I were sure he came not to quarrel, or to collect a debt, perchance?"

"I have no debts," said Shakespeare, smooth and sly, and yet proud. "'Tis a virtue my father enjoined upon me, yet more by precept than ensample. But I thank you, host, for your good care. An you always guard your guests so well, 'tis small wonder the Mermaid is in fashion among poets."

"Why sir, this is a quiet house. A man may hear his own voice here, and that's what poets like."

"We are rebuked. But proceed with the account of this brawl."

"I had rather forget it. Such a scandal hath not sullied my house before, and will not again, I trust. These four gentle-men——"

"Anonymous gentlemen," Drayton amended.

"Nay, I would not put such a word to them, sir, though they used me ill. These four gentlemen came late, demanding victuals and wine, and they took more victuals than wine. Cry your pardon, Master Shakespeare, but they declared they lived after the tradition of Sir John Falstaff."

"See, Will, what a corrupter of morals thou art."

"They sat here," the host continued, "at yonder table, till past two of the clock. In the morning. Yes, sir, so late as that. They sang and they drank and they denounced all manner of men in authority, stopping short only at the

Queen's name. Again and again I besought them to leave, but they laughed in my face. They smashed three stools and used them for fuel on the fire. I ask you, sir, what man requires a fire in July? 'Twas wanton mischief. And when at last they departed, they overthrew the tables, and marched out with rapiers drawn."

"I'll be bound you were glad to see them go."

"Truly I was, sir. But the mischief did not end there. The wine—'tis good wine, but an excess of it is potent—was alight in their blood. They attacked the watch in Friday Street, and drove them back to Paul's Churchyard, wounding and beating several of the poor fellows."

"And when the enquiry was prosecuted, they blamed all on the wine at the Mermaid?"

"They did indeed, and the Lord Keeper, he was one of the Star Chamber judges, was all for making me pay a fine of forty pounds. It was only when I brought testimony of my good name, that I was honest and did not suffer in my tavern either music nor games forbid by the law, that I was set free. The balance dipped in my favour, sirs, when I was able to prove that, upon the riot spilling forth into the street, I sent forthwith for the Constable."

"A fortunate deliverance. And here's to a peaceful future for you, host."

As the two poets lifted their cups of canary wine and prepared to drink, the door swung open, a burly man paused on the threshold, and in a roaring voice cried: "Ho, there. Stay the toast and I'll join ye in it."

"Master Jonson," the taverner exclaimed. "Welcome. Come in, sir. Sit. Canaries? Sack? Ale? Truly, I have a distinguished company tonight."

"'Twas distinguished ere I came," said Ben Jonson, making a clumsy burlesque of a bow at Shakespeare and Drayton. "Now 'tis scholarly to boot. What drink ye? The same will serve for me. And to whom do ye drink?"

"To our host and his future," said Drayton, who still

found Ben Jonson a noisy, disputatious fellow, but, under pressure from Shakespeare, had consented to tolerate his manners in consideration of his talents. "You heard he 'scaped the Star Chamber by the breadth of a hair?"

"By the breadth of his good conduct," Shakespeare amended. "You are a puritan among taverners," he said to Williamson, who had now returned to the table with a cup for Master Jonson.

"How so, sir?"

"Why, because of this brawl in your house the law now directs itself against drunkards. Is it not enacted that no taverner may receive company after nine o' the clock? And any man reputed to be a common drunkard may henceforward be bound over to keep the peace? And to keep the peace is not to be a drunkard? Wherefore, host, you have extirpated and sponged from existence the whole company of goodly wine-bibbers."

"This," said Drayton, "will not make you the better liked among your fellow taverners."

"Fret not, host," Jonson assured him. "This new law will have a briefer career than a drab's bantling. Proclaimed today, ignored tomorrow, and the day after forgotten. 'Tis too wide in its application. Administered seriously, it would bring nine citizens out of ten to book. Put it out of mind. And here's to you and the Mermaid. Floreant!"

All three drank to the host, who thanked them, and then hurried away to attend to his other guests. The discourse turned to poetry, to plays and to the penmen who made them. Ben Jonson being present, this meant that it turned chiefly to Ben Jonson's opinions, Ben Jonson's anecdotes, and Ben Jonson's experience of life. Whenever it strayed from these themes, it was shortly and forcibly fetched back. Drayton, never entirely at ease in Jonson's presence, added little but interjections to the talk, and Shakespeare, idly amused, maintaining his own private thoughts but uttering few of them, did but feed fuel to Jonson's fire to see how high and bright the flames would leap.

For a man so proud of his own work and abilities, so firm and forthright in his conceit of himself, Ben was strangely jealous. He would admit few to rank his equals or near equals, and had a rough, ready condemnation for any new poet whose name was mentioned in his presence. He rarely disdained to praise himself, even before serving maids and potmen, and would not hold back a jest for fear it might lose him a friend. He suspected the motives of others, and, although fond of stimulating his friends to call him Honest Ben, you might (Will Shakespeare thought) listen to his conversation for a month of Sundays without guessing there was another honest man in the world. Yet, for that his vices and virtues were not to be restrained, but leapt to shew themselves to the world, it was impossible not to like him—upon this condition only, that he was seen and heard not too often. A daily feast of Ben Jonson no man could stomach: taken at intervals, and spiced with the listener's unspoken disbelief, his conversation was good nutriment.

Ben now threw down, like a glove for a challenge, the proposition that the value of poetry resided in its meaning, and that all else, the accent of the verse, the tuneable sequence of words, their impact upon the fancy, was but useless ornament.

"By Heaven," exclaimed Drayton, "I have heard you maintain the exact contrary of this."

"You have not," said Ben, truculent and small-eyed under lowered brows.

"But I have, and I call Will here to witness it."

"No man," said Shakespeare softly, "may take an oath to Ben's meaning upon a particular occasion. Not Ben himself." Deftly he rescued the argument from the past by urging: "This new assertion needs enlargement. 'Tis too blunt. It grapples too much in too few words. For if the sense be the only value in verses, Ben, what's to distinguish between a good poet like thyself, and a bad one like——"

"Like Michael Drayton," Jonson interjected rudely.

Drayton turned away, his thin face drawn thinner than ever, his lips pale, his hands trembling.

"Tush," said Shakespeare. "Take no offence. Ben meant none, didst thou, Ben."

"'Twas but a rough jest."

"And a poor one," said Drayton.

"I'll agree to that," Jonson conceded.

"Then expound this thy proposition," Shakespeare urged him, gently persuasive.

"Why," said Jonson, "'tis all clear enough. Meaning resides in words, cannot exist apart from words. The better it is expressed the better it is. Ergo, the artifices of verse-making and phrasing are but a part, a quality, of meaning."

"It would be as just to argue that meaning is but another artifice of phrasing," Drayton replied.

"I could maintain that also," said Jonson, sitting back to cross one foot upon his knee, and smiling upon them equably, at which first Shakespeare and then Drayton burst forth in laughter.

"More canaries," called Shakespeare to the taverner. And to Drayton: "Ben's like a man with a shrew to wife, who hates and yet loves her. He cannot brook contradiction, and yet, if any agrees with his opinions, he's taken aback like a ship fetched to the wind. Hell shall have no torments to affright him. Peace and quiet would be the only damnation could punish him."

"You put me in mind," said Jonson, when he had drunk deep, and signed for his cup to be filled again, "of a cook who was much debauched, and when the priest warned him his evil courses would send him to hell, 'What is hell then?' quoth this cook—do ye know the story?"

His friends shook their heads.

"'Hell,' the minister said, 'is everlasting fire.' 'Pish,' said the cook, 'I shall not cease my drinking and wenching for that. I am a cook, and fire is my playfellow'."

Then, as if he tired of talking of the common sort, Ben

turned his attention to people in high places, and commended a great lord who, when he played at tennis, if he saw in the gallery an onlooker with a face which displeased him, would not shrink from losing the game but would strike the ball up at the gallery again and again, in the hope he might hit the face he liked not.

Lords put him in mind of Queens, and he railed against them, saying they were no better than other women, and often worse. Leaning forward to whisper (and now Will Shakespeare judged, from his sweating face and glazed eye, he had drunk overmuch) Ben inveighed against the Queen. He said the old woman made a fool of herself through vanity, and because she would not now suffer a looking glass in her presence, some of her maids once mocked her, painting her nose vermilion, she ne'er suspecting. An the Queen were a virgin, said Ben, it was perforce and against her will, due to a disability which made her incapable of a man: in despite of which she had tried many, but all in vain. Chastity, said Ben, was not to be looked for in royalty: the very word 'Harlot' was taken from the mother of William the Conqueror, whose name was Arlotte.

This was the very discomfort and hazard of loose talk, and Shakespeare strove to turn Jonson's attention back to poetry, mentioning Sir Philip Sidney's defence of the art, but Ben growled that Sidney's own verse lacked poetic decorum. Besides, he said, the man was doubtless high-minded and noble-souled: nevertheless his blood was foul and his face marred with pimples. Suddenly he began to speak of John Donne, as if he were a worthless fellow and his poetry contemptible: but when Shakespeare, calling to mind a street encounter with a tall braggart who had sent him reeling to the gutter, spoke of Donne as an ugly ruffian, Ben sprang to the defence.

"Why," he exclaimed, "in many ways, and excepting only myself, I esteem Jack Donne the first poet in the world. I have his verses called 'The Lost Chain,' by heart".

"Is he so accomplished? I saw but one poem once. It was strange, yet it had quality. I never heard that his work was printed."

"It is not. But there are copies of verses to be had. I'll procure all I can lay hand to, and thou shalt see them, Will, and marvel at them, to boot."

Shakespeare thanked him, but privately doubted if the promise, given so easily in drink, would be kept. Jonson talked on, while Drayton sat, courteous by nature, but scarce able to keep distaste from showing in his face. Will Shakespeare also, at the moment, was not attentive except to the secret course of his own speculations. He was marvelling that a man so hot-blooded as Ben Jonson should write in such cold fashion, shaping all to theories, producing from the brain without co-operation of the heart: whilst he himself, to the world a man of calm demeanour, smooth-faced and smiling, gentle-spoken, friendly to all, was inwardly for ever in tumult, seething, like an ill-tended cook-pot, with desires, affections, hatreds, dissatisfactions; and in his writing unable to escape himself, so that almost every line he put to paper was heavy freighted with his own emotions. Some men, he guessed, wrote sober, and some only when their minds were intoxicated by their fancy, as if the heart distilled potent syrups into the brain. Yet this was not to be discerned from their demeanour in the presence of others, else an observer might conclude Ben Jonson to be the author of ' Romeo and Juliet ' and of that play of ' Hamlet ' for which Dick Burbage was clamouring.

Here was a mystery, and if it were to be solved and expounded reasonably it could only be thuswise: every man who wrote was two men, and the man who did the writing had not the ability to shew himself to others. He inhabited the writer's flesh only when the writer was in solitude, pen in hand or meditating upon the work to be done. For all normal occasions, for the transaction of business, for eating, drinking, talking, another man, a stranger, must take his place. Here were Ben Jonson, Michael Drayton and Will Shakespeare gathered round a table in the Mermaid: all of them poets and make-plays, Yet not one of them was the same man who, in solitude, made the poems and plays. Ben was better in his writing than in his boastful conversation: poor Michael was a fellow of nobler quality, met like this, than when he laboured out his ponderous verses. And Will Shakespeare, the moment he opened his mouth in another man's presence, became a stranger to the Will Shakespeare for whose plays he was always ready, with due modesty, to receive compliments. We are not, he decided, three poets met together, but three usurpers; better or worse than the poets we have displaced, but bred of a different kind.

He was startled out of this meditation by a roar from Ben Jonson, who, having drunk too deep, must needs fall a-cursing all manner of young men striving for playhouse fame who shewed him insufficient respect. He began to thunder his great fists on the table, continuing his curses. The host came, timid-eyed and plainly hoping his house was not to be involved in another brawl. But his business was first with Shakespeare and, bending over him, he whispered: "This has just been delivered for you, sir, after vain application at your lodging."

Shakespeare rose and stepped apart to where he could read the message by candlelight. With Jonson's voice, at once maudlin and enraged, resounding in his ears, he broke the seals, unfolded the paper, and read: "The obstacle is removed to Dover, thence to Calais and beyond. You are expected, and shall be duly welcomed, this night."

There was no signature but he recognised the neat go-between hand of Peter Fender. Nell was rid of her husband again, and awaited him in Gracious Street. She would wait there in vain. He had done with all that furtive, humiliating lechery. The woman was put out of his life. This two months he had not seen her, and he was the cleaner and happier for the abstention. He had recovered the power to work again. Will Shakespeare, free of his dark mistress, was in health once more. His decision had been taken long since, and was not to be recanted. So his thoughts proceeded as he stood beside the candle fixed in the wall-bracket, the written paper still opened in his hand. But deeper, and more secret, more urgent, than thought, an unappeasable host of memories fevered through his blood, and resolution was sapped ere it declared itself.

Ben Jonson was still muttering over his wine. Drayton left him and came anxiously across the room.

"We should never have consented to his company," he said. "What shall we do?"

"Why, get him away before he draws sword or falls under the table. Come, take one arm, and I'll the other. I know where he lodges."

They paid the reckoning and dragged Jonson out of the tavern. The cool night air made him stagger, and a moment later he vomited over the paving stones.

"I'd as lief abandon him here to rot," said Drayton savagely. "He stinks. Now why a plague should a man overburden his stomach with wine in this beastly fashion?"

"Why, for misery."

"For misery?" Drayton repeated.

"Ay, for misery that he's only poor Ben Jonson and not Will Shakespeare or Michael Drayton."

"I think 'tis not me he envies."

"Could he but understand us now," Shakespeare said with a laugh, "he'd run us through. Ben envies no man. Ben alone of all the world hath no ambition, for to be Ben Jonson surpasseth all achievement. Come, he's empty as a cast shoe now. Let's get him home and to bed."

"And then to our own beds."

Shakespeare, hauling and supporting the heavy, stumbling body of Jonson, who slept as he was dragged along, thought himself more abject than this malodorous drunkard: whatever prudence, virtue and experience might counsel, he knew that it was not to his own bed he would return that night. Yet his mind lofted away for a moment. It was as if, remote, serene and comprehending all things, he looked down on himself, a weak fool escorting a drunken fool homeward and plaguing flesh and conscience with thoughts of desire. What his mind observed was a creature all inadequate who, knowing good from evil, preferred the worse; who, having all loveliness for his empery, chose the stale sweats of an adulterous bed. When the mind thus escaped the body, there was no pride left to it. All passions were stilled in that spaciousness of calm contemplation. Pity itself, even pity for the Will Shakespeare left to crawl along the narrow, darkened streets, was not human pity but an indwelling perception beyond tears and reproaches, cleansed and sweet like the first soft airs of spring when life renews itself. The two men who claimed the name of Will Shakespeare, never at peace, never wholly united, disputing ceaselessly for domination, were for a time sundered. From limitless heights of detachment one watched the other make a sorry progress, and could not grieve because he saw, prophetic soul, the petty scope, the infinitesmal vanity, of the other's turmoil, as if a stir in a leaf should seem to the insect clinging there to be a howling hurricane.

The moment of foreknowledge came and went. Will Shakespeare and Michael Drayton reached their journey's end, pitched Ben Jonson into bed, left him, and bade each other farewell. Drayton went yawning away to sleep: Shakespeare, in tears, to seek a joy he knew he would not find.

XVIII

AT THE core of enjoyment he found despair. Will Shakespeare, secretly abed again with his dark mistress, renewed all the adventurous triumphs of lust, but immediately afterward lapsed into self-contempt. Beyond the release of the body's tensions (and that toppled his spirit in a few moments from ecstasy to anguish) there was no satisfaction for him in these amorous couplings. Knowing all this, he was yet unable to free himself: his resolution was as helpless as the sword arms of the gentleman bewitched by the priestly conjurations of Friar Bacon in Robert Greene's play. He was a man under compulsion. Abject, he had crept back to Nell's arms, forswearing all his new made vows, as soon as she called him. Better to be a wine-flown brawler sallying forth from the Mermaid to disturb the civil peace, than one, all fair to outward view, who must evade his friends with lies and insincerities, that he might sidle withindoors to share an ignominious bed.

For, whiles Nell possessed him body, heart and spirit, whiles she had him enslaved, he went ever in doubt of her fidelity. Were he able to take her, use her, and between times forget her, as other men employed whores, he were a more brutish but a happier man. He could not do it, nor wish to do it. Even in the heat and tumult of the bed, some faculty in him, pride or fancy or aspiration, ached, in the little, silent, central cell from which his mind observed itself, for more than the excitement of desire, more than Nell could or would yield him. And again, suspecting that a woman who so furiously and resourcefully pleasured herself in the act, must esteem a lover only for the virility of his service, he tormented himself with jealousies. Absent from her, he suffered his imagination to picture her flagrant with other men, and discovered in his thoughts devices for testing her good faith; sudden questions shot into the midst of endearments: furtive watchings; unheralded appearances at the house in Gracious Street. Not once did he detect her unfaithful to him, but still suspicion cankered in his heart. Sometimes he thought that to discover her guilty would be a deliverance. Let her take another lover, and Will Shakespeare would quit her, and gladly. Meanwhile, these torments abased him. Peace and dignity had gone out of his life.

I should have been born with cool blood and a bent for chastity, he decided one day: or else, obtuse, clownish, calloused against all delicate perceptions. Given one nature or the other, he could be happy in virtue or in debauchery. The source of all his troubles was that, like an egg twin-yolked, he possessed not one nature but two. He could not enjoy lust naked and shameless while that part of him which was not lustful cried out for sweet affection and comely living: and again, he could not live orderly, confining his days to the unsmirched making of poesy, because his blood stormed with gross desires. Dubiety racked him. Proud of the treasuries of his mind (too proud to vaunt himself in speech, as Ben Jonson did), he secretly envied the poorest, most insignificant fellow who could guide all his life to a single aim, and be content. Part of his torment could be ascribed to these modern times, all speed and strain and complexity. The ancients lived simply, more brutal in their evil-doings, nobler in their goodness. The ancients were happy because they were less aware of themselves: prompted by instinct, they made no question but did and said as instinct enjoined. A gentleman could not live like that today. Incertainty governed all. The Queen's life drew to an end, and already the temper of her reign was changed. The age of valour was giving place to an age of malcontents. The mind was no longer an instrument devised to further action: the deed proposed, the mind analysed it ere it came to the doing, observed, recorded, sifted, passed judgment, and dubious judgment to boot, and thus sicklied all with the pale

cast of melancholy and ingrown dissatisfaction. Such was the
nature of the times, and if some men could ignore it and
plunge about the world, bloody, ambitious, lustful, as if all
were fixed at now, as if yesterday had never been, and tomorrow
must always tarry its coming, Will Shakespeare was not among
them. Being more complex, more sensitive, more aware, he
was their superior: and for the self-same reason, he was
cruelly disadvantaged—and knew it.

There the whip cut deepest. He knew his own shame,
however secret he might keep it from the world. He could
chart every peak and promontory of his ignominy, unpack
his sullied heart in words: words, words, words: and yet he
could not deliver himself. To dwell incarcerated behind stone
walls and iron bars was a punishment any man might fear,
but worse it was to lie pent in a prison intangible, knowing
in the self-same thought both the pains of confinement and
what the joy of freedom would be. From this misery he saw
no prospect of release but death or madness, for he believed
that his prison was his own nature. Yet it must surely end,
and soon: either his reason must be overthrown—he trembled
at the conjecture—or one part of his nature must extirpate
the other. He foresaw victory for the worser part. Knowing
himself unable to refuse whenever Nell called him to her, he
feared he would soon be wholly sunk in lustfulness. And late
one night he contrived to pose his dilemma and his fear in a
sonnet:

> Two loves I have of comfort and despair,
>   Which like two spirits do suggest me still:
> The better angel is a man right fair,
> The worser spirit a woman colour'd ill.
> To win me soon to hell, my female evil
> Tempteth my better angel from my side,
> And would corrupt my saint to be a devil,
> Wooing his purity with her foul pride.
> And whether that my angel be turn'd fiend

Suspect I may, yet not directly tell;
But being both from, me both to each friend,
I guess one angel in another's hell:
  Yet this shall I ne'er know, but live in doubt,
  Till my bad angel fire my good one out.

As always when the unruly circumstance of his thoughts
had been concentrated to a shape of words, however much of
the original splendour had escaped him, he enjoyed a measure
of satisfaction and peace. For a little while, some hours or
some days, the sonnet would not set to its mould, and he
would seek to amend a word here, a rhythm there; but the
thoughts were captured now, and there was comfort in that.
Lying on his bed afterward, his mind still repeating and for
the most part approving the lines, he was for a moment perturbed, and then amused, at a wanton speculation. By the
'better angel', the 'man right fair', he intended to represent
himself, the poet, as he had been before black-haired Nell came
to delight and degrade him; the poet of sweet fancies he was no
longer, and might never be again if this woman persisted in
her dominion over him. Now it occurred to him that, were
he ever to print these sonnets in their full sequence (and the
greater part of them had been copied and passed from hand
to hand already), a reader, deducing overmuch from the earlier
numbers professing an artificial friendship for Southampton,
might well assume the young Earl to be Will Shakespeare's
'better angel.' At first he resolved to amend the line, to make
all clear: then the notion of confusion and misunderstanding
began to please his embittered mood.

If any could conceive him speaking of Southampton, who
had frolicked through so many amours, as a "saint" endowed
with "purity," so much the worse for them. It was not for
Will Shakespeare to gloss and expound his every written word:
and were he to do so, or were he to live chaste as ice, he should
not escape calumny. Had not Dick Burbage told him once
that certain gentlemen, readers of the earlier sonnets, sur-

mised from them that the sonneteer must be given to un-
natural affections towards boys. Burbage said they backed
the deduction by pointing out that Will Shakespeare was
known to live soberly, apart from a wife in the country,
having no recourse either to drabs or a mistress. It seemed
he would have to blazon forth his relation with Nell to redeem
his name from slander. But he would not do it. There stood
his monument, his plays oft enacted and many of them in
print, however botched the versions. If any person acquainted
with these plays, and with those poor poems of Venus and
Lucrece, wherein the desire of man for woman was so faithfully set forth in rich diversity; if any one confronted with
such a testament could still believe Shakespeare a frequenter
of boys, he was beyond reach of reason. There were vices
aplenty to be laid to Will Shakespeare's accompt, but this was
not among them. Let the sonnet stand as it was written: let
gossip whisper what it pleased: and let an unhappy poet
slumber now, for the making of poetry exhausted energy, and
the world was no such upright a tribunal that he need justify
himself before it.

Sometimes Nell and he quarrelled, and, strangely, for all
the contempt in which he held himself and her, it was ever
she who provoked the conflict. Though she would not once
confess herself heart-bound to him, she was as voluptuous in
emotions as in bodily desires, and, for very wantoness and
pride, it seemed, delighted to range in an hour through all
the potentialities of love—except the simple avowals. Now
she would coy him with soft kisses, adorning him with the
garlands of her white arms: next she would complain that
he spared his wit, sat dull and dispirited in her presence, to
insult her: anon she mocked him, roused his desire, and for
spite would not suffer him near her; and again she ·sprang
from him, and paced the little room like a black pard cag'd,
her eyes afire, and venom spitting from her tongue, declaring
him incapable of understanding her mood, declaring herself
his mortal enemy. She knew that her reproaches, idly made,

for mere diversion's sake, had power to wound; once he saw her halt a sentence, unfinished, on her lips, glance at him with cruel eyes, and then, for sport, complete her utterance as she had not intended when she began it. She twisted out of his arms and said, "I hate——" There she paused, expanding the black centres of her eyes as she held his gaze, and then softened to his woe, to say: "I hate not you." And the poor fool spanielled across the room to thank her for an act of mercy.

To be fast in love with Nell meant that he was out of love with all else: with himself, with humankind, with all the natural ways of life. It was some measure of his humiliation that he pondered much on death, terrified and yet allured by the dread act which sundered soul from flesh, by the vast incertainty of all which followed the last gasping out of breath, by a myriad foul images of the wormy corruption going on under the earth in every graveyard. Death, by none to the evaded, looming ever larger at the avenue end as life progressed and the tale of a man's years, not to be arrested, mounted urgent behind him, thrusting him forward to the grave—death was the adversary of life, assured of victory and slowly stealing in, attaining mastery, inchmeal, and by towering comparison transmuting all the dearest values of life, diminishing them day by day. Once he sounded a trumpet call of defiance to death, in a sonnet which began "Poor soul the centre of my sinful earth": but a se'enight later it seemed a leger demain of words. Every morn that the sun rose, invading death stepped nearer. He could do no more to withstand it than to spoil its slow invasion of a few fine phrases for his play of 'Hamlet,' which was still inchoate, not of a piece, fine-finished here, rough-moulded there, and indifferently joined one part to the next.

Burbage, however, was to be put off no longer. They were old friends, and each ready to indulge the other: but the Globe needed a new piece by William Shakespeare. As it was already writ to a sufficient length, Burbage desired it to be put in rehearsal forthwith.

"But it goes lame and inadequate."

"Let me be the judge of that. Or else amend it."

"I cobble at it when I can. But I am tired, Dick."

"Thy mind's not on the playhouse these latter days."

Shakespeare sat silent. There was truth in his friend's complaint.

"Something, I know not what, hath thee sore perplexed," Burbage continued. "I'll not enquire too close. A man must bear some of his own troubles in privacy. But why not take holiday, from the town, from the playhouse, from all of us? A month in Stratford should restore thine energy."

"I have no wish to go to Stratford."

He spoke the words sharp and irritable, for the naming of his native town fetched into his mind tender and reproachful memories: of himself simpler and more innocent; of Anne in her past beauty, radiant to his love, and Anne now, grey-haired, a stranger, a neglected wife; of his dead son; of his two living daughters. Judith would be fifteen now, a maid, no more a child. Doubtless she and Susan found occasion sometimes to talk of their father and wonder what he did in London: that they must never know.

Stratford was far away. Here sat Dick Burbage labouring persuasions for the sake of his playhouse.

"Harken, Will," he said. "Let me have the scrip now, to read it through. Even though it be unfinished and not ready to be performed, it would pleasure me to study it. 'Tis the best of thee, thou say'st. Well then, I am all impatience. I can wait no longer to hold it and read it."

Burbage had his way, and the next morning he was abroad betimes, running up the stairs at his friend's lodging and thumping fists on the door to startle Will Shakespeare from sleep. No man cares to be so rudely awakened, or to gather his still slumberous wits to comprehend a spate of words in the cold grey morning. But Burbage's pleasure and praise sweetened the shock.

"Wait till I have it all perfected. There's much to be done yet."

"Ay, Will, thou shalt amend to thy heart's desire, but not till I have this scrip fair copied. Then all that thou alterest shall be incorporate, as we proceed. Meanwhile, I announce 'Hamlet' to be performed within the month."

"This was no part of our bargain."

"Call me a cozening rogue, Will, but I have read the play and I must have it. I promise thee: all amendments shall be put in. But even as it stands, t'is a marvel. It will make such a stir as London hath never known."

"Thou'lt play Hamlet thyself?"

"None shall take the part from me. It is the prince of tragical parts."

Suddenly dropping his voice, Burbage said, gently, almost timidly: "Will, thou'rt a strange fellow. When we two first struck a partnership, I did not look to get such a piece as this from thy pen. My belief is, there never was such a play made before. It embodies the spirit of the age. It gives voice to all that men capable of thought are thinking, or wishing they could think. It is more modern than the newest farthingale at Court."

"'Tis a piece," said Shakespeare, "hag-ridden with melancholy bewilderments."

"Like the age we live in, an age of discontented men, storming the gates of heaven not with prayers but angry questions. Folk will talk of this Hamlet night and day. The times are out of joint, and this play will set them to rights."

"'Twill need more than a play to do that. But you have given me a phrase I'll render thanks for. The times are out of joint! The time is out of joint! I'll remember that and put it to Hamlet's use."

"And we may have the play?" asked Burbage.

He could not be denied.

The players were set to con their parts, and the first arrangements made for rehearsals: but Will Shakespeare paid little heed and scarcely visited the playhouse. He was still absorbed in his own peculiar problem, rarely smiled, avoided company.

To Burbage and to all his friends it was plain he was sorely entangled in some love affair which did not prosper—but none knew the name of the woman.

"An I could find her," said Burbage, "I would wring her neck, as a housewife treats a chicken grown plump enough for the pot. There is not any crime I would refrain from to make our Will himself again."

But the poet, at whose explorative understanding even the shallowest-pated player set to learn his lines marvelled, lived in day-long perplexity, and could not comprehend himself at all. He now loathed desire, but all his rage and contempt did not abate his appetite for dark Nell. He was in no way proud of her, was not to be seen in her company abroad (for which she railed at him, yet, being married, she would not have it otherwise); against this, he must confess himself a jealous and suspicious lover. Her husband stayed absent: she continued a ready and skilful mistress: he had no cause to suspect her of harbouring another bedfellow: yet still he tortured himself with jealousy. Neither reason, honour nor self-esteem availed to ease his pain. Happiness came to him only in the supreme moments of desire consummating itself, when the hot pulses of his blood swept memory, foreboding and observation away into an oblivious ecstasy. For such moments Nell lived: they were the not-to-be-questioned justification of her existence, and, that they should come about as frequently as might be, she was willing to pay tribute with her soul. The end sanctified the means, and, so that she might hold her lover in her arms and get her joy of him, she would wade through a sea of deceits.

At times he called her a drab: she laughed in his face and kissed him in thanks for the contumely. But a drab she was not: her ardency was too superb in its purposeful, remorseless, unwavering aim. For her the whole value and meaning of life was enacted in bed: all else subserved that end. He could not emulate her in this concentration upon one experience. Absent from her, he did not wish to: but once in her arms, he was caught up into her orbit and whirled dizzily after her.

Yet he knew himself no reluctant partner in her lust, and his mind, as well as his blood, aspired to share some secret open to her, closed to him. The act of love was an act of mystery. For the most of men it was but a corporeal union, shameful, absurd, a tension stimulated to a climax, released, and relieved: well enough to mock it, wry-mouthed, with such a name as the beast with two backs. A woman apt to such an exercise might be dubbed a drab or a whore and the man, her partner, a whore-master. Like enough full many a couple blessed by the rites of holy matrimony got no more, expected no more, dreamed of no more, from the act. Had Nell offered him only this, she could not have enslaved him. He were free from her long since. Her power was that, lustful and provoking lust, she gave him a richness of experience beyond the furthest frontier of lust's empire. This alone marked her as other than a drab.

Locked in her arms, he scaled the heights of comprehension, leaving reason, logic, and even the tallest ventures of his fancy, far below: locked in her arms, he was a new man, a man exalted out of himself, charged with visionary powers, triumphant at the gates of ultimate understanding. That he never entered through those gates was not here nor there: to reach so far was to salute magnificence. What troubled him was that he did not know, probably would never know, where dwelt the mind of his Nell at these moments when her body lay closest to his. What did she think, what did she feel then, when, for him, thought and feeling were fused in a rapture of steepling, god-like enlightenment? If he questioned her afterward, she smiled but made no answer. Had she mocked him then—and her tongue had a tang—he could have comforted himself, deemed her one whose love was all of the body, and so put her out of mind and escaped thraldom. She would but smile and keep silence: and so he never knew. Locked in her arms, he was a creature exalted, mounted to the very threshold of the remotest mystery, but still perplexed, dubious, incomplete. And so rapture ebbed to an end: the body spent its fervour: the poor, inadequate, clumsy intelligence came back to contemplate the after-chill of passion, to fret itself with suspicions and self-contempt. Each time he quitted the house in Gracious Street he swore silent, unhappy oaths never to return: and always he returned to the familiar attempt upon the unattainable, to lie locked in her arms, to strain to a vision beyond visions, and to guess, blind with passion, what secret—or what commonplace, void of secrets—was enclosed in the dark heart of this dark woman, his mistress.

Only when 'Hamlet' was fairly put into rehearsal, did Will Shakespeare at last bestir himself. He came posting to the Globe with new passages he would have inserted, making Queen Gertrude no longer innocent of knowledge, making her seem in some sort accomplice in her husband's murder, and giving to Hamlet lines which, spoken by a son to his mother, cracked through decorum and soiled the very sanctuary of love between man and woman. Burbage shook his head over this new offering and doubted the lines would provoke to riot.

"'Tis true, Will," he urged, "the people delight in evil deeds and fearsome words. But they are provided already and plentiful. A touch of bawdiness is one thing: but here is no matter for laughter."

Others of the company sided with Burbage. They admired at the new play, but they feared its effect. "We shall see the boards torn down: we shall be whipped: we shall have stones whistling about our ears." To their astonishment Shakespeare, who had never been seen other than calm and courteous, lost temper, laid about him with curses, and swore that if they played not the piece as he wrote it, they should not play it at all.

Burbage gave way, yet even he did not at first perceive a further peril in these additional lines, when Hamlet addresses his mother:

Not this, by no means, that I bid you do:
Let the bloat king tempt you again to bed;
Pinch wanton on your cheek; call you his mouse.

Here was another devious insult to Ned Alleyn, who was known for his uxorious ways, and doted upon his wife, Henslowe's daughter, for all it had been rumoured he married her to further his ambition. Alleyn never shamed to fondle his wife in the gaze of other men: Alleyn was broad-faced and might well be called 'bloat'; Alleyn, moreover, rarely named his wife by her rightful name, preferring to dub her his mouse. Burbage thought Will had gone too far this time. Alleyn, heading the Admiral's men at the Rose, was a rival, and his acting had been mocked by Shakespeare before. But that was an old story. There was small need for Prince Hamlet, preparing the play within the play (a device taken over from Kyd, who had used it before in his 'Spanish Tragedy') to glance at Alleyn in his advice to the players: "O! it offends me to the soul to hear a robustious periwigged fellow tear a passion to tatters, to very rags, to split the ears of the groundlings." That might pass, however: it was part of the normal cut-and-thrust of playhouse rivalries. But to drag in by the ears these slights upon Alleyn's married life, this affronted decency. It was not like Will Shakespeare so to sustain malice: these days, it seemed, any consideration of love demented him.

To Arnim, who played the chief grave-digger, Burbage remarked sadly: "Hast noted the change in our Will of late?"

"Why, he is twelve months older, and perchance wiser, since last year."

"He is a different man. And this is a strange piece he hath furnished for the company."

"Passing strange," the clown retorted, "for it contains but a poor part, and a brief, for Arnim."

"Stranger than that. It affrights me at times, and hearing the sound of the words I have to utter, they ring in my ears

like the shrieks of an idiot in Bedlam. I fear all is not well
with our Shakespeare. He avoids company, frowns much,
looks on his friends as he had never seen them before, is ever
wrathful or melancholy. He suffers, and secretly."

"Yet," said Arnim, "this is a play to marvel at. I never
saw the like of it. If this be the fruit of his suffering, 'tis not
for us, who stand to profit, to succour him."

And so at last the play of ' Hamlet ' came to its first performance. Most of the private rooms in the galleries round
the playhouse were bespoke in advance, and long before the
time announced for the beginning the citizens came thronging
down the dusty roads of the Bankside to press in to the Globe,
taking their shillings and their twopences out of their purses
as they came abreast of the seat of custom. The players in
their tiring rooms, pulling on buskins, clearing their throats,
jostling for places in front of the mirror, were excited, jubilant,
quick to laugh or to quarrel, and yet apprehensive. That a new
play by Will Shakespeare should draw a crowd and fill the
Globe to the last inch of standing room, this did not surprise
them. In all the brief history of the playhouses there had
never been a maker of dramas, comedy, history or tragedy,
so popular as this Shakespeare. He was a nonpareil: the wonder
of the age. He could do no wrong. Or rather, hitherto, that
had been the way of it. But now, with this ' Hamlet ', all that
had been fixed and confident was turned to dubiety.

Many of the Globe company could remember the staging
of the old play on which Shakespeare had worked, itself a
renovation by Tom Kyd. Two of them had played in it. But
thus rewritten, it was not, they declared, recognisable. And
they were not to be convinced all the changes were for the
better. Doubtless the new version was richly found in poetry,
but it strained reason. The populace would not stomach overmuch of speech-making, unless it were heroical, by warrior
kings. Wiser to hold fast to the proved methods: a little love,
much murders, and a clown to trip up an old and drunken
man. Burbage sought to rally them. "There are deaths

sufficient in this 'Hamlet'," he declared. "Bawdy jests, also. As for the lack of love, what there is, is pitiful. We shall fetch tears to their eyes this afternoon, beshrew me, if we do not. But the Prince of Denmark is the play. Leave all to me. I'll drive this 'Hamlet' home to their hearts through eyes and ears. Canst not trust Dick Burbage?"

Each man of the company, himself vain, envious, dis-satisfied that he had inadequate opportunity to present his talents on the front stage, nevertheless took heart. If Burbage believed in the piece, 'twould be a success.

Secretly Burbage, himself perchance infect by all the self-examinations of the Prince he must so soon begin to enact, was not over-confident. Either this play of 'Hamlet' must utterly enthral the assembly, or else it failed abjectly. The Shakespearean reputation was enough to bring the people to the Globe. Having got them there, would the play be to their taste? To that question time alone could furnish an answer, but it would not now be long delayed. Already the shouts and laughter of the audience came nosily through to the tiring room; and the players held themselves yet a little more tense, grew brighter-eyed, talked louder and quicker. Such a communication of excitement was all to the good: where the onlookers obviously expected much, it was easier for the company to give their best.

Before the time was due, the gates had to be shut. Not another man, not the thinnest scrimshank 'prentice without meat to his ribs, could be squeezed into the great pit, on floor level, where all stood shoulder to shoulder, on three sides of the projecting stage, each sweating and complaining of his neighbour's sweat, chewing stored apples and sweetmeats, cracking jests, lifting an arm out of the crush to wave to a friend, and complaining that the play should be begun. Will Shakespeare, pale-faced, calm, not so remote in manner as of late, came round behind the recess of the rear stage to consult with Dick Burbage. Together they peeped out through chinks they made in the curtain with their fingers.

"Time we started," said Shakespeare.

Burbage, glancing expertly round the three tiers of galleries, declared himself well satisfied.

"There's not a seat empty," he whispered. "And divers notables have come to honour us. Yet look at yond merchant's wife, the one with the full bosom. What a plague doth she in that lower room? We could have sold that to an earl at the least. No matter. Her money is as good as his, yet she doth not lend grace to the occasion."

"Is she not right proud of her orange stuck with cloves," Shakespeare whispered back. "See how nicely she crooks her little finger as she holds it to her broad nostrils, and wrinkles her lip lest the stench of the multitude creep in sideways with the clove fragrance. Can none inform her this fashion went out with Harry the Eighth?"

"The balcony of that room is within leaping reach of the groundlings," said Burbage. "I look to see some bold fellow snatch her orange from her hand ere long."

"Forget it, Dick. Keep thy thoughts on my Prince Hamlet."

"Never fear. I have every line pat. I'll give the word now to make a start. Pox on 'em!" he burst out. "What are they doing now?"

Through the finger-parted curtain Will Shakespeare saw two of the playhouse servitors, down among the groundlings, dragging and belabouring a man on whom all around poured curses.

"'Tis a poor snatch-purse," he explained, "caught in the act."

"Ay, and the fools intend to make him a Knight of the Post. But I'll not have it. Shall a thief take the closest view of Richard Burbage in his glory? Am I to share the popular gaze with a vile conny-catcher?"

It was the custom at many playhouses, when a thief was found among the assembly, to drag him forth and rope him to one of the pillars at the side of the stage, so that, when there was no action toward, the groundlings might pelt him with rotten vegetables. Burbage, never indulgent to this practice, was determined it should be abrogated on this important afternoon, and sent word to have the snatch-purse haled out of sight, and either locked in a room till the constable should take him in charge, or despatched down the street with a kick and a curse.

When this was done, Burbage gave the signal: two trumpeters stepped out through the curtains and, standing beside the great painted board which announced the name of the play, blew a fanfare to indicate that the players were ready to present their entertainment.

The play began at Elsinore, with the sentries, helmeted, pausing as they spoke in turn to lean each on the staff of his pike. Next came Horatio and Marcellus, young players recently grown too burly and too rough of voice for women's parts. Their business was to discourse of "this dreaded sight twice seen of us," and so prepare the assembly for the entrance of the Ghost, Hamlet's father. These brief preliminaries were heard in attentive silence, for all knew that the sources of the plot, the roots from which all subsequent excitements must spring, were to be explained in the first passages of the play. But there was a momentary interruption, which set Will Shakespeare, lurking behind the rear stage among the players waiting for their entrances, trembling with fury and apprehension. Some rude fellow crushed among the groundlings, too drunken or too stupid to absorb a plain communication, caught at the notion of what was to come and complained in a loud tavern-brawler's voice that the ghost should appear first. In every good play that ever was, he declared, an there were a ghost, it had the prime right of entry: it should bob up in front, looking fearsome, and expound who it had been in life and why it might not lie quiet in the grave.

Fortunately, the younker who played Horatio kept his wits. He turned towards the interrupter and exclaimed: "Anon, sir, anon. Be patient, and the apparition shall visit you, never fear."

The whole assembly applauded this rebuke with laughter and clapped hands. The nearest neighbours of the brawler frowned him to silence. The play proceeded. At the end of the first scene, although some professed themselves disappointed that the Ghost, upon his two entrances, had spoken not a word, others thought it witty to answer these objectors with "Anon, sir, anon." All commended the ghostly king for his majestic port. Doubtless he would open his mouth, and soon, and to the point. Prince Hamlet's first line, spoken in the presence of Queen Gertrude and her new husband, but aside, as if to himself—"A little more than kin, and less than kind"—rang low but clear and momentous through the playhouse. The onlookers maintained a silence which, to Burbage's ear, promised success. He took heart and, left alone on the front stage, declaimed his first soliloquy with a deepening accent of scarce-restrainable despair:

> O God! God!
> How weary, stale, flat, and unprofitable
> Seem to me all the uses of this world.

Shakespeare would have had the lines softer spoken, letting the meaning and the sombre tune of the syllables, rather than the full-breathed power of the voice, achieve the effect. He turned away then and walked softly to the side wall of the structure behind the rear stage. Here, opening a door an inch or two, he could peep out on the assembly, and he smiled to note how the gorgeous-garbed young gentlemen in the upper rooms, leaning forward to gaze down at Hamlet in his solitary self-communion, drew back again when the last line was spoken, and altered their demeanour for the benefit of the masked ladies accompanying them. They strove to make themselves malcontents to the view, hollowing their cheeks, compressing their mouths to bitter straitness, imparting a bleak glare of disillusionment to their eyes, as if to say that they also, like Hamlet, put the foundations of all things to the question, suffered much, and were piteously misunderstood. I perceive, thought Shakespeare, that as I once created a myriad jewel-tongued Mercutios, so I shall people the town with melancholy Hamlets. I have ripped open my heart, and the consequence is—I am like to set another new fashion among the gallants.

A hand fell on his shoulder and, turning, he found Burbage, no more the brooding Prince of Denmark, but a man of affairs, assuring himself and all within hearing that the new venture revealed all the prospect of success.

"We have them on the hip, Will," he exclaimed. "They take it as a cat laps milk. I could feel their response nourishing me as I spoke. And this is but the beginning. Wait till I run my sword through the arras, wait till the rapier scene, wait till I die and am borne off to—what is it? What is it Fortinbras must say?"

"'The soldiers' music and the rites of war,'" Shakespeare quoted.

"Ay. A good line. Will, this play shall astonish all London. Nay, the whole world. But I am reminded—the drums for the last scene. One of them split but yesterday. I gave orders for its repair, but the fellow is forgetful. I'll not be carried off for my funeral to the tap of a cracked drum. I had better see to it while I have a few moments."

The apprehensions, the minor alarums, the uncertainties and brittle tempers behind the stage, smoothed away as it was seen that the tragedy now had the whole assembly in thrall. The story, bravely enacted in rolling speech and cunningly planned action, swept on through all its tensions, and scarce a climax failed of its full effect. The Ghost disclosed his evil tale of injury to Hamlet: the motive of revenge was firmly installed in the public mind: then came the subtle divagations proceeding from the nature of this strange Prince, by turns bloody-minded and compassionate; trammelled in doubts; devious in suspicions and stratagems; for ever striving to reconcile the apparent and the immediate to the wide spacious abstracts of his secret thoughts; now noble, now bawdy or brutal; now all earnest sincerity; and again, feigning madness and gullible simplicity for bloody ends. Ofelia, lending her pliable innocence to her father's designs, was warned and schooled for her base employment: a play within a play was promised, and thrust a new device, ready-ripe, into Hamlet's hand. These were novel complexities, over which Burbage had in rehearsal fretted: but now, enacted on the open stage, they were seen to divert and yet, postponing the full impact of the vengeful theme, holding the main action in suspense, to gather up its power for the delayed explosion.

Will Shakespeare left the players and made his way to one of the curtained rooms in the highest gallery. He bowed to the masked ladies and the gentlemen seated there, but, when they would have had him talk, simulated not to hear. Instead he took place behind one of the chairs, leaning his shoulder against the wall, and gave his whole attention to the play. The tall wooden building, arranged in circular tiers, with the stage cutting a small arc, was little changed since, ere it became the Globe on Bankside, it stood in Shoreditch. All the circling rooms were packed, line after line of attentive faces. In the pit below the artisans, apprentices and serving-men stood shoulder to shoulder, in marvelling silence.

From this lofty vantage point Will Shakespeare saw his play at a sharp angle, looking sideways on the stage and downwards from far above. Dick Burbage came on now, as Hamlet, in sable hose and doublet. As always for tragedy, the stage was hung with long black draperies, and against all these sombre cloths Burbage's broad face and hands appeared exceeding pallid. The chain on his breast glittered thin and golden. Sturdily built, from this angle he looked shorter than ever, a stout and somewhat clumsy Prince of Denmark. But he possessed the inward force to compel the respect of others. Even the groundlings, packed tight, their gaze upturned, round the three sides of the stage, breathing their own rank smells and standing on their own weary feet, neither jested nor shuffled, though on the stage all was words at present,

with never a jest, a sword drawn, or a buffet bestowed. Dick
Burbage had a tongue apt for the melodious rendering of
verses. He could play upon his voice skilfully as a musician
on the organ pipes, now lifting it to a solemn and swelling
resonance; now, after a judicious delay, letting it drop like
a plummet to whisper amid a painful silence; and again setting
it to a gallop of excitement. Yet every syllable came clear to
the ears, like the note of a true-struck bell.

He managed the soliloquy well enough, Shakespeare
allowed, standing motionless in the centre of the front stage
to enounce, Hamlet in session with his own thoughts:

> For in that sleep of death what dreams may come
> When we have shuffled off this mortal coil,
> Must give us pause.

At that Burbage permitted, or created, a suspense of silence,
the whole assembly bating breath, although Will Shakespeare
well knew that the player, who had everything to calculation,
was counting three, silently, in his head, to clock time. Then
abruptly Hamlet swung away, wandered towards the curtained
recess, speaking more quickly, and when he turned again to
give profile and full face to the spectators, his voice was harsh
with indignation against "the whips and scorns of time,
the oppressor's wrong, the proud man's contumely."

Dick's Hamlet, thought Shakespeare, is not mine: his
mesh is too wide, and much escapes him. Between his rages
and his tenderness 'twas hard to find a reconciliation within
the compass of one man's nature; and when, following the
scrip, he must feign madness, he brought feigning to the
threshold of apparent verity, and what could the tardy wits
here gathered at the Globe make of that? But it was a Hamlet
to move tears and amazement, a Hamlet apt to the playhouse,
and much to the liking of them that came to see and hear.

Next entered Ofelia, loosed upon Hamlet's solitary com-
munings, and the poet who had conjured her up, out of a
wench drowned in the Avon long since and out of his own

sorry bungling ventures with womankind, frowned at her entrance. He misliked the boy who played this part, vainer even than most of such boys, deft enough to ape the instructions given him, but lewd-eyed, a sniggerer in corners. Could play a wanton, but not Ofelia! And his voice was creamy where it should have been crisp. A poet must needs resent this compulsion to render women through chorister boys, who all too soon grew lump-shouldered, pimple-faced, and squeaked in the throat, and so outlived their usefulness. This boy was worse than most, for his conceit was soiled: he had no innocence in him; Ofelia was beyond his compass. And now, instead of giving her replies to Hamlet in bewildered maidenly fashion (for Ofelia may not guess how she is infect with all the wily heritage of women), he played as if the scene were roaring comedy, and as if his task were to nourish a clown ready to belch forth his favourite quips. The groundlings, and some of the gentles also, who should have known better, grinned at the lewdness. From horror designed to strike them aghast they obtained only easy laughter. This it was to be a poet and serve the playhouse: all was misunderstanding.

Will Shakespeare was so much enraged that he saw naught of the dumb show, the play within the play, nor knew that it was being enacted under his eyes. Only when the end of the scene came, the continuation of a silence, and then the slow release of tension, the shifting of cramped feet, the low mutter of comments, told him that this inset drama of his devisal had also commanded success. From the occupants of the room where he stood he received ready praises, and they seemed all of them flattered that he should choose their small society in which to observe this first performance of his tragedy. He answered politely, his mind absent, and unmoved by compliments so indiscriminate.

When Hamlet had spared the King at his prayers, and rash intruding Corambis had been slain behind the arras, the Queen was left alone with her son. The Queen was played by one who upon his private occasions aspired to be a fine

gentleman. This prompted him to swagger under his farthingale, and to pronounce his r's as they were w's. Shakespeare
gloomed down at him, and when the fellow went on to botch
one of his lines, turning "wag thy tongue in noise" to "rattle
thine intemperate tongue," thus bringing the measure of the
verses to confusion, the poet was moved to curse. But he
modulated his voice to a whisper, and the ladies and gentlemen
seated in front of him heard nothing, and never turned their
eyes away from the stage. Perchance one here and there
shuddered at the spectacle of a son rebuking his mother for
her new-married indulgences, but the lines which Burbage
had feared might provoke to riot passed without a cry of
protest from the assembly.

Ofelia returned, with her rosemary and rue, to sing her
piteous ditties, and again with her last injunction: "And of
all Christian souls! I pray God. God be wi' ye!" The boy-
player—perchance Burbage had given him a stiff rebuke?—
managed this more decorously. She was brought to the burial,
and Hamlet and Laertes leapt to quarrel in her grave. Yielding
the onlookers no pausing space to ask why Hamlet's revenge
should apparently be diverted from his usurping, adulterous
uncle to the grief-struck brother of a maiden misused, the tale
plunged forward again. Swordplay on full stage should be
to the liking of everyone, and it went well, with the stamp of
feet, the cries of the combatants, the clatter and flash of the
foils under the candles now lighted on all the multi-branched
brackets. For those with faculties to apprehend more than the
eye saw, more than was added to the dramatic expectation by
the stratagems of poisoned cups and a poisoned rapier point,
the clash of steel prefigured the clash of minds, the final
furious engagement of unhappy Hamlet with his destiny.
Deaths, swift in succession, strewed the stage. The Queen
drank poison. Laertes perished by his own foil, taken up in
error by Hamlet; the King was pierced with Hamlet's dagger,
revenge achieved at the last moment, by an afterthought.
Hamlet himself died more slowly, the poison in his wound

suffering him to make his last distracted farewells while, behind the stage, the noise of tramping feet and the single clap of a pistol shot announced the arrival of the Norwegian, Fortinbras.

"The rest is silence." Burbage spoke the words slow and solemn, as in anguish, as Hamlet were conscious of all fair projects uncompleted, frustrate, passing lame and unsatisfied to oblivion.

The drums beat to a crescendo, and never a false sound among them: Fortinbras marched in with flags and a sworded army, bearing torches, for by now the afternoon light had nearly faded. In the dusk, the smoky torch flames cast a blood-red radiance over the stage. The corpses were lifted shoulder-high and carried off, Hamlet last, while the drums slowed their beat to a funeral pace.

The stage was left empty. The play was come to its end. And still the assembly, sitting or standing, made no littlest noise. Shaking himself out of his concentration, Will Shakespeare looked round, alarmed, fearing that after all Burbage had been in error, and this his new play was to fail. But then the sudden stir below and around him, like an evening wind rustling through the field of corn at harvest time, brought different tidings. The applause swelled to a roar, and piercing it came great shouts of approval from the groundlings. His ears reverberated. He was dazed. He scarce knew where he stood, the while people turned their faces towards him, smiling and glad, and those in the room pressed round to offer their gratulations.

For a few moments he could not discern beginning from end of the sentences spoken to him, but at last he caught a phrase and could make sense of it. Yet the gentleman addressed not the author of the play, but his friend, saying: "The like of this I never saw. It excels all."

The one he spoke to made no immediate answer, but sat still on his chair awhile, gazing in front of him, as if he were still with Prince Hamlet and his misfortunes, rapt out of all the bustle and chatter of the little room. When at last he turned, he spoke direct to Shakespeare.

"Sir," he said, "my friend is in the right of it. This piece hath no equal in dramatical poesy. And yet that at which I marvel most is your comprehension of man, of each and all of us. You have such an understanding of our human nature, you must stand serene in wisdom."

Will Shakespeare bowed and, murmuring thanks on all sides, hurried away. That night he caroused with Burbage and the leading members of the company, and oft was toasted. He went to bed with his mind confused with drink and admiration, and then remembered again the stranger gentleman at the playhouse who had so gravely commended his wisdom, his understanding. Is this the truth, he asked himself? Is my Hamlet indeed an answer to all the questions he poses? A sorry answer, to slay and be slain. Let the multitude admire as it might, one man was not to be deceived. Hamlet was no more than a dramatical diversion for the stage, an old play made anew, and the Prince of Denmark a creature inadequate as the poet who made him, a compost of fine speeches come to naught, a king of shreds and patches. Wisdom was not serene, and how could a man achieve understanding of others who to himself was all mystery, contemptible too oft in action, in words a consummate evader, a will enslaved?

XIX

ON THE night of the seventh of February Nell sent for him to sup with her. Peter Fender was from home: they ate together, laughing at each other across the table. She pledged him more than once, her voice, always deep and flexible, roughened and yet like heavy bells melodiously chimed. This was a signal he had learned to recognise, this and the faint thickening of her lower lip, the golden lights in the dark of her eyes, and a slow deliberate richness in her movements. He was in the mood to match her desire and they scarce waited for the table to be cleared ere they retired, close clinging as they walked, side by side, to her room. But as he opened the door there rose a commotion from below, and a sound of voices. Nell parted her lips for one of her round, manlike curses, pushed him into the room, bade him await her there, and promised he should not wait long.

In the bedroom the moonlight shone from the window panes; thin silver beams speared through the shadows. He found the tinder box, made a light, and set it to the two candles. Then he drew the curtains. It was cold in this room. He walked to the bed and dropped his fingers on the silk coverlet stretched over the feather-filled coverlets: his thoughts derided him because all the proud empery of his mind was reduced to this small, flat theatre of amorous drama.

Soon he wearied of gazing upon a bed untenanted. He stood in the midst of the room, the cold air making his flesh shudder, and listened for her returning footsteps. They did not come. He heard only the sound of voices below stairs, quieter now but incessant, and all the small sudden noises, creaks and stirs and rustlings, of a large house in the night-time. The wretch left him in this icy solitude: she bewrayed him. He was half in mind to quit the room, to make his way to the long gallery and down the stairs, there either to rebuke her or to steal outdoors without a word, and so to punish her. A woman who turned back from the threshold of the bedroom deserved no less. But he wanted her: even while the teeth knocked in his head, and his hands and feet grew numb, he wanted her. He vowed he would wait another five minutes; or ten perchance: no more than that.

Making an impatient progress round the room, he saw, upon the iron-bound chest under the window, the small box of walnut wood in which, he knew, she kept such copies of his sonnets as he delivered to her. He had seen her oft unlock the box and lock it again, using a silver key clasped to a fine silver chain she wore round her throat. And so he was surprised, when he brushed his fingers against the box, to find it unlocked. He lifted the lid and then carried the box across the room to where the candles afforded a better light. He had a fancy to read through some of his poems again, for, although he kept his own fair copies, he had since amended certain of them. He needed an occupation to beguile this waiting time. It would interest him now to see again the early versions. Sitting on the edge of the bed, with the box beside him, he put in his hand and drew out a loose batch of manuscripts.

One sonnet he read from first line to last. Another he glanced at, and another. The fourth script astounded him: it was not a sonnet, and not in his hand. Yet the writing was not wholly strange. Jonson's it was not. Nor Chapman's, nor Spenser's, nor Drayton's, nor any poet's he could put name to. Leaving that question aside, he read what was written, scanning it fast, for its purport. It was strange stuff, hammer-rhymed and bluntly accented, but not cumbersome: a record, a bold celebration, of an adulterous amour.

> Was't not enough, that thou didst hazard us
> To paths in love so dark, so dangerous:
> And those so ambush'd round with household spies,
> And over all, thy husband's towering eyes

That flam'd with oily sweat of jealousy:
Yet went we not still on with constancy?
Have we not kept our guards, like spy on spy?
Had correspondence while the foe stood by?
Stol'n (more to sweeten them) our many blisses
Of meetings, conference, embracements, kisses?
Shadow'd with negligence and our most respects?
Varied our language through all dialects
Of becks, winks, looks, and often under-boards
Spoke dialogues with our feet far from our words?

When he had read so far, the question screaming through his mind was answered: he knew this clodpole style of poetry, and could put a name now to the man who had written it: Jack Donne. The same piratical fellow, gentleman by courtesy, ruffian by conduct, admired of Ben Jonson, who had once given Will Shakespeare a rough shoulder in the street and was ready to draw sword to eke out the quarrel. All these months, whiles Nell had been his loving mistress, jealousy had sentinelled up and down in his heart. Finding no stir or show of infidelity to report, jealousy had yet denounced her, and jealousy—these damnable verses proved it—was wiser than reason.

Jack Donne, the braggart Paul's man, had been her lover ere Will Shakespeare came to her bed: and likely he still was. Perchance he had arrived even now, hot in lust, and she, downstairs, was striving to turn him away with lies and feigned protests. Jack Donne had debauched her under her husband's nose; it was like the tearaway fellow to speak of sweat oily on the eyeball. He had deluded the poor cripple husband with his "becks, winks, looks," his foot-touchings beneath the table. Will Shakespeare she suffered to come to her only when the husband was away: but Jack Donne could have her even in the shadow of the poor cuckold's horns. She came to Will Shakespeare soiled with deceptions and the impress of other lovers: for if she entertained Donne, why not another, and another? A dozen perchance? But she had tripped this time, as every whore, soon or late, must trip: she had been surprised, perchance, or she had let her thoughts stray, and so forgot to lock the box wherein the poems of her rival lovers lay side by side. It should not be forgiven her either, that, having two poets to pay her tribute in verses, she should not keep the better offering apart from the worse.

Anger made his whole body shake, and when he dipped into the box again, lifting one script after another up to the candle flame to see which were his own and which his rival's, he could scarce hold the papers steady to read. Whatever happened hereafter, he must know the truth, the whole shameful truth here so secretly chronicled: every jot and word of it he must know ere Nell returned to the room. His trembling haste hindered the search, but he found another piece in the stranger handwriting, and noted one more gibe at the husband, who "swoln and pampered with great fare, Sits down, and snorts, cag'd in his basket chair." Then his jealousy fixed itself upon a poem bluntly entitled: ' To My Mistress Going to Bed ':

> Off with that girdle, like heaven's zone glistering,
> But a far fairer world encompassing.
> Unpin that spangled breastplate which you wear,
> That th'eyes of busy fools may be stopt there.
> Unlace yourself, for that harmonious chime
> Tells me from you, that now it is bed-time.

Thereafter his eyes skipped, jaundiced with sick hatred, impatiently eager for further wounds, down the many lines which followed, scarce making consecutive sense of them but absorbing their vile, hurtful, arrogant lechery. In this fashion Jack Donne celebrated his going to bed with dark-eyed Nell, and from his inky papers mocked Will Shakespeare who himself had hoped so to bed with her, and was waiting now in this chamber for that purpose. Jack Donne had had her first: haply had her now, when he chose; or haply had done with her, cast her like an outworn glove,, and grinned to see Will Shakespeare pick up and treasure what Jack Donne had soiled and thrown aside? And she—she was a dark-fleshed outrage flung in the face of all honourable living. Her every wanton word and glance, proceeding not from her heart, (she was as empty of that commodity as a stone of blood) but from the base, insatiable appetites of her body, was a blasphemy against true love. But she had exposed herself now for what she was: the word that fitted her should be hurled in her face: and then Will Shakespeare was a free man again.

Seated at the edge of the bed, he heard the sound of feet drawing nearer, and abruptly, as if he were the guilty one, crammed the papers back into the box, and sprang to his feet to move away from the bed. Ere he had taken a second stride, however, the door opened and his mistress entered.

"Will," she said. "Thou must come away, and at once."

"I'll make all speed anon."

"Nay, I am sorry for it, but the time for dalliance is not yet. Something untoward has occurred."

"For once you speak truth."

She saw the box lying on the bed, and looked at him, her eyes glittering narrow with questions.

He gave a quick answer to what she had not spoken: "The lock was not turned. You have been forgetful. Merely to pass the time of waiting, I have read certain poems I found therein."

"That was discourteous. And foolish."

"I thought to read only what I had myself writ. Instead —well, I found much enlightenment in these poems by your other lover."

"My other lover!" she repeated, uttering each word separately, spacing them with apprehensive pauses.

"I'll give him his name, for do not think, mistress, I am so ignorant whence my injury comes. I speak of certain amorous poems by one John Donne."

She was watching him intently, her arms wound tight

about her middle, one hand on the other elbow. She held herself very still, but she answered, easy and light: "True. Master Donne is the poet, or so said the gentleman who gave me these copies of verses."

"I am no more to be deceived. The poems were writ to you and of you. Have you not a husband to be betrayed, and a taste for lovers who can scribe you poems?"

"Why," she said, "I had not thought upon the similarity, but 'tis true I have a husband, and use him ill in that I have taken a lover. And that lover is a poet. His name is——"

"Jack Donne."

"There lies your error. His name is Will Shakespeare."

"Answer me these questions."

"So," she exclaimed. "I am to be put to the inquisition."

"I would I could stretch you on the rack." He paused. "Nay, I'm sorry for that. I meant less than I said. But I am a man much abused, wrought out of my proper nature."

"My thanks for the reprieve. I'm glad you would spare me the rack, and"—in the small gold glimmer of the candle-light she seemed to soften and glow as she spoke, renewing for a moment her old ardent familiarity—"if I must be stretched, Will, I'd fain it were done upon yonder bed."

He was not moved. "Ay, and Donne hath done it," he cried, savagely delighting in the rough play of words.

"You lie."

Her certitude astounded him. He fell at once inwardly to doubts.

"I am not jealous without cause," he said. "No other man could read such lines as I have read, a moment since, and keep so calm a front as I shew you now."

"Why, 'tis very true, the poems are not for the vulgar eye. They are curious, and shameless, I doubt not: but they have a power, and even a grace."

"You speak like a scholar addressing his academy."

"My interest in the poems is academic."

"How so?" he demanded. "You keep them in this box,

lying with those which I myself have writ to you. Wherefore
this proximity, if both be not from your lovers?"

"Thou'rt stupid tonight, Will. 'Tis not thy wont. These
verses by Master Donne are, as I said, not for the vulgar eye.
They have never been printed. I counted it a privilege to
secure fair copies of them. And, having them, I deemed it
wise they lie under lock and key."

"But you never showed them to me."

"The reason for that is simple. Though thy words deny
it, thine every action speaks it: thou'rt a jealous lover, Will."

"Perchance. 'Tis part of the penalty for loving intemperately. You say these are mere copies of verses, that Master
Donne is not your lover?"

"Will, thou'rt ignorant also. Dost not know that Master
Donne is a man reformed, forsworn to the pleasures of the
town, industrious in his duties of secretary to Sir Thomas
Egerton, and, as all gossips declare, lass-lorn for Sir Thomas's
young niece, a maiden of sixteen."

"Is this true?"

"It may easily be verified. And there's thy warranty, an
you doubt my word, that Master Donne is no lover of mine."

"But in the past?"

"Neither past, present or future," she told him proudly.

Yet were she lying, she would lie thus superbly.

"You say, a gentleman gave you the copy of these verses.
What gentleman is it gifts such written lechery to you, unless
he be your lover?"

For two seconds of ponderous silence she stood facing
him, before she laughed and answered: "I was foolish to say
'a gentleman.' I knew not what I spoke. These accusations
have destroyed my composure. I meant to say, my uncle!"

"Master Fender?"

"Even so. I have no other uncle. But Will, these suspicions
are not only unjust, they are untimely. I came to warn thee.
There's trouble afoot, and I fear thou goest in peril."

"How can this be?"

"Come, speak with my uncle. He has returned with ill news and waits below. He can unfold. the whole story. Oh, Will, why dost reproach me when I am thus all distraught with fears for thine especial safety. Come. We have wasted overmuch time already."

She took his hand and led him away.

The times were uneasy. No man could be assured today of his life tomorrow. There were factions in the realm, and the State struck at those it conceived it enemies, swift and with no nicety of enquiry. Will Shakespeare, as he followed his mistress down the steep stairs, was sore perturbed. But he remembered he had a question to put to Peter Fender, an important question, although for the nonce the form of it escaped his mind.

Nell, moving ahead of him, proved to have the more dependable memory, and he heard his question come from her own lips.

"Uncle," she cried, "here he is, but first, momentous though thy business be, first lend assurance to my good Will's doubts. Tell him that Master Donne's verses, which I have in my box, are but copies procured through thy kindness."

And Fender, silver-haired, silver-tongued, at once nodded his head, declaring that all Nell said was true in each particular.

Now Will Shakespeare would never know whether or not his Nell had been mistress to Jack Donne. Haply she deceived him, and, suggesting the answer in the question, ensured that her uncle should uphold her in her treachery. But equally, what she said, so feat and seeming thoughtless, might be the fruit of innocence, done because she loved her Will and could endure his distrust no longer.

Peter Fender put a term on these dubieties, his plump face unwontedly grave, his fingers gliding and gripping and twisting on a kerchief he held in front of him as he spoke.

"Your tragedy of King Richard the Second," he said, "it hath been performed this afternoon at the Globe?"

"I believe so."

"And it recounts the deposition and murder of the monarch?"

"'Tis long since I wrote it, and long since I saw it performed," the poet answered, "but such is the substance of the play."

"And you consented to this performance?"

"My consent was not needed or asked. The authority rests with the Chamberlain's company."

"In which you are a sharer?"

"Ay, and housekeeper in the playhouse."

"And author of the piece to boot," exclaimed Fender. "Master Shakespeare, you stand in peril of your life."

"Explain yourself. 'Tis true, there were passages in the piece to which the State took exception. Some feared that modern inferences might be drawn from old instances. I explained this was not in my mind when I writ, and the passages were struck out. 'Tis an old play now, and out of favour. The players would have sore labour conning their parts and rehearsing for this day's performance: I believe the request came only yesterday, and was backed by good monies. Else the company had never changed plan so suddenly."

He paused, and then asked: "You do not tell me some fool hath overlooked the passages struck out and let them be performed? Burbage would see to that. But he's absent. Phillips would bear the responsibility. Yet he would not make that error."

"What passages were included or omitted I know not. But the play hath been performed this day, and sore mischief will come of it."

"Still, I do not understand."

"You have been sadly to seek, Master Shakespeare, and 'tis said ignorance is no valid plea at law. Do you not even know which gentlemen procured the performance?"

"I was told, but I had other matters in hand. It escapes my memory now."

"The principal was Lord Mounteagle. He was himself present in the playhouse this afternoon, with Sir Christopher Blount, Sir Charles Percy, and Sir Gelly Meyrick. What doth that last name, at the least, convey?"

"Why, Meyrick is my lord Essex's man. His steward, I believe."

"Ay," groaned Fender. "They are all Essex's men."

With the name of the red-beard, pale-faced, turbulent young Earl, comprehension began to stir in Shakespeare's mind, and fear to keep it company. Essex, between times the Queen's favourite, was also secretly bespoken as the Queen's successor, perchance the Queen's rival even while she lived. He challenged the power of Robert Cecil, Burleigh's hunchback son, whom his followers called The Toad. Raleigh, Cecil's friend and and adviser, was known to be hot against him. Gossip had it that in his disastrous campaign in Ireland Essex had plotted high treason. It was certain that, rebuked in a letter by the Queen, he had returned uncommanded to England, ridden post to London and at Nonsuch palace burst in upon her majesty as she was dressing, her wrinkles unpainted and her scant hair, unwigged, about her face. For that he was mildly punished, being confined to the personal custody of the Lord Keeper. The Queen's heart was indulgent to the handsome Earl even though his looks had lately been marred by sickness, for he suffered from the stone: but the royal brain worked cool and deliberate, unmoved by emotions. Essex had access to her heart, but her brain was advised by Cecil. And now, it seemed, his followers had procured an extraordinary performance of the old play of a king deposed and killed: the treasonable purport and significance of this was plain now.

"Was my lord Essex at the Globe this afternoon?" Shakespeare demanded.

"Not he. The Privy Council summoned him to appear before them."

Shakespeare expelled a breath, full and sudden, a sign of apprehension relieved. It came prematurely.

"The Earl," said Fender, "hath refused to obey the Council."

"See," exclaimed Nell, breaking watchful silence at last, "what a dire and fearful time comes upon us. Will!" She caught him by the arm. "Thou must look to thy life and freedom. This performance involves thee near in conspiracy against the State."

Even then, still striving to adjust his introspective thoughts, turned all upon love and lust and the understanding of himself, to this abrupt invasion of politic affairs, he could pause to speculate upon the unfathomed nature of this woman. She feared for his safety: did that mean there was a true affection mingled with her desire for him? Her glistening eyes were solemn now, her fingers twitched as they clasped through the stuff of his sleeve, tight on his arm: and yet this bright alertness in her bearing might all be sprung from the excitement of impending danger. Women, it was said, loved a soldier because he bore the aura of danger and bloodshed about with him. The ancients aptly mated Mars with Venus.

"Was Southampton at the Globe?" he asked Fender. Southampton now, wearied of the patronage of poets, was known to stand high in the Essex faction.

"He lies with Essex in Essex House, together, rumour hath it, with Rutland, Mounteagle, Sandys, and a great company of gentlemen, armed and with armed retainers. The gates are guarded."

"Is this rebellion?"

At that awesome word, Fender nodded his head.

"And I am counted among these traitors?"

"I fear so."

"The faster, then, I return to my lodging, the faster I may clear my name."

Nell broke into open lamentation and protest.

"They will seek thee out there," she cried. "And the streets are unsafe. No man knows who is friend and who is enemy. There will be blood spilled this night. Thou must rest here, Will. For my sake, thou must stay and keep within doors."

"It hath not gone so far as that," he assured her. "These are rumours. I doubt not there is truth at the core of them, but much may be discounted. Your uncle hath been abroad: yet here we see him returned in safety."

"Ay, and glad to," said Fender. "I saw no broils, but alarums stir through the town. All honest citizens return to their houses."

"Then so must I."

"No," said Nell, importunate in distress. "Here thou'rt safe, and here shalt thou rest till danger be past."

He smiled at her. "This is kind, and I thank thee, Nell. But the house is not thine, and I cannot accept hospitality at one remove."

"You would be safer here," Fender murmured. "Beyond doubt. My only fear is——"

"I understand. You're wise. 'Tis like this, Nell. I am innocent of offence, but to all appearance involved. If I am sought and taken here, then thine uncle is involved also."

"But I'll not let thee go," she cried, weeping now and clinging to him, binding her arms about him, bending her head on his breast. "If this be rebellion, the Council will seek out first the men of bloody intent. Here is thy hiding-place. It grows late, and the streets will be unsafe. Here thou art and here thou stayest."

This sudden demonstration of concern appeared to awaken all Peter Fender's lubricious delight. His face creased into plump smiles again. He skipped around them, muttering benedictions. He assured Master Shakespeare of a thousand welcomes.

Only Shakespeare restrained his smiles. He reviled secretly the mean and evil nature of his thoughts, but could not evade their questionings. Did Nell keep him with her from pure concern for his safety, or because her desire for him, roused and then frustrate by the news Fender had brought, must forthwith be satisfied? There, crammed in the box in her room, John Donne's poems lay side by side with his; and in his heart suspicion and jealousy crawled like white abominable worms. Did she, out of some secret wisdom of her blood, fear to let his distrust grow in absence? Did she intend to bind him, who had half-escaped, the nearer to her by the prompt renewal of passion?

As he had expected, she came to his room that night, loose-gowned over her lacy nightdress, and with all her hair black clouded about her shoulders, stealing in on soft-slippered feet.

The next day was Sunday. Although the church bells (and there were a-many of them, and noisy, within earshot) rang out their customary summons, the folk moving through the streets were few, and those few went cautiously. At the house in Gracious Street, by the master's orders, the shutters were not unclasped from the windows on the lower floor nor the doors unbolted. Will Shakespeare and his Nell breakfasted with Peter Fender by candlelight. There was small stir without doors, yet the quietness seemed charged with foreboding.

Towards noon Fender came to report that one of the men-servants, discoursing through the shutter bars with a friend in the street, had obtained news of what passed beyond the Temple. At ten o'clock four of the Privy Councillors, including the Lord Chief Justice and the Lord Keeper, had appeared before Essex House, still held by a force of armed gentlemen. They had been admitted, but their retinue thrust back. Essex was heard by the crowd pressing under the great windows to declare his life in danger; and some of his followers had urged him to slay the Councillors and throw the Great Seal into the river. Later, it was said the Councillors were unharmed but detained as hostages.

"The issue of all this," said Fender, "will be violent and bloody."

As they sat to dinner, soon after noon, they were disturbed by a tumult of voices and marching feet outdoors. Peeping out sideways from the upper windows, they saw a company of men, two hundred or more, and by their apparel gentlemen of substance, marching boldly, like soldiers, up the street. Most of them were cloaked, but it could be seen that under their cloaks they carried not only swords but pistols and, some of them, muskets five feet long. At their head, but guarded on either side by a swordsman, went the Earl of Essex, anon solemn-eyed, anon smiling upon those who stared at him from windows and from the edges of the street. At every ten paces he lifted up his voice and shouted: "For the Queen! For the Queen! A plot is laid for my life!"

"This is novelty," Shakespeare whispered into Nell's ear, "to declare rebellion in the Queen's name!"

"He seeks to overthrow his enemies, Cecil and Raleigh," said Fender.

But Nell, staring at the Earl's trim red beard and pallid, anxious face, observed: "He is a proper man, and a comely. 'Twould be pity for treason to succeed, and yet pity for such a handsome traitor to come to harm."

Shakespeare, noting the moisture running down the Earl's temples and cheeks, answered: "And pity also to go to meet his fate in such a muck of sweat. Were my lord of Southampton here," he added, hurtfully mischievous, "thou wouldst see how bravely a gentleman may comport himself."

"Is he so handsome then?"

"Many women have thought so. Art unaware of his reputation?"

"But he is married now?" she objected.

"Who? Southampton? Ay. But an old dog is not so easy reformed."

"An he excels Essex, I would I might see him," Nell whispered.

"What happens now?" And Shakespeare nodded down to the street.

A knot of younger citizens and apprentices came thronging up out of an alley to stand and stare, and Essex halted for a moment to address them, beseeching them to arm themselves forthwith, else they could do him no service. The whitecoat trainbands, he declared, would rally to his side, and he was now on his way to Sheriff Smith's house, to ensure their complicity. One or two among the little crowd raised a cheer, but most stood in silence.

"I see none," said Shakespeare, "flying home to bring pike or sword to aid the cause. 'Tis doomed already."

"Yet he is a proper man," Nell maintained, opening the window now and leaning out to watch the rearguard of the little army as it pressed on into the city.

Half an hour afterward they hurried upstairs again to observe another occurrence in the street. This time it was horsemen, with heralds and trumpeters, and one superbly apparelled—either the Knight Marshall or the Garter King at Arms, Shakespeare declared—who read a proclamation, in the Queen's name, denouncing the Earl of Essex and his complices as traitors.

Thereafter several bands of pikemen and musketeers passed by, but all orderly and none acclaiming Essex. Before night-fall it was known that the Earl had failed to secure aid from the Sheriff and the trainbands and, with his small army much diminished (scenting disaster on the wind, many of them abandoned their arms in the streets and slunk away), was endeavouring to force his way back to Essex House. From Paul's came a whispering reverberation of noises, and presently the sounds of shots. A few minutes later—the street was shadowed with dusk now—men came running from Lombard Street, hot-faced and excited, and then, shamefaced, slowed their progress to a walking pace.

From one of these onlookers, inquisitive but not beyond the care of their own safety, the news was passed into the house, through the shutter bars, that the Bishop of London had caused a force to muster by the west gate of Paul's, with iron chains drawn across the street, to bar the rebels' way. Sir Christopher Blount, leading the assault at the Earl's command, had slain a man, but was himself sore wounded. A gentleman had been shot dead, and several citizens. A ball had passed through the Earl's hat; but he was unharmed. He had but twenty or thirty followers left to him, besides those still holding Essex House: and it seemed impossible he could make his way back there. Before midnight, although train-bandmen were patrolling the streets to reinforce the watch, they declared their chief duty was to safeguard honest citizens against cut-throats and snatchpurses who ever saw in times of civil disturbance their richest opportunities. Essex and his men had surrendered and were in custody of the law: the rebellion had flared and been quenched all in a single day.

The next morning it was safe to move abroad and possible, to some degree, to sort news from rumour. Shakespeare, thanking Peter Fender for the enforced hospitality, declared he must now appear in the places he frequented of custom, and meet any charges the performance of Richard II. might entail. He kissed Nell and made his way over London Bridge, where he shuddered to overhear a man, nodding up to the shrivelled heads on the poles, jest that there would soon be newcomers in that company. The Bankside streets were crowded with people, all striving to outdo competitors with reports of what they had seen, what they had heard, and what in their wisdom they had foretold before the event. Many tried to hold him in converse, but he hurried on to seek out Richard Burbage. He found him of good cheer.

"We may suffer a reprimand, Will, for this old play of thine, but no more than that. Our innocence is patent. Nay, that's not because I was myself absent and ignorant of what was toward. Essex and his men hoped to set treason alight through thy verses: but what could the company guess of that? Besides—saving thy vanity—there were none present at the performance, none to make the counting worth while, excepting the gentlemen who commanded it and paid for it."

"Nevertheless," Shakespeare objected, "there will be executions and imprisonings aplenty, and who will care if I pass to judgement in that sorry crowd?"

"Why, thou wert not out with the rebels? No man knew where to find thee, Will, but I was assured thou wouldst not be in mischief or foolishness."

Shakespeare laughed. "I was housebound from first to last."

"And have witnesses to prove it?"

"Two, and a half-dozen of servants."

"Then all's well. Fear not. Come, put it to the test. What in the devil's name have we, the Lord Chamberlain's Company, oft appearing at Court, to profit by lending ourselves to treason and rebellion? That's the question the Council will ask. Moreover, 'tis known thou'rt no friend to Southampton, whiles he is right hand to Essex."

"Is he taken too?"

"Ay, and like to lose his head, the poor fool."

Burbage, who had always a sifted store of inner knowledge, rendered a brief account of the last nocturnal hours of the rising. Essex, it seemed, unable to force his way through the City, turned away to Queenhithe with his few remaining followers and, taking the boats there, was rowed up river to the stairs of Essex House, and so rejoined Meyrick and Southampton, who still held the Councillors to hostage, except the Lord Chief Justice, already released. But the great house was a fortress now, besieged on all its landward sides; and presently the Lord Admiral, coming from Whitehall, established his men also in the gardens by the river. The rebellion was pent, and in hopeless case. Called on to surrender, Essex and Southampton parleyed for terms; determined to sally forth and die fighting; changed their minds again; and at last, at ten of the clock at night, the whole body of gentlemen came forth and, falling on their knees, delivered their swords to the Lord Admiral.

Essex and Southampton, because the night was dark and the river not passable under the bridge, had been confined till morning in the Archbishop's house: doubtless they were by now both in the Tower. The demeanour of the Queen had been a marvel to all: she had shewn herself no more disturbed than by a report of a brawl in Fleet Street, and had not moved from the table, hearing the first news at dinner, nor eaten less than was her custom. She and Cecil, Burbage confided, had known of the conspiracy long before it came to a head. Had

Essex been less proud, he had been wiser, and made a more formidable challenge for power. Had he been more resolute, and kept to a single purpose, he might have seized London, but even when he declared himself he was uncertain whether his appeal should be to the Court, to the Tower or to the City: with each in turn he failed, and his failure was the fruit of multiple purpose and indecision. In that, Shakespeare could understand him, and offer sympathy.

He grieved, too, that Southampton was taken and must stand trial: they had once been friends. It would strain sentiment and truth to make much of that friendship, ended long since: yet it was true that when Will Shakespeare was a young poet come to town, poor and of small reputation, Southampton, whatever his motive, whatever the narrow limits and gross blunders of his affection, had sponsored him. With Southampton's gift of a hundred pounds Shakespeare's first holding in the Chamberlain's company had been purchased: the debt was discharged, but upon it was built all his subsequent worldly fortune. He could do no less, he said now, than grieve for Southampton.

"Arrant nonsense," Burbage declared. "What was an hundred pounds to a man of such wealth? A mere nod to his steward, forgot as soon as made. He needed a poet in his retinue, and had it not been thee, Will, it had been another."

"Yet I it was. I cherished a grudge against him once, on another score: that I have long since put out of my mind. Indeed, I have lost the right to reproach him." For a moment Will's mind anguished back to a memory of himself, younger, simpler, romantical, faithfully pledged to the love of a lady in scarlet and white who would have naught of him but his verses and the cool colloquies of friendship.

He emerged from this brief retrospection to hear Burbage denouncing Southampton as no sudden traitor, no unfortunate misled by impulse. Nearly two years since in Ireland—and this was news known to Cecil and the Queen, but never bruited abroad—Southampton had helped Essex to a privy and traitorous discourse with the Earl of Tyrone, Hugh O'Neill, the very man Essex was charged to put down. Tyrone, his rebel head bare to the wind, sat his horse, up to its belly in the river, while Essex parleyed with him from the bank, and Southampton rode about to keep eavesdroppers away. Nevertheless, three men, hidden in the reeds, overheard what was said: not only the arrangement of a truce, shameful to the Queen's majesty, which Essex afterward published, but a further plot to make Tyrone viceroy of Ireland and Essex nothing other than King of England. To this plot Southampton was chief complice: no call therefore to pity him, said Burbage.

Yet Southampton's part in Will Shakespeare's life was not yet played out. It happened thus. The Council found the players guiltless of evil intent in the performance of ' Richard II.,' and Will Shakespeare was not even called to testify his innocence. Thomas Lee, a captain who had served under Essex in Ireland, and had borne messages to Tyrone, was taken in the palace, and confessed his intent of seizing the Queen's person and compel her to sign a warrant to release Essex from the Tower. He was speedily brought to trial and condemned. Four days later, Southampton and Essex were jointly arraigned at Westminster Hall. Southampton conducted himself well, and besought pardon so winningly that, although the Court could not but pass the dread sentence for high treason upon him, many that watched were moved to tears.

Essex was bold and outrageous, laughing aloud, jogging the earnest Southampton by the sleeve to listen to his whispered jests, and mocking the solemn utterances and classical comparisons of Francis Bacon. Yet that might be forgiven him, for had he not wearied the Queen, a few years since, with requests for Bacon's advancement: and, failing in that, gifted with an estate at Twickenham the man who now came to prosecute him unto the death? When his enemy, Sir Walter Raleigh, was called and the oath administered to him, Essex cried aloud: "What booteth it to swear the fox?" He charged Sir Robert Cecil that he had declared the Infanta of Spain held better title to the Crown than others. Yet he sobered towards the end of the trial, announced himself willing to die, but besought pardon for Southampton. The Court sat from nine in the morning till six, and both Earls were condemned as traitors to be hanged, bowelled and quartered.

When this news was divulged, it spread swifter than wind-blown fire through London, and the citizens, their wives and daughters also, thronged the streets to see Essex, for the last time, as he was escorted back from Westminster to the Tower. Will Shakespeare was at Peter Fender's house in Gracious Street when a servant maid came in, speaking so fast she could not catch her breath, to tell of the issue of the trial, the formation of the crowds, and say that at any moment the condemned men might pass by in the street.

Without a word, they all rose and went up the stairs to open the windows and look out.

"It is but twelve days," said Fender, "since we saw Essex from this place, armed and surrounded with his henchmen, in the pride of his rebellion."

"A small pride it was," Shakespeare amended, "and mixed with incertainty. Even then, methought, the pale flag of death showed in his face."

Nell seemed not to hear, for now the crowds lining the street grew silent and still, and the sound of feet marching to a monotone of drum taps reached their ears. Presently they could see a body of pikemen and musketeers, their bearded faces illumined by the light of the torches borne by men marching on the flanks, and in the midst, guarded against all hope of rescue (for there came murmurs of anger now, as well as of pity, from the people on the street) walked the two Earls side by side. Southampton marched staring before him, with dull eyes which seemed to see nothing. Essex went with his face downbent.

"God help them both!" said Shakespeare, and Peter Fender turned to him astonished, for pious exclamations were not often on his lips. But Nell said never a word, and Shakespeare saw her staring with avid, brilliant eyes, gold glistering amid their black, down to the street and the handsome rebels being marched to their death.

"He is a proper man, and a comely," she whispered.

Yet she could scarce discern the features of the Essex from here, for as he went he sank his jaw on his chest and looked at the ground. Nell's words echoed painfully for a protracted moment through Will Shakespeare's mind, as if their full purport escaped him. He thought to have assuaged this dissatisfaction when, out of a far-off memory, long lost, he fetched up just such another phrase of woman's commendation, spoken of himself by old Meg Candler, beside the Bank Croft in Stratford, that morning when he met Nan Hathaway in the mists. Meg—she was in her grave now—had appraised him as a farmer inspects cattle, and forthwith had begun her plot for marrying him to Nan. It was passing strange that after all these years he should hear the same words—surely they were the very same words?—spoken by dark Nell, who had usurped Nan's place in his heart, or at least in his bed.

But he had not yet come to the end of these surprises. The phrase still lingered in his mind.

"A proper man, and a comely," he repeated.

Why, this was what Nell had said of Essex only a few days earlier, when the Earl went, a free man, proclaiming rebellion through this same street down which he was now marched, unarmed and guarded, to await his death at the Tower. And Nell still admired the poor creature! Shakespeare glanced at her again, and his heart tightened painfully in his breast as he saw that her soft voluptuous gaze was bent not on Essex but on Southampton! He remembered himself praising Southampton to her, declaring him more handsome than Essex. Lightly given, jesting advice: and the perverse wench had taken it! She looked down on Henry Wriothesley as no woman should look, save on her lover. And who was her lover but Will Shakespeare? Unless it were Jack Donne? If curses, heartfelt but unspoken, could blast, the woman were cinders and ashes already as she leaned out of the window. She stared and stared as if she could not endure to have that spectacle move away from her, as if Southampton were some precious jewel she coveted. A plague on such an intemperate wench, glutting her desirous eyeballs upon one man after another! Jack Donne first. Will Shakespeare next. And now Southampton. Trust her to disdain Essex, who could not escape the block, and fix on Southampton, who, so said those that ought to know, would surely receive the Queen's pardon. And why, of all men, must she now choose one who had already done Will Shakespeare sufficient injuries? To the world, Southampton had bestowed benefits upon the prime poet of the age: only the poet knew the obverse of that story. Out upon Southampton! Dick Burbage was in the right of it: the fellow deserved no pity.

When the procession with its flaming torches was lost in the crowd surging out to follow, and Nell turned back to the room, she breathed deep, held herself erect, and her brown bosom, widely exposed, swelled and quivered. Shakespeare looked at her, and saw the pulse throbbing in her throat, the veins shewing azure at her temples, the darkness circling her eyes, mantling the upper and lower lids. He took her hand: she did not shake it off: she seemed unaware of his touch. Her fingers were hot and damp against his.

They returned to their supper. Nell was silent awhile, and when she spoke she mentioned Southampton compassionately. Shakespeare stared, realising she did not understand that only Essex was like to be executed. He did not enlighten her ignorance. She perplexed him. He was angry with jealousy and bewilderment, till she began to jest with him. She drank wine, as if she thirsted deep, and soon her cheeks were crimsoned. She called Shakespeare, openly before her uncle and the servants, her darling, her poppet, and her dainty delight. She held his foot between hers under the table, smiling the while into his eyes: that put him in mind of Jack Donne's poems, and questions still unanswered; he frowned. But she courted him so sweetly he could not harbour jealousy.

Peter Fender blessed them with his pimp's chuckles, and tripped away as soon as the meal was finished.

"I can read in thine eyes, Nell," her lover told her.

"What canst read?"

"One word, and that brief. Bed."

"This is a plea of benefit of clergy. Canst write as well as read?"

"An I take thy meaning, the answer is known already. But it shall be proven again."

"Then come," she said, rising and turning towards the door. There she halted, and swept her gown round her as she twisted to close him in an embrace. Her hands clipped him at waist and shoulder; she was supple and strong in his arms, bending backward as he leaned over her. He saw the slow voluptuous fall of the black-lashed lids over her eyes a moment ere his kiss found her mouth, which moved to his, hot and eager. When she drew back her head, but keeping herself close in his embrace, she opened her eyes again and, having her so near, he stared into the black pupils wide expanded. Through the streaming forests of his desire a single thought jerked its impulsive way: he had said he could read in her eyes a plain message of desire, but here, at this intimate advantage, he found only darkness, a blank enigma. She pressed her lips again to his: his own eyes were blinded now in her hair, and the perfume of it was sweet and sharp in his nostrils. Through all the interventions of their clothing, her body was beseeching him, adding its entreaties to the urgency of her mouth, endeavouring to overwhelm his mind, to put to oblivion all that was, more durably than flesh, Will Shakespeare.

Such surrender, fore-known and alluring, would come easily: yet his mind held obstinate, and then, the thought creating such a shock that his veins were of a sudden turned cold and from head to foot he shuddered, his mind reached out and surprised her secret. All this her excitement of desire, fixed upon him, sprang from sight of another. When Southampton—"a proper man, and a comely"—passed by to the

Tower and apparently to death, then had her desire awakened. She had no true pity for the Earl, only a meaningless gratitude because, being a headless corpse still suffered to walk the streets, he could make her thus burn and tremble with anticipated pleasure. The prospect of death, herself secure from it, cast a sorcerer's spell of lust upon her. Because she believed Southampton would die, not merely at the time appointed but now in her blood-fascinated imagination, she must sate herself with a man. Any man would serve, so he were not too uncleanly or too ugly. And why not ugly? Was not Jack Donne splay-nosed and beetle-browed? The prospect of death, violent, agonised death, was more potent with her than wine or endearments. Any man could do her all the service she required: but Will Shakespeare was at hand. Will Shakespeare was ever at hand, retained for that purpose. But of that servitude no more! All things attain an end!

With a cry, which came from his throat not deep nor wrathful but thin and strangled by horror, he wrenched himself out of her embrace.

"How now?" she demanded. "What ails thee?"

"Naught but this: I boasted I could read in your eyes, but I read wrong. There is in truth a single word inscribed there, and I should see it always were I ever to look again. The word is—blood."

He made haste to quit her then, and to quit the house, knowing he would never return. Astounded and disbelieving, she followed him to the stairs and caught at his sleeve.

"Blood!" she repeated. "What means that? Dost think me a murderess?"

"You have said it. You have recognised your kin."

He went to a tavern, and drank much, and talked much, and, finding the wine sour, pledged a silent toast to Henry Wriothesley, Earl of Southampton, sometime his friend, through whose unwitting interventions he had lost his solitary hope of love and had, this same evening, been delivered from thraldom to a woman coloured ill. Let the one debt cancel the other!

Book Four

JUDITH

XX

THE elm marked the borough boundary where it cut west, against all reasonable expectation, across the road to the Guild Chapel, and there turned south to the tithe barn. The elm was tall: it spread its firm-founded roots over the turf, and cast its cool shade wide. The elm was most conveniently placed. Whether it had been planted for a boundary mark, or, being already tall and notable, had attracted the boundary to it, none now could tell: were trees endowed with the power of reflection, doubtless the elm would be indifferent upon the problem. There was much virtue, and more consolation, in indifference: a man whose youth and maturity, though free from civil or martial strife, had been all turmoiled within by conflicting loyalties and desires, discovered in himself as he grew older a soft welcome to the encroachments of indifference. When the heart nor raged nor yearned nor joyed beyond tolerable measure, youth was past, but even the melancholy mourning over it held new and peaceful allurements. To sit here was to reign a king of inward content; to ease the shoulders against a tree trunk, to gaze on the sun-scorched spectacle of a fair summer's day, and yet to be cool in shadow, and cool in the mind. Pleasant was an epithet insufficient for such an occupation: it yielded the best rewards a man grown indifferent could look for, thus to sit and contemplate, and let idle meditations troop as they wished, remote, unhasting, and unhurtful

To have taken London town by storm, so far as a playhouse poet might be a successful captain of assault: change the figure. To have left upon London, that great and multitudinous capital, the persistent impress of the name of William Shakespeare: try again. To have made of London an oyster and swallowed it—that was Falstaff's phrase. Did Dick Burbage, enouncing the words upon the stage, ever remember they were filched from his own conversation? This silent, lazy grappling of expression upon thought was more than commonly discursive. Concluding it, he resolved that to triumph over London, by storm, by impress or by digestion, was much: but better to have returned here to Stratford, an armorial gentleman, a gentleman of property, substance and fame; and to doff all this acquirement like a cloak and sit alone, out of the sun, this was best of all.

Under the bank where the elm tree rooted, a narrow road-way ran, and when a passer-by, rare and unhurried, moved beneath, there was ever a respectful salute for Master Shake-speare. Beyond was the grass of the Bank Croft, here narrowed to a strip less than twenty yards wide: and beyond that ran the Avon river, smooth-surfaced, all its dark freight of mud bedazzled under the golden glitter of the sunshine.

If he listened intently, and excluded from his awareness the busy domestic chattering of the birds, the occasional sharp commotions from the Bear Inn and the Swan, diminished by distance, the lowing of cattle and such rustic sounds, he could detect the faint, rippling music of the river water under the bank, as it flowed around the sedges there. None of these sounds disturbed the presiding quiet of this late summer afternoon, in which even the bees, golden in the golden air, went drowsily about their labours. Beyond the river (it had seemed broad once, ere he saw the Thames) the meadows rose to a long ridge, and trees marked the route of the Oxford and London road. He would frequent that road in future as little as might be. Turning his head left, he could discern the long causey and the pointed arches of the Clopton bridge, and trace, as a succession of green stains patched on the grey, the herbs and grasses crannied between the stones. To the right, the narrow wooden spire of Holy Trinity church was lofted, as if upborne on the trees which hid the church from view. An a man stood up and walked across the road to the river bank he would see further, to the mill and the mill-bridge, and the flat spread of the fishing ground. An a man stood up and turned him round, he would see the narrow streets, the black-timbered walls, the close-clustering roofs of Stratford rising behind him, and mark the towers and turrets of the Gild Chapel, beside which stood his own fair property, repaired and amply walled and gardened, New Place. Yet a wise man chose but to sit and watch and let his thoughts meander as they would.

In the fields across the river a small brown figure proceeded slowly, the only movement in a landscape slumberous with sunshine, for everywhere the cattle lay in the shade. Suddenly the man in the fields stopped, and, watching him close, Will Shakespeare could see he was doffing his doublet to carry it on his arm. When the man moved on, he was no longer a dim and colourless figure, for the white sleeves of his shirt gleamed in the sun, and his waistcoat was of scarlet.

For him who watched from afar there was no gaiety in this new disclosure of colour: Will Shakespeare remembered that, nine years earlier, nine and a half years it must be now, the rebel Earl of Essex, divesting himself of doublet and gown, had kneeled to the block wearing such a scarlet waistcoat. Sir Walter Raleigh, against advice, had come to the Tower that day, making the excuse that he must be present to answer any accusations against himself uttered by the condemned man in his last moments. Raleigh had been roughly told he came to feed his eyes on the sight of his enemy's blood: and his own friends, fearing that gossip would make scandal of his appearance there, had urged him out of the throng pressing about the scaffold. Nevertheless, it was said, he looked on from a window in the armoury. Raleigh was widely and bitterly hated: more than once the mob would, unleashed, have had his life. He was a man of great enterprises and notable courage, proud, but authentically a poet, as few were who adopted the name. And now lesser men had triumphed over him, and he in turn lay condemned in the Tower these many years, for conspiracy against the Throne, having escaped the block only at the last moment. Since then there had been another plot against the Parliament, with one Guido Fawkes prepared to explode gunpowder. The times were more uneasy and fatal than ever. Death was ready to pounce on any man emerging out of the mob in London. Better to live quiet here, and let death come, in his own time, natural-wise and gentle. Better to sit by the river in Stratford than to be incarcerate by the Thames, like Raleigh, who doubtless looked out and thought on Essex in his scarlet waistcoat, and the blood spurting under the axe. Three blows it had needed to deliver Essex from the burden of life.

Raleigh, it was said, meditated oft and deep on death. Even Jack Donne, that ranging lover of women, now married and reformed, wrote only of God and the church and death. And Will Shakespeare in his time had riddled mortality through and through with words, till, like an old and useless sieve, the notion of death retained not a jot of significant meaning. Essex was dead: Southampton, his henchman, spared by Elizabeth, was freed from the Tower when Scottish James came south from Edinburgh, with all his furniture and a pack of place-seekers about him. The Queen was dead, having been Queen for forty-four years, only two less than the full count of Will Shakespeare's life down to this sunny summer's day. Almost to the last she had been vigorous, riding ten miles on horseback, and going to the hunt, all in the same day: a hard woman, and impervious to the inbiting cares which made a poet older and wearier than his years warranted. A poet had lost his Queen, for the which he suffered as a citizen. Yet in her stead he gained a King, even though it be but one mean, unpredictable, and oft ridiculous. A new monarch meant new royal favours, and the source of revenues persisted under another and more resounding name: the Lord Admiral's became the King's Men, and flourished still at the Globe.

From other deceases a poet suffered as a man, and that was more hardly borne. He had lost his father, soon after Essex:

his brother Edmund, a younker scarce known, had come to London, turned player, begotten a son out of matrimony, and both were lately dead. Within the year his mother died too. Neither Shakespearean vigour nor Arden pride availed when death came resolute and peremptory. And a man left un-parented in the midway of his life shivered the more in the chill blast to think there was no issue to continue his name. Yonder by Holy Trinity church lay little Hamnet, the only son of this bereft Will Shakespeare, eleven years old when he died. Had he lived, he were now a tall young man of twenty-five, twin to Judith. Yet all was not retreat. Life and death battled uncertainly through the family. Will Shakespeare was a grandfather this eighteen months, since his elder daughter, Susan, had borne a girl child to her husband, who was at least a gentleman and the son of a gentleman, come from Acton in the county of Middlesex. Will Shakespeare was also new-made an uncle, for his sister Joan, married to William Hart, the hatter, had now both son and daughter. Yet what were new births but fresh food for death? This was incon-sistent, a vain kicking against immovable pricks, a thoughtless carry-forward of youth's resentments into the later years when death, though never welcome, must surely seem but a prophecy ripening from the blossom of words into bitter but inevitable fruit. Added one to another, these considerations made of wisdom naught but a lesson in acquiesence.

A man no more than forty-six years of age should not harbour such uncomfortable thoughts. It was true that the three score years and ten promised in the scriptures were, upon average taken, not to be expected in these later days. Yet there were those who lived so long: and escaped dotage, to boot. The Queen had seen her seventieth year through. Bur-leigh was near eighty ere he died. A man with the better part of four years to run before he attained no more than fifty made himself absurd with such graveyard thoughts. Yet it was past denial that he had aged much of late. He had grown heavier in body, though still not stout: fuller fleshed, and

pouched round the jaws. Shaving his beard to leave but
moustaches, cut short and thin, and a tuft under the lower lip,
had not brought youth back to his face. His temples, ever
high, had encroached upon the crown of his head: his hair
receded, yielding further spoils to age, being interspersed
now with grey. He had lately sat for a portrait—a bad portrait
it turned out, and that not merely because it failed to flatter
him: he smiled now to recall the painter's puzzled face when
he asked that the doublet should be shewn one half facing
backward: "for," he had said, "I am a man ever in two minds,
all inward oppositions, and uncertain whither I go. Let the
doublet be symbolical!" Puzzled or not, the fellow had
painted the cloth better than the face.

Out upon it, he cried in his thoughts: I am no longer
entered in the lists of love. So that he cared not to please a
woman's amorous fancy (having been for many years but on
courteous, disinterested terms with his wife, Anne, who was
become white-haired and all engaged with her grandchild),
what mattered it that he had a bald head, a measured step, a
disposition to sit through the sunny afternoon and do nothing?
All his fellows were older now: Ben Jonson tamed out of his
unwisest truculence; Michael Drayton, disappointed at the
new court of King James, with the gold of his head transmuted
to silver; Dick Burbage, still playing and prospering, but
heavy-footed on the boards. Hot-foot-youth was crushing
them out of their old occupations. They that were wise and
fortunate, like Will Shakespeare, could withdraw a little,
warm themselves with contemplation of their own fame and
property. Poor Ben had not done so well for himself, and was
still fain to sell his books when debts beleaguered him: yet
even Ben had what he most desired, repute and flattery.

Nor could women have 'scaped the stealthy spoliation of
the years. What had become of a lady who once sat horse in
the courtyard of Southampton House, doubleted and hosed in
scarlet and white? Somewhere in the outlands of the north
she would be matron and mother now. Conceive her, with the

inward eye, garbed soberly in grey, seated as daylight gave place to dusk, and calling her children to her knee to tell them, but discreetly, how once on a time she had known the famed poet, Master Shakespeare, and spoken with him, and by privilege read certain of his poems ere they were printed. So was Will Shakespeare diminished to a theme for a mother's tattle, of which little children soon wearied, demanding to be told a livelier tale.

Those sonnets were printed now, however, printed this twelve-month and more. What call to hold them back when their ardours and anguishes no longer had power to hurt? All his sonnets were included in that book pell-mell, a hotchpotch: those writ by command to Southampton; those sprung with little occasion from a mood; those that were clean, addressed romantical to a disdainful lady: and those that were foul, reviling, even as they celebrated, the passions of the flesh. Set out in random sequence, with most of the clews to the maze misleading of intent, the sonnets would bewilder the enquiring reader. Thorpe, the printer, had not mended matters, copying certain scrips which were imperfect, and hastening the printing so that the poet, absent here in Stratford, could make no corrections. A man of forty-six need not look yet to the prospect of death. Time amply stretched before him; energy and interest would return, and here, in the quiet seclusion of New Place, he would presently to work, and render for the printer a full and faultless version of his plays and poems, the full toll of them.

Meanwhile, he wondered whether dark Nell—he had not seen her since the night Southampton and Essex marched by, condemned, to the Tower—ever read in print the sonnets writ to her? An her uncle, Peter Pandarus Fender, sustained his taste for the fashionable poets, he would surely expend fivepence on a little book by a man he had once pimped for? Nell, too, must be older, after these nine years. Her husband, haply, was dead? Had she married again, and, tiring of illicit pleasures abed, turned sober, borne children, reformed her ways, like

Jack Donne? Never now would Will Shakespeare know if Donne were indeed once her lover, or what substance there was to that pother of jealous hatreds evoked by two men's poems lying side by side in the same box. Nell had bedded with Donne, or else she had not bedded with him: and Will Shakespeare, grown somewhat bald and somewhat plump, neither knew nor cared. He could call her poor Nell now, in his thoughts, and think he had used her somewhat harshly, for doubtless she had been no worse than many another woman intemperate in blood and husbanded by a weakling. She was not of his kind; if she communioned only with his flesh and such part of his mind as answered to the flesh, the fault was in him, not in her. What passed between them, and was to ·him a torment in delight, an abasement cracking through every triumph, was doubtless for her no more than a natural sport. He was disposed now to indulgence, towards her and towards others he once had feared and hated: here was yet another sign that he detached himself from the turmoil of life. And any harm Nell had done him was richly counter-balanced by the plunder which his mind, energetic in retro-spective forays, had taken from their amour after Essex went by beneath the windows in Gracious Street and all kisses and embracements came to an end.

When first he escaped from Nell he found himself free only of a barren condition of despair, able to do no more for the playhouse than to take the stage again awhile in Ben Jonson's 'Sejanus', knowing that gossip considered him a poet come to a climax in his 'Hamlet', and there sucked dry. But the agonies of shame Nell brought him matured like wine within his mind: and now, sitting at the foot of an elm, to all appear-ance dazed with sunshine and sleep, he could feel his thoughts quicken as they recalled the three years which followed the accession of the new king. That had been the most furiously fruitful period of his life—and all the plays writ and performed in those three years were rooted in Nell or in the havoc she had cried within his soul. From wanton Nell came Cressida, and Pandarus was made in the image of her uncle: from Nell impassioned sprang his Cleopatra: from Nell with appetite whetted by sight of Southampton escorted to the Tower sprang Lady Macbeth: from the jealousies and sick suspicions she engendered in Will Shakespeare's mind came ' Measure for Measure ' and ' Othello '; from the torments she put him to rose all the screaming dementias of ' Lear ', writ when reason was like to split asunder beneath his skull. The fables, the framework of events upon which a poet must build, were there, in other books, in old plays, waiting to be taken and adapted: but the energy of invention, blowing like a three-year hurricane, had all its source in dark-eyed Nell. She might well be spared further imprecations, dismissed, nine years after their last parting, with an oldish man's indulgent smile.

These tragical pieces were all the best of him, save only ' Hamlet ', and in the making of that also Nell had a share. He had reached, though easy in his inward conceit, to but half the measure of his stature as a poet ere Nell came to him. This was passing strange, and held more than casual significance. In his youth he had oft toyed with the notion that good and evil are not so separable as preachers would have it, that consequences, though not to be evaded, cannot be predicted neither: he had mused upon fair lilies which grow out of mud. A young man perceives a notion, plucks it, holds it a moment, throws it away: years afterwards, when he is indifferent old, he finds what he has discarded come again to his hand, and understands at last its fuller purport. Nell had steeped him in mud, and he had cursed her for it: yet behold what later grew out of that mud, plays majestical and un-matched. Pause awhile: truth must not give place entirely to kind-heart compliments. These plays were writ not by Nell but by Will Shakespeare, and the poor lustful wench would be perplexed to trace her own lineaments in Lady Macbeth and in Cleopatra: the lily's roots are something less lovely than the flower. Will Shakespeare's retrospection, making plays

out of overpast experience, had kept only the heat and horror
of what, in the doing, had been all furtive degradation, adding
to it nobilities poor Nell could never dream on. She had
served her days—and her nights: there was enough bawdry
left in him to make him relish this gross amendment to the
thought.

Doubtless 'Hamlet' was the best of all these playhouse
tragedies. Divers were of that opinion. It was printed these
six years now in a tolerable version, to supplant that bastard
copy got out by a rascally printer the summer after the Queen's
death. Remembering that base piracy, his meditation turned
fretful, as if old wounds were grown angry again. He had
suffered oft from printers who asked permission neither from
author nor players, who paid no fee, and who cared not
whether what they issued were true to what the writer had
penned; but that his 'Hamlet' should appear to the world
so botched and misunderstood enraged him at the time, and
even now, when the fault had long been righted, stirred him
to reminiscent wrath.

One of the players, in need of a few shillings, must have
been bribed to treachery, for certain parts were almost per-
fectly rendered: but the play substantially was maimed from
start to finish. What was writ as prose appeared as verse, and
t'other way about. Some base fellow, hired for the purpose,
had stood in among the groundlings and secretly writ on his
tablets what he heard spoken from the stage. Had he heard
fair and recorded true, he had done less harm. But, pressed
for time, he turned stenographer, using some system of
symbols to shorten words: so that when the players spoke
slow, he caught the most of their phrases, but when they
spoke fast, he recorded in his own stale inadequate phrases
no more than the gist and sense of long periods. It was all
set to rights now, even the new and sweeter sounding names:
Polonius for Corambis, and Reynaldo for Montano. The
second printed 'Hamlet', a few printer's errors apart, recorded
the whole enlarged and revised scrip: too long for perform-

ance, but presenting all that Will Shakespeare had writ, and having writ, would not strike out for Dick Burbage nor any man.

He was startled out of his reverie to see his daughter Judith, straw-bonneted against the sun, gazing up at him from the roadway below.

"Why dost look, and say naught?" he asked.

"I feared to wake thee."

"That was kind."

Already, merely at her coming and the sound of her voice, his mood went weathercock to tenderness.

"But I was not asleep. I am not yet so old I must sleep after dinner," he told her.

"Yet, my dearest father, so still thou wert, I scarce dared breathe. And I could not see thine eyes, whether they were open or shut."

"Wert pleased to find me here?"

This was a fond, foolish custom he had taken to, like pushing a foot into an old, familiar slipper, ever gratefully received. Judith was his darling, and of late, the chief treasurer of his confidences: between them affection flowed calm and undisturbed, as the river flowed yonder: yet always he must seek out and engineer assurances of love from her lips.

"I am ever pleased to see thee, father."

He frowned as his mind, devious in its scrutinies, went about to discover a motive for these sweet-spoken words, and arraigned him that, whiles this girl grew through her childhood, he was commonly far away in London. He and she had made close acquaintance only these few late years: thus, for her, all about him was novelty, such as few fathers could hope to spring upon their children: for this cause she could truly say she was ever pleased to see him.

"Shall I go now? Have I disturbed you in your meditation? I meant no harm."

He stood up and was displeased to find his legs and his back stiff with aches. But he ran nimbly enough, and proud of the nimbleness, down the grassy bank, till he stood beside her in the roadway.

"Question for question," he said. "Am I a father so tyrannic that my daughter must go in fear of me, start timidly in my presence, swear she intends no harm if she but speaks to me?"

Judith looked at him then with eyes shaped and hazel-bright like his own. "Thou'rt ever kind and gentle to me, as thou well knowest."

"An I know it, then 'tis no secret from thee, child."

"Prithee do not interrupt upon my speech ere it be finished. 'Tis a fault thou'st reproved in me, but I see now it is inherited."

He caught up her hand and admired at the warm, firm touch of her fingers on his.

"I commended thee," she went on, "for a kind and gentle father, a very nonpareil of fathers, but with one exception."

"And that?"

She laughed. "When thou'rt at work, either pen in hand or silent in thought, upon thy poesies, and there enters Judith, thy fond, devoted daughter, then thou'rt like to be chuffish and surly."

"I fear me this is a true indictment. Whither now?"

"Home."

"I'll come with thee, child, an I may."

"Child!" She made a wry mouth as she repeated the word.

"Crave pardon that I treated such ripe years as thine irrevently. How many are they now?"

"Twenty-five."

Walking at her side, he remembered that a little while since he had made up the count, reckoning how Hamnet, his son, would speak and look were he not dead these many years. The boy had lain longer in the grave than he had walked the earth. And Judith, still unwed—but she must not throw away all her preciousness on the first comer—had become a grown woman. In his thoughts he saw her still a maid of sixteen: a foolish habit, and one he must learn to correct. Yet there

was in her speech and in her manner a simplicity which
marked her younger than her years: wise within, all innocent
to the world. She came late to full development, as he himself
had done in his youth, and might have so continued had he
never left Stratford.

At the foot of Walker's Street he paused and, nodding
towards the Clopton bridge, said: "The furthest arch, that
nearest the Banbury road—dost remember once I held thee up
to look on the water passing underneath?"

"That was the year Hamnet died I remember. The current
strikes against the bank and returns through the same arch.
I have demonstrated the strangeness to many since then, who
never noted what is always there to see."

"And I," he exclaimed, "have not thought on't again from
that day to this. I wonder what retained it in thy memory?"

"That's easy to answer. A visit from my father in those
days, even upon such an unhappy occasion, was an event of
moment, rare, surprising, and long to be talked on afterward."

"And now thy father is as everyday as the making of butter
or the washing of soiled pots?"

"Not so. Thou'rt more dear to me now, and we are better
known each to each—art seeking to trap me, to make me say
outright I love thee?"

"I believe I was. If it were a fault, forgive it. I can return
the declaration word for word."

She slid her hand into the crook of his arm, and they
turned and walking up the rising street towards the thatched
roof and grey garden walls of New Place.

"I have much to make amends for," he told her. "Nay,
every man of my age can say, in his heart at least, so much as
that, and know that all his effort will not repair the half of
what lies heavy on his conscience. I meant, to come closer to
the issue, I cannot have too much of thy society, Judith. All
thou'lt give, I shall be grateful for."

She made no answer, and presently he asked, anxious-faced:
"Have I said ought to offend?"

"Surely not. I was but in a consideration, and marvelling to myself. A father, I know, bears great affection toward his child, as the child owes him affection in duty. A duty lightly yielded, for me. But thou'rt a man highly placed in a world greater than any I know, famed in London, and esteemed by all in Stratford. There must be in thy memory and in that inventive mind, so strange to me, whole continents of experience I could never sight. This being so, wherefore dost desire the company of one, thy daughter perchance, but in all other sorts with no claim on thine attention?"

Thus Judith proved herself another of them who marvelled at a poet not that he writ so well, but that, confronted with blank paper, he should be able to cover it with inked words, any words, all out of his own invention. Her father put back his head and roared his laughter aloud.

"I could give thee a long, sophistical answer to that, but a short will suffice. I am not Will Shakespeare, the poet whose powers and reputation thou hast so courtier-like over-esteemed, during all my waking hours. Oft enough, for days, ay, and months together, the poet never indwells this ill-wearing flesh. And between visitations, my Judith, I am but Will Shakespeare of New Place, Stratford, a passable fellow, no more, if somewhat vain: and vain chiefly of his daughter's love for him."

"Then, father, thou wert not meditating upon some new piece for the playhouse when I came upon thee by the boundary elm? And my coming did not distract thee from thy work?"

"This question is a rebuke for idleness. I'll conceal naught. I have a new play in the making. Not a word writ as yet. And were I as diligent as thou deemest, I had been cogitating it into some sort of shape this afternoon. The truth is, I sat and thought of many things, but none of them so much as cousin-german to the play."

They came to the gate in the wall, opened it, and passed in. Will Shakespeare was ever a lover of gardens and a great questioner of gardeners, though himself of no notable skill or assiduity at the labours thereof. Now that he possessed these flower beds and orchards of his own, and had come to dwell in the house he had long held in freehold, the garden was his unwearying delight. Flower-beds were a new fashion, unknown in his childhood save at the greatest houses: wherefore he felt great pride to possess, besides orchards and a kitchen garden, an ingenious knot sheltered by trellised Lady's Bower and quaint-trimmed bushes of yew and rosemary. He could not now be restrained from walking round the paths once more, and Judith walked by his side, admiring at the tall yellow flower-de-luces, by some called iris, the clove carnations, the peonies, larkspurs and white lilies, and the tulips new fetched from Holland. As he went, pausing now to savour the fragrance of a damask rose, now to root up a weed, and anon to examine the mulberries, some of them already ripe enough to come away in the hand, the "passable fellow" talked to his daughter of the other Shakespeare, the poet, disclosing his mind as he would not and could not, in these days, to any other creature.

"This play that I intend," he said, "is not to be writ yet. There's another, of which parts are already complete, I must finish first, and soon, for 'tis to be called 'A Winter's Tale.' But the other, the better, must wait and ripen awhile. Like fruit, its season may not be enforced. It is not possible to abrogate treaties made with time. Ripeness is all. I have said that before: no matter. The new piece is to be set upon an island, and it shall have fairies in it, methinks, and a monster, a caged monster I could call cousin."

"Like the 'Midsummer Night's Dream'? I saw that when the players came to Stratford, the summer I was seventeen."

"Not so like, I fear me. Nor is the fable full of surprisals and excitements. It will not please thee much, child. I am a man much changed of late years, and it hath taken me long, overlong perchance, to make reckoning of the change. My passions are all spent. Once I was urgent and tumultuous within: now I am turned, like it or not, to the habit of contemplation. Some virtue hath gone out of me. And the strangeness, child, lies in this: I know my loss, and regret it not."

"Father, this asks more than I can give. Thou speakest what are enigmas to my ears. So much I must at once confess. But speak on, and haply I'll attain comprehension."

He looked at her, and she saw his love in his eyes. But he said: "Nay, I'd not have thee possess all the knowledge I have come by. Let it be magic to thee. Let it be magic," he repeated, as if to himself.

Then, briskly and cheerfully: "But think not I have confided forebodings of failure. What is lost is gone: call it dramatical energy. But I have much left, enough to eke out such further labours as I care to undertake. Poetry is left to me, though it be transformed all to contemplative calm. And still I have the ability to laugh and to make others laugh. This is more than nothing."

An upper window in the house was opened, and the thin mindless wail of a child unfed sounded through the garden.

"Susan is here," said Judith, "with her babe. Mother will be busy giving her endless counsel."

"Whiles we must go within and admire at a new tooth or a noise which, by kindness, might be construed into the first elements of an English word."

"Prophet!" said Judith, pointing up to the window where Mistress Anne Shakespeare, her mother, leaned out, whitehaired and benevolent, and beckoned them indoors.

XXI

THE SWAN INN faced the Bear across the width of Bridge Street and, on its other frontage, looked out on a wood yard and the bar-gated causeway leading to the Clopton bridge. Will Shakespeare, proceeding there, went long-cloaked against the nipping airs of the March evening. He was appointed to meet old friends, his fellows in the penman's trade, Ben Jonson and Michael Drayton. With neither of them had he encountered these several years. On his last visit to London (sixteen months since, in the November of 1614) he saw little of the playhouse poets, avoiding so far as possible the Bankside and the Globe, although his pieces continued to be performed there: but no new pieces. Since 'The Tempest', he furnished nothing for the King's Men, except a little weary carpentering of other poets' work: insertions and revisions.

He looked back now on four years with nothing writ, and no impulse in himself to write: nor did this barreness move him to regrets. His work was done, his reputation secured, and he had revenues sufficient to live as a gentleman. It should be ample occupation for his retirement to consider in leisurely sort, and carefully bring to fine perfection, each word examined and estimated with a jeweller's precision, the texture of all his poems and plays, so that the world might have them, collected authentical together, in a printed book. This, it was true, was a labour he for ever put off, pleading against the arraignments of his conscience that, with so much time before him, he could wait upon the suitable mood. More secretly, he went in doubt: in many of the plays, printed in haste and without warrant, there were gross errors easy to amend: but from the greater task, the final faceting of meaning and expression, the chase of the last perfection, his mind withdrew, timid and distrustful.

Almost it seemed that conscience called him, lethargic and aware of his own inadequacy, to revise the work of another man, a stranger more richly gifted than himself. Although it was possible for the Will Shakespeare of 1616 to smile at the private follies and contumacies of his past self, that younger Will Shakespeare had made poems and plays beyond the ken of him who now, bald-headed and broader-girthed, supplanted his title to the name and lived in gentlemanly ease at New Place in the town of Stratford-on-Avon. The wisdom of this older man amounted to—what had he concluded, once, the sum of wisdom to be?—a willing acceptance. Qualify or extend that to a knowledge of his own inadequacy. Therefore, possessing such knowledge, made humble by it, was it possible for the older man, grown out of passions and bereft of their energy, to con the work of the younger, and say: this is good and shall stand: this is indifferent and shall be struck out: more temerarious still, this can be improved and should be writ thus and thus? Crippled by such doubts, Will Shakespeare, who was now fifty-one years of age and older than that in his mind, was glad to clutch at the playhouse company's unwillingness yet to release their rights in the more popular plays; glad to postpone the start of these revisions to some day, unnamed and unlocated, in the future.

He had quit the playhouse and intended no return. Notwithstanding, it pleasured him much that Ben Jonson should come to Stratford this day, and that Michael Drayton, a Warwickshire man, should ride into the town that they might all three have a merry meeting. Ben was proud. Still indifferent poor, he had that afternoon carped a little in his admiration of New Place, and doubtless in his heart he envied his friend Shakespeare this solid manifestation of success: not, as he declared, that Ben Jonson, London born and bred, schooled at Westminster under Camden, could live anywhere but in London. Ben found little to praise in the town of Stratford: said its distinctions were but two, that Will Shakespeare chose to live there, rotting his brain on rustic chatter, and that Ben

Jonson lodged one night at the Swan. Ben was proud and would not stay at New Place, tempering the refusal (as he would not have troubled to do in his ruder, younger years) with a claim that inns were ever the most suitable resorts for poets to meet and discourse. "In thine own house, Will," he said, "thou'rt a man of family, a mere citizen of Stratford: at the Swan thou'lt be a poet again, Ben Jonson's peer."

So to the Swan now Shakespeare made his way, wondering if Drayton would remember another evening at another tavern, when he and Jonson and Shakespeare, and none else, discoursed over the wine. Nor Drayton nor Jonson would recall, for they did not know, how Will Shakespeare ended that sorry night, crawling back, foolish with gratitude, to the bed of a dark mistress who summoned him when her husband went away. Ben had drunk intemperate that night at the Mermaid: it was to be hoped he had mended his ways, for the tossing of pots, though it could provoke mirth on the stage, was elsewhere apt to be dreary, and, when it came to retching and quarrelling, hateful. Michael Drayton, never a frere of Ben Jonson, had loathed him that night as, with Will Shakespeare to take the other arm, he had lugged a foul-smelling brother poet out into Bread Street and home to bed. Drayton would be coming to the Swan this evening to pleasure Will Shakespeare and merely to tolerate Ben Jonson. Ben, did he know so much, would despise him for it. But they had all grown older: the peace would be kept. Then, remembering Drayton's face, paler even than of wont, and bleak with contempt, as he salvaged Jonson from the Mermaid, Shakespeare laughed aloud. A man passing on the other side of the High Street turned at the sound and gave him a respectful good-night.

All Stratford now was proud of its citizen, Will Shakespeare. The old wiseheads, who had prophesied calamities upon the head of a youth lacking all diligence, were dead now, most of them: and such as survived forgot their former denunciations when they saw who occupied New Place. This also Will Shakespeare remembered, as he passed the High Cross surmounted by its roofed house and turret and clock. And as he turned down towards the river, walking out from the black shadows thrown by the buildings in Middle Row, he remembered how, a youth instructed by his father to deliver gloves at this same Swan Inn, he had met with Hamnet Sadler in the mists, and persuaded him to complete the errand. That Will Shakespeare should marry Nan Hathaway, who had gone so long unwed, puzzled Hamnet. Hamnet would sometimes look resentful at Mistress Shakespeare as if her hair were still gold in place of white, and as if she were the one who had abandoned home and family. Hamnet sometimes, all dutiful, sat to read in one of his friend Shakespeare's printed plays: but all escaped him, meaning, accents, melody and wit. He was proud of his judgement, proud that Will had proved the worth of Stratford in London town; but why London should make a pother over verses so crazily fantasticate, this was past Hamnet Sadler's comprehension.

At the Swan, Shakespeare learned that Michael Drayton had but a moment since arrived, elegant and courteous.

"Thou'st weathered the years better than either Ben or me," Shakespeare told him.

"If the meaning of this," cried Jonson, jovial from inspecting the supper already coming from the ovens, "is that Michael hath not notably increased his girth, 'tis conceded. But consider my hair, ye dotards. Doth it not keep its colour? No silver flecking there, my masters."

"'Twould take more than time to wither thee," Drayton smiled at him.

Without speaking his conclusions, Shakespeare recalled that Ben's tawny hair had never possessed much colour to lose; and he noted Drayton did not draw a lip at the use of his first name. Friendship, not so readily given as in youth, baulked no more at petty offences. Age, being lazy, came easily by its virtues.

"Add to which," Drayton continued, "thou'rt youngest of the company. Wilt outlive us all."

Ben was pleased by that. When they sat to meat, he commended to them the reading of Quintilian and Horace, distinguished between the merits of the second Pliny and Tacitus, and smacked his lips upon an epigram of Petronius, which he repeated several times and insisted upon Englishing for Will Shakespeare's benefit, whose little Latin and less Greek, acquired upon the hard benches of the grammar school in this same town of Stratford, demanded his compassion.

"I had a good schoolmaster there," said Shakespeare. "One Simon Hunt. I can remember his teaching, saving your presence, Ben, better than the man himself, for when I was ten years older, in 'seventy four—that's forty years since."

"We talk like grandfathers," cried Ben.

"I am a grandfather."

"Put it out of mind. Tell on about this dominus who taught, as thou imaginest, passing well."

"Ay, but he did teach well. The test of Latin is not in the memory, as is thy belief: 'tis in what profit Latin can be put to in the English tongue."

"A contentious statement," cried Jonson, "masquerading half a truth as a whole. But I am in merciful mood. I forbear to crush thee. Proceed. What happed to this Simon schoolmaster of thine in 'seventy four?"

"He fled the country, having turned Papist. And for that, Ben, he must escape thy rebuke."

Jonson muttered that he was quit of his Roman errors long since, and Shakespeare continued: "Master Hunt, Father Hunt he became, died young in Rome. Or so I heard. After him came a Welshman, Jenkyns. His Latin was Welsh in enunciation, and he taught it as a sergeant-at-arms drills recruits. I have pictured him at his hic, haec, hoc, in my comedy of the Merry Wives. You will remember the passage?"

Looking at his friends, he saw Drayton nod, polite but evasive, and Ben turn his head away. They did not at all remember Will Shakespeare's comedy: their interest was all for what they themselves had writ. Drayton was too courteous or too modest to talk overmuch of himself, but such scruples could not restrain Ben Jonson, who began to tell how the Earl of Pembroke, out of esteem, sent him twenty pounds every year to buy books. Then he complained that not half of his comedies were in print.

When they had done eating and sat over the wine, Ben, with more colour now in his plump cheeks, grew censorious awhile, after his former fashion. He commended Drayton to his face for the intent and scope of his 'Polyalbion,' but said the execution lagged behind the promise, and the verses were too long. As for Will Shakespeare, he was a very paragon of poesy, but that he wanted, besides sound Latin and Greek, art. Next Ben must take off his signet ring and show them his device of a compass with one foot in the word Center, the other in the word Broken, which impresa he declared in all ways superior to Drayton's or to Shakespeare's falcon, spear and helmet. He was also of a mind to make mock of Will's high temples, and forthwith recounted a merry jest concerning a bald man who, enquiring of another why he grew his hair so long, was answered that it was to see if it would grow to seed that he might sow it on bald pates.

At this Drayton was fain to thrust back his chair from the table, but Shakespeare stilled his protest by commending the tale and laughing loud at it. Drayton, thereupon (in all innocence, for, Shakespeare was persuaded, he knew naught of Mistress Nell in Gracious Street) began to speak his opinion of the poem, 'The Anniversary,' by John Donne. If Ben roared again to the assault, at least it was not now against his friends at table. Silently they suffered him to speak his vinous censures, which, though protracted, amounted to the not uncommon opinion that 'The Anniversary' was profane and full of blasphemies; moreover, such an extolling of woman had been apter writ of the Virgin Mary.

As soon as he paused for breath, Drayton objected: "Yet I have heard thee put Donne first among living poets."

"As maybe: but not for this."

Shakespeare strove to turn the dispute with a question. "I am not well informed of what chances in London of late, and I have not read this poem of Master Donne's. Explain to me what it is, and the scandal thereof."

At this Ben grew jocund again and, with some interjected amendments from Drayton, he expounded the new jest of Jack Donne, who, it seemed, composed sundry elegies upon the death of one Elizabeth Drury, a maid of fourteen, the only surviving daughter of Sir Robert Drury, a gentleman of Suffolk. Upon this girl Donne had never cast eyes, nor so much as heard of her, till after she was dead. Yet he was moved to profound grief, composed his long poems, all in an ecstasy of mourning, and despatched them to the bereaved father, who chanced to be of surpassing wealth and, as a small return, gave the unworldly poet and his family a commodious set of chambers in his own London house, in Drury Lane. Ben saw in this a monstrous imposition, yet fit for laughter. Even Drayton's smile was sour.

"The most profligate wencher in town," cried Jonson, "is turned religious, and to good profit. 'Tis said he seeks out all his amorous verses, made in his hot youth, and with tearful lamentations burns them as they were heretics and he the grand inquisitor. Yet I doubt not he keeps secret copies."

At that Shakespeare stirred, discomfited by old memories, and then, smiling to himself, wondered if Jack Donne, reformed, no more piratical, had found his penitent way to a box standing in a bedroom in Gracious Street, and what he said when he discovered therein other poems than his own.

Drayton protested that Donne was become truly another man and, although his funereal courtship of Sir Robert Drury's riches might be scandalous, his professions of religion were sincere. Moreover, last year, the bold soldier of Cadiz, the swashing lover, had consummated his adoption of a better life by submitting himself for ordination as a priest.

"Why, so he is," said Jonson, in no way abashed. "I had forgot. He performs the office of curate in the parish of

Paddington. I believe that was my information. Come, more canaries. We'll drink to him. To holy Jack Donne. We shall see him a bishop yet, or Dean of St. Paul's at the least. He'll be more at ease in the prose of sermons than ever he was bursting out of the buskins of verse. Yet I fear me I see him brightening a lickerish eye as he leans over the pulpit and picks and chooses among his congregation to find the prettiest female face."

Drayton, aghast at this profanity, sought to maintain that Donne would make an exemplary parson, but Jonson roared him down and drank to his own toast, thrice. Will Shakespeare, no more than sipping at his wine for courtesy's sake, for he had lost the custom of London drinking and already the blood throbbed in his temples, paid little attention to what was said. Jack Donne was nothing to him now: he could sit here and suffer himself to speculate if black-haired Nell would be one of Donne's congregation, as pictured by Ben—and feel no tiniest pang of jealousy. Another passion had spent itself within him, leaving no wrack behind but printed words.

The conversation went on, with Jonson, as of old, having the main part. Sometimes Shakespeare threw a sentence or two into the flood tide, but he scarce heard what he said, sitting abstract and contemplative. His attention roused again when he heard his own name from Jonson's lips. Ben, he saw (though the wine had taken toll of his own sight) was sweating freely, and not from the warmth of the fire. He had the wide-eyed stare, not easily moved, of one who has drunk too freely. But what he had to say was shrewd enough, although it was to be his last lucid utterance of the evening. And it seemed that Ben, after all, had some of his friend's work in memory.

"Will here, he is a changed man also. Domestic peace and overmuch comfort have tamed his blood. It can be seen in the women he centres his later plays upon."

"What's amiss with them, Ben?"

"Why naught. They are very seemly and likeable females, but, to be blunt with thee, Will, they are but half alive. I'll tell thee what it is, thou'rt not intent upon them. And the reason for this is plain: thou'rt no longer in love with women."

Will Shakespeare considered this judgement. "In some sort, thou'st hit upon truth. Yet say not I have ceased to love women. Say rather, I have learned to love them after another fashion."

"And a better," said Drayton, who, crossed in love, remained a faithful, high-minded bachelor.

"Not a better," Ben declared. "Thou wert never a dramatist," he told Drayton roughly. "A passable poet, I'll concede, but never one to command the power of the playhouse, the energy of dramatic conflict. The change in Will—I perceive it now—is this: in his plays of late he no longer makes love to his women. Is't not so, Will? Thine approach to them is altered. Thou'rt grown"—he paused for the word—"paternal."

Here was a judgement to be considered; but being considered, it could not be gainsaid. Imogen perhaps escaped the scrutiny, but Marina in 'Pericles', Perdita in 'A Winter's Tale', and most certainly 'Miranda', though he had made them speak love to young men, were all presented as daughters: as his own daughter: as his own Judith.

Soon they decided they could talk no more. Shakespeare bade farewell to Michael Drayton, hard-pressed to conceal his yawns, and to Ben, who took his hand to wish him well and then forgot, and turned away to call for a last cup of wine. It might be a year, two years or three, or more, ere they met again; but now the wine worked potent in them. They parted with laughter, yet not reluctantly.

Walking home to New Place, Will Shakespeare blamed himself that his feet stumbled as he went. Time was when, invited to such a meeting as this now past, he would excuse himself, say he was in pain and could not come. Wiser to have held to that old and proven strategy: yet it had been churlish to refuse two old friends come so far to greet him. The after penalties of wine could be slept away. Let him to bed and all would be well. Yet it was strange to find himself shivering as with cold even while his head burned and his thoughts went dizzily about it and about. Sleep was the remedy this petty malady called for.

It was a strange notion of Ben's, that, of no intent, unsuspect by himself, he who had made out of fact and fancy so many women sweet to love, and had loved them as he made them, was now grown paternal in his poesy. There was a measure of truth in it, and he was not disposed to dispute, or to be ashamed. If he unwittingly thus paid tribute to Judith, she had all his dear love, and deserved it. Yet again, even that was in the past. Four years were gone since he had sent a play to the Globe, and the Globe, since then, burned down and rebuilt. Scarce a timber was left of the old Shoreditch Theatre, erected by Dick Burbage's father. It had been a bold enterprise, that night in the snow when they tore down the whole structure and carted it to the Bankside, to build it again as the Globe.

Judith, also, was gone from him. It would be vile to grudge her that freedom. Thomas Quiney, the vintner, was an husband unfit to match her: so much could be said of any man. Yet his affection towards her seemed sober and honest, and she had desired the marriage. Only a curmudgeonly father would stand in her way: but it was grief to see her go. Some malignant creature had since sworn an information against her and young Quiney, for the marriage took place the previous month, in a season forbid by canon law. The parson should have foreseen that. There must be no scandal. Some there were in Stratford who misliked the prosperity of the Shakespeare family: three years agone his other daughter, Susan, had been compelled, reluctantly, under advice, to protect her name in the church courts against a slander of incontinence. Susan, however, was a merry wench, quick-tongued and broad-tongued—which had given purchase to the slander. She was well able to conserve her own repute, even were her husband not skilled in the ways of the world.

It was for Judith her father feared. She was softer and finer in grain, simple, of a natural innocence. He fretted his feverish mind over her now, as he went wearily back to New Place, striving to guess whether she were as happy in her marriage as she professed, whether she would be with child and how soon, whether she would have son or daughter, and whether childbed would relent its worst torments for this his dearest daughter. Bootless to tell himself that time would disclose answers to all these questions: better to creep on slippered feet to bed and yield to slumber and to the hope that the next day would clear a mind dispirited and all awhirl with sick bewilderments.

But the next morning he woke in a fever, and scarce knew he lay shuddering in his own sweat, aware of little more in the world outside himself than that Nan, his good wife, ill-used by him, had brought his daughter Judith to help minister to his wants. After three days the fever abated, but left him feeble in body and in his mind strangely lethargic. Judith smiled to see him wake cool from a long sleep, and said he would soon be out and about. She showed him the sunshine spilling golden across the room from the windows: though it was burdensome to turn his head on the pillow, he looked to please her, and thanked her when she told him the wind was swung warm, the daffodils were all in flower, and the orchard trees in bud, the pink peeping through the green.

"'Twill make you well again when you go forth to see them," she said.

He engaged then to make his first excursion to the garden in her company, and said nothing of his fears, for he did not know whether it were the illusion of sickness or a veritable foreknowledge which made him feel the tides of death sweeping cold and irresistible through his body.

The fever returned, but in briefer visitations. In one of the cooler intervals, while his mind was calm, he asked his wife to send for Master Francis Collins, the attorney. Perceiving the dismay in her face, he bade her be of good cheer.

"Death may come as well to the young and the strong,"

he said, "as to such as myself. I requested Collins to draft me a will in January. 'Tis a duty I have neglected overlong. And I need occupation for these idle hours."

He made Anne promise not to tell Judith, however. Master Collins was precise and tedious as any other attorney, and what was told him in good plain English came out on paper in the complex language of the law, which had oft amused a younger Will Shakespeare but was now a weariness to a man lying sick unto his death. The first draft would need to be much revised, said Collins, if only to make new provision for Judith, married since the will was first put in project. Doubtless, her father thought, Thomas Quiney would be a good husband to her, and return love for love: but wiser to secure her against the future. Collins undertook to arrange a fund in trust for Judith. Susan, being the elder, and less prosperous in her marriage, should inherit New Place. Twenty-five shillings and eightpence should go each to Hamnet Sadler and William Reynolds, and to Dick Burbage, Heminge and Cundell at the Globe, that they might buy mourning rings. Ten pounds to the poor of Stratford. 'Twas customary, pious, and haply would be welcomed.

He remembered that Judith cherished a great affection for the broad silver gilt bowl. She should have it, and the rest of the plate could go to Elizabeth, Susan's little daughter, for when she grew to marriageable age. Collins had formerly explained that it was not necessary to specify inheritances for Anne: the law secured for her, as the surviving wife, a dower interest in one third of the whole estate, and residence in New Place. But Anne, he knew, desired to possess, beyond all possibility of dispute, the old bed in which her children had been born and in which she had slept since she and her husband lived separate. 'Twas a whim, a fond foolishness, but it should be observed, to please her. He called Collins back from the door and told him of Anne's request.

"I will see to it," the attorney said.

"Be sure you make no error, or else my wife will be

offended. I do not mean this bed, purchased since we came to New Place. The other, in the south room. You can see it an you wish."

"That will be unnecessary." And Collins came back to the table, dipped pen in ink, and made another note on his papers.

The next day the fever ran high, and urgently he demanded that Collins come again. The attorney arrived with the will drafted on three sheets, not a fair copy, he declared, for the amendments were all writ between lines, but it was adequate for the purposes of the law. He insisted that he must read it through from first to last to a man whose mind whirled hot and restless, weary, but uncontrolled in its furious haste; a man who could attend to no more than a phrase here and there; a man who was amused to hear himself described as "in perfect health and memory God be praised"; who feared there was something erroneous in the will concerning his wife Anne, but could not catch at it and durst not stay to dispute. Then in came Hamnet Sadler and three other substantial men of Stratford, walking, against their wont, soft-footed, to watch a sick Will Shakespeare summon his little strength for the task of scrawling his signature at the foot of three several sheets which he could scarce see as he thrust pen at them.

Thereafter he looked for death each coming night or morning, but death lingered on the way: while he lay thus waiting, his sister Joan lost her husband, William Hart. They did not tell him of this, and Judith attended the funeral sicker with expectation than with present grief. She knew herself to be with child now, and asked her mother to tell her father that, were the babe to prove a boy, it should be called after him, not William but Shakespeare Quiney. Being informed of this resolve, he whispered the name several times, and they saw pleasure brighten his pallid face.

When he was absolved for a space from fever, he taxed himself with unseemly fears, and almost believed he would presently rise from his bed and be about again. But when the fever came back he was lost to comfort, for, although the prospect of death had grown so familiar that the terror ebbed from it, reducing it to the likeness of sweet sleep, the spinning fantasies of his mind sped in such disorder that he feared to lose his reason ere he died. Amid the agitation of these bewilderments he remembered, as sharp as it had been yesterday, the death of Robert Greene, who, scarce knowing him, had dubbed him an "upstart crow." If he were dying, he was dying better found than Greene, not lousy nor poor, and with his family around him. Yet, like Greene, he was mortal sick of a fever sprung from a surfeit. He consoled himself, however, that he had taken no sour, cold pickled herrings, and the wine at the Swan had been canaries, not rhenish. The distinction seemed important.

In one of these feverish fits he at last called to mind what it was in the will that had troubled him: Collins had made him bequeath to Anne his ' second-best bed with the furniture.' Dull-witted lawyer not to detect the insult implicit in such a phrase ! Poor Nan had suffered over-much from her husband: she should not be exposed to such a posthumous contumely. The will must be recalled and amended. Then he forgot this annoyance, for there were other matters of import he must attend to ere he let life slip from him. His plays, which he had oft determined to revise for the printer, were left still imperfect, uncollected: some botched in print, some lying in script among the playhouse stores. It was fortunate Burbage had salved all the chests from the Globe when it was destroyed by fire.

The fever left him before he died. He had some clear-minded hours when he lay and could see about him in the room; the first flies of spring noisy under the ceiling; the poor helpless physician striving to look wise; Anne and Susan and Judith hiding grief behind tender smiles. He was too weak to stir a hand and, from the way they all bent over him when he spoke, he judged his voice had sunk to a mere piping.

Yet he heard his own words loud in his mind, which now was blessedly lucid and cool. At last he remembered that the physician was John Hall, Susan's husband, who had rid Michael Drayton of a tertian ague with an infusion of violets: he would not so easily cure his new patient!

Will Shakespeare's principal awareness was of himself as a man frustrate, vanquished. He had failed in all he set heart and mind to. He was a faulty husband to Anne, and a father who had long abandoned his children here in Stratford while he chambered and hunted fame in London. He was leaving no son to inherit his name. His plays had had their first flowering time in London, but slothfully he had neglected to perfect them for print, till now it was too late. And this was not unjust, for he who, arrogant under a modest demeanour, had held himself to be a master of words, which are the keys to wisdom, had never, save in transient illusions, come to a comprehension of life. Grasping at ultimate secrets, he found even the true nature of everyday events mysterious. And now came death, the simplest of events, the long dreaded, which answered, or silenced, all questions. There was only one marvel in all this: he was not embittered. Death found him, a poor prey, but ripe for the taking.

Yet even now vanity stirred within him. He saw on the table by the bedside a gilt hand-mirror, lying face down. It had been placed there, no doubt, for someone to test his failing life, to catch the exhalation of his last breath dimming the glass. At that thought, he felt his dry lips part in a smile. He asked for the mirror to be held in front of his face, and, at the third effort, Judith understood his desire. Staring at his own reflected image, he saw himself very pale, his lips cracked, and his face swollen. The dome of his temples seemed all the more bald by contrast with the rough grey beard covering lips and chin. A barber would shave the beard after he was dead. Yet, he thought, if they take a mask, for a monument, it shall grievously misrepresent me: I was not so bland and foolish in my heyday.

He was unconscious for nearly an hour ere the physician declared him dead: yet he stared up at the ceiling, while his breath came faint and slow, with wide-opened eyes. They remained open after he died, and Anne, his wife, went and fetched two silver coins. As she bent over him to draw down the lids over the blank eye-balls, she remembered a warm September afternoon in the greenwood, by the Avon, when this cold corpse had been young and eager, and she, timid to see the fervour in his eyes, had reached out her fingers and closed the lids ere his arms came urgent round her.

She did not begin to weep until she had dropped the coins softly into place.

THE END

AUTHOR'S POSTSCRIPT: HISTORICAL ORIGINS

THIS novel has been long in consideration—ten years at least. When I found the idea of it becoming urgent in my mind and taking more definite shape, I began to study in greater detail what is known of Shakespeare's life and of the lives of some of his contemporaries. The story, as it is now written, contains much of my own invention and interpretation, but all, I believe, conforming to recorded facts or developed from them and from a close study of Shakespearean texts.

I did not wish to write in the first person because that method has limitations which would, I foresaw, involve me in too many artifices in order to get the whole of the story told, unless I made Shakespeare himself the narrator—an undertaking I could not contemplate. Nevertheless, I felt I must adapt the technique of telling this story to the time in which it is set, so before I began to write, I set myself to find a suitable style, and to practise myself in it. Such a style, I decided, had several requirements. First; it should not be artificial, not wholly different from my normal way of writing, but a style evolved out of it, so that I could write the book freely and without self-consciousness. Second: as I had to render not only the speech but the thoughts and emotions of people living between 1580 and 1616, it must be a style in keeping with the period, such as would not grossly offend the eyes and ears of a scholar specialising in Elizabethan-Jacobean literature. Third: while I must, to fulfil the second requirement, employ many expressions and constructions not now in ordinary use, they should be made immediately intelligible to the modern reader. In brief, my style should *suggest* the period, but be free from obstructive archaisms. I have tried to avoid words or constructions which came into use after Shakespeare's death, and equally not to use old

words and expressions in senses which belong to later yea:
But I am not a scholar, and lack the scholar's patient care, as
well as his knowledge; so I dare not claim to have made no
anachronistic slips at all in my diction. For any errors I must
beg indulgence, and hope that none of them will seem
outrageous.

I cannot whole-heartedly regret my deficiencies in scholarship, for I suspect that, with a scholar's outlook to halt the
inventions of my mind, this novel would never have been
conceived, shaped, and at last realised on paper. On the other
hand, I am deeply grateful to many writers more learned than
I can ever hope to be, and part of this debt is acknowledged in
the bibliography. I am grateful not merely for the information I have garnered and put to my own uses in this story,
but for the sustained pleasure my vicarious researches have
brought me, for the enlargement of my private knowledge
and understanding.

It was an ambitious, perhaps a foolhardy, task to present the
life of Shakespeare in the form of a novel. I could not hope to
render an adequate account of him as an artist. The Shakespearean splendours must remain in his own words, and outside
the scope of the task I set myself: this was to tell the story of
his life so far as it is known and so far as I could more intimately
imagine it, affording myself and my readers no more than a
few glimpses into the less inaccessible quarters of his workshop,
his mind. If I seem to have gone about the job with insufficient
humility, that is in part explained by my conviction, held these
many years, that, whatever sort of a man William Shakespeare
was, he was not an abstract force but a human being.

I cannot hope to escape the charge that in making a life-
length portrait of Shakespeare I have to one degree or another
imputed to him thoughts and feelings which properly belong
to myself. The same accusation has been brought against
Mr. Bernard Shaw for his 'The Dark Lady of the Sonnets',
and against Frank Harris for a play which I have not read.
If I were to plead Not Guilty I should perhaps fail to convince

myself. There is a passage in this novel, towards the end of
Chapter XV. (it begins: "One morning he realised, what he
should have known from the first") in which I have put
Shakespeare himself into the same dilemma. It is easier to
attain an objective manner than an objective outlook; that
the two are often confused does not make the distinction less
important. Again, an objective outlook can at best be only
a comparative achievement, not an absolute. A man only
deceives himself if he imagines he can wholly escape from his
own personality, and every honest writer knows that strict
limits are set to his powers of thinking and feeling himself
into the stead of one of his own created characters. In miti-
gation of my offences, my only further plea is that I have
striven to draw Shakespeare (as I shall presently demonstrate
in detail) close to the evidence of records and his own printed
words, and that the Shakespeare of my story is very different
from the man I imagine myself to be.

The known facts of Shakespeare's external life may seem
scanty, but they are ampler than those of most poets of his
period, except Ben Jonson, whose conversations Drummond
of Hawthornden recorded, and Robert Greene, whose excesses
and notorious death produced a topical pamphlet. We know
a good deal more about Shakespeare than about Drayton,
Dekker and Marston, for example; and possibly many who
who have a general idea that his career is clouded with obscurity
will be surprised to find how much contemporary information
is available.

I reject all the theories which seek to prove that Shakespeare was Bacon, Oxford, Rutland or any one but Shakespeare.
This is not the place to expound the reasons for this rejection:
they would grow into a long and involved argument. Let it
suffice that I see no reason why a grammar school education
should debar a man from writing plays and poetry—there
are many parallels in the history of literature; that there are
in the Shakespearean text many references to his Stratford
days, including the observation of the river current from the

Clopton bridge, and to his acting experience; and that Robert Greene, Ben Jonson, Henry Chettle, Gabriel Harvey, John Manningham, John Webster, Francis Beaumont, and others who were alive when he was, had no doubt that the man who wrote Shakespeare's plays was Shakespeare.

My story conforms to the established facts of the life. The gap of several years between Shakespeare's probable migration from Stratford and his arrival in London I have left as a gap: and if Shakespeare in my story rarely thinks back to this lost period it is possibly because there is such a gap of years in my own personal history to which I only infrequently give a thought. To the known facts I have added certain conjectures of my own, the most important of which may be traced by the notes on the chapters given at the end of this Postscript. I have also used a large measure of invention in interpreting Shakespeare's inward life: for this I must bear responsibility. Principally, I suppose, I shall be called to account for the way I gloss the Sonnets by my characterisation of Southampton and by creating two women for Shakespeare to fall in love with.

In the absence of further information, it is impossible to trace the personal history on which the Sonnets were founded. That the best of them are personal, and not literary exercises, is hardly open to doubt. Those who think otherwise must, in my view, be lacking in experience and perception. What I have done is to deny the first assumption on which the reading of the Sonnets is usually based: that they are all of a piece, and, if restored to their rightful order, would unfold a unified story.

The first seventeen are addressed to a young man, presumably Southampton, though Pembroke, a Will Hughes, and others are candidates. To me these first sonnets lack the accent of sincerity and strong personal emotion. They are stiff with artifice and may fairly be regarded as literary or social exercises. I set them apart, and put out of mind an excessive friendship with Southampton or any other young man. If the rest of the Sonnets be examined without this preconception, they yield little or no clues to a friendship homosexual to one degree or another. And as there is in the Plays no indication of Shakespeare approving, or even being interested in, such friendships, I reject this as a key to an interpretation. I take him to be a man strongly, but normally, sexual.

Considered as a sequence, the Sonnets do not make sense. We may therefore fairly regard their arrangement as arbitrary and need not assume that any consecutive run of them is addressed to the same person. They may, however, be tentatively divided into five groups. 1. the early sonnets addressed to a young man urging him to marry. 2. those in which the poet is concerned chiefly with his own mood or with a general examination of human experience. 3. romantic love sonnets. 4. sensual and generally unhappy love sonnets addressed to a dark woman. 5. sonnets in which the poet complains that his friend has robbed him of his mistress. It is commonly assumed that the poems in this fifth group are linked with those written to or about the dark woman. I have taken another view. Deducing from the plays that Shakespeare was not homosexual, I have made him write the romantic love sonnets to a young woman for whom I invent no name beyond The Lady in Scarlet and White; and upon his love for her I make him found most of the heroines of his romantic comedies. To this love affair I attach the sonnets complaining of the loss of a mistress, and I have employed such a misunderstanding as he often uses in his plays to account for it.

The sonnet beginning 'Two loves have I' (set out in Chapter XVII.) belongs to this fifth group, and it is sometimes used to reinforce the homosexuality argument. In my story I make Shakespeare foresee this deduction and repudiate it. That the "man right fair" should be, not Southampton, but Shakespeare himself will not seem so far-fetched a fancy if the symbolism of 'The Tempest' is borne in mind. Such symbolism need not be made too specific or elaborated into a

symmetrical allegory, yet it is difficult to avoid the conclusion
that Prospero personifies Shakespeare's conception of himself
as an artist, while Ariel represents his poetic imagination,
and Caliban his grosser nature. Again, to read "better angel"
as, in our modern phrase, ' better self,' squares with the inward
conflict and dual nature of Hamlet, who may almost certainly
be taken as an intimate revelation of Shakespeare the man.
There is also, I believe, some probability in the way Shakespeare, in this story, mischievously sets out to confuse readers
of the Sonnets, and to cover up incidental disclosures of his
private life. Every creative writer who is not a confirmed
exhibitionist does this sort of thing on occasion: and in such
phrases as "I have made myself a motley to the view" and "for
daws to peck at" there is evidence that Shakespeare was sensitive, too late, to the effect of public exhibitions of his own
emotions.

Who the dark woman of the Sonnets was, no one knows.
Mr. Bernard Shaw made her Mary Fitton, a lady of the Court,
but in his Preface tells us that a portrait reveals her to have
been fair-haired. Dr. G. B. Harrison draws attention to a disreputable negress. There was also a Sir William Davenant
who liked to hint that he was the illegitimate son of Shakespeare, and on the strength of this the dark woman has been
identified as an inn-keeper's wife. These are all guesses, and
as no more is known of her than is revealed in the Sonnets,
I have thought myself free to invent her again as Mistress
Nell, and to make up a story for her conforming in its general.
tenour to the revelant sonnets. The most probable date for
the composition of these sonnets brings her into Shakespeare's
life about the time ' Hamlet ' was written, and thus I have
been able to shew Shakespeare first suffering a sensual passion,
complicated by a bout of sex-nausea, and then wresting his
tragedies out of the aftermath of humiliation.

There is no historical warrant for assuming that the dark
woman was the merchant's wife with whom John Donne had
a surreptitious love affair about 1596: but certain similarities

in the two stories, as recorded in verse by the poets, fascinated me. To cover myself I have left it uncertain in the reader's, as in my Shakespeare's mind, whether the dark woman had been Donne's mistress before she met Shakespeare, or whether she had in fact merely come into possession of copies of his poems.

The major heroines of the Plays I have sorted into three groups, who appear chronologically. First: the romantic and witty ladies of the early comedies (1592-1599), towards whom Shakespeare's attitude is more or less that of an admiring lover. They are derived, in my story, from the character I call the Lady in Scarlet and White, and (quoting Benedick in ' Much Ado ') Dear Lady Disdain. I hope it will be noted that Shakespeare, in my story, is aware that in making these heroines he is not merely copying nature, that his stage ladies are invested with a good deal of his own expressive splendour of mind which their original in real life possibly lacked. Second: from ' Hamlet ' (1600) to ' Antony and Cleopatra ' (1607) come the tragic heroines, women of a very different sort, either majestic like Lady Macbeth and Cleopatra, wanton like Cressida, or ill-used objects of masculine jealousy, like Ophelia and Desdemona. Towards these Shakespeare's attitude is not so simple: it is compounded of unstable elements of passion, sex-hatred, impatience, and reluctant admiration. Third: in his last writing years, set in plays which reveal dramatic urgency yielding to contemplative calm, we find Marina, Perdita and Miranda. These heroines, charming though they may be, lack both the wit and adventurous spirit of the romantic ladies, and the capacity for suffering of the tragic heroines. I make Ben Jonson (Chapter XX.) perceive this last alteration, and apply the adjective ' paternal ' to Shakespeare's new attitude towards his heroines.

This analysis of the Shakespearean women covers almost all the plays, the principal exception being the histories. Once I had these distinctions clear in my mind, I felt them to be both valid and significant. I may very well have taken the

idea, whole or in embryo, from some of my reading in Shakespearean criticism, but my memory is unable to trace the
origin and allow me to acknowledge it. It has become so
familiar to me that I cannot believe it to be my own discovery:
if it is, I must accept responsibility. Certainly I do not feel
disposed to apologise for emphasising Shakespeare's fatherly
outlook upon his later heroines.

It seems only fair for an historical novelist to make plain
which parts of his narrative are founded on fact and which
are invention or surmise, and perhaps this can be most conveniently set out in these notes, chapter by chapter.

Chapter I. There are no records of attendances at the
Grammar School in Shakespeare's time, but almost certainly he
was educated there from his seventh year onwards, under Simon
Hunt and Thomas Jenkyns. The schoolroom is still in use. The
Welsh schoolmaster's method of teaching grammar is based on
a passage in ' The Merry Wives of Windsor ', IV. i. The ritual
game which Will plays with Hamnet Sadler is intended to be
a foreshadowing of the references to Philippi in ' Julius Cæsar '.
The drowning of Kate Hamlet, from which Ophelia's end is
probably derived, is taken from the records.

Chapter II. John Shakespeare, father of William, is described
in contemporary documents as a yeoman, a glover and a
whittawer, i.e. a curer of skins. The authorities which make
him a butcher and a wool-dealer are of later date, 1681 and
1709 respectively. He certainly sold barley and timber. John
Sadler, his nephew Hamnet (after whom and his wife Judith,
Shakespeare's twin children seem to have been named),
Richard Field (a printer who later issued ' Venus and Adonis '),
all the Shakespeare family in this story, and Anne Hathaway,
are historical persons. Meg Candler is partly developed from
the Nurse in ' Romeo and Juliet.' The topographical detail
in Stratford, and later in London, has been verified from
maps, drawings, histories and personal visits.

Chapter III. John Shakespeare's troubles with debts and
lawsuits can be traced in the Stratford record. Anne Hathaway,

probably daughter to Richard Hathaway (who died in 1581) was at least eight years older than William Shakespeare. They were married towards the end of 1582, by licence issued from Worcester. Their daughter Susannah was baptised on the 26th May in the following year. And on the 2nd February 1585 the twins, Judith and Hamnet, were baptised. Shakespeare's mixture of ardour and high-mindedness with a strong sensuality, as depicted in this chapter, is drawn from his early poems. I show him from the first a man often at war with himself, given to debating problems of conduct in his own mind, because he invests so many of his heroes, notably Hamlet, with this characteristic.

Chapter IV. The personality of Anne, and the release of sensuality she effected in her husband, are my own deductions from the few bare facts known about the marriage, the poet's migration from Stratford, and the amorous passages in his early work. The legend that Shakespeare in his youth was in trouble with Sir Thomas Lucy of Charlecote, over deer-stealing, and later revenged himself by references in the 'Merry Wives', comes from a manuscript dated between 1688 and 1708, and is expanded in Nicholas Rowe's short 'Life', 1709. It has probably some foundation in fact, but cannot be taken as history. I have therefore avoided detail and used the anecdote only as a passing reference. The date when Shakespeare left Stratford is not known, and there is a gap in the record between 1584 and 1592 when Thomas Nashe and Robert Greene made mention in print of his plays.

Chapter V. The description of this hot day in August; the scene in St. Paul's Cathedral—later burned down in the Great Fire and replaced by Wren's; the rogues's slang; London bridge; details of personal appearances; the theatrical and literary references, are based on contemporary pamphlets by Greene, Nashe and Gabriel Harvey. 'Cutting' Ball was in fact Greene's henchman, Ball's sister his mistress, and Fortunatus his illegitimate son by her.

Chapter VI. Edward Alleyn, actor and son-in-law to Philip

Henslowe of the Rose theatre, founded Dulwich College. His character and his professional abilities are here presented unfavourably, perhaps unfairly. The narrative is, however, developed from passages in Shakespeare and others of his contemporaries which scholars regard as references to Alleyn: we may thus suppose that Shakespeare's view of him was not very different. The death of Robert Greene in the house of Mistress Isam is recounted in Gabriel Harvey's 'Four Letters and Certain Sonnets' (1592): he was "attended by lice"; begged "a penny pot of Malmesie"; had taken too much "pickle herring"; borrowed Master Isam's shirt; died in debt; and was crowned by Mistress Isam with bays. The supposition that from this death-bed Shakespeare took a hint for the end of his Falstaff—"babbled of green fields"—is my own. A tradition associates Richard Burbage with the part of Richard III., but for my purposes I have preferred Alleyn.

Chapter VII. John Florio, best known as the translator of Montaigne's Essays, was born in England of Italian parentage. He spent some years in Southampton's household and is assumed to have been tutor or (as I have made him) secretary to the young Earl. His helpful friendliness towards Shakespeare is presumed from the fact that Southampton was Shakespeare's patron. I do not know the name of Southampton's steward, or even if anyone knows it: thus I am responsible for calling him Hollis and making him in part the original of Malvolio. The character of Southampton is here drawn from contemporary scandals and from his later political and military adventures. 'Wriothesley' is pronounced 'Rosely'—two syllables. Greene's and Chettle's references to Shakespeare are, I hope, self-explanatory in the story, and can be read in the original pamphlets reprinted under Dr. G. B. Harrison's editorship. The costume worn by the Lady in Scarlet and White should not be taken as derived from Shakespearean heroines who disguise themselves as pages: ladies of the period sometimes wore breeches and doublet when they went riding, hunting or hawking. The surmise that Anne Hathaway was, in part at least, the original of the Venus in her husband's poem cannot be proved, but has been made by others before me.

Chapter VIII. Little is known of the character of Richard Burbage, the actor who is traditionally regarded as the ' creator ' of such Shakespearean rôles as Hamlet and Macbeth. I have therefore based my rendering of him chiefly on his portrait in the Dulwich Gallery, and a little upon Nigel Playfair's conjectural essay in ' The Great Tudors.' The account of Marlowe's end is founded on Dr. Leslie Hotson's ' The Death of Christopher Marlowe ' and on contemporary records abstracted by Dr. G. B. Harrison in his ' Elizabethan Journals.'

Chapter IX. The latter part of the conversation between Shakespeare and the Lady in Scarlet and White is derived from ' As You Like It ' Act III. Scene II.

Chapter X. The similarities between the Montague-Capulet feud and the Danvers-Long brawl in which Southampton was involved are pointed out by many critics; also the changes which Shakespeare made when he turned Arthur Brooke's poem into a play.

Chapter XI. It is an assumption, but one backed by most of the authorities, that the passage in ' Willobie and his Avisa ' refers to Shakespeare and Southampton. But it is not necessary to conclude that it reveals events as they actually occurred. I have taken it that this anecdote, as such gossip often does to-day, garbles the facts. Burbage, in the part of Nick Bottom, burlesqueing Alleyn's style of acting, is taken from the common stock of criticism. But, so far as I know, it is my own suggestion that Shakespeare may have got the first notion of Bottom and the play acted by the "rude mechanicals" from Nashe's ' The Unfortunate Traveller.' The changing of the name of Sir John Oldcastle to Falstaff is noted in Dr. G. B. Harrison's ' Elizabethan Journals '; also the apprentices' riots, and the events of the Queen's grand climacteric year. Of Shakespeare's son, Hamnet, nothing is known beyond the baptismal and burial entries in the Stratford parish register. Those parts of this story which deal with him, and with other members of the Shakespeare family, are therefore almost entirely invented. For the reference to the strange flow of the current under the Clopton bridge (described in ' Lucrece ') I am indebted to Dr. Caroline Spurgeon's ' Shakespeare's Imagery.'

Chapter XII. The street encounter between John Donne and Shakespeare is fictitious: it is by no means unlikely, however, that in the then small world of London they knew each other, at least by sight and reputation. The portrait of Donne in these pages is intentionally biased and incomplete: those who do not know him otherwise should consult a biography and his poems. The mild snobbery and pride in his rank as gentleman with which I invest Shakespeare is in keeping with the period and with several passages in the plays. In quoting the Grant of Arms I have not, as elsewhere, modernised the spelling because, I fancy, the heraldic jargon was even then antiquated. When I make Shakespeare so determined to acquire property and economic security, I deduce from his known purchases and his will: it seems legitimate to ascribe this ambition to the effect on him of seeing his father debt-ridden and so many other dramatists living and dying in disreputable poverty. He was almost alone among the playhouse poets of his time in escaping imprisonment. The historical events in this chapter, including Ben Jonson's imprisonment in the Marshalsea, are based on the ' Elizabethan Journals ': the purchase of New Place is taken from records. The bricked well shaft may still be seen among the foundations in the garden. The visit of Drayton and Shakespeare to Jonson in prison is fictitious.

Chapter XIII. Again the history, including Ben Jonson's duel and trial, and the removal of the playhouse from Shoreditch to the Bankside, is based on the ' Elizabethan Journals.' Those who care to may easily consult this and judge for themselves whether or not I have played fair in expanding a few lines into this narrative.

Chapter XIV. The character and the acting style of Arnim are deduced from the change in Shakespeare's clowns marked by Feste in ' Twelfth Night.' William Kemp, the supplanted comedian, has left a pamphlet, ' Nine Days Wonder ' (1600) describing his dancing journey from London to Norwich: out of a few unintentional disclosures in this I have been able to make this sketch of him as man and as player. That Shakespeare's ' Hamlet ' is a rewriting of an old play, probably by Thomas Kyd and itself not original, is the usual critical conclusion. Peter Fender is a fictitious character, derived from Pandarus in ' Troilus and Cressida.' Some of his conversation runs close to dialogue in the play.

Chapter XV. It will be seen that, although I have invented freely, Mistress Nell in this and other chapters conforms to what Shakespeare tells us of the dark woman in the Sonnets. Thus, using the numbering in the original and standard editions, we find she plays the virginals (128); she has black eyes and a dark skin (132); she lies to him (138); she is younger than he and makes him feel older than his years (138); she sleeps with him (138); when he asks her to say that she loves him, she refuses (140); she is not the sort of woman he normally finds attractive (141); she makes him sin and makes him suffer (141); she has been unfaithful to her husband with other men (142); she torments him by pretending to say that she hates him (145); she makes him "frantic mad" (147); she compels him to examine his conscience (151); she has broken her "bed-vow" (152).

Chapter XVI. The story of the composition of Hamlet as it is given here is based on Dr. G. B. Harrison's Introduction to his reprint of the 1603 edition in his Bodley Head Quartos. To the best of my knowledge I am the first to suggest that Shakespeare, writing the scene in which Hamlet discovers his uncle at his prayers, may have taken a hint from Nashe's ' The Unfortunate Traveller ': but quite possibly I have read, and forgotten where I read, the suggestion that Hamlet's refusal to kill was intended by Shakespeare as a piece of characteristic self-deception in a man much given to post-poning action. In making Shakespeare use Polonius (first called Corambis) as a burlesque of Bacon's essay style, I am also, so far as I know, first in the field. It is a guess, but it amuses me, and if it irritates the Baconians I am not so sorry as doubtless I ought to be. For a reasonable and convincing explanation of Hamlet's harsh behaviour to Ophelia I am indebted to Dr. Dover Wilson's 'What Happens in "Hamlet"'.

Chapter XVII. There is no historical origin for this meeting at the Mermaid tavern between Shakespeare, Jonson and Drayton (of whose private life little is known: but there is a stimulating portrait in the National Portrait Gallery, near that of Ben Jonson). The legend of a poets' club meeting at this tavern seems to have grown from Francis Beaumont's lines to Jonson:

> What things have we seen
> Done at the Mermaid! heard words that have been
> So nimble, and so full of subtle flame,
> As if that every one from whence they came
> Had meant to put his whole wit in a jest,
> And had resolved to live a fool the rest
> Of his dull life.

But the tavern existed in Bread Street, the taverner's name was Williamson, and he was in trouble early in July 1600 over the brawl here described. In view of Beaumont's tribute, it seems reasonable to suppose that the Mermaid was in favour with the playhouse poets, though not necessarily used as a club. If the worst side of Ben Jonson's character is shewn in this story, it should be remembered that Drummond of Hawthornden (who thought his conversation worth recording) declares that Jonson was "a great lover and praiser of himself, a contemner and scorner of others, given rather to losse a friend, than a jest, jealous of every word and action of those about him (especiallie after drink)." Part of the dialogue in this chapter is derived from Drummond's record.

Chapter XVIII. The suggestion that the lines in ' Hamlet ' about " the bloat king" may refer to Alleyn is my own, sprung from certain of Alleyn's letters to his wife, in which he calls her Mouse.

Chapter XIX. The account of the Essex rebellion and the trial of the two Earls is founded on the ' Elizabethan Journals ' and on Professor J. E. Neale's ' Queen Elizabeth."

Chapter XX. In 1623, after Shakespeare's death, his plays were collected for the first time, in a volume now known as the First Folio. Heminges and Condell, two members of his playhouse company, assisted in making the collection. It has prefatory poems by Ben Jonson, and, on the title page, an indifferent engraving by Martin Droeshout. For this engraving there must presumably have been an original portrait, painted in Shakespeare's lifetime. The engraving shews the poet wearing a curious doublet, of which the left half appears to be drawn back to front. This has given rise to some extraordinary speculations from those who cannot believe that Shakespeare was Shakespeare. I think my suggestion is as plausible as any of theirs: that the back-to-front doublet may have been so painted at Shakespeare's request, to symbolise mockingly that view of himself, as a man in whom two natures were at war, which is constantly indicated in the Play and in the Sonnets. The story of the pirated version of ' Hamlet ' comes from Dr. G. B. Harrison's reprint in the Bodley Head Quartos. The word ' stenographer ' and the reference to a shorthand system are not anachronisms. Nothing but the barest biographical details (baptism, marriage, a will, burial date) is known of Shakespeare's younger daughter, Judith. The scenes between her and her father are therefore to be read wholly as fiction, but fiction based on deductions from the later plays—and from human nature. All the bushes, orchard trees and flowering plants (including the new fangled tulips) here ascribed to the garden in New Place were in favour at the time.

Chapter XXI. John Ward, vicar of Stratford-on-Avon,

entered in his dairy about 1661-3: "Shakespear, Drayton and Ben Jonson, had a merry meeting, and itt seems drank too hard, for Shakespear died of a feavour there contracted." This is evidence nearly fifty years after the event, but recorded on the spot. There is no good reason to reject it. For the conversation between the poets I have again drawn a little on Drummond, but the references to Shakespeare's schoolmasters come from putting together Stratford records and Act IV. Scene I. of the ' Merry Wives.' The discussion of Donne is wholly fiction, but, of course, as I make Ben Jonson prophesy, Donne did live to become Dean of St. Paul's, and after concluding his life in piety left instructions for his son to publish his early erotic poems. Shakespeare's will, the death of William Hart, the naming of Judith's son (who died before he was six months old) as Shakespeare Quiney, John Hall's successful doctoring of Michael Drayton, are all from records. The bust over the poet's tomb in the parish church at Stratford is by some held to have been made from a death mask: if this was so, the swelling and coarsening of the face after a mortal "feavour", combined with the artistic deficiencies of the sculptor, may account for the disappointing effect of the bust. I have just inspected, in my own parish church, two heads in a very similar monument, erected thirty years later: and, although this church is near London, where, presumably, the best sculptors were to be found, and although the family had plenty of money to spend, the two busts are just as blank and inexpressive as the famous one at Stratford.

For making Shakespeare die, not embittered, but with a sense of frustration and unfulfilment, I must take responsibility. Perhaps I shall find more approval for the charitable suggestion of how he came to leave to his wife his "second-best bed"; my version at least accords with the absence of bitterness and cynicism from his later plays.

BIBLIOGRAPHY

I HAVE read too many books on Shakespeare, many of them good ones, to allow me to make here a full list. Instead I set out those I have had by me during the immediate preparation and writing of the story.

TEXTS

Tragedies, Comedies, Histories and Poems of William Shakespeare. (Oxford text.) Oxford University Press.

The Bodley Head Quartos. Edited by Dr. G. B. Harrison:

The Tragicall Historie of Hamlet Prince of Denmarke. William Shakespeare. 1603.

A Notable Discovery of Coosnage & The Second Part of Conny-catching. Robert Greene. 1591-1592.

The Thirde and Last Part of Conny-catching & A Disputation Between a Hee Conny-catcher and a Shee Conny-catcher. Robert Greene. 1592.

The Blacke Bookes Messenger, Cuthert Conny-catcher & The Defence of Conny-catching. Robert Greene. 1592.

Greene's Groatsworth of Witte & The Repentance of Robert Greene. 1592.

Foure Letters and certaine Sonnets. Gabriel Harvey. 1592.

Kind-Hartes Dreame. Henry Chettle. 1592. *Nine Daies Wonder.* William Kemp. 1600.

Pierce Pennilesse, His Supplication to the Divell. Thomas Nashe. 1592.

Discoveries. Ben Jonson. 1641. *& Notes of Conversations with Ben Jonson* made by William Drummond of Hawthornden, January 1619.

The Unfortunate Traveller. Thomas Nashe. 1594.

Percy Reprints. Basil Blackwell.

The Works of Christopher Marlowe. (Clarendon Press.)

The Plays of Ben Jonson. Mermaid Series.

The Plays of Beaumont and Fletcher. Mermaid Series.

383

The Poems of John Donne. Everyman Library.

The Essayes of Francis Bacon Lord Verulam. Everyman Library.

Five Elizabethan Tragedies. World's Classics.

Five Elizabethan Comedies. World's Classics.

Six Plays By Contemporaries of Shakespeare. World's Classics.

Elizabethan Prose. Edited by Michael Roberts. Cape.

HISTORY AND BIOGRAPHY

A Short Life of Shakespeare, abridged by Charles Williams from Sir Edmund Chambers's *William Shakespeare*. (Clarendon Press.)

Shakespeare's England. Two Volumes. Clarendon Press.

The Elizabethan Journals. 1591-1603. G. B. Harrison. Routledge.

Shakespeare at Work. G. B. Harrison. Routledge.

Shakespeare's Fellows. G. B. Harrison. Bodley Head.

The Death of Christopher Marlowe. J. Leslie Hotson. Nonesuch Press.

Chart of Plays 1584-1623. W. P. Barrett. Cambridge University Press.

Queen Elizabeth. J. E. Neale. Cape.

The Great Tudors. Edited Katharine Garvin. Nicholson and Watson.

James I. Charles Williams. Barker.

John Donne. Hugh l'Anson Fausset. Cape.

CRITICISM

What Happens in Hamlet. J. Dover Wilson. Cambridge University Press.

The Essential Shakespeare. J. Dover Wilson. Cambridge University Press.

Shakespeare. John Middleton Murry. Cape.

Shakespeare's Imagery. Caroline Spurgeon. Cambridge University Press.

A Shakespeare Glossary. C. T. Onions. Clarendon Press.

GENTLEMAN OF STRATFORD
was first published in September, 1939,
the week war broke out. Because of
paper rationing and the necessity to keep
Mr. Brophy's war novels in print, this
remarkable story of the life of William
Shakespeare has not been available for
several years, although copies in the
second-hand market have changed hands at
fantastically high prices. Meanwhile its
reputation has spread and increased,
largely by word of mouth. It is now all
re-issued in a substantial edition.